Blood
of the
King

Khirro's Journey Book 1

By
Bruce Blake

Bruce Blake

Dedication

So often we hear that a novel is not the work of just one person that it has become a cliche, but cliches are what they are because of the unavoidable truth they hold. This book is dedicated to all the people who worked hard to help bring it together: Ella for her editing and encouragement; Travis for another eye-catching cover; everyone who read it and gave me feedback prior to its release; Lynne for always being a critic and a fan; and especially to my wonderful wife just for being.

Special thanks to Rob Antonishen for creating the map of Khirro's world. Check him out at http://www.cartocopia.com/

Bruce Blake

Cast of Characters (in order of appearance)

Khirro – A farmer conscripted into the King's army

Braymon – King of Erechania

Emeline – Khirro's love

Jowyn – a soldier of the King's army and friend to Khirro

The Shaman/Bale – King Braymon's healer, a magician.

Gendred – an Erechanian soldier, one of the elite Shadowmen

Rudric – a general in the King's army and member of the Kingsblade

The Necromancer/Darestat – an outlaw magician, the only one able to raise the dead

Ghaul – an Erechanian soldier who joins Khirro on his journey

Elyea – a whore who joins Khirro's journey

Therrador Montmarr – advisor to King Braymon

Graymon – Therrador's son

Suath – a one-eyed mercenary

Maes – a midget and brother of Athryn who joins Khirro's Journey

Alicando – a troubadour

Athryn – a magician, brother of Maes, who joins

5

Khirro's Journey

Aryann – a whore and friend of Elyea's

Leigha – a whore and friend of Elyea's

Despina – a whore and friend of Elyea's

Imlip – door-keeper of the cult of magic

Shyn – a border guard who joins Khirro's journey

Monos – the first Necromancer

Shyctem – the first king

Lord Emon Turesti – High Chancellor of Erechania

Sir Alton Sienhin – commander of the king's army

Hu Dondon – Lord Chamberlain of Erechania

Hahn Perdaro – Voice of the People of Erechania

Sir Matte Eliden – a senior soldier in the king's army and friend of Therrador

The Archon/Sheyndust – magician and leader of the Kanosee

High Confessor Aurna – high priest of the Order of the Four Gods

Seerna – Therrador's late wife

1

Khirro blinked.

Wispy smoke floated across an otherwise unspoiled sky, marring it, capturing his attention, bringing him to focus. He realized there was nothing but sky and the smudge of gray—no smells, no sounds, nothing.

Smells returned first, all of them familiar—dirt and stone and dust, the scents of his life that had always been there.

The farm, then. I'm on the farm.

That didn't feel right, didn't explain the streak of smoke. Memories were faint, distant, as though seen through the wrong end of an eyeglass. It couldn't be the farm, he'd left home months before...but for where?

Sound crept back into Khirro's world. A man's voice floated to him on the summer air, then more voices—not shouts of reverie but cries of anger and pain. Like a dam bursting, the clash of metal on metal added to the din.

The sounds jarred Khirro and memories flooded back

like the tide filling a hole in the sand. Consciousness slammed down on him, brutal and unflinching. On his left, a sheer stone wall rose thirty feet or more; his right arm dangled over untold nothing. He moved his head to see and pain flooded his body, filling every joint and crevice, leaving no portion free from its touch. Something wet on his forehead and face, the taste of blood on his swollen tongue. The feel of it all filled in the last holes in his recollection: the invasion, the fight on the wall, the king and his men coming to his rescue. He'd tried to fight alongside the elite knights, but he was only a farmer forced to dress up in armor and wear a sword.

There'd be no harvest this year, not for him.

He spat weakly to clear his mouth; bloody saliva ran down his cheek into his ear. Ragged breath caught in his throat as he remembered the warrior breaching the wall, a huge man dressed in closed helm and black chain mail splashed red—paint or blood, Khirro couldn't tell. The man easily bested him, forced him back until he stumbled over a fallen knight. He recalled the fellow's pained groan as his foot struck his ribs, then he was tumbling end over end down the stairs, desperate to keep from going over the edge to the courtyard seventy feet below.

So that's where he was—lying on the first landing, precariously close to death, as King Braymon and his guard defended the fortress from a Kanosee army.

King Braymon.

8

Everything hurt: back, arms and legs, hips. His head pounded. Warm blood oozed down his forehead from above his hairline. His throat worked futilely; it was a struggle to draw breath. Instead of his lungs expanding in his chest, panic grew in their place. He'd survived a bombardment of fireballs and the first Kanosee breach of the fortress wall; how ironic it would be to die falling down the stairs.

When he could breathe again, he gasped air past the bloody taste on his tongue like a man breaking the surface of a lake after a long dive. He took inventory of his body, wiggling his fingers and toes, flexing his muscles. They hurt, every one of them, but they all worked.

What do I do now?

The thought was fuzzy, as though spoken by someone with a mouthful of cotton. Another thought came fast on the heels of the first: *The king needs me.* Even warriors as fierce as King Braymon of Erechania and his guard couldn't defeat so many. He wanted to get up and rush to his king's side, to stand against the enemy, but more than the pains in his body kept him from it.

He thought of Emeline, and of his unborn child. His heart contracted.

Idiot! All you had to do was push over a couple of ladders. What kind of soldier are you?

He was no soldier, that was the answer. Spade and hoe were his tools, horse and plow, not sword and dirk and

9

catapult. But he had a duty, and he'd made a promise to Jowyn before the hellfire claimed his life. Khirro scrambled away from the edge; his head smacked the stone landing sending a fresh jolt of pain through his temples.

I don't want to end up like Jowyn.

Fighting sounds tumbled over the edge of the walk thirty feet above, carried to Khirro on a hot summer breeze that petered out long before it reached him. The thought of King Braymon and his guards fighting for their lives filled him with guilt. He heard the king's voice call for aid. Someone answered, far away and small, and Khirro felt relief. The clangs and clatters intensified and the king called out again, but this time his cry cut short. Khirro gasped and held his breath, waiting for a sign of what had happened.

He should be at the king's side, repelling invaders. He was no one's equal with a weapon, but another sword was a sword nonetheless. Pain flared as he tensed his muscles and his body tilted dangerously in the direction of the painful death awaiting at the bottom of the wall. He scrambled a few inches away from the edge, sweat beading on his brow, leather breast piece scraping on stone stair. A couple of deep breaths pained his ribs but slowed his racing heart. Part of him wondered if he could just stay there, wait for the battle to end. His sword arm would be of such little use to the king, anyway, perhaps more of a hindrance. *Live to fight another day,* as the saying went.

His father, a lifetime farmer who never hefted a sword, would said that was a coward's saying. His father still considered himself the best judge of such things, but ever since the accident that cost him his arm, everything Khirro did made him a coward, or useless, or no good.

He wouldn't prove his father right.

Khirro stared up the wall at the sky, its promise of summer seeming so far away now. He gathered his strength, drew a few short, sharp breaths. The muscles in his shoulders and back bunched painfully. He stopped and released them, allowing his body to go limp again as a figure appeared at the edge of the wall above.

The angle and distance made it difficult to see the man until he leaned forward and peered directly down at Khirro. The black breastplate splashed with red made him unmistakably the same man who nearly killed him. Khirro stared up, mimicking a corpse, as anger filled his chest, partially directed at the invader for his actions, partly at himself for playing the coward his father accused him of being.

The man disappeared from sight, but only long enough for Khirro to release his held breath and half-draw another. When he returned, the Kanosee warrior held a limp form in his arms. Sunlight glinted on steel plate as, impossibly, he hefted the armored body above his head, presenting it to the heavens as if an offering to the Gods.

Something caught the man's attention and he looked

11

away for a second then hurriedly, ungracefully, heaved the body over the edge.

Time slowed as the limp body twisted through the air toward Khirro. He saw the blood caked on lobstered gauntlets, dents and scuffs on silver plate.,an enameled pattern scrolling across the top of the breastplate. The armor seemed familiar but his pounding head gave no help in recognizing it as the limp form tumbled toward him.

At the last moment, instinct overpowered shock, fear and pain, and Khirro rolled to the right, teetering dangerously on the landing's edge. The body hit the stone floor beside him.

The slam of armor against stone was nearly deafening, but not loud enough to mask the sickening pop of bones snapping within. The body bounced once and came to rest, some part of it pressed against Khirro's back, threatening to push him over the precipice. He wriggled painfully away from the edge, pushing against the unmoving body behind him.

The sounds of fighting renewed. Soldiers must have pushed past the burning catapult that had barricaded them, rushing to engage the enemy and save their king.

Where were they five minutes ago?

Khirro put the thought from his mind. He lived, after all; it was more than he could say for the man lying beside him.

Khirro lay still for a minute, unsure what to do. If he

stayed put, he'd forfeit his life to a Kanosee sword as surely as if he rejoined the fray. His eyes flickered from the wall walk above to the stairs. He saw no one. If there was a best time to move—to go *somewhere*, to do *something*—it was likely now, while the enemy was freshly engaged. He turned his head, looked at the man lying dead beside him.

The man's cheek pressed against the stone landing was curiously flat, crushed by the fall. His eyes were closed; blood ran across his closed eyelids from a gash on his clean-shaven scalp. A scrollwork of enameled ivy crawled out from the corner of his silver breastplate and across his epaulet. Khirro stopped breathing.

King Braymon!

It was the king dead beside him, the man who had rescued him from the red-splashed Kanosee soldier, leaping into the fight to save a lowly farmer-turned-soldier without regard for his own safety.

The king. The man who ruled the kingdom.

While Khirro had chosen to cower on the landing, struggling to find his courage as others fought for the kingdom, Braymon hadn't hesitated a second.

And now the king was dead, and there was no one to blame but Khirro.

Guilt stirred his gut. What would this mean to the kingdom? To the war? His head swam. Did this mean he could return home, or would it mean more fighting? He thought of Emeline. It was easy to remember why he

Bruce Blake

hadn't risen after his fall down the stairs when he thought of her and of the child she carried. He only wanted to return to her, to go back to the farm and live out his life in peace and quiet. If Emeline would have him back.

The clang of steel and the shouts and screams of men fell on him like violent rain. He didn't know how long he lay there listening and thinking, mourning and celebrating, awash in guilt and remorse and relief when another sound caught his attention. He held his breath.

A footstep on the stair?

His eyes darted toward the stone steps, but he couldn't see beyond the king's leg twisted at an unbelievable angle. He dared not turn his head for fear a man clad in a red-splattered breast plate may be leering at him from the stair, waiting for an excuse to fall upon him and finish the job. Thirty seconds crawled by, a minute. Khirro began to think he'd heard his own breath. For a while there was only the sound of fighting, then it came again. Not a footstep, but a groan, small and weak, but close. Khirro waited, listening, hoping. Dreading. Then another sound, a whisper.

Haltingly, Khirro moved his gaze back to the face of his king, the man who saved him, the man who so many years ago, saved the entire kingdom.

He looked into the open eyes of King Braymon.

2

A helm clattered off the wall walk, bouncing end over

14

end down the stairs. It hit Khirro's foot, startling him and sending a jolt of pain up his leg. When he looked to see what hit him, he recognized the dead eyes of a member of the king's guard staring back at him from within the helm. A pained grimace twisted the face, blood dripped from severed tendons and ragged veins. Khirro recoiled, pain flashing down his spine. He kicked at the head, the sound of his armor scraping stone impossibly loud in his ears. His toe contacted the helmet painfully, sending it spinning across the landing. It trailed off blood spatters as it rolled to the edge then disappeared over the brink. Khirro breathed a sigh of relief.

"Help me."

Khirro flinched. The king's plea came again, a breathy whisper barely audible above the sounds of battle. Chickens ran about after their heads were removed, but nothing could speak without life remaining within. Khirro shifted painfully onto his side.

"My king," he whispered.

Braymon lay in a tangled heap, hips wrenched farther than possible, one arm pinned beneath him, the other twisted behind. Blood streamed from his shaven head onto his cheeks and into his eyes, a mask of red through which little flesh showed. He blinked clearing his vision, a slow, lethargic movement, then directed his gaze toward Khirro. A pained smile twitched his lips; it quickly turned to a grimace.

15

Bruce Blake

"I thought you lost, lad."

The blood drained from Khirro's cheeks.

"No, your highness. I... I was knocked unconscious. I've only just woken to find you here beside me." The lie tasted more bitter than the coppery tang of blood on his tongue.

Braymon coughed a fine spray of bloody spittle. Khirro knew it meant something inside him was bleeding.

"I've not much time. I need your help."

"I owe you my life."

"Then you can return the favor."

Fear lumped into a mass at the back of Khirro's throat. "What can I do?"

"The healer will know I've fallen," Braymon said coughing again, face strained with the effort. "Take me to him."

Relief. He didn't ask to be avenged or dragged back to the battle to die a soldier's death. Khirro glanced at the blood pooling beneath the king's contorted body, flowing from some unseen spot under his plate mail, and pushed himself up to kneel beside Braymon to better assess his condition. The battle raged above but no one appeared on the stair.

"You shouldn't be moved," Khirro said after consideration. The way the king's body twisted upon itself made him feel sick. "It would mean your life."

Braymon shook his head minutely. "It matters not. I must get to the healer before the warmth has left my body

16

or all is lost."

"I don't think--"

"Soldier," Braymon said with a tone of command befitting a king. "If you do this thing, all else will be forgiven."

Khirro gaped at the king's words. He fought to keep tears at bay as guilt siphoned the strength from his limbs. His mouth moved trying to form the words to apologize for not rejoining the fight, to beg forgiveness, to explain, but his constricted throat choked them. Instead, he nodded.

"You'll have to remove my armor to carry me."

Khirro stripped the king's armor as quickly and quietly as his hurts allowed. Each time he shifted the king, Braymon's face contorted with deeper levels of pain, but he never cried out, and each piece of armor Khirro removed revealed more horror. The king's blood-soaked underclothes stuck to him like a second skin; the jagged end of a bone punched through the flesh of one thigh; a loop of intestines protruded from a long cut in his abdomen. As he uncovered each injury, Khirro felt more grateful to be alive and whole and his own injuries seemed less significant. By the time he finished removing all the pieces, the king's eyes were closed, his face taut with pain, cheeks pale. Khirro had to look closely to ensure he still drew breath.

"We've no time to lose." Braymon said in a strained

17

whisper. "Take me to the center keep."

Khirro stood, teeth gritted against his own meager pain. He reached for Braymon but stopped, unsure how to proceed. He saw no way to pick up the injured man.

"Don't concern yourself with my pain, it will end soon enough. Put me over your shoulder."

A shudder wracked Khirro's spine as he paused to look around. A few men ran about the courtyard below, but they were distant. Above, the fighting reached the top of the stairs. Two Kanosee soldiers—one wearing gray leather, the other the black breast plate splashed with red—hacked at soldiers of the king's army who tried to keep them from the stairway. Khirro hoped they'd hold them long enough. He bent and hooked the king by the armpits, struggling to pull the dead weight from the ground. The king clenched his jaw, every muscle he could control straining to help.

Finally, the king's limp form flopped over Khirro's shoulder. He imagined he felt the soft flesh of his innards through his leather armor and his stomach flipped, forcing bile into his mouth. He swallowed it. The pain proved too much for the king and a cry tore from Braymon's bloodied lips as his broken body pressed against Khirro's shoulder.

Khirro looked back up the stairs, hoping no one heard. At first he thought the Gods with him as the fight continued, but one of the Erechanians fell and as the gray leather-clad Kanosee pulled his sword from the man, he leaned toward his companion and pointed down the stair.

A sword flashed and the man fell, but Khirro saw no more as he turned and rushed down the stairs, focusing on his feet hitting each one and not over-balancing under the king's weight.

By the time he reached the bottom of the final flight, Khirro's back and legs ached, his pulse beat in his temple as his breath came in ragged gasps. If he didn't pause to catch his wind, he wouldn't get much further. He stood at the foot of the switchback staircase, half-bent, and watched a pebble strike the ground near his foot. Khirro looked at it without understanding, his fatigued mind reeling from lack of oxygen, but realization came quickly. He twisted awkwardly, ignoring the pain in his back, to look up the stairs. Halfway down, the black and red mailed soldier hurried toward him, battle axe in hand.

Khirro moved into the courtyard, tired legs burning with effort. Each step jostled strangled moans from the king. Braymon's breath was alarmingly shallow and Khirro could find nowhere to lay his hand without it coming away sticky with the king's blood.

A ball of hellfire arced over the wall and landed a few yards away, showering them with sparks. Fire smeared across the courtyard, igniting the tinder-dry grass, cutting off his path to the center keep. Sweat or blood stung Khirro's eyes as he glanced up at the fire, looking through the wavering heat and smoke, and amended his course, veering toward a closer building. It wasn't where the king had requested, but he had to find a place to make a stand.

Make a stand. The thought made him shudder. *I hope the door isn't barred.*

As they approached, the world slowed to dream time and everything leaped to new levels of clarity: fires burned brighter, sounds became clearer. The king's breath rasped in his ears, blood pounded in his own head. Another sound hammered above all else: footsteps closing in, gaining ground fast. And a smell. It overpowered the sooty stink of fires and the stale odor of sweat and dried piss. Rank and sweet, earthy and rotten, it smelled of the dead.

Hope drained from Khirro like candle wax pooling into panic at the pit of his stomach, leaving behind a quickly solidifying trail of fear. His mind swirled. The foot race was lost, no doubt of that.

What do I do?

Face the soldier? He'd be dead before he drew his dirk. Surrender? The Kanosee would take no prisoners. But did the warrior pursue *him* or was he simply after Braymon?

What if he dropped the king?

Khirro gritted his teeth, biting back the thought. He let the king down once, he wouldn't do it again. A day ago, he told Jowyn the king deserved his loyalty, not his life, but he could no longer make that argument. Braymon could have waited, sacrificing one man to ensure his own safety, but he didn't. Instead, he threw himself into the fray knowing it might mean his end. If a monarch would sacrifice himself

20

to save a dirt farmer, how could the farmer hesitate at saving the king?

With each step Khirro expected to feel steel in his back, ending his flight and his life. A cry rose behind him, deep and wild. Khirro echoed it, crying out with effort, putting everything into pumping his exhausted legs. Ahead, a door swung open and a figure appeared on the threshold, distracting him. Khirro's feet tangled and he fell forward, tumbling awkwardly as he twisted to protect the king. His shoulder hit the ground painfully. The king's body shifted forward, sandwiching Khirro's head against the ground, blurring his vision. He rolled to his back, reached for his scabbard, found it empty, and had only a second to realize his weapon lay on the wall walk where he'd stumbled down the stairs before his pursuer was on him.

Khirro tried to struggle up, but his arm was trapped beneath King Braymon. The Kanosee soldier sent him back to the ground with a kick to the midsection and put his foot on Khirro's chest, pinning him. Writhing and wriggling beneath the pressure, Khirro grabbed the enemy's boot in both hands and tried unsuccessfully to move it. He looked up at the warrior, at his black mail splashed with red, at his menacing closed-face helm, at his massive axe, and his limbs went numb. For the second time in a day, death stared Khirro directly in the eye, and Khirro was afraid.

The Kanosee stared back at Khirro from behind his

visor, breath rattling against the steel. Khirro looked from the black helm to the battle axe and saw star bursts of rust dotting the blade, chips and gouges marking its edge. What soldier carried a weapon so old and neglected? It would split his skull nonetheless. Khirro gritted his teeth, determined to take the deathblow like a man but, to his surprise, the Kanosee released the haft with one hand and lifted his visor instead of raising the axe.

The face beneath the visor may once have belonged to a man, but the flesh was rotted and decayed, leaving behind a parody of a man's features: a black-edged hole in one cheek revealed crooked yellow teeth; the right eye socket stood empty and inflamed; tattered flesh hung from cheek and jaw and forehead. Strands of hair, gray and stringy, escaped from under the helm, plastered by dried blood and pus to what was left of the mottled gray flesh patch-worked across its face. Khirro recoiled. If the thing's foot wasn't pinning breath inside his body, he would have had to fight to keep his gorge from rising. He squirmed under the thing's boot, grabbing and pushing; it didn't move. Tears squeezed from his eyes as he struggled to move, to breathe.

The enemy leaned over, leering at him, and something dripped onto Khirro's face—sweat or saliva or blood. He gagged and his captor laughed.

Khirro's resolution faltered, his mouth opened in a scream. The soldier—the creature—smiled, its lipless mouth twisted in a grin that might easily have passed for growl. Goose flesh puckered Khirro's skin, his stomach knotted. The thing straightened, grasped the haft of the axe with both hands, and laid the blade's edge on Khirro's shoulder. Cold steel pressed against his cheek, its rusty smell filling his nostrils. A weak cry burbled from Khirro's lips, unheard by any save himself and the creature raised the axe skyward as Khirro closed his eyes, whispering prayers to Gods he'd not bothered with since childhood. Memories of Emeline fought their way through his panic, first of her smiling, happy, then angry and accusing. So much had happened, so much was left undone.

What am I doing here? Why does it have to end like this?

He wished he was anywhere but here: tending fields, slaughtering cows, at the end of his father's switch for something done wrong. Anywhere.

Light flashed bright enough to shine red through Khirro's lids. A sound like canvas tearing. The pressure on his chest lessened then disappeared. Something hit the ground near Khirro and the stench of burnt hair filled the air. He tensed, awaiting the deathblow, lying helpless pinned beneath the king.

Dread-filled seconds passed, then the king's weight lifted. Khirro raised his arms in defense, peeked through slitted lids. A black-robed figure leaned toward him—the man from the doorway. He saw nothing beneath the man's

23

Bruce Blake

cowl: no face, no mask. The hood cast an inscrutable shadow even in the bright sunlight.

"Bring him," the robed man said.

Hands grabbed Khirro, dragged him into the darkness beyond the wooden door. It swung closed behind them, leaving Khirro blind in the night-dark room.

3

The face of the dead warrior floated before Khirro's eyes, lipless mouth pulled into a sneer, yellow teeth sharp and dangerous. Blood and pus seeped from its eyes and nostrils forming drops at the tip of its putrid nose. One drop lengthened into a string, separated, and landed square in the middle of Khirro's forehead.

Khirro woke with a start, eye lids snapping open, breath short. There was no dead man threatening him, no rotted face, no blood-splashed mail. Instead, guttering torches threw dancing shadows against the walls of a windowless room. Khirro struggled to control his breathing and kept his head down as he lay on the dirt floor. From behind hooded eyes he observed figures moving, but who or how many, he didn't know. His first memory was of the monstrous Kanosee soldier, then he recalled the black-robed man. And there had been others.

Khirro inched his hand toward the dirk hidden in his boot-top but pain in his shoulder kept him from drawing it —dislocated, perhaps broken. With no other choice, Khirro

24

lay at the mercy of whoever dragged him here. After all that had happened, it didn't surprise him he felt more relief than fear.

One figure he saw and recognized—the body of the king prone in the middle of the floor. Minutes passed and he came to realize there were three other men in the room. The black-robed figure bent over the king, whispering and gesturing. The king's healer, he guessed. A shiver ran the length of Khirro's spine. Rumor said this man was more than just a healer, something darker and deadlier who dabbled in arts outlawed in Erechania. Khirro hadn't believed the stories until the flash of light felled his undead pursuer.

The other two men wore heavy armor. The taller of the two wore silver and gold plate embossed with the crossed sword and lightning insignia of the Kingsblade—the King's personal guard—the other's armor was plain black plate marked and dented with use.

"Little life remains in the king," the healer said without looking up. "Give me the vial, Gendred."

The man in black plate pulled a glass vial from his belt and passed it to the healer. Gendred. Khirro had heard the name but never seen the man—few had, fewer had and lived. He was a Shadowman, one of an elite group of fighter-assassins Khirro had thought more fable than reality. On quiet watches, fantastic tales of the Shadowmen passed from soldier to soldier, building their legend. It

25

became the goal of any good warrior to be drafted into their brotherhood. The thought never crossed Khirro's mind.

"The boy lives," Gendred growled looking sideways at Khirro, his pock-marked face turned down in a sour look. Nothing about him looked friendly.

"Leave him," the healer said. "I'll deal with him later."

He held his hand above the king's head, a whispered chant of rhythmic cadence coming from beneath the darkened hood. Khirro shifted to watch, his movement drawing a glare from the Shadowman. The third man stood against the far wall, arms folded across his chest, concern showing in the blue eyes peering from beneath bushy red brows.

The healer's chant increased in volume, his pale hand shook. He spoke dusty, archaic words foreign to Khirro, unsettling, and he squirmed on the dirt floor in spite of himself. The king's eyes stared wide and glassy at the high ceiling as it collected oily smoke twisting up from the torches. To Khirro, it looked as though Braymon had already passed to the fields of the dead, but the healer's incantation continued.

The king gasped, his body jerked.

Startled, Khirro jumped, a bolt of pain lancing through his arm. The healer held the vial between thumb and index finger over Braymon's torso, open end toward the king. Braymon's back arched as though drawn toward the vial and Khirro held his breath. Gendred and the man of the Kingsblade watched silently. Above the king's head, the healer's hand quaked; the hand holding the vial remained steady.

It was just a single drop first, so small Khirro barely noticed. Another drop followed, then another. Khirro drew a sharp breath as the droplets expanded to a thin stream flowing from the king upward to the vial. Somehow, the blood from the king's wounds collected at his midsection, concentrating in one place to defy the Gods' laws. The fine stream of blood filled the vial as the healer continued chanting.

The container approached fullness and the stream waned, became droplets again, then stopped. The healer kept chanting as he turned the vial right side up, then his words ceased. The king's body spasmed then moved no more, the end of the healer's words releasing him to the fields of the dead. The officer of the Kingsblade and Gendred bowed their heads and kept their silence. Sadness gripped Khirro's chest, surprising him.

"Weep not for your king," the healer said as he stood. He drew a cork from somewhere in his sleeve and capped the vial then waved his fingers around it and spoke more foreign words. Then he said, "All I need to retrieve the king from the fields of the dead is here in my hand."

The warriors raised their eyes. Khirro wiped a tear from his face, hoping the men hadn't seen, and looked at the

27

vial, too. The flickering torchlight lent it a dull crimson glow.

"We must dispose of the king's flesh," the healer said. "No one can know the king has fallen."

"What of this one, then, Shaman?"

Gendred gestured toward Khirro, speaking of him as though he wasn't in the room, but Khirro barely noticed.

The rumors about the healer are true.

The healer turned his gaze toward Khirro. Something flickered beneath the cowl, impossibly far away. A shiver galloped up Khirro's spine.

"What is your name, soldier?"

"Kh-Khirro."

"Khirro has done the kingdom a great service." He paused as the torches flickered and spat in their sconces, then continued, his voice quiet, serious. "You have seen much."

Khirro shook his head.

They mean to kill me.

But he'd risked his life to bring the king to them, surely that meant something. He fought the urge to crawl away from their gazes, to seek refuge in a shadowy corner of the room.

"I won't tell anyone," he squeaked.

The healer chuckled, a sound like stone rubbed against stone.

"Of course you won't," he said still looking at Khirro.

Then, over his shoulder to the other men: "Bring him with us."

Khirro's chest felt as though it dropped into his stomach.

Bring him with us? Bring me where?

He stared into the blackness beneath the hood, searching for answers, but it revealed nothing. A horrible feeling flooded his aching body, one he'd never have expected: he found himself thinking he'd have been better off at the end of the monster's axe.

"That wouldn't be wise," the Shadowman said without looking at Khirro. His voice held the taut tone of a man containing his anger. It wouldn't be long before Khirro realized it sounded thus because it was the truth of it. "He looks more farmer than fighter."

"But he's a trained soldier of the king's army," the other man said and Khirro realized he knew him. They called him Rudric. He'd been one of the men leading Khirro's training.

"Hmph. He'll slow us down at best, more likely get us killed. I have no desire to waste my time saving his skin at every turn."

Blood rushed to Khirro's face. He'd managed to get the king here with a monstrous creature at his heels. Didn't that prove he was no longer a novice? He opened his mouth to protest the Shadowman's words but snapped it shut remembering his blunders on the wall walk which had led to Braymon's death. His ego shrank like a snail pulling its head into its shell.

"He has seen too much for us to leave him," Rudric said.

Does he mean they should spare me or kill me?

"And he'll be a burden if we take him," Gendred added.

He means to kill me.

The healer looked at them. "Would you kill the man who has kept hope alive? Would you kill the man who has given us the opportunity to bring back our king?"

Gendred opened his mouth to protest, but the healer raised a hand, stopping him. The vial was gone from his grasp, disappeared somewhere into his robe.

"Bring him with us."

Rudric nodded, accepting the healer's command, but Gendred remained motionless, the muscles of his jaw flexing as he ground his teeth.

"Bring me where?" Khirro fought hard to keep his voice from trembling.

"We are bound for Lakesh," the healer answered.

Khirro's breath caught in his throat.

Lakesh. The haunted land.

4

The healer dabbed a poultice on the short gash above Khirro's right eye. Whatever he applied to the wounds felt like nothing Khirro had experienced before—the cuts and bruises tingled with an unsettling but not unpleasant warmth; his flesh convulsed and quivered each time the poultice touched him. In his head, he heard his mother telling his four-year-old-self the story of a wizard who befriended a boy so he could cook him in a pie to feed his pet troll for dessert. In the story, the boy found himself in that predicament because he hadn't listened to his mother, of course.

At that moment, Khirro could identify with the boy in the story.

"Relax," the healer said noticing the tension in his limbs. "I will not hurt you."

Khirro let out a shuddering breath, forcing his muscles to unknot. Despite being only inches away, the darkness shrouding the healer's face revealed nothing. Occasionally, Khirro thought he saw a glint as torchlight caught the healer's eye, but it was gone so quickly, he couldn't be sure he saw even that.

"You needn't take me with you, Master Sha-- Master Healer," Khirro said. "The king saved my life. I wouldn't betray him."

With Rudric and Gendred gone bearing the king's body away in a canvas sack, the room gathered his words and cast them into the space above to reverberate in the ceiling. The Shaman finished up with the gash on his forehead and moved to an abrasion on his cheek.

"None can know of our journey." He leaned close and

31

Khirro smelled the scent of his breath: sweet and musty, acrid and mild—mint, cinnamon, and mold. It changed with each word so Khirro couldn't identify any one odor. "It may not seem it, given our destination, but I take you with us to protect you."

"But I'd never tell."

"If you are with us, there is no chance a pint of ale or a pretty girl loosens your tongue. There are those who would do anything to find out what you know."

Khirro shifted uncomfortably at the healer's words. "I have a lady who's with child. Can't I return to her, leave this all behind.?"

The healer paused as though considering his request. The thought of returning home bolstered Khirro only slightly. There would be struggles there, too, but of a vastly different nature.

"Our enemies are resourceful. It will not be long before they discover the king has fallen. If your involvement is discovered, neither you nor your family is safe. It is better for all if you are with us."

"But what if they find out anyway? They could still go after my family."

"For what, Khirro? You would never know they threatened those you love, so they would gain nothing from it."

Khirro noticed tension crawling back into his muscles at the Shaman's words: for his family to be safe, he must allow them to drag him to the cursed earth of Lakesh. The healer returned to his ministrations while Khirro's thoughts strayed to Emeline. The thought of her made his heart ache. He wondered if he'd see her again, if they would ever live their lives together—a question in need of answer whether the haunted land lurked in his future or not.

"Why Lakesh, Master Healer?"

"You watched as I drew the last living blood from the king." He moved his attention to a cut on Khirro's forearm. "With this, the king may be raised from the fields of the dead, but I have not the skills to perform such acts. Only the Necromancer possesses such ability."

"But...Lakesh. Is there no one else?"

Khirro shuddered. Lakesh—the haunted land, the cursed earth, country of magic and shadows and evil. The name alone instilled fear. People said no man who crossed the Little Sea into Lakesh ever returned.

"There is only one Necromancer, can only ever be one, and he is the only one who can do what needs be done. You will be safe with me, for I have safe passage through the dark land. Darestat was once my master, you see."

Khirro's eyes widened although this revelation no longer surprised him. "So it's true. You're more than a Master Healer."

"Yes. I am Bale, the king's Shaman."

"Did the king know?"

"Of course. It was the king's plan to be raised if he fell. The drawing of lifeblood is something no mere healer can do."

The Shaman rolled Khirro on his side facing the wall to work on his back, applying the poultice and murmuring the occasional unrecognizable word under his breath. His cold, strong hands made Khirro tense as they fell silent again. The dark magic made his hurts feel better, but what would it mean in the future? Could it taint him? If he could walk away from this evil, he would, but doing so would mean his life, maybe others.

When he completed his work, the Shaman stood and gestured for Khirro to do the same. With teeth gritted against the expected pain, Khirro pushed himself first to a sitting position, then rose to his feet. His tendons creaked, joints popped, but his injuries felt like they had occurred a week or more before and were in the final stages of healing.

"How...?" he began but stopped. *This is magic*. He didn't want to know any more about it.

"The entire kingdom is in your debt, though they may never know it."

Khirro's lips twitched into a self-conscious smile. Despite the fear and shame, confusion and embarrassment, pride dwelled within him. He *had* done something heroic, hadn't he? Someone else might have left the king there, but he'd done the right thing.

34

The door swung open, startling Khirro out of his self-congratulation, and Rudric and Gendred entered, their faces damp with sweat.

"The deed is done," Rudric said in a reverent tone. Gendred said nothing, his face frozen in the same stern expression that never seemed to leave it.

"And none saw you? The body will not be discovered?"

"There is naught to find but ashes and bone," Gendred snapped and cast a seething glance at Khirro. "You needn't question *me*, Shaman."

The air in the room became heavy and thick. To avoid confrontation, Khirro went to where his clothes and armor lay in a heap. He dressed hurriedly, promising himself to wash the acidic smell of urine from his breeches the first time they were near water. He pulled his leather cuirass on, cinching the straps when a thought came to him.

"Armor."

The three men looked at him; Khirro raised his eyes from his buckles as they regarded him.

"The king's armor lays abandoned on the stairs to the North tower."

Gendred spat a curse into the cloying air. The Shaman moved toward the door, robe swaying with the movement. He waved his hand, rippling the air, and stood rigid, staring at the door.

"It is too late. We must go."

Gendred glowered at Khirro, plainly blaming him for

the oversight. Khirro averted his eyes from the grim-faced warrior, directing his attention instead to fumbling with the straps of his cuirass. He nearly jumped when a hand touched his shoulder. He looked up nervously, fearing retribution, but it was Rudric standing before him, not Gendred.

"It's all right. You did what needed to be done. No man could expect more." He stepped back to survey Khirro. "You lost your helm and sword in the fight."

"What good is a sword to a farmer?" Gendred snorted.

Rudric ignored him. "I'll get you replacements."

Khirro nodded, thanking him with a barely perceptible smile. The officer of the Kingsblade stole from the room, returning moments later with a short sword and an open-faced helm. Rudric handed them to him with a shrug.

"Closest I could find. The previous owner won't miss them."

"Thank you." Khirro wondered who the previous owner had been and what happened to him. "You needn't have troubled yourself."

"You're a hero of the kingdom." Rudric put his hand on Khirro's shoulder again. "It's no trouble."

Gendred interrupted their exchange with a disgusted grunt. "How do you propose to leave this place, Shaman? Shall we march out the door to the rear gate? Two officers, a magic man and a farmer shouldn't attract much attention."

The Shaman ignored Gendred's baiting and moved to the wall at the back of the room.

"The king's armor has been discovered," Gendred continued. "Perhaps they'll return it to us, then hang us as traitors to the crown."

"Hold your tongue for once, Gendred," Rudric said, his tone calm but icy, the voice of command. Gendred sneered but fell silent. Watching their exchange, even Khirro saw the hostility between them seething beneath the surface. Perhaps only duty kept them from each others' throats.

The Shaman raised his arms, the wide sleeves of his robe falling back from long fingers, veins showing blue beneath translucent flesh. He muttered indistinguishable words, then placed his hand on first one stone, then another, then a third. A section of wall before him swung inward revealing a passage leading into darkness. Khirro squinted but inky blackness devoured the light only a few feet beyond the opening. The Shaman didn't say anything, didn't tell them to follow, he simply stepped across the threshold into the passage. The dark engulfed him as completely as it did the light from the torches, making it seem like the black-clad healer vanished.

Gendred took a torch from its wall sconce and plunged into the passage after the Shaman, the flame barely holding the darkness at bay. Rudric plucked another torch from the wall and ushered Khirro into the passage before him.

Damp, cool air touched Khirro's face. It smelled of

earth and mold, of ancient times and long gone people.
The passageway must have lain unused for many years,
maybe centuries, forgotten.

What other secrets does the Shaman keep?

Khirro put one tentative foot in front of the other, eyes
on Gendred's torch bobbing ahead of him, Rudric's torch
close behind lighting his way. He looked over his shoulder,
past the officer, and saw the dull gray square of doorway
disappear as the wall swung closed with the sound of rock
grinding on rock, shutting out the room, closing on his life
and everything he knew.

5

The soldier sat on the top stair cleaning blood from his
sword, listening to the groans of wounded men strewn on
the walk around him. He shifted and slid the blade into its
scabbard. Men moved along the wall walk making repairs,
tending the injured and collecting the dead. Most of them
made a wide berth around him, avoiding a man wearing
the garb of the king's guard. A few archers remained at the
parapet launching arrows at the retreating Kanosee, but
they had pulled back beyond bow range. The fight had
been fierce but, despite the wall breach, they'd repelled
the invaders.

For now.

Farther down the wall walk, soldiers scavenged the
fallen enemy for whatever they might keep or sell. He

sneered. How could they act that way? Where was their honor? On the battlefield, in the heat of the fight when life and death were at stake, such things were done for survival, not for personal gain. Bury them or burn them, don't rob them. He spat in their direction and turned his head away.

When the Kanosee soldiers breached the wall, it had required all his focus to stay alive, and he lost track of the king in the melee. The last time he saw Braymon, he was engaged with one of the monstrosities summoned to swell the Kanosee ranks. The tide of battle engulfed the soldier, distracting him from his assignment until a fresh troop of Erechanians joined the fray, driving the invaders from the wall, setting the ladders alight with urns of burning pitch. The stench of burnt flesh had threatened to empty the soldier's stomach; he might have known some of those men, as he may have known some he slew himself. When his thoughts had cleared of the fog of battle, the king was gone. The cloaked man wouldn't be happy he failed, but he'd have other opportunities.

The soldier stood, stretched, and glanced down the stair at the landing below, a glint of sunlight on metal catching his attention. Near the wall, crowded at the corner of the landing, he saw a suit of plate—Erechanian and of high quality, but he couldn't get a good view. He hurried down the stairs for a closer look.

Puddled blood, dried and brown, stained the landing.

Bruce Blake

He surveyed the scene with a practiced eye and surmised two men had lain here, one gravely injured. His gaze followed the trail of blood descending the stair and the story became clear: one man injured, the other stripped his armor to carry him to safety. The warrior shook his head. How many men died trying to save one fallen soldier when the entire fortress was in peril? He half-smiled at the novice mistake and went to the heap of plate, shifting it with the toe of his boot. Dirty, scuffed, caked with dried blood inside and out. Through the flaking gore and dust of battle, a pattern was evident on the breast plate. He brushed grime away with a gloved hand and revealed a scrollwork of enameled ivy. His eyes widened.

The armor belonged to the king.

It must have been he who was seriously wounded, carried to safety by some faithful soldier. His stomach clenched. How would he find the king and complete his task now? Anger rose in the soldier; he despised failure, had been trained since birth that it meant weakness. A boot scuffed on a stair below and he stood, muscles tensed, hand on sword hilt.

"Ye! What 'ave we 'ere?" The man ascending the stairs halted as he saw the soldier standing over the pile of armor. "Anythin' valuable?"

"Not sure."

The soldier kept his voice purposely low to draw the man closer. With the king fallen, he had little time. The

40

cloaked man had told him what would happen if the king fell and the Shaman performed his abomination, had explained how they would get out of the fortress. He needed to find a way to intercept them before they got too far. This man might be the way.

"I can't see, ya damn fool. Move outta me way!"

The soldier shifted, keeping his king's guard insignia hidden, and made space for the other man to sidle in beside him. The man did as the soldier had moments before, crouching, wiping dirt away for a better look and to gauge the armor's value. The soldier loosened his dagger in its sheath.

"Gods, look at this. Must be worth a fortune."

He brushed away more dirt, then stopped, hand hovering above an exposed loop of ivy spilling across the breastplate. The soldier's dagger slid free.

"What is it?"

"The king," the man said, a note of shock in his words. He stood, half turning toward the soldier. "It's the king's pl--"

The soldier's blade touched the man's throat, cutting off his words as the sharp edge pressed flesh hard enough to draw blood.

"Don't cry out. I'll open your throat before a sound escapes."

The man's eyes widened and his breathing stopped; the soldier knew he'd do whatever he said. This man was no warrior, he clung too tightly to life.

"There are tunnels leading from the fortress. Do you know how to access them?"

The man didn't respond at first, so the soldier pressed more firmly and a drop of blood rolled down the man's his neck. He nodded once, a quick, mute movement intended to keep the dagger's edge from slicing deeper into his throat.

"Take me." The soldier spun the man around, facing him down the stairs, deftly moving the blade from his throat and inserting the tip through the seam in his leather armor. "Don't betray me or I'll gut you like the pig you are."

They descended to the courtyard five flights below, beads of sweat running down the man's neck, mixing with the blood. They were nearly at the bottom when the man next spoke.

"Why? Why do you betray your king?"

"Not my king," the soldier growled and jabbed the knife further into the man's ribs. "Looks can be deceiving."

They crossed the courtyard, bodies pressed close hiding the dagger between them. Soldiers and workers passed by, too distracted with their own business of repairs and clean-up to notice anything awry. The soldier breathed deep, inhaling familiar fumes of battle, and raised his eyes to the sun. Many hours yet remained in the day, encouraging him. He'd find the king.

His mission would yet be completed.

6

Spitting and sputtering, Khirro plucked another spider web from his face. He'd lost track of how many times he'd pulled the unseen traps of their silky strands from his face, as he lost track of how much time passed while they followed the tunnel. It sloped down gently at first but soon fell away at an angle steep enough to necessitate careful footing. Not long before this last arachnid's snare, the tunnel leveled, then began to climb again. The tingling heat in Khirro's wounds intensified as the four men walked, silent and purposeful.

What did he do to me?

What little pain lurked beneath the heat was less than the ache of effort burning in his thighs. Keeping pace with Gendred and the Shaman proved difficult, but Rudric stayed close, the light cast by his torch opening a circle six feet in diameter around them. Beyond it lay impenetrable gloom. Occasionally, the air quality in the tunnel changed as they went by passage openings, but they never veered from their path. Khirro peered into the solid darkness as they passed each one, only once divining anything in the pitch black—a glimpse of movement that wasn't the scurry of a rat or mouse, but something larger shuffling in the gloom. Startled, Khirro misstepped and nearly fell, but Rudric caught him by the arm, ushered him forward. After

43

that, Khirro's eyes didn't stray from Gendred's ring of light leading the way as the ascent went on and on. Torch smoke clung to Khirro's lungs with each breath, clogging his chest and stretching time impossibly long.

"How much farther?" he said over his shoulder to Rudric trying to make it sound like he was not panting as he spoke. "It seems we've been walking all day."

"Quiet," Gendred barked from ahead. Khirro received no other answer.

More sloped floor passed beneath their feet; Khirro calculated the passage must have been excavated beneath the lowest levels of the fortress, below the dungeon. As he marveled at what depth into the earth they must have traveled, the upward grade eased, then leveled. His lungs ached with thankful anticipation—even the horse-and-human stink of the fortress would be a relief after the claustrophobic tunnel. No torch smoke would seek his airways outside the cursed tunnel, no unseen things shuffling about in the dark, no spider webs waiting to ambush his face. Instead, he'd feel the sun on his face and breathe fresh air to cleanse his chest. So many years living the agrarian life made him take such things for granted, but a few hours of underground isolation reminded him how much a part of his life the elements were.

Distracted, Khirro watched his feet as they walked the last stretch of unknown distance, unable to discern the outline of his shoes in the dark as he imagined the warmth of the day and the relief in his lungs. He didn't notice Gendred stop and looked up too late to avoid walking into the man's back. Their armor and weapons clattered together with unnatural volume; Gendred whirled faster than Khirro had seen a man move.

The warrior's hand shot out of the dark with unerring design, grasping Khirro's throat, stopping his breath instantly. Thoughts of sunlight and fresh air fled as his hands clutched at his captor's grasp and met an arm chiseled of granite. The dancing torch flames snaked shadows across Gendred's emotionless face, mutating his expression into something fiendish.

He's going to kill me.

Rudric spoke a word and the Shadowman released his hold. Khirro gasped, head hung to avoid Gendred's gaze. Now, even the oily, smoke-filled air felt good.

When Khirro looked up again, Gendred had moved away. He might have stood there forever watching the warrior's outline recede, afraid to follow, if not for Rudric's hand on his shoulder prompting him forward. A few yards ahead, the Shaman stood in the center of the tunnel, flickering torch light engulfing his figure in writhing specters, making it impossible to tell if he moved or stood still. Whispered words crept along the tunnel walls, keeping to the shadows where they couldn't be heard, and the air grew heavy.

Light burst into the passageway and everything

45

disappeared: walls, men, the dark. Khirro threw his hands up to protect his eyes from the explosion of light which felt like the sun came down to settle amongst them. He blinked again and again, but his eyes resisted clarity after the long, dark walk underground. A gentle push from Rudric urged him on and he took a tentative step, not sure if he should be more afraid of the incredible light or of walking into Gendred again.

When the Shaman used magic to fell the undead creature, there had been light, but there was something more, too. A smell of energy expended. This time, the smell differed. Instead of ripped plasma and indescribable things, the smell was familiar.

Fresh air.

Five paces and the oppressive blackness and stale air disappeared. Revitalizing warmth bathed Khirro's face and clean air filled his lungs. He breathed deeply once, twice; each breath forced the stink of the torches from his chest. Squinting, he lowered his hands, eyes slowly adjusting to the light. As his vision cleared, relief filled his chest, fortifying his limbs, and he momentarily forgot his predicament.

Khirro surveyed the area as warmth and sunlight filled him. A vast meadow stretched before them, thigh high grass lush and green in places, burnt yellow by the summer sun in others. Patches of flowers dotted the ocean of grass: purple heather, white daisies and orange poppies waved in the scant breeze. Distant hillocks rose and fell like frozen waves. To their right, the dark stone of the massive fortress wall rose, casting little shadow in the midday sun, an impressive sight even to someone who had lived behind that wall for the past months.

Rudric pushed past Khirro, extinguished his torch and threw it back into the yawning mouth of the tunnel. Gendred did the same. Khirro turned to look back at the tunnel they'd vacated and his scabbard banged against the Shadowman's leg.

"Watch it," Gendred growled, but Khirro's attention was on a piece of earth as it slid over the opening in the hillock, transforming it back into one amongst many.

"The hills," Khirro said turning to Rudric. "I hadn't noticed them before. They're quite unusual."

"Not hills: barrows. Every man, woman and child who's met their end at the Isthmus fortress lies beneath them." He looked at them with reverence, a soldier silently paying his respect to fallen comrades. "There will soon be more."

They observed them together in a silence that felt uncomfortable to Khirro. He thought of the thing shuffling in the dark, his mind conjuring visions of something dead but not dead, like the thing that nearly killed him in the courtyard. Shivering, he shook his head to loosen the thought. He didn't want to think of dead soldiers—there was too much chance he'd soon be one of them, though it was unlikely his body would ever be found and buried

47

here.

"There's one fallen soldier who won't be among them," Khirro said breaking the moment. "King Braymon."

Rudric half-smiled. "Only his body is lost. We will ensure Braymon's return."

Khirro opened his mouth to ask a question but the Shaman spoke before the words cleared his lips.

"Stealth is needed. Following the road or seawall will be risky. We cannot chance being stopped and interrogated. The fewer who know of our passing, the less perilous our journey will be."

"And how do you suggest we cross the plain without being seen?" Gendred asked appraising the area around them.

At their backs, smoke rose skyward from cook fires and smithies of the village outside the fortress gates. The plain stretched on to farms on one side and to the seawall many leagues ahead—all of it would be patrolled.

"There's a drainage ditch ahead. It will provide us cover," Rudric said. "The sun will have dried it by this time of year."

The Shaman nodded. "It is less than a league from here. We will stay close to the base of the wall until we reach the ditch. We cannot be seen or the alarm will be raised"

Gendred grunted and immediately started for the wall without waiting for the others. The Shaman fell in with him, robe fluttering and waving as he moved. Rudric prompted Khirro forward and they followed, though the pace Gendred set once again proved quicker than he could comfortably maintain. Even though Rudric could likely match the Shadowman's speed, he stayed with Khirro, whose respect and like for the man increased. As they walked, the question which had occurred to him a few minutes earlier returned to Khirro: *if the king's body is gone, but we restore his spirit, what body will he have?* He decided to keep it to himself for the moment.

They reached the foot of the wall and Khirro paused to take in its immensity. From its base, the wall seemed to go up forever, not stopping until it reached the Gods. It was obviously huge from inside, but buildings and stairways and towers divided its surface into smaller, less meaningful portions. Only from here could its size truly be appreciated.

"Keep moving." Rudric's words jarred him from his thoughts. "We've no time to lose."

Khirro peered up the wall again and sighed. Soon it would be far behind and he'd likely never see it again. He hated the place, wanted only to be home every second he'd been behind the wall, but now wished he could stay.

He followed Rudric. Gendred and the Shaman had gotten farther ahead, sometimes appearing at the top of a hillock, then disappearing down the other side, swallowed by the barrows.

"How far is it , General?" Khirro asked after a while.

"Not far. Beyond the next barrow. And, given our circumstances, I think it best you call me Rudric."

Khirro nodded, stifling a smile that one of the highest ranking men in the king's army wanted him to call him by his first name. How different Rudric was from the Shadowman who accompanied them.

"How come Gendred dislikes me so much, Rudric?" Khirro asked trying out the name. It felt odd in his mouth, but its use made him happy, proud.

Rudric chuckled. "Gendred dislikes everyone. Don't take it to heart, he's harmless." Khirro doubted that. "It took years before he and I--"

Something cut Rudric's words short and stopped him mid-step. Khirro halted, too, and looked into the general's intense face.

"What is it?"

Rudric put his finger to his lips, silencing Khirro, who heard nothing for long seconds except the sound of his own blood pulsing in his ears as he held his breath. Then, ahead of them from the other side of the last large barrow, came a yell. The sound of metal contacting metal followed quickly, then silence again, the sound cut off like a hand clamped over a mouth.

Rudric drew his sword and leaped forward. Left behind, Khirro drew the short sword Rudric had found him, the feel of it clumsy and uncomfortable in his hand. No sword ever sat comfortably in his grip, but this one was too light, its hilt smaller than what he used in practice. Khirro loped up the barrow feeling weighed down by his leather and light mail. Rudric quickly outdistanced him despite his much heavier plate, disappearing over the crest of a hill. Khirro reached the top seconds later and stopped to gaze incredulously at the sight at the foot of the hillock. The blood drained from his limbs.

At the bottom of the slope, on the edge of the drainage ditch, eight Kanosee soldiers engaged Gendred while two others lay dead at his feet. A few yards away, the Shaman struggled with a huge fighter garbed in black mail splashed with red paint. A shimmering cloud distorted the figures and enveloped the area around them. Sparks flew as Gendred parried blows and struck his own, but Khirro heard nothing of the battle. Meadow birds sang, grasshoppers chirruped, his leather armor creaked as he drew breath, but no sounds emanated from the fight. Rudric skidded to a halt short of the haze.

"Bale has cast a spell of silence," he called over his shoulder. "There will be no aid from the fortress. Hurry."

He sprang through the undulating gleam of the Shaman's spell without slowing, and slammed into the undead soldier gripping the Shaman's wrists. The three of them tumbled to the ground, but Rudric darted up in an instant and brought his heavy sword down across the creature's neck. Its head rolled across a narrow band of grass and over the edge into the ditch beyond.

Khirro scudded down the hill. Behind the diaphanous curtain, he saw Rudric say something to the Shaman, then rush to Gendred's aid. When Khirro reached the edge of the spell, he hesitated. Only five Kanosee soldiers remained.

They have things under control.

Haltingly, Khirro put his hand through the shimmering air, steeling himself for pain, but there was not so much as a tickle. He let out his breath and shivered. The Shaman's hands danced and moved, readying a spell and he remembered how his pursuer had fallen dead in the courtyard.

I'll wait for him to cast his spell. I'd only be in the way. Whatever spell he casts will end the fight.

A Kanosee soldier stumbled out of the fray and nearly tripped over one of his fallen comrades. He stopped, wiped blood from his face, then bent and plucked a bow from the dead soldier's hand, an arrow from the quiver on his back, and faced the Shaman. Khirro called a warning but his words bounced back from the hazy invocation and died in the summer air as the enemy soldier sited the Shaman. The weapon in Khirro's hand felt suddenly foreign, the weight of the short sword great. He looked toward the others.

What if the Kanosee prevail? The thought made him both fearful and morbidly hopeful. *If they all die, there's no reason for me to go to the haunted land.*

He shook his head, dispelling the thought, and reached a hand through the glistening shell, staring at it as it penetrated. If nothing else, he owed the king his life.

Too late.

A flash of movement caught his eye. He looked up and saw the Shaman's incantation die on his lips, his hands cease moving as he slumped forward, falling awkwardly around the arrow piercing his chest. Khirro gaped at the Shaman lying in a heap on the grass.

The Kanosee soldier nocked another arrow. Gendred saw him and shouted—Khirro saw his mouth move—but in the instant of distraction another Kanosee soldier's sword glanced off Gendred's parry, the edge finding a sliver of flesh between epaulet and helm. Blood squirted, but Gendred fought on, impaling the man. He wrenched his sword free of the enemy's belly and lurched toward the bowman.

Three wobbling strides passed beneath his feet before one of the two Kanosee remaining in close combat cut him down. Gendred stumbled, sword falling from his hand, his balance holding for an instant before he pitched face first to the blood stained grass.

The archer loosed his arrow. It struck Rudric in the shoulder, piercing his plate mail and knocking him back a step. With a grimace of pain and effort, he chopped down the man who felled Gendred leaving one Kanosee soldier in close combat with him as the bowman drew another

53

arrow.

Thoughts of home and safety fled Khirro's mind. If Rudric died, he'd be left alone with the enemy and the Kanosee surely wouldn't let him live. He burst through the spell's shimmering veil, swapping gentle bird song, rustling grass and the sound of his pulse beating in his ears for the biting clang of steel on steel, the howl of a battle cry.

It took an instant to realize the scream of rage belonged to him.

He rushed at the bowman, who spun toward his cry, startled. The Kanosee archer nocked his arrow quickly and released without benefit of aim, acting purely out of self-preservation.

Pain seared Khirro's thigh and he pitched forward. His shoulder struck the ground, jolting more agony through his body. He lay on the grass, teeth clenched, hand going unconsciously to the wound in his leg. The arrow had pierced the fleshy outside of his right thigh, just missing bone; the head protruded through the back with the shaft buried to the flights at the front. He cringed, stomach roiling.

This must be how father felt when he lost his arm.

Pain filled his body, pounding and pulsing through his veins, the sound of it clouding his mind. He might have cried out, but couldn't be sure. For a moment, his world was only the wound in his leg and the misery it inflicted.

Slowly, the blood-colored cloud receded from his eyes, from his ears—like a blanket pulled back from a child to wake him—and the world returned.

Khirro heard his name shouted and remembered where he was, what was happening. He struggled to his knees and searched for his one remaining ally, saw the fallen Shaman, the dead soldiers. Sweat streamed from under Rudric's helm as he fought a Kanosee soldier clad in the black-and-red mail of the undead; the general's left arm dangled uselessly as he wielded his huge broad sword with the other hand. To Khirro's right, the archer nocked an arrow and sited Rudric, awaiting his opportunity to let fly and end the fray. Khirro struggled toward him on hands and knees. Everything happened at once.

The undead monster swung his sword.

Rudric dodged and returned a blow, catching the Kanosee across the neck, sending his head tumbling from his shoulders.

The bowman drew back as Khirro lunged forward, swinging his short sword in a frantic arc. He missed by a foot and tumbled to the grass at the archer's feet, breath knocked from his chest.

The Kanosee archer loosed his arrow as Rudric took a step toward him.

The arrow pierced Rudric's throat, stopping him mid-stride. He wobbled like a man spun around and made dizzy, then his knees buckled and he folded to the ground, dead.

Struggling to draw air, Khirro scrambled to his knees, eyes wide, heart racing. The enemy kicked him in the chest and sent him reeling onto his back. His head hit the ground knocking his helm free. The sky loomed above him, bluer than he remembered it ever being. No clouds marred its smoothness as it stretched on forever, leading to the fields of the dead where he would soon go.

The sky disappeared as the shadow of the Kanosee soldier fell across him. Khirro squinted but couldn't see the face of the silhouette standing against that beautiful sky, an inky shape with nocked arrow and drawn bow.

"Death be yours, Erechanian pig," the bowman growled as he straddled Khirro. He drew the bowstring to its fullest. Khirro raised his arms knowing the attempt to defend himself would prove futile.

A second passed. In that small space—more time than Khirro thought left in his life—he heard a sound like a stone thrown against leather followed by a splash of dirt against his cheek, then a gurgling from the archer's lips.

Khirro lowered his arms.

The bow hung limply at the side of the black silhouette and a new appendage had grown from the man's chest. The archer lurched to one side and Khirro could see again. It wasn't a new arm sprouting from his chest, but a sword penetrating from behind. The bow fell from his hand, his body thrown roughly aside as the sword pulled free. Khirro expected Rudric or Gendred, even King Braymon, miraculously coming to his rescue, but the man standing over him was none of them.

Khirro gasped in as much air as his lungs could take as breath finally returned. He stared up at the man standing over him. His clean shaven face looked back impassively, blood dripped from his sword.

Khirro scrambled away, the arrow protruding from his thigh catching the ground and sending a fresh wave of pain coursing along his leg. He fell back, face pinched with agony. The man—his rescuer? his killer?—took a step toward him.

"Don't be afraid," he said. "I'm on your side."

Khirro looked at the man through a haze of pain. Did he speak the truth? Should he thank him or defend himself? He touched the hilt of the dagger hanging from his belt but didn't draw it.

"Who are you?" Khirro rasped, his lungs thankful for air and not wanting to waste it on words. The man's armor bore Erechanian markings.

"Are there any others?" The soldier looked around, then back at Khirro who shook his head. He switched his sword from his left hand to his right and offered to help Khirro up. "All right. Let's see if anyone lives."

Khirro stared at the man's hand without accepting it, not knowing if he truly meant to help him.

What choice do I have?

Fresh blood ran down his thigh as the man pulled him to his feet. The muscles of his jaw bunched as he bit down against the pain.

"You're wounded."

He set his sword aside and pulled a long knife from his belt. With two strokes, he removed the fletching from the shaft.

"What are you--?"

"Brace yourself."

Before Khirro could, he pulled the arrow through his thigh with one swift movement. Khirro cried out, swaying on rubbery legs, and the man caught him by the arm, steadying him. When he regained his balance, the man removed a pack from his back and drew a strip of cloth from it to wrap Khirro's wound and stem the flow of blood.

"What's your name? Why do you help me?"

"I'm called Ghaul." The man pulled his pack back on. "I serve the king as you do, but there will be time for talk later. We should check your friends quickly, there may be more Kanosee about. I'll check the robed man."

"No," Khirro responded without knowing why he objected.

Something inside him—perhaps something as simple as a sense of responsibility—told him to protect the Shaman and the item he carried. Ghaul shrugged and went to where Gendred lay amongst the tall grass burnt red with the Shadowman's blood. Khirro's leg pulsed with pain as he hobbled to the Shaman's side.

Blood soaked the magic man's cloak. Khirro stood over him, an unexpected sense of loss churning his gut, tightening his throat. The three men performed their heroics to save the king, he knew, but they also saved his life and for that he owed them.

If only I'd joined the fight sooner, maybe they'd still be alive. If only I'd been brave.

"Khirro."

Little more than the sound of breath passing lips, the word startled Khirro and sent goose flesh crawling down his arms.

"Khirro. What's happened?"

The Shaman coughed bloody spittle from the dark depths of his cowl. His hands shaking, Khirro reached out and pushed the hood back. The Shaman's sallow skin stretched thin on his hairless skull, blue veins drawing a grim map of some unknown country. His open eyes stared skyward—one black with no pupil or iris, the other red. His purple lips quivered with each pained breath.

"Rudric and Gendred have fallen."

The Shaman closed his eyes. He coughed again spattering bright blood across his pallid cheek. His head rocked back and forth slightly in protest or denial or both.

"Can you heal yourself?"

"No."

Khirro looked up and down the healer's prone form. "What can I do? How can I help?"

"You cannot help me." As the Shaman spoke his face contorted and his body tensed then went limp.

"Where did they come from?"

"They found the tunnels, came out at the drainage ditch."

Khirro glanced at the ditch and the small opening in the fortress wall feeding it. The iron gate that should have covered it hung from one hinge, canted at an awkward angle. Khirro's breath shortened in realization there was nothing to stop more Kanosee coming through to kill them all.

"The entrance is sealed," the Shaman said reading Khirro's thoughts. He took a shuddering breath and air gurgled through the wound in his chest. "Take this."

Khirro didn't see the Shaman move his hand, yet he held the vial, arm shaking as his strength waned. Khirro stared, mesmerized by the crimson fluid ebbing and flowing inside with the quake of the magic man's hand.

"No." He shook his head as much to tear his eyes from the vial as to indicate dissent. "I can't."

"You must."

"I'm not strong enough or brave enough. I'll return to the fortress. I'll get someone capable."

Khirro went to stand, but the Shaman gripped his wrist. Khirro winced, surprised the injured man still had such strength.

"No time," the Shaman rasped. "You're the only hope."

"I can't do it."

Khirro's head sagged, unable to meet the Shaman's mismatched eyes. Another gurgling breath shuddered the man's body. His strength flagged and the hand holding the vial slumped to the grass, though he maintained his grip on Khirro's wrist with the other. The vial rolled from his fingertips and came to rest against Khirro's boot with a soft clink.

"Come close."

Khirro hesitated, worried the man might still be dangerous.

It wouldn't make sense for him to harm me.

He chastised himself. This man kept him alive when Gendred would have killed him.

Khirro leaned close to the magic man's swollen lips, close enough they brushed his ear as the fallen healer whispered non-sensical words. Khirro listened, brow furrowed, attempting to hear the quiet voice, comprehend the words. It took only a few seconds for him to understand why the Shaman beckoned him.

"Gods!"

Khirro pulled away, but the healer grasped him by the back of his neck, pulled him close with strength impossible for a dying man. Unintelligible words flowed from the Shaman's lips as Khirro struggled to get free and images flashed through his mind: a wizened old man, an ancient stone keep, a ruby dragon, vast forests, uncountable hills, windswept waters, unknown towns, and finally the meadow outside the fortress walls. Vivid and real, it seemed as though he saw them right here, right now. Sweat beaded Khirro's brow, his hands shook. The Shaman completed the incantation and released him. Khirro fell back.

"What have you done?" Khirro demanded with shaking voice. "What have you done to me?"

The Shaman's eyes slipped shut. Only his lips moved as he spoke. "He who seeks entrance to the keep must face the keeper alone."

Khirro shook his head. "What have you done?"

"I've shown you the way to Darestat the Necromancer."

"I won't go," he insisted, voice louder. He glanced over his shoulder—Ghaul continued his search of a fallen Kanosee soldier, unaware of the exchange. "I told you I won't. I'll find someone else."

A pinched smile contorted the Shaman's lips into an ugly purple gash across his face. "You have no choice, Khirro."

He stared at the magic man, wanting to believe he hadn't heard his words. He crawled closer to the Shaman again. "What do you mean?"

"You're bound to save your king." The Shaman coughed another gout of blood.

62

"No. This can't be."

Breath rattled from the Shaman's throat, the gurgling in his chest ceased. Khirro looked past the fallen man, his attention drawn away as the shimmering curtain of air surrounding them faded. Meadow sparrows chirped, but, to Khirro's ears, it wasn't the happy sound that makes one glad to be alive, not now. Perhaps not ever again.

"Your friends are dead."

Khirro whirled at the sound of the man's voice, grabbing for his dirk. Ghaul took a step back, holding his hands up defensively.

"Whoa! Hold on, friend. What's the matter?"

Khirro's strength fled and he fell to his side on the grass, hand contacting the warm glass vial. Ghaul rushed to his side.

"Are you all right?"

Against every feeling in his body and thought in his head, Khirro closed his hand around the glass vessel containing the king's blood. He'd rather have gotten up and run from it, or hurled it as far as he could, but something made him tuck it under his tunic.

"I'm cursed," he said in a voice so calm it surprised him. "The Shaman has sentenced me to death."

7

Khirro sat cross-legged in the grass by the Shaman's body watching the blood within the vial move as he rolled

63

it back and forth on flattened palm. The urge to squeeze his fingers around it, choke it, throw it away had diminished to an almost forgotten thought in the wake of an inexplicable desire to protect it. The Shaman's curse had done this to him.

"What's that?"

He closed his fingers around the vessel, hiding it close to his chest. "Nothing. A bauble."

"Is this thing the reason you traipsed about the meadow with a Shaman and two warriors?"

Khirro's eyes narrowed. "What are you doing here?"

"I'm from a village to the north, near the mountains. When the king's men came to collect men to defend the fortress, I was ill with fever, so they left me behind. When the fever broke, I donned my armor, mounted my horse and came to fight for king and country. Only by the will of the Gods did I come upon you with a Kanosee arrow shoved up your nose. A little more gratitude might be in order."

"I know a man from the mountains," Khirro said recalling Tandel's brogue, absent from this man's voice. "What village?"

"Epoli."

"Never heard of it."

"I've probably never heard of yours, either."

"What of your horse?" Khirro snapped. He stood, hugging the king's blood to his chest.

"Perhaps the Shaman's spell scared him off. Magic will do that to some beasts."

"Quite a coincidence you came to this place the same time as the enemy."

"Do you think me an agent of those Kanosee dogs?" Ghaul drew his sword and Khirro shrank back, but instead of the threatening, he dropped the blade at Khirro's feet. "If I'm a soldier of Kanos, why didn't I let him kill you? Then I'd have taken your bauble and anything else I wanted."

Khirro opened his mouth but found nothing to say. Could it be coincidence this man happened across a fight while thousands inside the fortress knew nothing of it? He felt his cheeks turn red, embarrassed by his suspicion. Sunlight glinted off the steel of Ghaul's blade; seeing it lying there convinced him. If he undertook this journey—and, truthfully, he had no choice in the matter—the aid of someone deft with a sword would be invaluable.

"I'm sorry. I should be thanking you for saving my life, not questioning your loyalty. It's just... I don't want to go to Lakesh."

Ghaul's eyebrows dropped, fashioning a frown. "Lakesh? Why would you go there?"

"The Shaman cursed me to complete the task he set out to accomplish. I'm the only one left."

"What are you talking about? You make no sense."

Uncurling his fingers, Khirro extended his palm. The

dark red liquid shifted inside the vial with the shake of his unsteady hand.

"So?" Ghaul shrugged.

"It's blood."

"Whose?"

Khirro hesitated. "The king's."

Ghaul's eyes widened. "Braymon?"

Khirro nodded.

"The king fell in battle." Khirro's gut twinged as he said it, but he didn't elaborate. No one needed to know more than that. "The Shaman extracted his blood. I was to accompany them to Lakesh, to Darestat the Necromancer."

"I don't understand."

"He can bring the king back. He's the only one who can."

Ghaul sucked air in sharply through his teeth. "Raise the king."

The soldier shook his head and moved away, pacing to the nearby body of a Kanosee soldier clad in black and red mail. With a flick of his toe he sent the helm rolling from the rotted head.

"But what of this? The Kanosee fight alongside an army of the dead. Who but the Necromancer could raise such soldiers?"

Khirro forced wobbly legs to carry him to Ghaul's side, to look at the severed head. One vacant eye socket stared skyward, its jaw hung askew. It hadn't occurred to Khirro to wonder from where these living corpses had come. He'd been too worried about his own skin to ponder why theirs was decomposed.

"Maybe someone else has discovered the secret of recreating life," he ventured without conviction. He didn't need to look up to know Ghaul shook his head. Khirro said nothing for a time, afraid his tightening throat would choke his words.

Ghaul broke the silence, restating the Shaman's words. "Legend says there can be only one Necromancer."

Khirro took a slow, deep breath and released it. "The man who is supposed to be the savior of the kingdom is in league with the enemy and I'm cursed to journey into his grasp."

"Don't go."

"I have no choice."

Khirro stared at the undead soldier's head, imagining his own face there instead. Ghaul put his hand on Khirro's shoulder reassuringly, startling him.

"I'll come with you."

Relief and confusion furrowed Khirro's brow as he turned toward the stranger and saw the determination on his face.

"But why? There is nothing to gain, only danger and death."

"It isn't coincidence that brought me here at this time—the Gods have intervened. I came to serve my king and this may be the only way."

"We may never return to Erechania. Not alive." *Why am I arguing with him? Let him come.*

"A warrior expects neither life nor death, only to serve."

Khirro sighed and felt as though a weight lifted from his shoulders, though a wisp of suspicion still tickled the back of his mind. He set it aside in favor of self-preservation.

"Thank you."

"All there is left is finding this Necromancer."

"The Shaman showed me the way."

"A map?"

"No. He put it in my mind when he cursed me."

"I guess that makes you invaluable to the success of this task." He slapped Khirro on the shoulder and smiled, but Khirro couldn't find it in himself to return the gesture. "We should go or we'll soon be discovered." Ghaul bent over the nearest corpse, searching the body. "We'll need supplies. Take anything we can use."

"We were going to follow the drainage ditch. It'll take us to the forest and then Vendaria."

"Fine." Ghaul removed the quiver from the Kanosee archer. "Search the Shaman, he may carry something useful."

Khirro went to the magician lying on his side, the thought of searching him sitting cold and uncomfortable in his head. His attempt to open the magician's robe failed as the arrow which had penetrated his chest held it fast. He groaned realizing he'd have to remove it.

Remembering what Ghaul had done to pull the arrow from his leg, Khirro unsheathed his dirk and sheared the flights from the shaft. He moved behind the Shaman and grasped the end protruding from between his shoulder blades with both hands but quickly let go, his fingers sticky with drying blood. He stared at them, partly numb, partly repulsed. The blood smear left the lines of his palms white. A hand reader would easily read his future and probably tell him more blood was to come.

My life has suddenly become all about blood.

Khirro wiped his palms on his breeches, flinching at the pain in his leg, then gripped the shaft again, throat clenched to quell his rising gorge. He pulled, moving the arrow only little, then tried again with little success. With a shuddering breath, he jammed his foot against the small of the Shaman's back and yanked. The arrow came free with a wet sucking noise. Khirro threw the shaft aside and fell to his knees, retching. When he looked up, Ghaul was staring at him. Khirro waved dismissively and turned back to the magician.

The Shaman's robe hid no armor beneath, only under clothes soaked with enough blood, Khirro couldn't guess what color they'd been. There were no pockets sewn in the robe and nothing hung around his neck. He pulled the edge of the robe back and was surprised to find a belt around his waist, a scabbard hung from it. The black leather case wasn't embossed or decorated. Fine work, if plain. He undid the buckle, careful not to touch the bloody clothes or cooling flesh, and pulled it free. Standing, he removed his own sword belt and replaced it with the Shaman's.

The belt sat comfortably at his hip, reassuring, but wearing it felt wrong. He loosed the long sword from its sheath and pulled clear a few inches of blade unlike any he'd ever seen—black steel highlighted by red scrollwork. He unsheathed more of the blade—the runes ran the length of the blade.

"Anything?" Ghaul asked.

Khirro dropped the sword back into the scabbard and whirled to face him like a man caught stealing.

"Just his sword," he said defensively.

Why did he feel like a thief? The Shaman wouldn't miss it. In fact, if it helped complete his cursed task, he'd probably want him to have it. He put his hand on its hilt, more to keep it from leaping from its place than with any intent to draw it.

"Good. That will do you better than a short sword. Here."

He tossed him a sheathed dagger and Khirro barely released the sword in time to catch it. Gendred's dagger felt heavy in his hand, not comfortable like the sword. Guilt made the weapon feel weighty.

"We shouldn't take these. They're not ours."

70

Ghaul shook his head. "This a matter of survival, not personal gain."

"But I--"

"They gave their lives for their king and country, for this journey. Certainly they wouldn't hesitate to give a few of their belongings."

Khirro sighed and tucked the dagger into his belt. Ghaul was right—he shouldn't feel bad pilfering from his dead fellows. They'd have given everything for their king. In fact, they had.

"Now this he might not have wanted to give up to me," Ghaul said with a laugh as he brandished the fallen Kanosee archer's bow. He slung it over his shoulder and spat on the corpse. "I hope the shithawks have a good meal of your balls, pig."

High overhead, two dark shapes circled. The smell of blood had already attracted carrion feeders, and the birds would eventually attract attention from the fortress.

"Let's go before they swoop down and take our eyes by mistake."

Ghaul climbed down into the ditch first, moving with the athleticism of a practiced soldier. Khirro slid down the side painfully, skidding against the dirt side and coming to a jarring stop at the bottom. He gritted his teeth, determined not to cry out.

The trench's earthy odor reminded Khirro of home where the aroma of turned dirt was a constant in his life.

His family would be readying for the summer harvest, storing some away and taking the rest to market to trade for meats and staples they'd need for winter. The thought made his heart ache. Emeline would be with her parents doing the same. He longed to be there, to tend to her while her belly swelled. At least she'd be safe.

I hope.

Khirro breathed in the normally comforting smell but it offered no solace this time. He swayed on his injured leg, grappling for balance, then started after Ghaul.

Don't dwell on the past, it holds only sadness now.

Easy to think, difficult to do.

He didn't want to think of his future, either, for the complete unknown of it held only dread. As the fortress wall receded behind, his boots splashed in a trickle of water snaking down the middle of the trench. He tottered along the bottom of the ditch trying to calm his spinning head and a sound came to his ears, a rumble as if distant thunder spoke to him. He glanced up at the cloudless sky, confused for a moment before he identified the sound as hooves beating dry ground.

"They're coming," Ghaul said.

8

The sounds were small and far away. Khirro stopped to listen while his companion continued along the dusty path, pace unchanged. Sunlight streamed over the edge of

the ditch though they walked in shadow. Early evening.
They had a head start on their pursuers.

King's soldiers or Kanosee?

The death birds might have drawn their attention, but
more likely one of the regular patrols discovered the
battleground. Or maybe the Kanosee come through the
drainage system again without the Shaman's magic to hold
them back.

No, too much noise to be the enemy.

Khirro scrambled up the side of the ditch, careful of his
aching leg, and hoisted himself above the edge. He heard
shouts and the sound of horses, but the tall grass blocked
his view. He pushed himself up farther, straining to see.
Another inch higher and his eyes would be clear of the
grass.

A hand gripped his belt, yanked him back and brought
him tumbling from his perch. His back slammed against
the ground, leaving him gazing again at the clear blue sky.
He wished he could float away into it, leave behind the
pain in his leg, the fear of the curse, flee from the vial at his
breast and the pool of water collecting at his shoulder.
Then Ghaul's silhouette blocked his freedom.

"Are you trying to get us killed? We'll be easy enough to
track in this dirt. Would you make their task easier by
signaling them?"

Khirro shook his head as the water soaking his breeches
and the fresh pain in his tail bone erased thoughts of a

better place. This was the only place for him, the only place he could be. And Ghaul was right—had Khirro seen them, then they might have seen him, too.

Why can't I think more like a soldier? More like Ghaul.

"I wanted to see who it is."

"King's soldiers. They'll be on our trail soon. We mustn't waste our lead."

Ghaul offered his hand and Khirro took it. The warrior hoisted him to his feet, spun on his heel and continued without waiting.

"How much farther before the ditch ends?" Khirro brushed dirt from his breeches, grimacing at the pain in his rump and his leg as he hurried to catch up.

"Not far. The sides are not so steep anymore."

The yellow grass-trimmed edge—well above their heads when they entered the ditch—had dipped to Ghaul's height. Khirro shook his head, frustrated he hadn't noticed the change. He'd been trained as a soldier of the king, endured the same hardships as other recruits, even as Ghaul had at some point, yet still couldn't make his head work in the manner of a soldier. How far apart to plant corn or when to harvest crops he knew without putting thought to it, but observing his surroundings or remembering not to reveal his location were things yet beyond him. He hoped time would improve his skills, but there wasn't time for practice, not when everything was life or death. If a crop languished in the ground too long, there would be other crops and other years, other farmers from whom to purchase food. The same couldn't be said of a soldier. One mistake could end everything.

Why did the Shaman think I could do this?

As Gendred said: a dirt farmer would do nothing but get in the way. If he could release himself from this curse, pass it on to someone else, he'd do so without second thought. A real warrior like Ghaul would be better suited.

Khirro reached beneath his jerkin and brought the vial from its hiding place, held it up toward the sky. The sun shone through it, turning it into a glowing liquid ruby.

The king's blood. The fate of a kingdom in a small glass vial.

"Ghaul?" His companion responded with a grunt but neither stopped nor turned toward him. "How long have you been a soldier?"

"I am the son of a soldier's son. Ten summers had tanned my skin when I joined the town garrison."

"I'm not a soldier. My place is digging in the earth, providing for my family, selling my crops at market." He rolled the vial in his fingers watching the blood ebb and flow.

"A noble profession when there's no war." With Ghaul's back to him, Khirro couldn't gauge the sincerity of his words. "But these are dark times, the darkest you or I have seen. I was barely out of swaddling clothes when Braymon took the crown."

"Have you fought before?"

"Your archer friend is not the first blood my sword has tasted."

"When war comes, they make a farmer become a soldier," Khirro said curling his fingers about the vial. The feel of it gave him comfort. "But when war is ended, no one asks the warrior to become a farmer."

"Better for both of us." Ghaul chuckled. "The kingdom will always need protecting, as its people will always need feeding. Neither is more important than the other, each of us is a small part of the greater whole."

Khirro considered his words. Perhaps he did mean what he said.

"Do you know how far apart to plant corn? When to harvest potatoes?"

This time Ghaul stopped. Khirro hid the vial behind his injured thigh without knowing why. Something in him made him want to protect it—all the time, at any cost.

"They grow in the ground and they're ready when they sit upon my plate, that's all I know. Do you know how many ways you can kill a man with your bare hands? I'm no better with a plow than you are with a spear, but if I needed to know, I'd learn. It's our lot to do what's asked of us."

Khirro couldn't dispute Ghaul's words. It seemed his companion may be more than the average soldier—not just a killing machine bred to serve. Perhaps, with Ghaul's help, he would reach the Necromancer, and perhaps the kingdom could be saved. A warm feeling spread through Khirro, calming him, but he quickly realized it wasn't emotion or certainty, duty or loyalty. The feeling didn't emanate from his heart or his head or his gut. Instead, the feeling flowed from his leg.

No, not from my leg—into my leg. The vial.

Ghaul started moving again, talking to Khirro over his shoulder.

"We approach the end, then there's some distance to the forest. We have to move swiftly."

Khirro nodded but didn't immediately follow. The mute heat flowed into the muscle of his thigh, flooding his leg with warmth like the Shaman's poultice had imparted upon his wounds, though this time it ran deeper, warmer. He didn't want to move in case it ended the sensation.

"Khirro?"

He shook his head, refocusing on the man in front of him. "What?"

"We'll have to run. Can you do that?"

Nodding, Khirro said he could.

The ditch shallowed. The shadows that dogged them through their flight gave way to sun. Grass spilled down the sides, reaching for the rill of waste water struggling its way to freedom. Then the ditch ended abruptly, the water disappearing in a patch of muddy ground. A sweeping hill of grass fell away, ending in tangled brambles held in check by forest beyond.

"Elevation will hide us a short while," Ghaul said as he surveyed their path. "But we must make the forest before they reach this spot."

"Two men can move faster than many."

"Even when one has an arrow hole in his leg?"

"It feels alright."

"They'll be on horse. If they've found our tracks in the ditch, it won't be difficult for them to follow."

Frowning, Khirro watched Ghaul bound down the hill, then turned his attention to the vial.

Why did I take it out?

He'd considered giving it to the warrior, reasoning it would be safer in the hands of a man able to defend it, but found the thought of parting with it unbearable. He slipped the vial back into its hiding place, its gentle warmth pulsing briefly before disappearing to become just a piece of glass pressed against his chest. Khirro started down the hill, the pain in his leg fading to a tolerable ache.

When he reached the edge of the snarled brambles, Khirro looked back over his shoulder. No soldiers stood at the top, but they weren't far behind. Even now, he felt the dull thump of hooves in the earth beneath his feet. High overhead, death birds circled and swooped, dots against the cerulean sky, upset at having their dinner of fresh man flesh interrupted. The soldiers would take the bodies of Rudric, Gendred and the Shaman and bury them in the

78

barrows at the foot of the fortress wall, but the enemy would be left to rot. The buzzards would yet eat. Khirro thought of the undead creatures with their rotted flesh and shriveled fingers and grinned.

They won't make much of a meal.

The neighing of a warhorse interrupted his thoughts. Khirro turned and rushed into the brambles, heedless of the thorns grasping for his flesh.

9

"Did they see us?"

As dusk deepened to night, they glimpsed their pursuers at the crest of the hill. Khirro didn't doubt they were soldiers of the king.

"I don't think so. The brambles will slow them. They'll likely stop for the night and pick up our trail in the morning."

Branches whipped off Ghaul as he broke the trail, thorny twigs slapping against Khirro's arms and chest. A barb raked his face drawing warm blood to run down his cheek.

"Can't we stop? They were Erechanian. We needn't fear them."

"And how would you explain the vial you carry? Or the trail of dead behind us? They'll want someone to blame, Khirro. The king is dead."

The thicket thinned to a rocky swath before the trees

began. Khirro wiped blood from his cheek and trotted to catch up to his companion.

"I'll explain what happened."

"Why should they believe you? You could be a Kanosee soldier dressed in Erechanian mail. You slew the Shaman, stole the king's blood for you own purpose. You have the Shaman's sword in case there's any doubt."

Khirro grasped the scabbard at his belt, a fresh wave of guilt torturing him.

"But I didn't."

"Then maybe they'll kill you for a spy, or think you killed the king yourself. Do you know the penalty for regicide? You'd pray for them to kill you quickly."

Khirro ground his teeth. *There has to be a way.*

"They'd have to believe both of us. Why would we lie?"

"For your life. Maybe they'll deduce you followed the Shaman and his friends, ambushed them with the other Kanosee, and killed them all yourself."

"All I'd have to do is show them how I wield a sword to convince them otherwise. I'd have been no match for either Rudric or Gendred on their own, never mind both."

"They won't ask for a demonstration. You'd be dead before your steel cleared the scabbard. As soon as we fled, we became guilty of anything they want to accuse us." Ghaul stepped over a moss covered log. "It won't be a stretch for them to add the deaths of Braymon and the Shaman together to come up with a likely reason for you to have done it."

"Rudric and Gendred disposed of the king's body. They will only have found his armor." *Maybe he's right.*

"Worse. The king's missing and you carry a vial of his blood. How's that look for treason?"

Khirro fell quiet as they picked their way beneath enormous hemlock and fir trees and through the shrubs crowding the forest floor: salal and ivy, skunk cabbage and salmon berry bushes. Somewhere above the branches would be a half-moon, Khirro knew, and stars arranged in constellations his father taught him before he lost his arm and stopped speaking to his eldest son. The outdoors normally calmed his soul, but not on this night, not with his countrymen coming to lynch him.

How could this have happened?

"Why would a Kanosee spy want a vial of the king's blood?" Khirro moved through the underbrush, careful not to trip on roots and runners that grasped for his foot like human fingers.

"What good is it to you?"

"The Necromancer. The Shaman said he could bring the king back."

"Right. Did you see the undead fighting beside the Kanosee? Imagine if Braymon was one of them and led the Kanosee forces against his own subjects. The war would end."

"I hadn't thought of that."

Khirro's head swirled. His own countrymen on his trail, the undead soldiers, the Necromancer. The last thought stopped him in his tracks. Ghaul traveled another three steps before he noticed.

"What is it?"

"All are against us." Khirro swallowed hard, felt the pulse beat at his throat in spite of the feeling that all the blood had drained from his head. He suppressed a tremor in his knees. "Our own people pursue us. The enemy will be after us if they know what we have. And the man we seek has sided with them. Why would he help us?"

"All we can do is follow the Shaman's wishes and hope for the best. Let's get on with it before our pursuers hear your whimpering and relieve us of our problems." Ghaul strode back to Khirro and put his hand on his shoulder. It did nothing to reassure him. "For now, we're the only ones who know of your burden. Let's keep it that way."

Khirro's stomach churned. At best, he'd be branded a traitor, at worst: a king slayer. And that was if his own people caught them. What if the enemy found them instead? In the space of a few hours, the most dangerous option—going to Lakesh—had become the best one. Khirro expected the fear and dread the name Lakesh provoked, but he felt something else, too. This task meant more than feeding people. No matter what happened, he'd never guide a plow again. His life had been irrevocably changed when the king came to rest on the landing beside him. He

Blood of the King

was a warrior now, like it or not. The last hope for the realm.

The thought made him want to vomit.

***

The night passed in silence, disturbed only by rustling brush and the snap of twigs underfoot. Night under the trees wasn't like night on the farm, the darkness was deeper, claustrophobic. Khirro fumbled for the hilt of the Shaman's sword when shapes loomed only to find no more threat than an overturned stump or fallen log. Thankfully, the darkness hid his trepidation from Ghaul. After a time, he got used to the screech of the owl and the skittering of tiny feet hiding from it. Something larger followed them for a while, keeping its distance—they both noted it but didn't speak of it. As night lightened with the dawn, the noise ceased without approaching closer.

When the interwoven branches above their heads parted, Khirro glimpsed the dark sky fading to midnight blue. His favorite time of day. Most mornings, his day would start at this time, full of promise. His brother would still be sleeping, forsaking the farmer's life, convinced there were better things for him, though he never tried to discover what. Many times Khirro tilled soil or fed animals with teeth clenched in anger at his brother. He felt the same this morning knowing he slept safe at home, but he missed him, too.

"There's a stream ahead," Ghaul said, the first words

either had spoken in hours. "We'll rest there, slake our thirst and change your bandage."

Khirro hadn't thought about his wound in a long while. The pain and limp he'd carried along the drainage ditch were gone.

Walking must have been good for it.

The stream's gurgle reached Khirro's ears as evergreens gave way to smaller deciduous trees. The brush thinned until the forest paused at a glade carpeted with flowers all the way to the water, each species of flora a different shade of gray awaiting the life-giving sun to coax them open and give them color. At the edge of the stream a spotted deer raised its head but bolted into the forest before Ghaul removed the bow from his shoulder.

"Damn. I'd have enjoyed venison for breakfast."

They hurried across the clearing, knelt at the edge of the stream. Khirro wiped his hands on his breeches as Ghaul leaned forward, immersing his face in the water. Khirro watched him for a moment, then did the same. The first gulp of cold water hurt his head, but his throat was thankful for the wetting. He took a deep draught, drinking until his lungs begged for air. When he'd had enough, Ghaul was already standing.

"Much time has passed since anyone's been here," he said surveying their surroundings. "All the better for us."

Khirro inhaled the stream's crispness and the perfume of blossoming flowers, then washed his hands in the cold water, splashed some on his face It stung the tender scratch where the thorn had caught him. He touched it lightly and his finger came away with fresh blood.

"Let's change your dressing." Ghaul dropped his pack from his back. "It would do the kingdom no good if the only man who could find the Necromancer lost his leg to the blood sickness. Lakesh is a long way to hop."

Grinning though he didn't find the prospect funny, Khirro moved to a large rock on the bank of the stream where he sat and flexed his leg.

"It feels good."

"Numb from walking."

Ghaul unwound the bandage from Khirro's thigh with a surprisingly gentle touch for a battle-hardened warrior. Dried blood stuck the strip of cloth to itself and Khirro thought of his father. He'd watched him scream and curse as mother changed the bandage where his arm had been. *'You're no son of mine,'* he screamed as the gauze pulled painfully away.

Khirro shook his head and concentrated on Ghaul removing the dressing.

The warrior pulled the last of the bandage away from his leg, then scooped water from the stream with cupped hands. He splashed it on Khirro's leg, washing away much of the dried blood. No fresh blood flowed to replace it.

"How badly does it hurt?"

"Not at all."

Ghaul shook his head. "Something's wrong. It should still be bleeding."

"It feels fine."

"Bleeding clears impurities. I better have a look."

Khirro stood, removed the Shaman's sword belt and set it aside on the rock, then dropped his breeches to his knees. Ghaul examined his leg.

"Gods. How can this be?"

"What? What is it?"

Ghaul stepped away, eyes narrowed with suspicion. "What manner of man are you?"

Concerned, Khirro hobbled to the stream and dropped to his knees. He splashed water across his thigh, washing away the last of the dried blood and saw a puckered pink scar where the wound should have been. He brushed it with his fingertips, first lightly, then pushed on it more firmly. No pain.

"I'm no manner of man," he said looking up at Ghaul and remembered the warmth in his thigh when he held the vial of the king's blood. "I mean, I think I know how this happened."

He stood and tied his breeches. Ghaul watched, wary as Khirro reached into his jerkin and pulled out the vial. The glass was cool to the touch and he doubted his memory.

"What are you doing?"

Khirro didn't answer. Instead, he raised the vial and touched it to the scratch on his cheek. It warmed immediately. A tingling spread across his face, uncomfortable like an itch he couldn't find when he went to scratch it, and chased his doubt before it. Ghaul watched, eyebrows slanted in unvoiced question. When the warmth faded, Khirro lowered the vial.

"Well?"

Ghaul's expression lost its edge, shifting to something like wonder. He stepped closer to Khirro, reaching out tentatively. His fingertips brushed his cheek then drew away.

"Gone," he whispered.

"It's the Shaman's spell. Whatever he did to keep the king's blood alive, to sustain it, must spill from the vial."

"Let me see it."

An instant of panic flashed through Khirro's mind, then temptation.

I could give it to him and leave. I could return to the farm. To Emeline.

He extended his hand, visions of home dancing before his eyes. Ghaul took the vial, holding it between two fingers.

"It looks like a vial of blood, nothing more."

Sweat broke on Khirro's brow. The thoughts of home, Emeline, and the farm, disappeared. His gut churned.

The Shaman's curse won't let me.

"Give it back," he croaked, his throat suddenly dry.

Ghaul hesitated, looked like he'd refuse. Khirro's eyes

87

flickered to his sword belt lying on the rock, then back to the warrior. He couldn't reach it fast enough. Ghaul closed his fingers around the vial, holding it in his fist. Then he laughed.

"I don't want your vial, Khirro," he said tossing it back nonchalantly. Khirro bobbled it but kept it from dropping. "I don't know how to find the Necromancer."

Relief calmed Khirro's gut, but sadness tempered it. Maybe he'd never be able to return home. He tucked the vial back into its spot.

"Sorry." He retrieved his sword belt from the rock.

Ghaul shrugged. "No need to be. But next time you eye your weapon, you will be."

10

They ate hard cheese and dark bread from Ghaul's pack, but didn't sleep. Khirro begged for rest, but Ghaul insisted they push on while they had a chance to increase their lead.

"The glade is too open," Ghaul said as they followed the stream south west. "We'll find somewhere less obvious to rest soon."

Soon turned out to be more than three hours later. The sky had lightened to bright morning blue, the sun promising another hot day when it peeked through the branches overhead. They stopped at a huge fallen tree, charred by fire and hollowed by time. A perfect place to sleep unnoticed. Khirro surprised himself by offering to take the first watch. He felt good. A bit of food and a splash of water had done wonders to refresh him.

Ghaul had been sleeping for an hour when a black bear lumbered by, two cubs cantering along behind. Khirro watched in awe and fear as they passed; Mama bear sniffed the air once and glanced his direction but otherwise ignored him. He'd never seen a bear before. Cows and goats, pigs and chickens were as close as he came to wildlife. He told Ghaul excitedly about his sighting when he woke an hour later. The warrior seemed less than impressed.

When Ghaul woke Khirro, the sun was hidden above the trees, so he couldn't tell how long he'd slept. His companion's expression told him immediately he wasn't waking him because the time had come to move on.

"Wha--?" he began, but Ghaul silenced him with a gesture. More gestures followed, but Khirro's sleep fogged head couldn't immediately grasp their meaning. It took a moment to realize Ghaul had heard something.

Birds chirped, insects buzzed; Khirro heard no other sounds as they listened. Minutes passed. Could Ghaul have been mistaken? A smile tugged at Khirro's lips at the thought.

Mighty warrior hearing things.

Then there was a noise, small and far off. It wasn't the sounds he'd been afraid to hear—no clanking armor, neighing horses, or men shouting that they'd discovered the trail.

It was a woman's voice.

Tension released from Khirro's shoulders; Ghaul looked at him, shaking his head. He signaled the direction the sound came from and moved from beneath the hollow tree, presumably expecting Khirro to follow. After collecting the items he'd removed for sleep, he did. They picked their way through the brush quickly and carefully, striving for silence, a task Ghaul accomplished much better than Khirro.

As they drew nearer the sound's source, other voices joined the woman's. Khirro heard at least two, perhaps three, all of them men. The woman's tone suggested anger, though the tangle of trees and shrubs muffled her words as surely as they hid the group from view. Ghaul took the bow from his shoulder and plucked an arrow from the quiver; Khirro drew the black and red blade. When Ghaul saw the sword, his forehead creased and he glanced a questioning look at Khirro but quickly turned his attention back to the sounds before them.

At the top of a short rise, the trees thinned and the ground dropped away in a gentle slope. A clearing spread out beyond the edge of the forest, not unlike the one at which they'd stopped. Three men laughed and cat-called the naked woman standing in the middle of their rough circle. She seemed unconcerned by her nudity.

Ghaul motioned Khirro to take cover behind a fallen cedar claimed by moss. Khirro crouched and stole a glance over the top of the log. The woman stood almost as tall as the men surrounding her, red hair spilling down her bare back. He averted his eyes from her nakedness, feeling a hot blush rise in his cheeks, but looked again when she shouted.

"Give me my money." She wagged a finger at the biggest of the men, a stocky fellow with thick black beard and powerful arms. Her breasts jiggled with the movement. "Nothing's free. Pay me what you owe me."

The man laughed, caught her by the arm and pulled her into a bear hug, arms pinned at her sides. He kissed her on the lips as she struggled to get free, then he pushed her across the circle into the waiting arms of another, this man young with an eager look in his eyes. He repeated his fellow's actions. Each time she pulled free, they pushed her stumbling into the arms of another man. Her curses and cries of anger rang through the forest. As she fell into the arms of the first man again, he pressed his body against hers.

"One more for the road, I think," he boomed, laughing, but his laughter turned quickly to a cry of pain. He pushed the woman away and looked down at his own dagger sticking from his thigh, a dark patch of red spreading down his breeches.

"You bitch."

91

He grabbed the knife hilt in his right hand and jerked the blade free as his free hand flashed out and caught the woman across the face. She tumbled to the ground, but when she looked up brushing hair from her face, she smiled defiantly showing teeth red with blood.

Ghaul signaled to Khirro and rose from his crouch, began to move away.

He wants to leave. We can't leave her to these animals.

Khirro grabbed his shoulder.

"We have to do something," he whispered.

The bearded man stood over the woman, hands clenched into fists as the others chided him on. Ghaul's expression told Khirro they didn't have time for this foolishness, that a search party was after their heads, but Khirro held his gaze without wavering. After a few seconds, Ghaul gave in.

"Go over there, quickly. Shout and throw rocks when you see my first arrow fly. Make it sound like you're more than one man. Go. Hurry."

Khirro stole from tree to tree, stooping to pick up rocks on the way. His movement was far from silent but he doubted the men would notice anything but the naked woman.

"It's time you got that payment you deserve, whore."

Khirro heard the bearded man's words as he found cover behind a fir tree within throwing range. The man sheathed his dagger and drew his sword, raising it skyward. The woman kicked him in the groin; he howled and stumbled back a step, his compatriots' laughter adding to his ire. Anger contorting his face, the bearded man growled and raised his sword again. The woman scrambled to get away, but the other men blocked her path.

When the arrow pierced his shoulder, the bearded man's expression changed from fury to surprise. His sword hit the ground and he fell to his knees. Khirro took the cue, yelling and launching rocks toward the group, not worrying about aiming but still trying not to hit the woman. Caught off guard, the men panicked.

When Ghaul skewered the second man through the thigh, they'd had enough of their unseen enemy.

The uninjured man collected his companions and ran toward their whinnying and prancing horses picketed at the far end of the clearing. Khirro caught the bearded man in the back of the head with a good-sized stone and smiled, satisfied. The man with the arrow in his thigh fell screaming in agony as he attempted to mount his spooked steed. His fellows didn't stop to help as they crashed into the forest without looking back. The man dragged himself to his horse, struggled into the saddle, and took off hanging from his horse at a dangerous angle. Khirro smiled, an unfamiliar feeling of triumph tingling his arms and legs with a flood of adrenaline.

So this is what it feels like to be a real soldier.

He rushed into the clearing, hooting and hollering after

93

them. Ghaul did the same and they came together to watch the men disappear into the trees.

"They're afraid of us and the rest of our company," Ghaul said sweeping his arm across the empty meadow. "They won't be back anytime soon."

The woman stared at them, suspicion burning in her eyes as they approached. She pulled herself to a sitting position, knees hugged to her chest, blood running down her chin from her split lip. She watched them but said nothing.

"Are you all right?" Khirro asked when they were a few yards from her.

"Take what you will of me," she said, neither fear nor resignation in her voice.

Ghaul laughed. "There is naught we want of you, my lady, except perhaps your thanks and direction to the nearest village."

Her brow wrinkled beneath the red hair spilling across her forehead as though she didn't understand what he'd said. Or didn't believe it.

"Thank you," she said hesitantly.

In spite of her unkempt hair and the blood on her chin, Khirro found her beautiful. Freckles peppered her cheeks and shoulders. She searched their faces with eyes shining green like the ocean and almost as deep.

Ghaul offered her his hand and something twinged in Khirro's belly—Ghaul hadn't wanted to stop yet now proffered aid. The woman placed her hand in his without reservation, allowing him to pull her to her feet. She stretched while Ghaul appraised her appreciatively. She either didn't notice or didn't care as she made no attempt to cover herself. Embarrassment spread across Khirro's cheeks.

"I'm Ghaul. My companion his Khirro."

"Elyea." Her gaze darted back and forth between them. *She's looking at our armor.* "Why would two men be hiding in the forest? Are you deserters? I've had enough of deserters today."

"Oh no, my lady," Khirro said. "Not deserters. We're--"

"Misplaced wanderers in need of clothing and supplies," Ghaul interrupted. "This is why we need your help. Could you direct us to the nearest village?"

She nodded. "I'll take you."

"But where are your clothes, my lady?" Khirro asked.

He attempted to keep his eyes from the curve of her hip, the swell of her breasts, the patch of red hair between her legs, but found it difficult. She smiled.

"Does my body cause you discomfort, brave rescuer?" She canted her hips, her smile spreading from her lips to her eyes.

"No," Khirro replied, fire burning in his cheeks. "I thought you'd be more comfortable clothed." He looked at his feet.

"I'm comfortable either way, but I see you're not."

She strode to where her frock hung on the low branch of a tree, her steps slow, purposeful and full of grace. Khirro raised his eyes to watch her heart shaped buttocks swing side to side as she went. Ghaul made an 'mmm' sound in the back of his throat.

"One thing we need to get straight if I'm to help you: my name is Elyea. No more 'my lady' shite. I am no man's lady."

She pulled the dress unhurriedly over her head, the shapeless shift disguising her curves as she stood erect and elegant, wiping the blood from her chin with it. She returned at the same deliberate pace, curtseying as she reached them.

"Is that better?"

"Better for my friend," Ghaul said continuing to eye her. "He's shy."

"I'm not shy. I... I'm married," Khirro bumbled.

Elyea moved to him, put her hand on his chest; it brushed the vial hidden beneath. She smiled—most of the blood was gone from her teeth. "You're not the first married man to see me unclothed."

The redness rushed back to his cheeks, sweat jumped to his brow and he took a step away. Ghaul laughed.

"Why were those men treating you that way?" Khirro asked, desperate to change the subject.

"When I completed the work they contracted me for, they refused to pay."

"But what of your clothes? Did they rape you?" The word prodded a cold finger into Khirro's heart.

"No, Khirro. I told you: I completed the work for which I was hired."

Ghaul chuckled again. "Don't you see, Khirro? Our lady friend is a harlot."

"I prefer the term 'courtesan'. I guess your friend hasn't met a woman such as I, Ghaul."

"I suppose not."

Khirro wanted to ask her why a woman like her would sell her body for pocket change, but he held his tongue. He didn't know her; it wasn't his place to question her.

"Those men would have killed you," he said instead.

Elyea shrugged. "Hazards of the job. A girl has to put food in the pantry. Now, do you or don't you need someone to take you to the village?"

Ghaul bowed, gesturing toward the forest with a sweep of his arm. "Lead on, my lady."

"Elyea," she insisted, then started toward the south end of the clearing, her white dress swaying. Sun shone through the thin material, outlining the shape of her legs beneath.

"But what of those men?" Khirro asked keeping pace a couple of steps behind. "What if they come back?"

"They won't come back," Ghaul said, eyes tracking the sway of the woman's hips.

"How can you be sure?"

"Men like them are cowards," Elyea said over her shoulder. "And two of them are in need of a good surgeon, thanks to you."

"Not just us," Ghaul said. "You did some cutting yourself, my lady."

"Elyea."

Ghaul smiled as she quickened her pace.

"Quite a woman," Ghaul said to Khirro in a hushed voice. "But be wary. I'm loathe to trust a harlot."

"We saved her life. She wouldn't do anything to harm us."

Ghaul grunted noncommittally.

They were correct—Khirro had never met a harlot, or a courtesan, or a whore. His village was too small to support such trade, though some told rumors that the widow Breadmaker sold more than bannock to passing merchants and wanderers. Khirro didn't know if the stories were true —she'd only offered him bread. The differences between Elyea and the widow Breadmaker were like comparing a destrier to a used up donkey.

Elyea had gotten farther ahead, so she stopped and looked over her shoulder.

"Are you two coming or are you going to spend your day looking at my ass?"

***

They followed the gurgling stream as it twisted and turned, mimicking Khirro's thoughts.

Trust her, don't trust her?

They wouldn't reach their destination without supplies, so they had little choice. Ghaul and Elyea walked together, talking and laughing, leaving him trailing behind to ponder his thoughts and wish he could talk to a woman like her as easily. He watched the courtesan pick her way across rocks and through underbrush with lithe grace despite the loose sandals snapping against her heel. From time to time, Ghaul or Elyea would cast a question or comment over their shoulder to which he replied with a smile or nod—as few words as possible—then return to his ruminations.

Did we take too long? Are the pursuers closing in?

Ghaul didn't seem concerned.

"In my experience," Elyea said loud enough to involve Khirro in the discussion, "two men wear arms and armor wandering alone in the forest is unusual. My guess would be they're either deserters or in love with one another. Which are you?"

Shocked by both allegations, Khirro opened his mouth to protest, but Ghaul's snort of laughter cut him off.

"Neither. We're simply two men who lost their way."

"Um-hmm. And where were you going?"

Panic flashed in Khirro as he thought Ghaul would reveal everything. Words jumped from his mouth unbidden. "We can't say."

Elyea stopped and Khirro almost walked into her. She looked into his face and he turned away from her scrutiny, regretting his words. He didn't look to Ghaul for help, he knew what kind of expression he'd find there.

"What do you mean 'you can't tell me'?"

"Yes, what do you mean, Khirro?"

He felt their gazes on him, their questioning looks. Too many times he spoke without thinking; it always caused him trouble.

"It's just that-- It's because..." He chewed his bottom lip. "I can't."

"Take no offence, Elyea. Khirro holds our journey as one of great importance and we don't know you well."

"And I don't know you, yet you want me to take you to my village. You could be deserters, or spies, or Kanosee."

"We're not." Khirro's heart sank.

Elyea crossed her arms; faint lines showed on the bridge of her nose as her brows turned down in anger.

"Show us to the village." Ghaul's soothing tone surprised Khirro—he'd have expected a demand. "Where we're headed after that isn't your concern."

"Don't tell me my concerns. I'm no strumpet swayed by your honey tones. *You* should be concerned. Finding yourself lost in the forest would be bad; being found by the garrison and branded deserters would be worse."

Ghaul's demeanor changed instantly and he reached for his dagger. Elyea stepped back, body tense.

Bad to worse.

Khirro hadn't wanted to help this woman only to have

Ghaul kill her in a stupid dispute he caused. He rested his hand on his companion's forearm.

"We mean no harm," Khirro said.

"That's not how it looks." She tilted her head toward Ghaul. He released his knife.

"I can't tell you where we're going. It would be very dangerous for us."

He wanted to tell her, to put an end to this stupidity, but the Shaman's curse moved and roiled in his gut, keeping him from speaking the truth.

"Then you'll find your own way. And good luck to you."

"But you must--"

"I must do nothing. If you want my assistance, you'll tell me where you're going." Her eyes bore deep into him, unblinking, unrelenting. "And don't lie to me, Khirro. My profession requires I know when a man lies to me."

Khirro looked to Ghaul for guidance, but he neither moved nor spoke. The soldier's hand no longer rested on the knife hilt, but it looked like it could be there again in less than a blink. Khirro sighed, his shoulders slumped. The sensation in his belly intensified.

"Look at me, Khirro, not him. He'd sooner slice me than tell the truth."

A bark of laughter erupted from Ghaul, startling Khirro. "Tell her, Khirro. We have no time for this."

Hesitantly, Khirro nodded.

"What I tell you can never pass your lips to another."

Elyea rolled her eyes.

"Promise." Khirro was aware he must sound like a child preparing to tell a secret to a *friend—'Cross your heart and hope to die'*—but she seemed to hear the severity in his words.

"I swear I'll tell no one."

Khirro regarded her, searching her face for insincerity, deceit, and detected none, but wouldn't someone who mastered detecting the lies of others be adept at hiding her own truths? He hesitated, unsure, until he imagined the beat of hooves closing in on them. He reached under his jerkin and removed the vial, holding it in his fist for a few seconds, not wanting to let it go. It felt like diving from a cliff—he'd committed and hoped nothing dangerous lay beneath the water. He released his grasp, offering the vial for her to see. Elyea uncrossed her arms and stood straighter.

"What is it?" She reached out to touch it; he drew his hand away. "Wine?"

"No. Not wine."

"What then?" She didn't look displeased by his refusal, but stepped closer for a better look. She squinted at the vial rolling on his palm, its contents lapping the sides. She looked up at Khirro. "Blood?"

He nodded.

"Whose?"

He fought the urge to look to Ghaul for advice—this

choice was his to make. The Shaman bonded him to this journey, not Ghaul. It should never have been Ghaul's decision.

"It's the blood of the king."

Birds chirped, the stream gurgled, but three people stood in silence staring at the vial in Khirro's hand. Then the words came tumbling forth in an unstoppable torrent. It felt right to tell.

"We're bound for Lakesh—the keep of the Necromancer, Darestat. A Shaman's curse made this journey mine, to bring the blood so the king might be raised from the dead to lead Erechania to victory."

He told her of Braymon's fall and his escape, of the escape through the tunnel, the fight in the meadow and his flight with Ghaul.

"Braymon has fallen?"

He nodded, wondering if she'd heard all he said. "Yes."

She pushed through a shrub and slumped down on a log as though her legs refused to bear the weight of his news. Khirro moved toward her but stopped at the sight of tears gleaming on her cheek. A woman's tears were foreign things to him; his mother never shed a tear where he could see, perhaps never did at all. Not until the day with Emeline had he seen, and been the cause of, a woman's tears. Only once, on the day Emeline told what had happened that night.

"Why does a harlot care so much for a king?"

Ghaul's tone held no tenderness or understanding. Khirro shook thoughts of Emeline from his mind and followed his companion to Elyea's side. The woman didn't answer at first, instead drawing a shuddering breath and wiping her eyes on her arm, composing herself. She looked up, green eyes rimmed red, gazing into the sun-dappled forest.

"I owe Braymon my life." Her voice trembled. "I'd seen eight summers when he took the throne. His first act was to release those forced into servitude. His ascension meant I no longer had to serve as concubine to a tyrant."

Khirro's breath stopped half-drawn. "Eight years old?"

"I'd been there three years when Braymon rescued me. I owe him everything." She bowed her head.

A child of five. Khirro saw the horrible memories on her face, could only imagine what she must have endured. *How terrible it must have been for her.*

"He rescued you from a life as concubine to the king so you could be courtesan to the common man?"

The lack of empathy in Ghaul's voice turned Khirro's head; Elyea's reaction was similar, but more extreme. She stood abruptly, face to face with the soldier, her expression hard.

"He did terrible things to me," she snarled. "Don't you see the difference between being forced into something and choosing it? Are you a soldier because you chose it, or because you were told to be one?"

Ghaul stood straighter. "I was born a soldier."

His words further enraged her. "And what of you?" she snapped at Khirro.

"I'm no warrior," he responded quietly, not knowing how to calm her.

"Do you enjoy being forced to be one?"

"No. I've already seen things no man should have to see in his lifetime. I'd rather be home with Emeline, tending my farm. But it's my duty to be here."

"At six years I was fucked by the king and told it was my duty."

Khirro stared. He had no answer to such atrocity. The inhumanity of it didn't enervate Ghaul.

"And now?" the soldier asked.

For a moment Khirro thought she'd strike Ghaul, but the anger drained from her limbs. Perhaps the burden of her memories wore her down. How could they not?

"Now I make a living I enjoy with customers of my own choosing."

Ghaul's mouth curled into a smirk. "You didn't choose so well last time."

"That's what I get for offering my services to wanderers."

A look passed between them that Khirro didn't understand and the last of her fury fell away. Ghaul opened his mouth to say something else, but this time it was Khirro's turn to cut him short.

105

"I'm sorry for what happened to you," he said, knowing it could never be enough. "But we must be going. There are men following us."

Elyea's eyes met his, thanked him for the sentiment.

"Of course. It does us no good to tarry. Let's get to the village for supplies, take some rest, then we'll make for the Vendarian border at first light."

Ghaul caught her by the elbow as she went to leave. "What do you mean *we*? The only *we* is Khirro and I."

"You'll need my help."

Ghaul snorted. "We need no help."

"The journey will be dangerous," Khirro added. "No place for a woman."

He regretted his words the second they left his mouth.

"I'm no mere woman." She scowled and pulled her arm from Ghaul's grasp. "And I'm not giving you a choice. You'll need all the help you can get. And I know someone else who would be interested in your journey."

She looked at them defiantly, daring them to contradict her. Neither did. She picked her way nimbly through the brush as Ghaul shot Khirro a derisive look. They said nothing. Khirro purposely didn't look at his companion as they followed the woman, knowing he should feel that telling her of their journey was a mistake, but he didn't. Surprise, fear and exhilaration mixed into a muddle in his mind, but no regret. It felt right, but only time would tell. Amongst all the confusion, one question declared itself in his mind above all others:

Who did she intend to tell?

11

Therrador rested his chin on his fist, elbows propped on the marble table; veins of red ran through the white surface of the table's twenty foot length. In the centuries it had sat in the council room at the palace of Achtindel, much had been discussed and decided at this table: wars declared, lives forfeit and spared, plots plotted and taxes declared. Stroking his braided beard, Therrador wondered if the ancient marble had ever seen a conversation as was about to take place. Had it seen the kingdom betrayed? History suggested not.

Only hours earlier, a rider reached the capital bearing the tale of a dead Shaman, empty armor and a missing king. Concern bordering on panic had shown on the messenger's face and in his words, so Therrador sent him to a cell rather than risk his knowledge spilled over too many pints of ale. The king's discarded armor suggested Braymon's fall. Bale's body, along with Rudric and Gendred's, found outside the fortress walls told him they collected the king's blood, as Braymon planned. Such information made public would lead to panic, and panic would hinder everything.

But what of the Kanosee who was supposed to see to Braymon's death? What became of him?

107

They'd found dead Kanosee soldiers with Rudric and the others, but he couldn't know if any of them were the man—he didn't know who he was. Those arrangements had been left to others.

Therrador sighed. He'd miss Rudric; they'd spent much time together over the years and Therrador found him a pleasing conversation. The world would be a better place without that bastard Gendred.

"What happened?" he whispered aloud. "Where is the vial?"

"Did you say somethin' Da?"

Therrador looked up at the five-year-old boy peering from behind the tapestry hung to hide his private antechamber. His expression softened and a sad smile nearly won its way onto his lips.

He looks so much like his mother.

"Dada was talking to himself, Graymon." He spread his arms and the boy ran into his embrace. "I thought I told you to wait in the other room for me."

The boy waved his carved wooden dragon near his father's head, acting as though he didn't hear him, pretending the toy flew like a real dragon.

"Graymon?"

"I bored, Da." The toy dragon attacked his father's arm; a wooden tooth dug into Therrador's skin. "Play with me."

Therrador grasped the boy's shoulders, held him at arm's length and spoke gently. "Da is busy, we can play when I'm done. Can you go back into the other room for me?"

"Rrraaarrr."

The toy dragon flew out of his hands in the direction of the tapestry. Therrador spun him around, sending him on his way with a tap on the bum.

"That's my boy."

As the boy disappeared behind the velvet arras, Therrador's smile disappeared, too. All that had been put in motion brought the taste of bile to the back of his throat, but it must be done. Erechania would always remember Braymon the Brave and one day they would exult Graymon the Great; he only hoped they would eventually forgive or forget Therrador the Traitor. He lowered his eyes back to the marble table top shot with red, lost in his thoughts until a sound made him look up.

The fifteen-foot high cedar doors swung inward with a belabored creak and a guard in shining silver chain mail and green-and-gold cape entered, ornamental pole axe in hand. He opened his mouth to pardon the interruption but the man he led in pushed past him, sending him off balance and interrupting the act. The guard recovered, grasped his weapon with both hands and advanced on the intruder but Therrador rose, stopping him with a gesture.

"Leave us."

He waved his hand and the guardsman bowed at the waist, eyes steady on the other man, and backed out, closing the door with a soft thud. The intruder stopped a yard shy of Therrador, removed his helm and nodded instead of bowing. He didn't speak. His close-cropped gray hair couldn't hide the scars criss-crossing his scalp, spilling down his face over the deep wrinkles earned through decades spent fighting in the name of whoever paid him the most. His lone granite-colored eye stared unwavering while the other socket sat empty for all to see. Plain gray armor, as pitted and worn as his face, but fitting him as comfortably as if he'd been born in it, completed his drab yet menacing appearance. Everything about him spoke of business, and his business was death.

"Suath," Therrador said forcing a welcoming smile. "How long has it been?"

The man didn't answer. No surprise—Therrador expected no reply. More than a man of few words, the mercenary only spoke when absolutely necessary.

"Too long, I guess, but I need of your services."

Suath nodded, remained silent.

"Someone has something which belongs to me. I want it back."

The man's presence brought a sheen of sweat to Therrador's palms. He wanted to look away, to turn his gaze on anything but the uncaring gray eye and the pink, puckered flesh of the mercenary's empty socket. Legend said he'd lost the eye while being tortured and, when he won his freedom, Suath took both the torturer's eyes before killing him. People whispered that he carried all three eyes—his one and the torturer's two—as good luck charms. Therrador suppressed a shudder.

"I have good men on the trail already, but this task is of the utmost importance. I need you to retrieve this item and bring it back. No questions asked."

"At what cost?" the mercenary asked, his voice deep, grating—a voice that made Therrador wish he didn't speak at all.

"Whatever it takes."

"What is it?"

"A vial."

Therrador waited for the next, obvious question, but Suath didn't seem to care what the vial contained.

"How much?"

"This is why I sent for you: you only care about the money."

Therrador nodded with satisfaction and used the opportunity to break from Suath's gaze. He cast a glance toward the tapestry hiding the ante-room's entrance. It hadn't moved. *Good boy.*

"And the killing. How much?"

"Thirty gold now." He pulled a leather pouch from his belt and tossed it onto the marble table with a clink. Two gold coins rolled out onto the white and red surface. "Fifty more when the vial is in my hands."

Suath nodded. His head moved so slightly, Therrador

didn't know he'd agreed until he retrieved the pouch and
stray coins from the table. The mercenary tucked it into his
jerkin without counting the coins then waited for
Therrador to say more.

"You can pick up their trail in Inehsul."

The man answered with a blink, then turned and strode
toward the carven doors. Therrador felt a vice release from
his head when their gazes finally parted.

"Another ten coins if you bring me the head of the
thief."

Suath stopped halfway to the door and replied without
turning: "Heads are poor company."

"Twenty coins, then," Therrador said annoyed to be
speaking to the man's back. Would he treat the king thus?
Probably. "But no one can know of your task."

The mercenary slid his helm on, hiding scars and hair
and wrinkles, and continued toward the door. The room
seemed to sigh its relief at his leaving, along with
Therrador.

"Don't fail me, Suath."

The mercenary stopped, hand on the door handle, and
pivoted toward Therrador, his one eye blazing. He stared a
moment before his laughter boomed down the hall, deep
and echoing, a chilling sound Therrador hadn't thought
the man capable of creating.

"I won't fail you. Your killing will be done," he growled
and then nodded past Therrador. "And I see the child

hidden behind the curtain, so don't you be failing me, neither."

Therrador's heart jumped in his chest and he spun to look at the tapestry. The edge swung ever so slightly, like someone had just left. He faced the mercenary, a threat ready on his lips, but by then Suath was gone, the door left open behind him. The guard peered in.

"Let them know I'm ready to break my fast," Therrador snapped. The soldier saluted and hurriedly pulled the door closed.

"What did the man mean, Da?"

Graymon's head peered from behind the tapestry, blond locks tussled. Therrador slumped into the chair and gestured for his son to sit with him. When the boy climbed onto his lap, the nearness of him quashed a chill threatening to creep up his spine.

"Nothing, son. A jest, nothing more."

It would be hours before the vision of Suath's naked eye socket left his mind. Part of him wished never to see it again, but there would be at least once more. If anyone in the land could return the vial to him, Suath could.

The thought did little to make him feel better.

12

The scent of cloves and garlic mingled with the smell of fresh baked bread. Tomatoes, melons, carrots and peppers arranged in colorful patterns occupied bins sitting on the ground and atop makeshift tables. The marketplace at Inehsul was larger than in Khirro's village, with more variety of wares and many more people. Men called out from stalls, beckoning passers-by to peruse their selection of cloths and perfumes. Other booths offered trinkets and beads, clothing, and housewares. One displayed charms and amulets promising health, wealth, or love—a long line of desperation led to that one.

Khirro adjusted the tunic Elyea had acquired for him. It hung too long on him, didn't fit in the shoulders, and he found himself missing the reassuring weight of armor. Funny how quickly one gets used to something after a few days and a little danger. Elyea had suggested that wandering Inehsul dressed as soldiers would attract unwanted attention, so they'd left their arms and armor hidden amongst a stand of pines.

"Where did you get these?" Khirro asked pushing up the sleeves of the tunic.

A sly smile crept across her face. "It's my job to talk men out of their clothes."

As they wandered the market purchasing food to fill the packs Elyea had brought, Khirro still wondered if telling her had been the right decision. Beyond Ghaul, he didn't know how to tell who to trust. The effort she put in—acquiring clothes and packs, paying for much of the food—eased his concern a bit.

Only time will tell.

A canvas tent, larger than all the others, blocked the road at the far end of the marketplace. A pitchman standing on a crate shouted above the din of people milling about the tent's entrance, hollering about the juggler, the jester, the troubadour and the story spinner, and a man called Athryn who would perform wonders to leave the crowd astounded and amazed. Elyea weaved her way through the marketplace crowd toward the tent while Khirro and Ghaul hurried to follow.

"Where are we going?" She didn't answer Khirro's question, though he was sure she heard.

"What are you doing?" Ghaul demanded, as anxious as Khirro to leave the village and its possibility of discovery. "We have no time for foolishness."

"There's always time for entertainment."

She grabbed Ghaul by the wrist, pulling him along until they stood beside the pitchman. Khirro followed, forcing his way through the crowd, apologizing as he passed.

"Child," the man roared, abandoning his pitch to favor her with a broad smile. "We haven't seen you in so long."

"Too long."

He bent down to speak into her ear and whatever he said made her smile. She whispered in response, the man nodded, and Elyea kissed his cheek. Waving her in with a sweep of his arm, he pulled aside the tent flap and she pulled Ghaul through while beckoning Khirro to follow. Some of the people waiting to gain entrance noticed them bypassing the queue.

"Whore," one woman muttered.

"Slut," called out another.

"Who do we have to fuck to get into the show?" a man said.

Their comments made Khirro's cheeks burn, but Elyea either didn't notice or didn't care. Either way, she appeared to be well known in Inehsul.

They entered into air thick and hot, rank with the smell of canvas and the stink of sweat. People sat on rows of creaking benches, fanning themselves with anything they could find: hats, skirt hems, work gloves. Elyea guided her companions to a spot in the last row where they squeezed into a space meant for two. The man beside them grumbled about his lack of room. Elyea smiled sweetly and he said no more.

Khirro shifted in his seat attempting to keep his knees from pressing into the back of the woman seated in front of him; the rows of benches were packed so tightly the front row's knees pressed against the low stage erected there. Atop the platform, a child clad in bright colors and odd patterns cantered about.

Someone should get him down before the performance begins. He glanced around and saw there were no other children in the tent. *I won't let my child act like that.*

As Khirro watched, he realized the person in piebald clothing and shoes with bells on the turned up toes was no child, but the smallest man he'd ever seen. All his parts were proportionate, nothing misshapen or stunted, the jester was simply a small man. He wore a constant look of surprise as he ran about the stage, tripping over one unlikely object after another, or sometimes nothing at all. The audience cheered each pratfall, hooting and hollering and calling the jester names. Khirro smiled at the little man's antics. It felt good to smile.

He overheard Ghaul ask Elyea: "How did you get us in?"

"The doorman is a friend of mine. I traveled with the troupe a few times."

Khirro wondered what she meant by 'traveled with'. Ghaul put words to his thought.

"As their courtesan?"

"No." She slapped his thigh playfully without taking her eyes from the performer. "I performed. I'm a dancer."

Khirro thought of the graceful ease she showed navigating the forest, traversing tangles of branches and twists of brambles like it was second nature. He could easily see her gliding across the stage, the antithesis to the clumsy jester.

"But why are we here? We should move on."

Someone shushed Ghaul, but the warrior's angry look made the man cower. The jester didn't speak as he stumbled about, his body hitting the stage the only noise he produced, and Khirro wondered why the man would bother telling Ghaul to be quiet.

117

"Have patience, Ghaul," Elyea replied. "Enjoy the show."

Ghaul looked as though he would say something else but relented. Khirro smirked. He imagined Elyea often got her way.

The little man's performance ended as he blundered from the stage to raucous laughter and applause. Next came the juggler: a tall, slender man with dark hair pulled back in a tight ponytail. He began his act tossing about three bean bags, then five, then ten, using every part of his body to keep them in the air: hands, feet, back, head. He graduated to sticks and rocks, then knives. For his finale, he juggled a double-edged axe, an egg and a lit torch. The audience gasped and oohed as the items spun and flew; Khirro gasped and oohed along with them, the performance making him forget their journey. The torch licked the roof of the tent on a final high spin and the man caught it with a flourish and a bow, ending his performance. The crowd cheered and Khirro clapped while Ghaul sat silent on the other side of Elyea.

A man with a lute in his hands and a purple feather bobbing from his felt hat took the stage, his features delicate enough he might pass for a woman but for his whip-thin mustache. The crowd went silent with the first chord he strummed. He sang of knights and dragons, maidens and heroes, of loves won and lost and regained again, all in a voice smooth and sweet like virgin honey.

Women dabbed the corners of their eyes as he sang; men shifted uncomfortably in their seats. One woman shouted a marriage proposal eliciting a glare from the man beside her. Khirro listened, appreciating the purity of the singer's voice, but the heat distracted him, made him fidgety. He stole glances at Elyea watching the troubadour. She smiled, sometimes sang along, but no tears needed dabbing during the sad ballads, lust didn't smolder beneath as it seemed to do for many of the other women. When she turned to meet Khirro's gaze, he looked away, blushing like a child caught stealing treats.

The singer finished his act. Women applauded wildly while the men sat, arms crossed, pretending to be relieved it was over. The performer bowed deeply, feather brushing the face of a woman in the front row, then left the stage.

A minute passed as the stage remained empty. A murmur started in one corner near the stage, and spread across the crowd. Khirro fidgeted, wondering if the show was done. The minute stretched on and the whisper grew to a mutter, then a grumble, the crowd agitated by the wait and the heat, but no one got left. As the noise grew to a crescendo, a flash of light on the stage silenced the grumble. Smoke billowed, catching in the peak of the tent, then dissipated to leave a man standing stage center, back to the audience. A black velvet cape cascaded from his shoulders, brushing the floor. The tent and all its occupants waited, breathless with anticipation, until a

119

Bruce Blake

shout from the back made them jump.

"Ladies and gentleman," the pitchman announced. "The amazing, astounding, awe-inspiring... Athryn!"

The man spun around, arms extended, cape spread to reveal its blood red lining. The crowd cheered. Khirro stared. The wide sleeves of the man's white shirt billowed; his blond hair was pulled back in a ponytail. His garb was impressive, but it was the polished silver mask covering his face that grabbed Khirro's attention. Anyone looking at him wouldn't see his face, only themselves, twisted and distorted by the contours of cheek and nose.

The applause continued while the man released the edge of his cape and rolled up his sleeves revealing forearms tattooed with black scrollwork. He raised his arms above his head and the crowd settled. With a flick of his wrist, a coin appeared between his fingers. He tossed the copper into the crowd causing a scuffle, then performed the same act with the other hand.

A magician!

If not for the things he'd seen the Shaman do, Khirro would have expected to go to his grave without witnessing a feat of magic. For as long as he'd been alive, the practice of magic was outlawed in Erechania, except in service of the king. He turned to Elyea.

"How?"

She shrugged. "He won't tell me."

"No, I mean how come he hasn't been arrested?"

120

"He does nothing wrong, Khirro." She rested a comforting hand on his knee; her touch returned the heat to his cheeks. "He does nothing but parlor tricks and illusions in public. There's no harm in a little sleight-of-hand." She removed her hand and the feeling of guilt and pleasure it had brought went with it.

An illusionist. Trickery, not magic. Khirro settled into his seat, relieved no one would burst into the tent to arrest the man.

For a half-hour, the illusionist made things appear, then disappear, only to pull them from an audience member's ear or from under their seat. He tore up a sheet of paper and made it whole again. A length of rope writhed about like a snake of its own accord until he cut it with a dagger which appeared out of nowhere, then he made the cord intact again. With each trick, the audience oohed and ahhed, gasped and catcalled. The greater their reactions, the more fervent his performance. Khirro stared, awe preventing him from joining the crowd's appreciation. It wasn't true magic, but it was impressive.

The time came for the finale. The illusionist surveyed the audience, his mirrored mask reflecting their distorted faces back at them, and a hush fell as he spoke for the first time.

"For my final feat, I shall need the assistance of a woman of unsurpassed beauty."

A forest of female arms thrusting into the air blocked

Khirro's view of the stage. It looked as though every woman in the tent wanted to be chosen.

"Fool yourselves not, m'ladies, this requires bravery as well as beauty. There is danger involved."

A few hands dropped. The illusionist made a show of searching the audience and each time his gaze passed a section of women, their arms stretched higher. Finally he pointed toward the back of the tent. Khirro felt a twinge: it looked like the magician pointed at him.

"At the back. Would the strawberry-haired goddess please honor me?"

Elyea popped to her feet and skipped down the aisle, a whisper from the crowd following her as she made her way to the stage. Khirro stared after her, an unexpected finger of dread poking at his mind.

He said it could be dangerous.

"What's your name, lass?" The illusionist offered his hand to help her on to the stage.

"Whore," a woman yelled. The illusionist trained his gaze on the heckler, the emotionless face cast upon his mask chastising her. The audience fell silent.

"There is no judgment in this tent," he said, voice quiet but firm. "We are all people in the eyes of the Gods." He turned his attention to Elyea again. "Your name?"

"Elyea."

She smiled widely looking every bit the goddess, then curtsied in the direction of the woman who'd called out the epithet. A few men in the audience snickered.

"Are you afraid, Elyea?" Her smile didn't falter as she shook her head. "Fear is not always a bad thing. Much like the pain of a hot object keeps us from getting hurt, so fear keeps us safe from dangers."

He grasped her shoulders and positioned her center stage facing the audience. Appreciation for the curve of her body, the fall of her hair, dulled the dread tickling Khirro's gut.

"Fear of entering the woods at night keeps us from encountering the foraging bear. Fear of the stage keeps us from embarrassment before our peers."

He gestured to the audience. Khirro nodded at his words—he'd become well acquainted with fear over the days since the Kanosee launched their attack against the Isthmus Fortress. And it only got worse from there.

The illusionist moved to the back of the stage, reached behind the curtain, and pulled out a velvet blanket of purple so dark it might have been black.

"But sometimes fear keeps us from experiencing new things, things that might change our lives forever." He shook the shroud out with a snap. "Fear not, my lady."

"Elyea."

"Fear not, Elyea. This will not hurt. All that is required of you is stand there looking beautiful, something at which I can see you are well practiced."

At the front of the stage, he whirled the velvet cover

123

around his head with a flourish, showing the lighter purple lining for the audience to see there was nothing unusual about it. The muscles in Khirro's thighs tightened, his breath shallowed.

"Close your eyes," the illusionist instructed. "Keep your arms at your sides."

He spun the cerement over her head and it floated down like an autumn leaf fallen from a tree, covering her completely. All movement in the tent ceased save for the illusionist stalking around Elyea's covered form, gesturing and whispering. Women stopped fanning themselves, men leaned forward in their seats. It seemed the entire audience held its breath.

The illusionist's gesticulations held an authenticity that reminded Khirro of the Shaman. His movements might simply be masterful showmanship, but Khirro felt there was more to it. A shiver ran down his spine as the Shaman's pale skin came to mind, and the black sword hidden in the brush at the edge of the village. The things he'd seen would change the way he looked at the world forever.

A flutter at the right of the stage drew Khirro's attention. He looked closer and saw the jester peering out from a crack between the canvas and the curtain.

A fellow entertainer enjoying the act or part of the trick?

He watched the illusionist more intently, glancing

occasionally at the little man. The other tricks had been beyond his understanding, but perhaps he could figure out how he performed this legerdemain.

Athryn circled Elyea once more, his gestures more pronounced. With a final grand motion, he swept the cloth away. The crowd sucked in its breath with a collective whoosh and Khirro's jaw dropped. Only empty air remained where Elyea had stood beneath the purple cover. Scattered claps broke the silence, quickly multiplying until the tent exploded with applause. The audience jumped to their feet showing their admiration. Khirro remained seated.

"Don't bring the harlot back," the woman in front of Khirro shouted, her words barely audible over the din.

It quickly became apparent the woman would have her wish. The illusionist spread his arms and bowed deeply three times—once to the right, once to the middle, once to the left—then exited through the center of the curtain at the rear of the stage.

Khirro looked at Ghaul, a concerned question forming on his lips, but it never left his mouth. The pitchman from the entrance leaned in and whispered something to Ghaul who nodded and rose. Khirro scrambled after them, pushing by the still clapping crowd as the man led them from the tent, past the dissipating mob that had crowded the doorway when they arrived, and around to the back. He lifted a flap and ushered them inside but didn't follow.

125

The backstage area was small and only slightly cooler than the front. Ornate rugs covered the ground; the only piece of furniture was a cushioned divan upon which Elyea lay, eyes closed and face pale. Khirro's heart jumped in his chest when he saw her and he moved forward, but the troubadour stepped in blocking his way.

"You must be Elyea's friends, yes? I am Alicando." He doffed his hat and bowed, the great purple feather sweeping against the ground. "Welcome."

With the man standing so close, Khirro felt anything but welcome.

"Let them through, Alicando."

The illusionist crouched at Elyea's side swabbing her brow with a damp cloth, his cape splayed on the floor beneath him. Beside them, the little jester sat cross-legged as the juggler wrapped a bandage around his forearm. A trickle of blood ran from under the cloth, snaking down his wrist and between his fingers. The singer stepped out of their path, his dainty lips turned up in a grin. Ghaul glared at him as they moved past, but the smile didn't falter.

"Is she all right?"

The illusionist's sleeves were still rolled up and Khirro clearly saw the tattoos twisting across his flesh, disappearing beneath his shirt, and for a second he thought he saw them slither like snakes. The illusion quickly passed. These were no colorful decorations but flowing black letters and words in unrecognizable languages. The illusionist looked at him, the reflection in his mask distorting Khirro's face into something both comical and hideous. He looked into the man's blue eyes but found his gaze slipping back to examine his own twisted features.

"Yes. She only needs to rest. It is a simple bit of entertainment, but an exhausting one."

Elyea's eyelids fluttered at the sound of voices. She looked first at Khirro, then over his shoulder at Ghaul.

"Not a bad trick, eh?"

Khirro grasped her hand in both of his. "Are you hurt?"

"No, only tired."

"How did you do it?" Ghaul asked.

The illusionist stood and faced the warrior leaving Khirro relieved he was no longer tempted to look upon the misshapen version of himself. He felt as though the mask showed him a piece of his soul he didn't want to know existed.

"A craftsman does not reveal his secrets," Athryn said moving to the exit, cape swirling with his movements. "Take care of the lady and get some rest yourselves. We will meet on the morrow."

Ghaul went to follow him out, but the troubadour blocked his way.

"It is always best to do as Athryn says, yes?"

Ghaul glowered but didn't challenge him further.

"We'll be meeting with no one tomorrow," he growled returning to his companions.

The jester and the juggler rose and followed the illusionist out leaving only the troubadour standing watch. Elyea sat up on the divan and took her hand from Khirro's.

"Alicando is right. We should listen to what Athryn has to say. He may be of more help than you know, Ghaul." She rose uncertainly, steadying herself with a hand on Khirro's shoulder. "I have friends outside town we can stay with. We'll be safe and they'll give us supplies and a place to sleep."

She led them past the troubadour, who smiled broadly as Ghaul bumped him on the way out. For a moment, Khirro thought they might come to blows, but the singer continued grinning as Elyea pulled the soldier away.

Who is this Athryn and what does he want with us?

Elyea led them toward the outskirts of Inehsul to collect their armor and weapons. Khirro looked at his feet as they walked and sighed deeply. He'd soon find out if telling Elyea the truth had been the right decision or not.

13

To Khirro's discomfort, but not his surprise, the place outside town turned out to be Inehsul's version of a brothel. Three women shared the thatched-roof cottage, each of them employed in the art of satisfying men. Aryann, the youngest, was a pretty blonde with small hands and close-set eyes. Khirro doubted she'd seen her sixteenth summer.

"She's only had two customers so far," Elyea explained, "and one of them asked for his money back."

"That's not true." Aryann blushed and protested. "At least, it wasn't my fault. It was my moon time."

The second woman, Leigha, wore her raven hair in a tight bun at the back of her head. She looked about Elyea's age and the formless shift she wore hid the pudginess she claimed her customers loved.

"There's more of me to love," she said winking at them. "But if you want a little extra cushion, you have to come during the week: I don't see customers on the holy days."

"Are you sure that's not just laziness?" Elyea teased.

"Hmph. After five days of men worshipping at this temple," she said spreading her arms, "don't you think I should go to temple, too?"

"Don't believe her," the third woman said—an older woman named Despina. "She doesn't accept payment on weekends, that doesn't mean she doesn't satisfy the odd man here and there."

"Oh honey, there's nothing odd about them."

Despina was the matron, easily old enough to be Elyea's mother or Aryann's grandmother. The dress cinched beyond reason at her waist struggled valiantly to contain her enormous bosom—a battle it was losing. Still an attractive woman, Khirro guessed the brown tresses spilling down her back were a wig. And she liked to talk.

"I have customers who've been with me nie thirty years," she said after the introductions were done. "I haven't taken a new customer in years."

"Wow." Khirro nodded and smiled politely, impressed she'd been in the business longer than he'd been alive.

"Mind you, you're the sort of lad who might tempt me into taking a new client." She prodded Khirro with her elbow and laughed hard enough he thought her corset might explode.

"I have someone waiting for me at home, my lady."

"Most of 'em do, love. Most of 'em do."

The women welcomed them enthusiastically, surprising Khirro: he'd thought women of their profession might be less inclined toward graciousness to men in their off hours, but they doted over them preparing dinner, providing supplies and acting genuinely delighted to do so. The sexual innuendoes and suggestive comments came fast and furious, making Khirro fidget and blush constantly, but the atmosphere looked to relax Ghaul, something he hadn't yet seen from his companion..

Thank goodness for that.

They sat at the wooden table by the fireplace in the large, open room serving as kitchen, dining and living area, eating fresh baked bread and bowls of steaming stew full to the brim with bawdy tales and laughter. When they finished, their hostesses cleared away the earthenware dishes and busied themselves leaving Khirro and his companions to talk on their own.

"Your friends are wonderful," Khirro commented. "And good cooks."

Ghaul grunted agreement as he watched Aryann cross the room to the doorway, water bucket in hand. She smiled at him as she exited.

"I doubt that." Elyea nudged Ghaul playfully; he grinned. "More likely everything was taken as payment. Times are lean when men are off making war. One can't afford to refuse a customer, whether they pay with cash or bread."

"But what of the men in the clearing?" Khirro asked. "Shouldn't they have been off making war?"

"I didn't ask why they were here. A deserter's coin is as good as an honest man's."

What about a coward's coin? Is it as good?

"In my trade, you learn not to ask questions. It's best that way."

"That wasn't the case with us, though, was it?" Ghaul scoffed. "We couldn't stop you asking questions."

"There was no danger you were customers, they're rarely so chivalrous."

She smiled and Ghaul chuckled, but Khirro had trouble finding the humor. What kind of life was it to sell yourself and live in fear of those buying your services? People buying his produce never caused him anxiety; he never worried someone would beat him over a potato.

After the dishes were cleared, Leigha disappeared into the lone room at the back of the hut and Despina whistled as she tidied the pantry. Ghaul pulled dagger and whetstone from his belt and began sliding the blade along its rough surface. The grating sound set Khirro's teeth on edge.

"What of this Athryn?" Ghaul asked as he honed the knife. "What's his interest in us?"

"It's not my place to say." Elyea leaned back in her chair and the thin material of her dress pulled tight across her breasts; Khirro glanced once, then looked away, silently chastising himself. "I'm sure he'll tell you tomorrow."

"And if we decide not to go?"

"What do you have to lose, Ghaul? If he offers nothing of interest, we go on our way. But if he proves useful..."

"She's right," Khirro said as he watched Ghaul store the honing stone and twirl the knife in his fingers. "It can't hurt."

He could imagine the warrior's thoughts: *You've already revealed our secret to one person too many'.* His eyes had carried the accusation since they met Elyea, though he hadn't said it. Not yet.

"Let's hope it doesn't."

He jabbed the point of his knife into the table as Aryann struggled through the door, both hands grasping the handle of the pail as water splashed over the edge. Ghaul rose to help, dagger wobbling in the table top. She smiled and the corner of his mouth twitched. Despina strode across the room, cloth in hand.

"It looks like Aryann will get some much needed practice tonight," she said pulling Ghaul's dagger from the table and brushing away the crumbs left from dinner. Aryann shot her an embarrassed look, then broke into a bigger smile. "That solves part of our sleeping arrangements. I've decided I'll sacrifice—you can sleep with me, Khirro." She winked at him and Elyea laughed.

"Very kind of you, my lady. I'd be honored, but there's Emeline to think of, and my child." Khirro shifted in his chair, the muscles in his neck tensing as he waited to see if he offended his hostess.

"This Emeline must be quite a woman for you to pass this up." Despina cupped her enormous breasts and jiggled them at him.

Quite a woman. He turned his eyes toward the table, picked at the grain of the wood with his fingernail rather than look at the others. *She deserves better than the likes of me.*

Leigha reentered the room, saving him from further embarrassment and interrupting his guilt.

"Leave the poor man alone, Despina. Can't you see you're scaring him?"

The tight bun was gone from her hair, leaving her tresses hanging to her waist; she must have chosen the

133

dress she wore for the way it showed her generous curves. She crossed the room and threw her arms around Khirro's neck, brushing his cheek with hers.

"You can take my hammock. I won't be needing it tonight."

She kissed him hard on the cheek then released him. Unconsciously, Khirro's hand went to the spot she kissed and the corners of his mouth struggled into a smile.

Leigha waved her fingers as she sauntered out the door, hips swinging a wide arc. "See you in the morning."

"Bah," Despina said with a laugh. "I guess I'll be sharing my bed with you again, Elyea. You best behave yourself, trollop. No freebies for the likes of you."

"And none for you either, old one. Don't think I owe you because you fed me."

Khirro and Elyea helped Despina finish tidying while Ghaul and Aryann retired to the only private room. When he finally lay down in the borrowed hammock, sleep didn't come immediately, though Khirro was as tired as if it was the middle of harvest season. Too much had happened in the last few days for sleep to be easy: too many worries, too many questions about Elyea, Athryn, and what lay ahead. As he finally quieted his racing mind and started to doze, the hut's thin walls proved his nemesis. Aryann sounded to be taking full advantage of the opportunity to practice, and made no secret of it. Khirro lay in the dark, listening, partly curious, partly embarrassed. Khirro shifted

onto his side, facing the wall, and put his hand to his ear
and allowed memories of Emeline to claw his heart.

***

Someone quite cunning had taken great pains to hide
the building. They were only a dozen yards from the
windowless stone walls before Khirro noticed it.

The plain gray walls rose unexpectedly out of a stand of
cottonwood trees shedding their fibers in a soft white veil
dancing in the sun. Branches nuzzled the keep's walls in
the slight morning breeze, each movement of leaf and twig
giving the illusion the structure disappeared only to
reappear again a second later. Khirro blinked hard to
dispel the illusion, but it remained until they drew closer.
Elyea led them toward the south wall which showed no
window or door.

"What is this place?" he asked.

"This is where the cult of magic resides."

Khirro stopped in his tracks.

"There's no such thing."

Besides dragons, giants and ogres, the bedtime stories
Khirro's mother told her young son had included wizards
and the cult of magic. But they were stories, tales of
renegade practitioners hiding their talents from the law as
they performed evil acts against the innocent.

"Yet, here we stand." Ghaul pulled him by the arm.
"Let's go. You're the one who said it couldn't hurt to
come."

Khirro resisted, thinking of the things little boys had been turned into in his mother's stories: frogs, lizards, goblins, stone. They were fanciful tales and myths but, in his heart, he believed a little. Bushes rustled a few yards from them, startling Khirro. He tensed, expecting a wyvern to take flight, or an ogre to charge them, but it was a partridge breaking cover, making for the blue sky. He took a couple of hurried steps to catch up to his companions.

Pitted by time and blackened by flame, the huge oak door set in the center of the wall hung on brass hinges showing a patina of verdigris. Khirro clenched his teeth, jaw muscles knotting. The door wasn't there a moment ago.

How can a door appear out of thin air? The small part of him that believed his mother's stories stirred.

The strange appearance didn't give Elyea a moment's hesitation as she stepped up to the door, placed her hand on a stone to the right of it, and closed her eyes. Birds chirped, the air stirred. Nothing happened for ten seconds, then wood grated against stone and ancient hinges creaked. The door swung inward onto a dark hall where there stood no one to pull it open.

"How did you...?" Khirro began.

"I'm no magician, Khirro. I asked the door-keeper for entrance and he granted it." She patted the rock upon which her hand still lay. "We are old friends, he and I."

"But there's no one here." Khirro rubbed his temple,

his fingers finding a droplet of sweat.

Elyea stepped through the doorway. "There is, but he's not what you're used to. Imlip has been door-keeper so well for so long, he has become one with the stone. He gave his life to protect this sanctuary."

She held her hand out, beckoning. Ghaul stepped across the threshold, but Khirro hesitated.

"Come, farmer. There's nothing to fear but your own thoughts."

Not long ago, being called 'farmer' had made him proud, but the word felt different now, made him bristle with feelings of inadequacy. Had he changed so quickly? Or was it because the words came from her?

He stepped up to the doorway, staring hard at the stone to the right. It was gray and coarse and unmoving like every other stone in every other wall. As he moved through the door, he brushed his fingertips against the spot where Elyea had laid her hand. His fingers found the surface fleshy and soft but firm, and it was warm—not like it had been warmed by the sun but as though heat radiated from within. He pulled away with a gasp and stepped through the doorway to retreat from this Imlip. The old hinges creaked shut, trapping them in the dimly lit hall.

14

Elyea led them down the hall and through another oaken door into a sparsely furnished room lit by an

137

opening in the ceiling forty feet overhead. Shadows crouched in the corners where the sun didn't reach, making Khirro uneasy.

They moved to the sunlit center of the room where the illusionist lounged on an overstuffed couch, a white cloth with holes cut for eyes and mouth covering his face instead of the silvered mask he wore during his performance the previous day.

Why doesn't he want anyone to know who he is?

The little man sat on a wool rug at the illusionist's feet, quill in hand and a pot of ink at his side as he scribbled on a piece of bark. He wore doeskin breeches and a loose cotton shirt instead of a jester's motley; he didn't interrupt his task to look up at them.

"I am Athryn. The little one is Maes," the illusionist said rising from the sofa and crossing the room to Elyea, embracing her. "You were wonderful yesterday, little bird. As always."

"It was fun." Elyea smiled and stepped aside, moving like she'd introduce her companions, but Athryn spoke before she could.

"Let me see it, Khirro."

"How do you know me?" Khirro stepped back, hand moving unconsciously to his chest.

"I have known of you since you made company with Bale. And I know what you carry."

"Bale." Khirro spoke the word as though it was foreign.

138

A vision of the Shaman's blood-spattered, ashen face flashed through his mind. "The Shaman."

Athryn nodded. "Yes, the Shaman. We were friends once, fellow students, but our paths diverged."

"How do you know all this, devil?" Ghaul grasped the hilt of his sword.

"There is no reason to fear, Ghaul. I am a friend." His eyes narrowed as he watched for further movement from the warrior but Ghaul neither released his sword nor drew it. Athryn turned his attention back to Khirro. "Let me see the vial."

A corner of Khirro's mind told him he should fear this man, but his heart wouldn't allow it, though he didn't know why. A pulse of warmth touched his chest, as though the king's blood in the vial hidden there spoke to him, giving permission to reveal it to this man. He looked at Elyea, who nodded softly, then at Ghaul whose eyes didn't shift from the illusionist. Athryn waited patiently, the long sleeves of his shirt hiding the tattoos slithering up his arms as the mask hid his face. Everything about the man was enigmatic, mysterious, yet Khirro still reached beneath his jerkin and pulled forth the vial, holding it out for the illusionist. Athryn made no move to take it.

"Maes," he called.

The jester abandoned his writings and rose from the rug. He didn't trip or stumble as he walked to the illusionist's side and Khirro felt silly this surprised him—of course he wasn't a clumsy oaf, but a performer, like Athryn. Maes held out his hand. Khirro looked down into kind, dark eyes and a face framed by thick black hair. The day before, the patchwork costume had overshadowed the man's features. As Khirro handed him the vial, he realized he hadn't noticed the labyrinth of scars on his forearm, either.

What happened to him?

"No," Ghaul said. "We don't know if we can trust them."

He loosened his sword in its scabbard and this time Athryn's body tensed, but Khirro saw no weapons on either him or Maes.

"It's all right," Khirro said.

He heard Elyea suck breath in through her teeth as the little man rolled the vial through his fingers. Khirro saw scars marring his hands; two of his fingers were without nails. Maes held the vial up and peered through the translucent fluid for a few seconds, then replaced it in Khirro's hand, nodded to Athryn and returned to his spot on the rug. With the vial back in Khirro's possession, Ghaul released his sword. Tension drained from Athryn and Elyea released her held breath.

"It is true, then," Athryn said as Khirro replaced the phial in its hiding place. "You carry the fate of the kingdom at your breast."

"What's your interest in all this?" Ghaul growled, but

Khirro barely heard.

The fate of the kingdom.

Here, in this room with a hole in the ceiling, the enormity, the importance of the task with which he was cursed struck full force. The weight of the sky pressed down upon him and the room wavered before his eyes. His companions, the gray walls and scattered furnishings were replaced by a crowd of people dressed in tattered clothing; a tide of soldiers clad in black mail splashed with blood and red paint swept through them, slashing and chopping; fields and villages burned in the background as women and children were put to the sword. Among them: his parents, Emeline, and a child he would never know.

He carried their fates in a vial pressed against his heart.

Through a fog he heard Ghaul and Athryn exchange words but they meant nothing to him. The room dimmed, he swayed on weakened legs. For a moment he expected everything to disappear and hoped for darkness. If it did, perhaps he'd wake in his own bed at his own farm and find this all a bad dream. A hand at his elbow dashed his hopes and brought him back to the room with the hole in the ceiling. More words, this time Elyea's voice.

"What?"

"I asked if you're all right."

Khirro closed his eyes and wiped the back of his hand across his brow. It came away damp with sweat. He breathed deeply and opened his eyes to find a distressed look on Elyea's face. Her concern warmed his heart.

"Yes, I'm fine. I'll sit a moment, though."

Elyea glanced at Athryn and, with his nodded consent, led Khirro to the settee behind Maes.

"What's the matter, Khirro?" Ghaul asked.

"I... I felt a little light headed. I'm fine now."

"Keep an eye on our guest, Maes," Athryn said. The little man nodded, his shirt shifting with the movement, and Khirro noted more scars—fine white lines on his neck, disappearing beneath the cloth. Khirro shuddered.

No one spoke. Elyea stood at Khirro's side, her hand resting on his shoulder making him feel both comforted and uncomfortable at the same time. He fidgeted beneath her touch. It seemed natural for her to lay her hand upon a man, but it was anything but to him. Athryn clapped his hands sharply, startling Khirro from Maes' scars and Elyea's touch. A man appeared from behind a tapestry that Khirro wouldn't have guessed hid a doorway.

"Prepare horses for everyone," Athryn said to the juggler when he entered the room, his long dark hair loose about his shoulders. "And food. We leave within the hour."

The illusionist's words didn't surprise Khirro. The thought of Athryn joining them caused peace in him instead of the trepidation he felt at revealing their intent to Elyea, though he didn't know why. Safety in numbers, perhaps. Or maybe because of the illusionist's connection to the Shaman. No matter the reason, Ghaul didn't share his ease.

"We appreciate the use of your horses," Ghaul said, the forced restraint in his voice too obvious to fool anyone. "But our party has already swollen to one more than it should be. We have no room for a performer of parlor tricks."

"I am no mere illusionist, and you will be joined by two of us. I go nowhere without Maes." The little man halted scribbling and looked up.

The muscles in Ghaul's jaw knotted, his fingers curled into fists. "You don't even know where we go, prestidigitator."

"Lakesh. You seek Darestat to raise the king and deliver Erechania."

Ghaul glanced at Elyea, eyes smoldering. Her gaze held steady, neither confirming nor denying his thought.

"She did not tell me, nor did Khirro."

"Cease your trickery and lies, illusionist. We have no need of your company, or that of a clumsy midget."

The warrior's words finally affected Athryn and he threw back his cape, exposing the sword hidden beneath. Ghaul's hand went to his weapon and he freed an inch of steel from the scabbard. The air in the room suddenly grew heavier and Khirro worried he might lose touch again.

"Wait," Elyea said. "There's no reason for this."

"Sit down, harlot," Ghaul growled.

"Enough, Ghaul," Khirro said taking offense at his

143

words even if Elyea didn't. He leaned forward on the couch. "This journey is mine, and I say they can join us."

The warrior's eyes flickered from Athryn to Khirro and back. "It may be your journey, but it is my life. And look at you: you're not well."

"I'm fine. My strength has returned."

"But what of him?" Ghaul gestured toward Athryn with his free hand. "Do you expect me to trust a man who doesn't reveal his face in the privacy of his own residence?"

Khirro pushed himself up on shaky legs, looked at Ghaul and Athryn, then Elyea and Maes, hoping someone would do or say something because he didn't know what to do next. Athryn must have seen the desperation in his eyes.

He raised his hand, gripped the white cloth mask and pulled it slowly from his face with a performer's dramatic flair. Elyea sucked in a surprised breath; Ghaul's stern look softened; Khirro felt a sinking at the pit of his stomach. Only Maes didn't react as Athryn revealed that he didn't wear the mask to disguise his identity but to hide the pink scar covering most of his features. The flesh around his left eye was all that remained untouched, the single eyebrow the only hair on his face, as the smooth, shiny skin stopped short of the blond hair he wore in a ponytail as he had the day before.

Athryn said nothing as they stared. His piercing blue eyes glowed, gauging their reactions. Khirro felt he should say something, but nothing came to mind. Elyea finally broke the tense silence.

"How did this happen?"

"Dragonfire."

Khirro saw Ghaul's expression shift again, this time to disbelief. "Dragonfire? If you speak the truth, prove it."

The illusionist said nothing as Khirro looked questioningly at Ghaul. The warrior folded his arms across his chest.

"A man who survives the touch of dragonfire retains a portion of the dragon's magic. If Athryn speaks the truth, he should be able to show us more than hiding coins on the back of his hand or making a woman disappear through a trap door."

"I didn't--" Elyea protested, but Athryn held up his hand to stop her.

"Let him show us," Khirro said, curiosity making him forget his bout of vertigo.

Athryn nodded. From the corner of his eye, Khirro saw Maes lay his quill and bark aside. The illusionist closed his eyes, head bowed. His lips moved whispering words Khirro had never heard before. A chill crawled up his spine.

The air in the chamber stirred and a gentle draft touched Khirro's skin as though a door was left ajar. He ignored it, but as Athryn's words continued, the draft became a breeze. Khirro looked around the room. The door remained closed, the tapestry didn't move. Overhead, the branches stretching across the hole in the ceiling didn't sway.

How...?

A movement drew Khirro's gaze away from the illusionist. Maes had stood, a dagger in his hand. Khirro's heart jumped.

Ghaul was right.

He wanted to warn the others but couldn't find his tongue. The breeze intensified, concentrating in front of Athryn at the center of the room, swirling into a whirlwind, flapping his cloak about his body. The temperature dropped and the illusionist's breath became visible as his whispers continued, words drowned by the howling wind. The whirlwind became a tornado, spinning in place, intensifying until it became opaque. Khirro looked from Athryn to Maes—the small man had made no move toward him or his companions.

The wind stopped abruptly and Athryn's cloak fell back to his sides, yet the tornado remained. Khirro squinted.

No, not a tornado.

Something solid had replaced the tornado, spinning in place like a coin set on edge. Khirro gaped. As the revolutions slowed, it resolved into the shape of a shield. Ghaul stretched out his hand but pulled away like a man who'd touched fire when his fingers brushed it. The disturbance set it wobbling and it clattered to the floor.

Tentatively, Ghaul reached out again, but this time didn't draw away when he touched it.

"It's real." His fingers touched bands of hammered copper and bronze criss-crossing the surface of the oval shield. "Did you create this?"

"No." Athryn's eyes were open. He pulled the cloth mask back into place as he answered. "I brought it here, but I did not create it."

"How?" Khirro managed to ask.

"I cannot explain, but it should quell your concerns." He picked the shield up from the floor. "This is for you, Khirro."

When Khirro could only stare at the offering, Maes took it from the magician and brought it to him. The small man no longer held the jeweled dagger; a trickle of blood flowed down his arm from a cut on his left bicep.

"What happened to you, Maes?"

Elyea pulled a cloth from her bodice and dabbed the cut on Maes' arm as Khirro accepted the shield, but the jester didn't respond. The shield was real—heavy and solid. It held no warmth or vibration, nothing to make him believe it a magic shield.

"It is necessary," Athryn answered on his behalf.

"What do you mean?" Ghaul shifted to look at the wound on Maes' arm.

"Magic requires payment. Energy drawn requires energy paid."

147

Khirro looked from the little man's bloody arm to Athryn, the blood draining from his face. All those rumors and stories dismissed as flights of fancy instantly became true, shifting his life into another dimension. A life of potatoes and beans sounded less complicated than one where wizards and dragons existed, but now it felt so far away.

"All is ready." The troubadour parted the tapestry and entered the room. "Shall I be coming with you to sing a traveling song?" He eyed Elyea and smiled.

"Not this time," Athryn said. "We leave immediately."

Khirro looked at him, his head spinning. This display, this new reality, left him with no words to speak, no idea what to do. He glanced at Ghaul.

"Why do you wish to accompany us?" the soldier asked.

"I dreamed a future without the king and it is not one I desire to live."

"But Braymon outlawed magic," Ghaul pointed out. "Why would you want him back if it means living a lie?"

"His law was a facade to placate the people and discourage show-offs. The cult of magic exists everywhere, meeting secretly, but Braymon knew and let it be thus." Athryn adjusted his mask and brushed wind-thrown dirt from his cloak. "In Kanos, Healers, Shamans and Sorcerers not in the employ of the Archon are hunted down and drowned like rats. An Erechania ruled by the Kanosee becomes a dangerous place for the likes of me."

Khirro nodded. Ghaul shifted uncomfortably from foot to foot.

"It sounds like you'll be joining us," the warrior said begrudgingly. Khirro wondered why. "We should go."

"Yes." Athryn moved toward the oaken door; Maes followed, leaving his writing implements scattered on the floor. Khirro glanced at them and saw the letters he'd scrawled on the light brown bark resembled the ones covering Athryn's arms. "We have a great distance to travel."

"I have a bad feeling," Ghaul said when the performers had left the room. "I've never trusted magicians."

Before the Shaman, Khirro had never known a magician, so he didn't share Ghaul's sentiment. Something felt right, even comforting, about the two men joining them. The vial of blood warmed against his chest as they followed the magician and jester from the roofless chamber. The dimness of the hall didn't quash his good feelings and, when they emerged into bright sunlight to find Athryn and Maes standing with horses readied, hope flooded Khirro. With Ghaul's blade and Athryn's magic on their side, perhaps they had a chance to succeed.

Or, at the very least, survive.

15

In the week since leaving Inehsul and the strange keep in the woods, there had been no particular need for a magician or a very small man, but Khirro still felt thankful Athryn and Maes had joined them. More travelers meant shorter watches and more plentiful sleep, though the performers always took watch together. Khirro felt better for the extra rest.

The magician knew the area, leading them along little used paths and around towns and villages to avoid attention. With a day's ride left to the Vendarian border, one town remained between them and Erechania's southern neighbor. The war raging in the north meant they couldn't know what reception might await across the border, so it wouldn't be safe to resupply in Vendaria. Neither was Tasgarad a safe haven, but it was their last opportunity before leaving the kingdom. As the headquarters of the border patrol, the town would be crawling with whatever Erechanian troops hadn't been called to war at the Isthmus or to reinforce the Sea Wall.

"Care will be needed," Athryn said as Khirro readied himself for sleep the night before their arrival in Tasgarad. "We will be better off to get in and out unnoticed."

Khirro nodded and laid his head down, listening as Athryn and Ghaul planned the best route in and out of town and where to cross the border. He listened a minute, disappointed they didn't seek his opinion even knowing he had nothing of value to add. What did a farmer know of such things?

Nothing.

He put it from his mind and turned his attention to sleep. Not so long ago, fear might have caused him to lay awake, tossing and turning the entire night, but not this night. Sleep claimed him and dreams usurped fear's power.

His dreams began as they did most nights, as he willed them to: a fall harvest, a babe in his arms and Emeline at his side. But this dream faded, replaced by one new and unfamiliar. Huge trees towered about him in an unknown forest. Night enveloped him and dense foliage deepened the darkness so he saw nothing more than limbs and trunks. He didn't know where he was or why, only that he shouldn't stay. Feet heavy with fear, he pushed his way through the brush. Twigs snapped under his footsteps, leaves rustled past his face, all startlingly loud in the silent dream forest, but he pushed on, less concerned with the noise than with finding a way out. The underbrush neither thinned nor became more dense; all the trees looked the same.

Am I going anywhere?

He stopped, took a moment to search for his bearings. The rustle of leaves continued after his movements ceased. A spear of panic lanced through his chest, so severe his sleeping body jerked with it. This was no echo or trick of the wind.

Something in the forest followed him.

Khirro pushed on, moving more quickly. He cast a look

over his shoulder and a gnarled root sent him tumbling to the ground, his fingers sinking into earthy smelling loam. He scrambled to his feet, stumbled forward, the sound louder, closer. Limbs whipped his face and grabbed his clothes, holding him back, impeding his escape. Now he heard breathing behind him, closing in. Ahead, a sliver of light through the trees beckoned. He ran for a long time, his pursuer gaining ground as the light drew no closer. Finally, he burst from the forest, the last tangle of underbrush snagging his foot, sending him to the ground again.

He came to rest on the rocky shore of a pristine lake. The moon reflected on its smooth surface, cutting a yellow crescent across the otherwise featureless lake. The instant he saw it, Khirro recognized his surroundings. He'd seen this lake when the Shaman gripped his hand.

Lakesh.

He had no time for despair as the brush shivered and shook, pulling his attention from the beautiful scene. He reached for his sword, but found an empty scabbard at his side. He scrambled away, stopping when his hand touched cool water. Breath held, he awaited his pursuer, the damp lakeshore soaking his breeches. In a dream, especially a dream taking place in Lakesh, anything could come out of the trees.

An animal Khirro had never seen before emerged from the forest. Muscle rippled beneath black and white striped fur and a tail equal to the length of its sleek body trailed behind. Yellow eyes stared from a huge head topped by pointed ears. Here stood another creature from his mother's stories, though this one he always dreamed to be real, living in one of the southern kingdoms he'd never visit. Before him stood a tyger: beautiful, ferocious, an eater-of-men. Khirro shifted, water lapping up the back of his hand, and wondered if the beast could swim.

The big cat approached, its lips pulled back revealing pointed teeth designed for tearing flesh. Khirro reached for the dagger at his hip, then the dirk in his boot: neither were there. His dream had left him unarmed in the presence of a monster. It moved forward, halting a yard from Khirro, and settled on its haunches. It regarded him with eyes that might have been human, save for the color and the head holding them.

"Fear not, Khirro."

The voice startled him. His eyes flitted around him, searching for the source, then flickered back to the beast. There was nothing there but the tyger, the lake, the moon, and the trees. None of them could have spoken.

"I'll not harm you."

He realized two things at once: the voice was his own, though he hadn't spoken, and his mind heard the words, not his ears. He shook his head, attempting to shake the voice from it. A breeze sent wavelets rolling across the lake.

"Wh... who are you?"

153

"I am the reason you're here."

The tyger's intense eyes seemed to look right into him, and the feeling of it chased fear from him. He suddenly knew the beast meant no harm. He pushed himself to a sitting position, withdrawing his hand from the lake. The sitting tyger's head stood higher than his.

"Why are we here?"

"So you know you are not alone."

The tyger tilted its head, long whiskers quivering, its eyes never wavering from Khirro's. The breeze stirring the lake ceased, the water calmed. Somewhere in the distance a cricket sang, the first sound Khirro heard in the dream not created by himself or the tyger.

"Will you help me?" he asked.

"When I am needed, I will be there."

The tyger rose and turned toward the forest, its tail brushing Khirro's face. He marveled at the size of the creature—it must have measured more than six meters from tip of nose to end of tail. It sauntered to the edge of the trees, hips swaying and tail flicking, then crouched and sprang gracefully away, swallowed by the forest. The urge to follow tugged at Khirro and he stood, took a step toward the trees. No sound followed the tyger's passing, leaving only the lonely cricket song to disturb the silent night. He wanted to follow, but a certainty that the big cat wasn't the only creature lurking amongst the trees stayed his step.

Khirro sat back down and leaned back, his head in the water sending ripples racing across its smooth surface. He stared up at the slivered moon and the clear black sky. Stars he didn't recognize winked and shimmered as he slowly exhaled and closed his eyes. Immediately, visions of Emeline returned, but she was different, her hair red instead of brown, her face freckled. When she spoke, he couldn't hear her words but knew the voice didn't belong to her, either. Elyea's voice, Elyea's hair, Elyea's face. Khirro opened his eyes.

The moon and lake were gone, disappeared like the tyger, as had the cricket's ballad. Instead, branches hung over him, sunlight streaming through the foliage. The smell of mossy earth was strong in his nostrils.

"Are you all right?"

He blinked and looked at Elyea knowing he no longer dreamed. Her hair hung down, framing her face, the morning sun shining behind creating the illusion she glowed.

"You called out in your sleep," she said. "You were dreaming."

"Yes," he replied, but said no more for fear of losing the peaceful feeling sating his spirit.

"It's time to go. Maes made food to break our fast. You can eat in the saddle."

Khirro smiled at her, still not speaking.

"Are you sure you're all right?"

"Yes," he said again. "Thank you."

She gave him an odd look, then turned and walked to her horse, leaving him to collect himself. He watched as she went, thinking of the white tyger and its words, of the pristine lake and of how Emeline's face became Elyea's. The empty ache of loneliness so often permeating his heart upon waking was absent this morning. He slipped his hand beneath his tunic and touched the vial hidden by his heart, its warmth flowing into his fingers. He pushed himself to his feet, rested and fortified, ready for whatever the day might bring.

16

A low haze of dust hung over Tasgarad's streets, kicked up by people, horses and wagons hurrying all directions. Stone buildings stood beside waddle and daub huts lining the streets, giving the town a feel of being caught between village and burgeoning city. Tents abutted the town's perimeter, most housing traveling merchants or entertainers, many of them from Vendaria and other points further south, here to sell their wares.

The group rode down the main street together, keeping their horses to a walk, Khirro and Ghaul wearing cloaks over their armor. Athryn had suggested leaving their leather and mail hidden rather than wear it, but Ghaul would have none of it. With soldiers about, he was unwilling to disarm. Athryn conceded but warned they'd have to be careful if they wanted to make it through Tasgarad without attracting attention. He hoped to make the border by nightfall, slip past the guard posts in the dark, and be well into Vendaria by morning light.

"Take Khirro and Ghaul, Elyea. Purchase as much food as you can carry." Athryn pulled a leather pouch from beneath his cape and handed it to her. "Maes and I have other matters to attend to. We will meet you on the south side of town at midday."

Khirro waved as Athryn turned the horse the two men shared down a side street, leaving them to stock their supplies at the market. Ghaul grunted as they left, his way of saying he mistrusted the pair.

"How long have you known Athryn, Elyea?" Khirro asked hoping for an answer to quell his companion's misgiving.

"Many years. When I was concubine of the king, he'd come to me in secret and distract me from my pain with sleight-of-hand. I didn't realize it at the time, but he likely used magic to heal my wounds at the same time."

"That doesn't mean I should trust him," Ghaul snarled.

"No, I suppose not, but I do."

She guided her horse around a throng of soldiers crooning a discordant song as they staggered across the street outside a public house. One of them eyed the three riders, but quickly rejoined his comrades in their bawdy ballad.

Bruce Blake

"And what of that damned pet midget of his? Why does the boy not speak?"

"Don't jest about him," Elyea warned, her voice serious. "Maes was also forced to serve in the king's court. The king was no less cruel with entertainers than with his concubines. Maes doesn't speak because the king took his tongue."

"Gods." Khirro had assumed the little man born unable to speak. "Why would anyone do such a thing?"

"I don't know. Athryn won't speak of it. One day, before Braymon fought to free the kingdom, Athryn ceased coming to my chambers. It wasn't until years later we crossed paths again. That Maes' tongue had been removed was all he would tell me then, and he has told me no more since."

A watchman's eyes followed them as they rode past the guard house at the market entrance. If he noticed the bulkiness of their clothes or wondered at the shield lashed to Khirro's saddle, he didn't stop them. The lanes ahead, clogged by merchants and shoppers, were too narrow for horses so they guided their steeds to a nearby tree to picket them. A boy of no more than eight summers sat nearby, idly tossing pebbles at a stump. Elyea knelt before him, said something Khirro didn't hear, then took a copper from the pouch Athryn had given her. The boy nodded excitedly and took the coin, a broad smile on his tanned face.

158

"The horses will be safe," Elyea said as she returned. They took their packs from the horses and strode into the churning throng of market-goers.

Color and sound nearly overwhelmed Khirro as they waded into the marketplace, easily three times the size of Inehsul's, which had been much bigger than the one in his own town. Khirro stared in awe at tents of green, purple or blue, some striped with white, all crowded so closely they left only enough room between for a line of customers to file past. The people bustling amongst them jostled for the best pick of produce or examined a merchant's offerings. Each time Khirro moved, someone else bumped against the sword hidden beneath his cloak or his leather chest piece. Every person seemed a threat to their journey and he found himself wishing they'd taken Athryn's advice.

"One thing I don't understand," Ghaul said, his words diverting Khirro's attention from the worries brought by the spectacle around him. "Why does Athryn have so much concern for this midget? Would the world be a worse place if there were one fewer?"

"Would it be worse for one fewer smart mouthed fighting man?"

"You know what I mean."

Elyea shook her head, sighed. "Maes is Athryn's twin brother."

"Twin?"

"Yes. Maes is the older of the two, but only by a few

159

moments."

"If this Athryn is so good and compassionate, why does he make his brother injure himself for the sake of a little trickery?"

Khirro interrupted their conversation to have Elyea pay for a package of salt pork. She took a coin from the pouch, then returned to speaking with Ghaul as Khirro stored the purchase in his pack.

"There is much I don't know about these two," she said. "But I don't believe Athryn makes Maes do anything."

"There's much you don't know, and yet you trust them," Ghaul scoffed.

Elyea stopped, the tide of people flowing past as she turned to Ghaul, her face grave. "I trust them with my life. I'd be dead if not for them."

"Hmph. If you trust them such, I guess we have no choice. But I'll keep my eyes on them nonetheless. A magician is never to be trusted."

"We should get potatoes and corn," Khirro said changing the subject. "It's their season, the flavor will be excellent."

Fruits and vegetables lay displayed on stand after stand, some varieties even Khirro hadn't seen before. As they wandered the stalls, Khirro explained to Elyea how different vegetables were planted and harvested, what time of year was best for which ones, and how to tell where melons were grown by the tint of their rind. His concern dissipated, eased by these familiar things and by Elyea's appreciation of his knowledge.

Ghaul vetoed most of his selections because there would be edible vegetation in the forest, therefore no reason to waste space in their packs. Khirro deferred to his experience and they spent Athryn's coin on dried meats, hard cheese, dark bread, and a quiver of arrows. When the money was spent and their packs full, they made their way back to the horses. Khirro pondered their journey as they walked. He'd never been this far south and knew little of Vendaria. He'd met merchants from the country, and knew they spoke their own language, but beyond that, all was a mystery. One couldn't tell a Vendarian from an Erechanian except for their language and accent when speaking the common tongue—much like it was impossible to tell a Kanosee from either of them.

They reached the horses and found the lad still pitching stones at the stump. He jumped up when he saw them and gestured excitedly toward their horses and gear, showing them how well he'd done the job. Elyea took the last copper from Athryn's pouch and flipped it to him. The boy caught it and ran off without a word of thanks, disappearing into the market to spend his new found wealth. Elyea laughed, delighted by the boy's enthusiasm as they removed their packs and secured them to their steeds.

"Oy," a voice boomed behind them. "I know you,

wench."

Startled, Khirro spun around. Out of the corner of his eye, he noticed Ghaul's hand go to the hilt of his sword.

A man built like a barrel approached them on thick legs protruding from his massive body. Khirro found it hard to believe the border guard found a hauberk large enough to fit the man, yet he wore their colors. Elyea glanced at Ghaul and Khirro then back at the man, his mane of black hair and dense beard all but obscuring his features.

"I don't think you do, good soldier."

"Yeah, I does." The man snorted and spat on the ground in front of Elyea; she took a step back. The odor of stale beer wafted from him. "You're the whore from Inehsul."

"You're mistaken. Move along." Ghaul stepped between them, but the man pushed him aside as though only a child.

"We have unfinished business, we does." He grabbed Elyea's arm. "I passed out before we was done, but you took your payment from me while I slept."

He yanked her arm, dragging her toward the guard house. Elyea dug her heels into the ground, shaking her head and protesting, but the mountainous man ignored her. Khirro took a step after them then stopped, not sure what he could do.

"No," Elyea protested trying to free her arm. The man

pulled her along, her feet digging furrows in the ground.

"You need to be taught a lesson, whore. You can't treat a man that way. You can't--"

He stopped, body stiffening. Elyea pulled away as his grip slackened, the crowd pushing by as he swayed on his legs. The big man looked down; Khirro followed his gaze to the hilt of Ghaul's dagger protruding from his side. The soldier slumped as Ghaul wrenched the blade free, catching him about the waist and guiding him to where the horses were tethered. A woman looked at them questioningly as she passed.

"My friend had too much drink, I'm afraid," Ghaul explained with a smile.

The woman gave him a scornful look—barely after noon and this man was too inebriated to stand on his own. She continued on her way without noticing the bloody blade in Ghaul's hand.

"What did you--?" Khirro began.

"Help me, he's heavy."

Reluctantly, Khirro grabbed the man's arm and directed him to a spot under the chestnut tree by the horses. Blood bubbled at his lips as he moaned, his head sagged forward.

"On the horses, quick," Elyea urged loosing the reins.

Khirro watched the man's life drain out onto the ground, mesmerized and appalled he was watching yet another man die.

How did this happen?

One moment they were purchasing supplies, the next a man's life was ending.

"Now, Khirro," Ghaul commanded. "Calmly. Don't attract attention."

His trance broken, Khirro slipped a foot into a stirrup and glanced again at the bulky soldier with the thick black beard, his eyes now closed. If not for the dark patch spreading on the ground beside him, the man may have fallen asleep under a tree on a hot summer day.

Death can look so peaceful.

Khirro pulled himself into the saddle.

They guided their steeds back toward the market gate at a forced pace, faster than they'd entered but not reckless enough to garner attention. Khirro felt eyes following as they departed, accusing them. He shifted in the saddle, looked over his shoulder at people as they passed and wondered if they knew what happened. Ghaul rode ahead, the bloody knife hidden beneath his cloak. As they rode through the gate, Ghaul nodded to the guard, and then they were in the less crowded street beyond.

"Stay calm." Elyea pulled her mount even with Khirro's. "Go right at the next lane and we'll be out of sight."

He nodded and prompted his steed on. With a few yards left between them and the corner, a woman's scream made Khirro twist in the saddle, straining to see. A guard rushed from the guardhouse, pushing through the crowd toward a woman standing by the dead man. She lifted her head and pointed toward them. Other soldiers broke from the crowd and ran to their horses.

"Go!"

Ghaul's horse sprang forward as he dug his heels into its sides. Elyea followed, her mount kicking up a veil of dust from the parched ground. Khirro had time to see several soldiers urge their horses down the street before his own mount surged forward. People dove out of their way as they thundered along the boulevard and around the corner onto the narrower lane. He kept his eyes on Elyea ahead, not knowing where they'd go, how they'd escape.

"Follow me," she cried over her shoulder, the beating hooves all but drowning her out.

People cowered against the rough walls of buildings as they raced past. Khirro choked the reins, each powerful stride shifting him in his seat. Elyea slowed rounding another corner and Khirro glanced back. Their pursuers were past the first corner, closing ground.

The deserted street they veered on to was narrower than the last. Hoof beats clattered on the cobble stones, echoed from the close walls, multiplying their trio into a platoon on the run.

A figure appeared in the lane ahead.

Khirro stretched, nearly sacrificing his seat to see past Elyea and Ghaul. Maes stood in the middle of the avenue, signaling them into an alley. They reined in their horses and followed his direction, crowding into the tight space where Athryn waited.

"Stop. Be silent."

The magician looked to Maes as he entered behind them; the little man nodded, drew his dirk, then pulled up the leg of his breeches and pressed the blade against the flesh of his calf. Athryn began a whispered chant as Maes cut his leg. Khirro cringed at the sight of fresh blood.

A sere breath of wind coughed down the alley, standing the hairs at the back of Khirro's neck on end. The air grew hazy, like distant heat shimmering on a sweltering day. The opacity swirled about them, concentrating at the mouth of the alley, first solidifying, then changing color to match the walls around it. Athryn's incantation continued, the only sound other than the panting of the horses.

Hoof beats broke the calm. Khirro held his breath and stroked his horse's mane to calm him as the sound grew louder. A rider passed, oblivious to them hidden behind the illusory wall. Another went by, then another. A cloud of dust wafted into the alley. Finally, two more riders galloped past and the sounds receded. Athryn chanted until the noise of pursuit disappeared, then his whispers ceased and the conjured barrier disappeared. The magician rushed to his brother's side, pulled a bandage from the pouch on his belt.

"They will soon realize they have been deceived," he said as he wound gauze around Maes' leg. "We must make for the forest to the south. Stay close to me and we should

166

be safe."

He boosted Maes into the saddle and swung himself up. Khirro's heart raced, keeping time with the pounding hooves as they spurred their horses down the street in the direction their pursuers had gone. No one spoke as they rode from the alley, soon turning toward the southern town limits and the forest. Beyond lay the Vendarian border with its line of guard towers. After that, a potentially hostile country, and then the cursed land.

As he bounced along in the saddle trying to keep from falling, Khirro wondered if he'd ever feel safe again.

17

Colorful dresses and frilled undergarments hung limply from the line strung between two trees with no wind to make them flutter. Suath watched, his patience honed through years spent lying in wait for the enemy. In this case, the variety of clothing on the line told him the enemy was three women. Gathering information from one person could be difficult but, with more than one, the job should be easy.

One of them would tell him what he wanted to know.

A young blonde emerged from the waddle and daub cottage to check the laundry, her hair pinned up in a tussled nest at the back of her head. The mercenary didn't move. He needed to know where they all were, choose the right time before showing himself, otherwise it could be

167

dangerous and messy. He hadn't survived this long by making things dangerous and messy. He watched as she ran her hand down the fronts of the dresses; finding them still damp, she left them hanging and returned to the hut's shaded interior.

Suath shifted slightly, keeping himself alert. Eager to pick up the trail before it grew cold, he'd ridden two days without stopping except to feed and water his horse. He didn't dare drift off now. There would be time to nap once he returned to the saddle.

Another hour passed before an older woman waddled out the door, a wooden bucket swinging in her grip. On her way to the well, she passed a few feet from the bush hiding Suath. The mercenary didn't so much as flinch. The woman—perhaps the young one's grandmother—fished water from the well, then struggled back to the cottage, slopping water over the lip of the pail to be quickly absorbed by the parched ground. Suath could have easily reached out and taken her. He didn't.

Two accounted for, one to go.

He put thoughts of his quarry's increasing lead from his mind, breathing quietly through his nose. He could make up the time spent waiting, but it would be more difficult if he had to fight his way out of town because of impatience.

The sun had reached its zenith when the third woman appeared. By then, the blonde had retrieved the laundry and the old one had hung a fresh batch. Both of them were in the house when the last resident walked out of the woods, a man in tow. They crossed the yard, giggling. The woman's disheveled hair fell across her pudgy face still caked with day-old make-up. The man caught her by the arm, spun her toward him, and drew her in for a kiss, but she pushed him away, admonishing him with the shake of her finger.

"You got your money's worth already," she said playfully.

The man dipped his fingers into a pocket and pulled out a copper. The woman smiled and kissed him, took the copper and tucked it into her bodice.

Whores. No wonder the town's women gave them up so easily—he didn't have to spend a penny to get the information he needed to find them. Normally, when a one-eyed man in well-used armor asks questions, it takes money or threats to get an answer. The threats Suath didn't mind handing out, but he didn't like parting with his coin.

The man watched the dark-haired harlot disappear into the shack, waved good-bye as she entered. He stared at the closed door for a moment before spinning on his heel and striding toward the bush hiding Suath. The mercenary pounced, dagger opening the man's throat before surprise registered. Blood spurted from the wound, thirstily absorbed by the dry dirt the same way the water had been.

Messy.

Suath chastised himself as he concealed the man's corpse in the bush where he'd hidden. The door of the hut opened and the mercenary squatted by his victim. The dark-haired one came out and walked past, oblivious to the mercenary and her dead lover concealed in the brush, unaware of the bloody dirt sticking to the sole of her foot. She went to the well and retrieved some water then drew a cloth from her bodice and dipped it into the pail. She hiked up her dress and removed her undergarment. Suath stared at the patch of black hair between her legs, quelling the stirring he felt as she bathed her woman parts. No time for lust, this was the time to make his move.

The mercenary emerged silently, the dagger in his hand still dripping blood. She didn't notice him until he was too near for her to react. The cloth dropped from her hand, her mouth opened.

"No sound." He flashed the bloody blade before her eyes. "Or you'll get what your boyfriend got."

Tears came quickly to the woman's eyes, the corners of her mouth pulled taut, but she did as he said and kept her tongue still. Suath pressed his blade against her throat, the keen edge drawing blood to trickle down her alabaster skin and blossom into a rose as it soaked into her lace bodice. The mercenary pushed her toward the door; she went without resistance.

"Open it," he whispered. She did and they stepped into the dim interior. "Call your friends."

He tightened his grip on her arm and felt her flinch. Tears ran down her pretty face and he fought the urge to lean close, lick them from her cheek. Nothing tasted so sweet as tears shed in fear. She opened her mouth, throat working against the knife held there, but no sound emerged. He squeezed again and she whimpered.

"Despina," she called, voice cracking. "Aryann."

No one answered.

"Again," Suath growled. Her hair smelled of sweat and honeysuckle. He wanted to bury his nose in it.

"Despina. Aryann," she called again, voice steadier but high and tight. "Can you please come here?"

The old one came first, wiping her hands on an apron strung about her waist.

"Leigha? Are you all right? You sound as though..."

Her words and steps halted as she saw the knife at the dark-haired one's throat. The young blonde came after her, but the old one put out her arm, keeping her behind her.

"What's happening?" the blonde asked.

"Don't speak," Suath commanded, his voice calm and even. No point inciting them, they would be panicking soon enough.

"What have you done, Leigha?" The old one remained composed in spite of the scene before her.

Not the first time she's been threatened with a blade.

Grown men had pissed their pants at the sight of him, yet she kept calm. The old whore showed more balls than most. The pudgy one shook her head in answer to the question sending a fresh trickle of blood down her neck.

"What do you want?"

"The vial."

The pretty one peered out from behind her grandmother's broad back. "What does he mean?" she squeaked, tears flowing.

The old one's gaze held steady on him as she answered, her voice still even and firm.

"We have no vial. You've made a mistake."

Suath almost smiled. *This one won't cry. Not until the blood flows.*

"A woman," the mercenary said, "a whore like you. She passed this way with two men—strangers."

"There has been no one here," the old one said but the gasp from the blonde confirmed what he already knew. The pudgy woman wriggled against his grip. He pulled her close against him, pressing the bulge in his breeches against her pillowy ass.

"Lies. The young one knows. Where did they go?"

He pushed against the dark-haired one's back, ushering her closer to her friends, stopped her a few feet from them.

"Tell me or the fat one dies."

"It's okay," the young one said stepping from behind the other. Tears streaked her smooth cheeks, her voice quaked as she spoke. "Everything will be all right, Leigha."

The old one moved to keep the blonde behind her, protected, and Suath saw what he needed to do. He drew the blade across Leigha's throat sending a fountain of blood splashing across her friends. While they gaped in horror, he grabbed the blonde's wrist, pulled her to him. The old one tried to fight him; he punched her in the face and she stumbled back.

"Where?" he asked, the calmness gone from his voice.

Impatience tingled his limbs. He wanted to be done with this before the pudgy one's body grew cold. At his feet, she gurgled through a mouthful of blood. The blonde sobbed and shook in his grasp.

"South," the old one shouted, blood streaming from her nose, her composure finally broken. "She took them to the entertainers."

"How many?"

"Just the three of them."

"Horses?"

The old one's eyes dropped to the dark-haired woman on the floor. Blood still pulsed from the slash in her throat but she no longer moved.

"Horses?" he asked again, more insistent. The pudgy one's eyes were going glassy. The grandmother shook her head. "Where are these entertainers?"

She shook her head, crying now. "Don't hurt my Aryann."

"Where are the entertainers?"

"South—outside of town. I don't know where."

"And then?"

She squeezed her eyes closed, shaking her head. Suath waited until she opened her eyes again, then dragged the point of his dagger down the blonde's cheek. She screamed.

"Tasgarad," the old one squealed. "They're going to Tasgarad."

Suath nodded.

He lunged, burying his dagger to the hilt in the old one's eye, then spun the blonde around and slid his blade into her belly, drawing it upward to her breast bone. She gasped and coughed, spattering his breastplate with blood, then slumped to the floor between the other whores as he withdrew the knife. Suath bent over and wiped the blade on her dress then put his hand on the pudgy one's leg.

"Warm enough."

He pulled her dress up above her waist. As he removed his sword belt, he saw the blonde looking at him, tears still running from her eyes. He smiled at her as he removed his breastplate and the shirt beneath. Uncountable white scars criss-crossed his chest. He searched across the ridged landscape of scars with his fingers until he found a clear spot, then brought the tip of his dagger to it and made four new incisions.

"One for each of you," he told the blonde, "and one for the fat one's lover."

He set his blade purposely on the floor just out of the blonde's reach, removed his breeches and knelt between the dark-haired one's legs.

"It's okay," he said, though he doubted the pretty one heard him anymore. "You can watch."

***

Sitting on the edge of the well, Suath used the cloth the dark-haired one had used to clean herself to wipe blood from his boots, then cleaned his dagger, sheathed it, and tossed the blood-soaked cloth down to the dark water below. Gray smoke snaked its way from the thatched roof of the whores' house, but he didn't hurry. A few of the men from town would want to rush to extinguish a fire in this particular hut, but their women wouldn't let them. He snickered at the thought of those self-righteous town's people putting less value on the lives of whores because of how they earned their living. Didn't they know all their lives were worthless?

Suath rose and walked into the woods, leaving behind his thoughts of the town and the dark-haired whore. His quarry had three days head start, but he had a horse. If he hurried, he might catch them before they reached the border.

The vial would be in his hands soon.

18

The rough land of low scrub through which they rode

from Tasgarad became new-growth forest littered with brush, slowing their progress. A fire had ravaged this area many years before, leaving blackened stumps and logs scattered throughout—burnt-out skeletons laid to rest beside their replacements. Khirro supposed there were roads through the woods, but they avoided them. The only people traversing them would be soldiers or merchants escorted by soldiers and nothing good would come of any encounter.

Khirro coaxed his horse forward to ride beside Ghaul.

"Why did you do that?" He kept his voice low so the others wouldn't hear.

"Do what?"

"Kill that man in Tasgarad. He was a soldier of the king."

"Use your head, Khirro," Ghaul said making no attempt to conceal his words from anyone. "Forget what he may have done to Elyea, what would have happened had he alerted the guards? What would they think of us carrying the blood of the king toward the Vendarian border? Do you forget we're hunted men?"

Khirro neither answered Ghaul's question nor met his angry look. Killing came too easily to this man for Khirro's liking, but it may be exactly this which would keep him alive.

There must have been another solution.

Ahead, Elyea and Athryn's mounts leaped over a fallen

tree. A moment later, Khirro's did the same, nearly unseating him.

"They wouldn't have known I carry the king's blood," he said, blushing after his rough landing.

"True, but a vial of blood in your pocket, no matter whose, would have raised questions we couldn't answer. When soldiers don't get answers, they employ crueler means to get what they want, and you are the worst kind of liar: a bad one."

"Ghaul's right. It's far better one drunken lout dies than our mission be discovered." Elyea slowed her horse to join them and poked a finger at Ghaul's shoulder. "Though I could have taken care of myself."

Ghaul harrumphed. "Of course you could, m'lady. I forgot we ride with the warrior harlot of Inehsul."

"I've kept myself safe from worse threats than him—or you." Her tone remained playful but Khirro saw the pride burning in her eyes.

"That sounds like a challenge." Ghaul raised an eyebrow as he guided his horse past a thorny bramble brimming with over-ripe blackberries. He plucked one from the tangle and popped it into his mouth.

"No, simply a fact."

"And would you have taken care of yourself in the same manner when first Khirro and I came upon you?"

"I'd have handled them without problem had two fools throwing stones not interrupted."

"Such gratitude." Ghaul smiled, teeth purple with berry juice.

"I need the aid of no man."

She urged her horse forward, rejoining the magician and his brother, ending the conversation.

"Women," Ghaul mock whispered, intending for Elyea to hear. "What are we to do with them?"

She ignored him.

They pushed on for several more hours with little more conversation before Athryn called a halt. Khirro glanced at the sun dipping toward the horizon and judged that an hour remained until sunset.

"The border is a few leagues from here." Athryn lowered Maes from their horse, then slid from the saddle. "We will rest a while."

They unsaddled and fed the horses before settling to partake of the food purchased in Tasgarad. The pork tasted tough and bitter to Khirro's tongue, but it would do as well as anything to return his strength. As he ate, he watched Athryn cut bite-sized pieces and hand them to Maes who accepted them with a nod. They seemed so different from the men performing in Inehsul, more real than the larger-than-life figures commanding the stage under that sweltering tent. As he watched the tenderness with which they shared their meal, questions came to his mind. He swallowed a mouthful of salt pork and asked the first.

"How did you know we'd be in that lane?"

Athryn looked up from cutting a chunk of hard cheese for Maes, his flesh-colored cloth mask inscrutable. His blue-gray eyes held Khirro's gaze for a moment before he answered.

"Does it matter?"

Khirro shrugged. "I guess not. It's just... I don't understand how this all works."

"It is not to be understood, Khirro. Accept it is and be glad it works for you, not against you."

"But it's not all working for me. We wouldn't be here if it wasn't for sorcery."

Khirro thought of the undead thing standing over him, threatening to end his life and a shudder ran down his spine. He'd let a detail of this journey slip from his mind: the only practitioner of magic capable of animating those dead soldiers and the man they needed to raise Braymon were one and the same.

"What do you know of Darestat?"

"The most powerful sorcerer there is. The only man who can raise the king. Why do you ask?"

"I saw strange things at the Isthmus Fortress."

"'Strange things' is an understatement in my estimation," Ghaul said through a mouthful of bread. "Your words could only be deemed accurate if you consider walking dead men a 'strange thing'."

Khirro nodded. He didn't want to dredge up these

179

memories, but he needed answers.

"It's as Ghaul said: dead men fought alongside the living Kanosee. Walking corpses with flesh hanging from their bones and the stink of rot on them. One of them killed Braymon. And Bale." His voice sank to a whisper. "And nearly me."

"Ugly bastards," Ghaul commented as he sliced a bite of cheese.

"How many, Khirro?"

"I don't know. I saw only a handful, but the Kanosee army numbered in the tens of thousands."

"One is too many, if my opinion is wanted." Ghaul wiped his knife on his breeches and replaced it in his boot.

"Darestat does not meddle in the trivialities of men. He has never lent his hand to sway a war."

"If this Necromancer doesn't meddle in man's affairs, why do we risk our lives to take the blood of the king to him?" Ghaul's eyes narrowed. "He won't help us, especially if he sides with the Kanosee."

"There is a difference between raising the dead and animating a corpse." Athryn shook his head. "He will aid us, but not for the sake of the kingdom or Braymon. He will do it because Bale was his student once."

"The Shaman is dead," Khirro said. The pit of his stomach twisted and writhed, upset by salt pork and dread. "How will he know Bale sent us?"

"He will know."

Maes wandered to a nearby tree and dropped his breeches to relieve himself—scars even blemished his buttocks. Khirro looked away from the little man to the magician, his eyes diverted in deep thought, and noticed for the first time how frustrating it could be when a man's face is hidden. Elyea sat beside Khirro and rested her hand on his forearm.

"Everything will be okay," she said. He tried to smile a thanks to her for the reassurance, but concern waylaid his intent.

"Tell me more of these undead soldiers," Athryn said returning from his thoughts.

"There's no more to tell. I spent my time defending myself or fleeing." His eyes flickered to Elyea, but he saw none of the judgment in her expression he might have seen from someone else. "They were decomposed, but not skeletons. And fierce fighters."

"Recently dead." Athryn nodded. "Without fear of death, the re-animated make superior warriors. Do you recall anything else?"

After a moment's thought, Khirro said he didn't.

"You certainly are a farmer." Ghaul shook his head and laughed. "A soldier is trained to observe his foes. The undead fighters wore black chain mail splashed with red paint, as though splattered with blood."

The mask didn't hide the way Athryn's eyes widened in surprise.

181

"Black with red? These are the markings of Sheyndust, Shaman of the Kanosee. I did not think Sheyndust capable of such an act. It would take much more power than I have, or Bale had."

Ghaul snorted. "Either someone has learned a new trick, or we ride into the grasp of our enemy."

"Animating the dead is the act of someone striving toward necromancy. This does not bode well for the kingdom."

Maes returned to his brother's side, tapped him on the shoulder and pointed toward the sky. Athryn nodded.

"It is time to continue." He rose and brushed bread crumbs from his breeches. "Night will be upon us soon."

Khirro saddled his horse, stomach churning. If Darestat was swelling the Kanosee ranks with soldiers of the dead, they'd be riding to their deaths, no doubt of that. But what did it mean if Sheyndust possessed the ability to bring forth the dead? He swung into the saddle and allowed his horse to follow the others. Thoughts of Emeline sprang to his mind, and of his farm, but the image appeared vague, unclear, like a child's drawing left in the sun too long, the lines had faded.

Will they eventually disappear?

A hand on his arm roused him and he turned to Elyea riding beside him.

"All will turn out." The small action settled his gut a bit; Emeline disappeared from his thoughts. "Have faith.

Athryn knows what he's doing. Besides, the Gods smile on people like you."

He smiled thinly. "And what of people like you?"

"Some of us have to take care of ourselves."

***

They concealed themselves in the thin brush at the edge of the swath of cleared land separating the two kingdoms. The bare tract stood five hundred meters wide and stretched the length of the border, the trees cut down centuries before to provide wood to build the guard towers dotting the frontier. Originally built to discourage bandits and refugees, the kingdoms maintained the non-barrier more out of habit than need. During wartime, however, no doubt the border guards would be more wary.

A fingernail moon cast sparse light as they watched torches flicker in tower windows and a foot patrol pass between the towers at irregular intervals. After an hour's observation, a whispered discussion between Athryn and Ghaul decided they'd attempt the crossing one by one. They'd already let the horses go knowing they couldn't sneak them across the border.

Ghaul glanced at the sky and Khirro followed his gaze: clear, as it had been for a month. No wisp of cloud hid the moon. Ghaul looked at the others, then nodded silently. They tightened straps and secured loose items then, without a word, Ghaul broke cover, moving swiftly across the field, crouched low and halting at the slightest hint of movement. Khirro reminded himself to breathe as he watched Ghaul zig-zag over the bare expanse, choosing a path which took him farthest from the towers. After a few minutes, Athryn sent Elyea and Maes.

A finger of fear prodded Khirro's heart, shaking him. It didn't matter who they were or why they were here, any soldier manning the outposts wouldn't ask questions before launching an arrow or swinging a sword. He glanced over his shoulder in the direction they'd come, wondered how difficult it would be to find one of the horses and make his way home.

That's why Athryn will send me next: they don't trust me.

A burst of anger flared but quickly disappeared.

I thought of leaving. They shouldn't trust me.

Elyea and Maes stopped suddenly and dove to the ground. Khirro's breath caught in his throat, anger and fear forgotten. He squinted into the night but saw no sentry, darkness and distance obscuring all save outlines and shapes. A tense moment passed. Ghaul's form had disappeared long ago and he assumed he'd reached the forest on the other side—the forest of Vendaria. Beside Khirro, Athryn's lips moved, forming a wordless whisper of breath. As if in answer, Maes rose, helped Elyea to her feet, and they continued, darkness swallowing them after another minute.

Khirro jumped when Athryn touched his shoulder.

"It is time," he whispered. His black cloth mask and the cowl of his black cloak covering his blond hair concealed all but the scant glint of moonlight in his eyes; Khirro might not have noticed him crouched beside him.

Khirro's heart climbed into his throat, threatening his breath; Athryn urged him forward with a gentle push. Out of the brush, Khirro felt like he'd been thrust naked into the middle of a busy marketplace, exposed and vulnerable. He crouched low, scuttled across the field. His foot struck a rock, kicking it away, and he stopped, listening, not breathing. When he heard no other sounds, he moved forward again more slowly, the weight of pack and shield on his back suddenly immense. The stillness of the night amplified every creak of his armor to ear shattering levels. In his mind, an unseen voice challenged him, the whistle of an arrow cloaked in darkness came to pierce his heart. He stopped, kneeling, pausing to catch the breath which had fled him.

To Khirro's right, a guard tower loomed, slivers of light leaking through shuttered windows and under closed door. He looked left and made out the next watch tower in the line a little farther away. His legs didn't want to move but Khirro forced them to creep forward, eyes pinned to the near guard post. Each step brought more confidence and he straightened, moved more quickly expecting the guard tower door to swing inward at any second.

Directly between the two towers, his foot caught in a clump of weeds and he pitched forward to the ground.

Khirro turned his shoulder, took the fall on his back. The clank of shield impacting ground seemed as loud as a clap of thunder. He rolled off it, came to a halt lying on his chest, sweat cold on his forehead. Afraid to breathe, he strained listening for any sound of men but heard only crickets chirruping and an owl call out a question that went unanswered.

No noise from the guard post, no door or window thrown open.

Carefully, Khirro rose. A figure to his left startled him and he turned toward it but it moved with him. He moved again and it did, too. With a sigh, he chastised himself for fearing his dim shadow and started toward the forest, careful of his footing. The yards of bare ground before him seemed to stretch on forever. His pack grew heavier with each step as panic grew within him. What if he reached the trees and couldn't find the others?

What if this is a trap?

When he finally reached the brush, he crouched and glanced around but didn't see his companions.

They've been discovered.

He searched for them, the bushes rustling with his movements, desperation festering in his stomach tempting him to shout for Ghaul. He parted his lips to call out when a hand covered his mouth, pulled him to the ground.

186

Khirro clamored for his sword, unable to reach it. He ceased thrashing when Ghaul's face appeared before his, a finger held up to his frowning lips.

Relief drained the tension from Khirro's limbs and he grinned sheepishly, a smile Ghaul didn't return. He imagined what the soldier must be thinking, but it didn't matter, he was safe—for now. He clambered to his feet with no help from Ghaul, and scanned the darkness for Athryn crossing to join them, avoiding thoughts of the tongue lashing he'd have to endure from Ghaul later. His clumsiness had endangered them all, a trend he had to stop.

I'll learn from this, be more careful next time.

Minutes passed, unease growing in Khirro as he waited. He shifted from one foot to the other, crossed his arms and uncrossed them, eyes darting, seeing nothing of the magician crossing the open land. But why did he feel so unsettled? If any of them could cross the border undetected, it was Athryn. Peering intently into the dark, Khirro ignored the growing notion something was amiss. He shifted again, careful to move noiselessly. The unease spread from his head and chest into his limbs, manifesting physically, weighing them down.

Something was very wrong.

As Athryn finally pushed through the brush, Khirro realized what. He slipped his hand beneath his tunic, hoping he guessed wrong, already knowing what he'd find.

Gone.

Ghaul tapped his shoulder, signaled him to follow. Khirro shook his head and the warrior gestured again. Embarrassed and afraid, Khirro didn't want to tell but had no other choice.

"The vial's gone."

Ghaul's face first slackened with surprise then went stern in anger.

"You dropped it?"

Khirro nodded minutely. With a shake of his head, Ghaul turned to the others and told them what happened. Without waiting for them to add their accusing looks to Ghaul's, Khirro slipped shield and pack from his back and moved quickly back onto the open ground before they could stop him or he changed his mind. The Shaman made the vial his responsibility, for better or for worse, so he'd fix this.

After only a few paces, an out-of-place, insistent bird call caught his attention. He looked around at Ghaul motioning him back but Khirro shook his head and continued, hurrying back along his previous path as quickly as he dared. Ghaul would be angry with him for ignoring him, but he was already angry anyway. He put the thought from his mind as the guard posts loomed and he searched for the spot where he fell. He must have lost the vial when he rolled on the ground.

What if I broke it?

188

The thought startled Khirro and he touched his chest: no damp spot on his tunic. Gods be with him, the vial had only come free. He fell to hands and knees, scanning the dirt and brittle grass, picking up scraps of wood and rocks and tossing them aside.

The sound of wood scraping against wood froze him in his spot—it was the sound of a bar withdrawn from its place on a door. Khirro flattened, pressing his belly to the dirt. The door opened, torchlight flooded onto the brown scrub grass. A figure stood framed in the doorway, pole arm in hand.

"Who goes there?"

The man sounded stern and threatening but Khirro thought he heard a slur in the words, the result of one too many drinks. He held his breath, body tensed. A reflection of the torchlight off something lying on the ground a few yards away caught his eye.

The vial.

"I said 'who's there'?"

The guard stepped forward from the doorway, brandishing his weapon. Stretched upon the ground, Khirro couldn't reach his sword, though it would be suicide if he did. The guard took another step.

"It is I, Shyn," another voice said, surprising both Khirro and the border guard. A tall man clad in Erechanian leathers stepped into the light cast by the guard's torch. His hand didn't linger near the sword hanging at his side.

189

"What are you doing here?" the border guard asked derisively, his threatening stance relaxing at the sight of the other man.

"Patrol," the second man replied. "Go back to your merry-making. I'll protect the border for you."

The man's foot came to rest inches from the vial. Another step and he might shatter it. Part of Khirro hoped he did.

"Go back where you belong, Shyn. The border is no place for the likes of you." The guard spit in the dirt, a line of saliva trailing down his chin. "Go back to Tasgarad and concern yourself with drunks and thieves and whores. Leave the soldiering to real soldiers." He retreated, slamming the door behind him, giving the other man no opportunity to reply.

Shyn stood his ground, fists clenched, fierce gaze burning into the closed door. To Khirro it felt a long time he lay on his belly unmoving, breath shallow as he waited for the man's next action. After a time he crouched, wrapped his fingers around the vial and stood again. Khirro's heart jumped into his throat. The man strode to where Khirro lay struggling not to squirm at his approach.

"Is this what you're looking for?"

Khirro looked up at the man, blinking. No anger or threat showed on his face, his hand held no weapon. Still, Khirro neither moved nor spoke. Shyn knelt before him, offering him the vessel.

If he knew I was here, why didn't he give me away?

"I don't know what this contains, but it must be important for five of you to risk your lives like this."

Khirro took the vial from the man's big hand. Calm flowed into him, down his arm and into his chest. He wanted to thank the man, but fear and confusion kept him from speaking.

"Where are your friends?"

Khirro gestured toward the forest with his chin. The soldier nodded without looking.

"I'll take you to them. Stay behind me and no one will see you."

He offered Khirro his hand, helping him to his feet. The man stood a head taller than Khirro, making it easy to hide behind him. Carefully matching stride, they passed the tower without challenge but, when they reached the tree line, Ghaul stepped from behind a high bush, an arrow aimed at Shyn.

"Let him go," he ordered, voice low and dripping with threat. Ghaul wouldn't hesitate to kill his rescuer.

"I'm not his captive." Khirro put himself between the two men

"Move, Khirro. Don't get between my bow and an enemy. You'll not like the outcome."

"He saved me when I was sure to be discovered."

Ghaul pulled the arrow back further, the bowstring creaking. Athryn emerged from cover and rested his hand

191

on Ghaul's shoulder.

"Come," he whispered gesturing for them to follow.

Khirro led Shyn warily past Ghaul who stepped away to keep his arrow trained on the big man. Athryn led them deeper into the forest, Maes and Elyea hand-in-hand behind the others as they picked their way through fallen trees and tangled brush in the dim moonlight. Ghaul's bow didn't waver from Shyn's back. With the magician satisfied they had put enough distance between themselves and the guard post, he spoke again.

"Who are you? Why did you save Khirro?"

Shyn looked from Athryn to Ghaul. "Tell him to lower his bow. I'll harm no one. You can have my sword as proof, if you like."

"Don't trust him," Ghaul said through gritted teeth.

Athryn ignored him and nodded to Maes. The small man went to their captive and took his sword. Shyn looked a giant beside the jester.

"Lower your bow," Athryn said. Ghaul acquiesced reluctantly. "Who are you?"

"Shyn," he replied with a short bow. "A soldier of King Braymon's army."

"But why did you help Khirro?" Elyea asked. "Doesn't the border guard keep people from crossing without permission?"

"Aye, but the guard has been turned into a collection of fools and jackasses of late, with all the officers and good soldiers taken north to bolster the Isthmus."

"That explains why you're still here," Ghaul grunted. Shyn didn't react.

"It doesn't explain why you helped Khirro." Elyea shot Ghaul an angry look.

"I saw what happened in Tasgarad." He glanced from one companion to the next, his eyes shining an unusual shade of yellow, his complexion ashen in the wan light. "I would be no servant of the king if I let a magician, two fighters, a woman and a midget go on their way without finding out what they were doing."

"See? He means to turn us in," Ghaul barked, half-raising his bow. Athryn lifted his hand, stilling him.

"I just passed up the perfect opportunity for that, didn't I?"

Ghaul frowned, jaw muscles bulging, but said nothing. Khirro glanced from one to the other, wondering who would come out on top should it come to a fight. He'd seen how savage Ghaul could be, but Shyn was taller, bigger and must have great skill to have followed them so far, so closely, without notice. He hoped they wouldn't find out.

"But why?" Khirro asked.

"An unregistered magician wouldn't perform magic in public without just cause. No soldiers of Erechania would be associated with a sorcerer not of royal decree. I can see no explanation for the woman and the little one. You're either up to great evil or great good."

"The difference is likely a matter of perception, Shyn," Athryn said. "But either way, you are correct."

"Never mind that," Ghaul snapped. "We can't trust him. We should kill him."

The vial at Khirro's breast blazed suddenly, startling him.

"No," he exclaimed before he knew what he was saying. "There's much bloodshed to come. Let's not kill for the sake of killing."

"If we let him go, he'll reveal us," Ghaul argued. "Speak some sense to the farmer, Athryn."

There's that word again.

Khirro ground his teeth. What would it take to show Ghaul he wasn't the farmer he met two weeks ago? It wasn't his fault the vial came free when he fell, it might have happened to any of them.

"We can bring him with us, see if he can be trusted," Khirro said looking to Athryn. The magician glanced from Khirro to Shyn, then to Ghaul, but didn't speak. "If he proves trustworthy, we can use his sword. If not, we can let him go when we're too far from here for it to matter."

"We're at war, Khirro. No one can be trusted."

"Khirro speaks sense, Ghaul," Athryn said finally, then turned to Shyn; Khirro wondered what the border guard thought of this masked man. "You will accompany us. I will keep your weapons and you will be bound, but you will be alive. We will decide your final fate when we are safely away from the border."

"This is a mistake," Ghaul grated.

"No." Khirro's tone betrayed more of his anger than he intended. "This man had me at his mercy, now he deserves ours."

He looked at the border guard but his face revealed neither relief nor fear, he simply nodded his thanks.

***

No lush forest or serene lake surrounded him in the dream this time, no slivered moon, no rocky shore. Khirro lay face down in dry grass, silence and darkness weighing on him, pinning him. Somewhere, somebody was searching for him; he knew this though he saw nothing but the grass before his eyes and heard naught but the wind bending its long blades. He wanted to stand and search out his pursuer, but knew it could mean his life. He lay there alone, afraid, staring at the ground.

"You chose your path well."

The voice didn't surprise Khirro. He craned his neck to see the tyger stretched out beside him, belly pressed to the ground in the same manner as his own. Its black and white striped body dwarfed his, its hot breath warmed his face and stirred the short whiskers grown on his cheeks in the past weeks.

"But I don't know what path I've chosen."

"It matters not if you recognize the path, or that a

195

choice must be made. Trust." The tyger's head moved forward, its wet nose brushing Khirro's. "Follow our heart."

"Our heart?"

But the tyger was gone.

Khirro stood, thinking about the creature's words and forgetting his earlier fear. Before him stood a one-eyed man, his face marked by uncountable fights. Khirro moved to his left to escape, but the man moved with him. He went right and the man matched him. Every move Khirro made, the man did the same, the two of them moving as though dissimilar reflections in a looking glass. Khirro reached for the hilt of his sword, but didn't draw it as the other man did the same. Not knowing what else to do, Khirro closed his eyes, squeezed them tight and wished to awaken from the dream.

When he opened them, still asleep and dreaming, the man had disappeared. The field around him blazed, the tinder-dry grass consumed by flame sending gray smoke billowing up to cloud the moonless sky. Khirro spun and ran from the blaze with the heavy, awkward legs of dreams, heat pressing at his back. He cried out—in anguish, in fear, for help, for anything—and the tyger appeared, loping easily along beside him.

"Beware the man with one eye," it said in his head as they ran. "Fear not the fire."

Somewhere above, a bird of prey cried out, its shriek

drowning the snap and crackle of the conflagration.

Khirro woke with cold sweat streaming from his forehead and his hand clutched to his chest. He pushed himself to his elbows, breathed deeply to keep shivers from rattling his spine. Nearby, Shyn sat with his back against the trunk of a fir tree, hands bound behind him. Their eyes met, but neither spoke. Khirro lowered himself, rolled onto his side and closed his eyes again. When sleep reclaimed him, he dreamed of a giant gray falcon rescuing him from the fire, soaring above the flames, through the smoke, to safety and freedom.

A much better dream.

19

Shyn leaned his head back against the rough tree bark and cast his eyes skyward. Khirro had seen him do this a number of times during their hushed conversations of the last three days, each time a wistfulness seemed to cloud the border guard's eyes.

"I'd seen but thirteen summers when I left my home," he said looking at Khirro again.

"Why did you leave?"

"I no longer wanted to be there. And they no longer wanted me there. I spent a year wandering, fending for myself, before joining the King's army."

"At fourteen."

"Big for my age."

197

Shyn shifted, the rope holding his hands creaked with the movement. Khirro wished he could loosen the knots but knew Ghaul wouldn't hear of it. He'd grown to like the big border guard, learning much about him in hushed discussions they shared as Khirro sat watch with Shyn lashed to a tree.

"The army was good to me at first. I felt things I hadn't felt at home: accepted, needed. But it was short-lived. Eventually, people turn on you when you're different. When they did, I was sent to the border like a broken tool discarded at the back of the barn."

"Different? Because of your size?"

Shyn shook his head and looked toward the blue sky again. Khirro shared some of his own upbringing, even telling Shyn about his father's accident and a much-edited version of what happened with Emeline and how he came to be a soldier, then felt guilty he hadn't shared completely. The similarity in their circumstances made Khirro feel a kinship toward this man.

"One day, I'll get back to Emeline. When all this is done. When the fighting is finished. And then I'll--"

"Enough. It's time."

Ghaul's words startled Khirro. While talking with Shyn, he hadn't noticed him cross the glade toward them. Khirro stood.

"Time for what?"

"We agreed to bring him far enough from the border

he'd be no threat to us, then let him go. I only agreed because you have no stomach for killing, farmer. Gods help us."

"I trust him. We've spoken and I think he can aid us."

Ghaul barked a derisive laugh. "What's wrong with your head? It's a spy's job to earn your trust."

Khirro glanced at Shyn and felt a twinge that the man should be party to this conversation, so he led Ghaul to where Elyea sat with Maes and Athryn, far enough away the border guard wouldn't hear. Elyea rose from her seat and laid a hand on Ghaul's arm to calm him, but he shook it off. Athryn watched in silence, his expressionless mask hiding his thoughts.

Why does he wear it when it's just us? It's only a scar. What else is he hiding?

"Why do you think he should join us?" Elyea asked.

Khirro looked at her, his heart palpitating as it always did when his eyes met hers. "I'm not sure." His latest dream of the tyger came to mind, but a dream of a beast advising him to trust his heart wouldn't convince the others. More likely the opposite. "He protected me when he could have turned us in. We treat him like a prisoner yet he holds us no ill. Having another sword arm wouldn't be a bad thing."

"Depends on who the sword ends up buried in,"' Ghaul said.

"If he intended to harm us, it would have been simpler

199

for us to be taken to the gallows in Tasgarad."

"True," Athryn said. Maes crouched beside his brother, moving dirt with a stick, disinterested in the conversation. "But perhaps he has a different agenda."

"Let me prove myself."

They looked at their captive tied to a tree ten yards away. *How did he hear us?*

"How did he--" Elyea began.

"Good ears," Shyn answered before she finished. They moved to him, Ghaul gripping the hilt of his sword. Maes remained behind drawing shapes in the dirt.

"What manner of trick is this?" Ghaul asked. "Are you also a man of magic?"

Shyn laughed. "No, not a magician. Ask Athryn, he'll tell you."

"I would know a practitioner. He is not."

"What I am is a man of unusual qualities who could aid in your journey, as Khirro says."

"Why should we trust you?" Elyea asked, arms crossed.

Ghaul looked as though he'd say something as well, but Maes pushed his way between them, interrupting. He approached Shyn, looked him in the eyes for a moment, then sat cross-legged on the ground beside him. The little man had done nothing like this before; in fact, Khirro couldn't remember Maes interacting with the soldier at all. Athryn didn't retrieve his brother from Shyn's side.

"Don't trust me," Shyn said glancing at Maes then back

at the rest of them. "I wouldn't if I were you. Not yet." He shifted his position, attempting to find a more comfortable spot. Ghaul tensed at the movement, pulling an inch of steel from his scabbard. Maes didn't flinch. "Do any of you know where to find the closest Vendarian town?"

"No," Khirro said. Elyea shook her head. Ghaul looked like he wouldn't admit to shitting in the forest.

"Neither do I," Shyn confessed. "Release me. I'll locate it and return to you with horses. If I do this, you'll know I can be trusted."

Ghaul shook his head. "If he's a Vendarian spy, he'll bring a company to slaughter us."

"No," Khirro said searching deep in Shyn's gaze. "The border guard knew him. They didn't like him, but they accepted his word."

"No matter why we let him go—to prove his trustworthiness or to rid ourselves of him—he could bring soldiers," Elyea said.

"Then we should kill him and take no chances," Ghaul said.

"We kill no one," Athryn said. He looked at Maes sitting comfortably beside the man. "He has done nothing to warrant his death."

"You've nothing to lose," Shyn said without any note of pleading or desperation. "If I don't come back, you lose nothing—you're already lost and traveling by foot—and you'd be rid of me."

Bruce Blake

"Not lost," Khirro mumbled feeling embarrassed. The Shaman put a path in his head, but he hadn't recognized anything since they crossed the border. He had no idea where they were but couldn't admit it to the others.

Shyn looked at them, waiting. His eyes held Ghaul's first, fearless despite the soldier's grip on his sword. After a few seconds, as they remained silent, his gaze fell on Athryn, then Elyea, and finally Khirro.

Athryn broke the silence. "Maes?"

The small man stood and went to his brother, extending his hand. Athryn took the collection of items offered—to Khirro's eye it looked to be an assortment of pebbles and small sticks, perhaps a bug as well—random items he'd picked off the ground. With the items delivered, Maes wandered away to pick berries from a nearby bush. The magician peered at the items, then tossed them to the ground and brushed dirt from his hands.

"It is as he speaks," Athryn said. "If he returns with horses, I will gladly welcome them, and him."

"No," Ghaul protested. "He can't be trusted."

Khirro looked at Ghaul. There was no reason for him to be disagreeable at letting Shyn go, it had been their plan from the start. If he returned with horses, all the better. What was it that--

He never planned to release him. He always intended to kill him.

"Let him go." Khirro's voice came out flat as he stared

202

hard at Ghaul; the warrior looked back, unwavering.

"Do as you will." Ghaul slammed his sword back into the scabbard. "But if next I see him without horses for us, his head will be mine."

He stalked away kicking decayed needles from his path as he went. Khirro went to Shyn and untied his hands.

"Get his weapons, Elyea," he called over his shoulder then turned back to the border guard. "We've seen no sign of civilization since we crossed the border. How will you know where to go?"

"I don't know where to go." He rubbed the rope burns on his wrists. Elyea lay Shyn's sword belt and dagger on the ground beside Khirro, then stepped away.

"We'll supply you with some food, but we can't spare much. Your trek may be a long one."

"Keep your food, I'm an excellent hunter." Shyn rose, took the sword belt Khirro offered and buckled it around his waist. He stretched his back and wiped dirt from the seat of his pants. "I'm also swift. I'll be back sooner than you think."

"You saved me once. We're even now." Khirro offered his hand and Shyn shook it. "I'll understand if you don't come back, you have no reason to. But don't return with soldiers or without horses. I can't stop Ghaul from fulfilling his promise."

"I'll return as promised. I don't know why, but I feel like I'm meant to join your journey." He shook his head minutely. "Gods know why."

Shyn bent at the waist, tucked his fingers into the top of his boot and retrieved a thin-bladed stiletto from some secret compartment within.

"Take this," he said offering it to Khirro. "Hide it somewhere near the vial. Just in case."

Khirro took the small knife and slid it into his breast pocket beside the vial, the steel clinking quietly against the glass, then Shyn went into the forest, picking his way deftly through the underbrush. After a minute, he disappeared into the dense brush.

"Fear not, Khirro." Athryn's voice was a whisper meant only for them. "Maes says he can be trusted."

Khirro looked at the magician and the confusion his words caused must have been plain on his face because Athryn answered the question running through his mind before he asked it.

"Maes may not speak, but he knows people. Worry not."

Athryn left to help his brother pick berries, leaving Khirro staring after Shyn. Behind him, Elyea joined Ghaul in breaking camp. After a minute, he went to help and everything was soon packed.

They walked through the forest, the scrape of boots on ground, the clink of armor and weapons and the rustle of brush the only sound to mark their passing. Maes popped red berries into his mouth as he walked, occasionally offering them to his companions. Khirro accepted and found the berries juicy and sour with an unfamiliar but satisfying flavor. He wiped a line of juice from his chin as his mind wandered. He thought about Athryn and Maes and the nature of their relationship: brothers, but somehow more. Concern for Ghaul's propensity for violence came to mind. He had been a soldier his entire life, Khirro reasoned, so he supposed it was simply a matter of training, but it went against Khirro's way.

Perhaps that's why we've been brought together.

They tempered one another—he made Ghaul more humane and Ghaul made him see things from a soldier's point of view; a good team despite and because of their differences. Without Ghaul, he wouldn't have made it even this far.

He glanced at Elyea walking ahead, hips swaying pleasingly. So beautiful, so confident. Embarrassed, Khirro quickly put the encroaching thoughts from his head and thought of Shyn instead, wondering if they should trust him, if he would return as promised. The memory of the dream tyger's words made him feel only slightly more comfortable.

Am I insane to take comfort from the words of a dream?

He didn't think so, but wouldn't tell the others, anyway. As he pondered the most recent dream, the screech of a bird overhead caught his attention. Through the tree branches, he glimpsed a gray falcon soaring high above. It circled over them, giving Khirro an opportunity to marvel at its size. His lips parted to tell the others, but it streaked off north-west at an incredible speed. His mouth remained open as he watched it disappear in the distance. It was the bird of prey from his dream.

A shiver ran down Khirro's spine.

20

Rain began the day after they released Shyn.

When clouds first gathered, they praised the Gods. As the first droplets fell—gentle to start, then gaining in tempo and force—they raised their faces skyward and let the rain wash weeks of sticky heat from their skin. Athryn removed his white cloth mask to feel the refreshing moisture pelt his scarred face. Elyea stole away into the forest on her own. When more than a few minutes passed, Khirro followed, worried for her safety, and came upon her dancing naked in a glade, water streaming from her strawberry hair in rivulets down her back and between her breasts. He watched for a while, enraptured, feeling something more than the embarrassment he'd felt when he first saw her unclothed. This time, when their eyes met, he didn't avert his gaze and she didn't attempt to hide herself. He enjoyed her beauty a moment before he left. She emerged from the forest ten minutes later, wet but clothed, and they exchanged looks and smiles, but nothing else: a secret for them to share.

Two days later, no one danced or tilted their faces to the heavens. They cursed the Gods instead of praising them.

"There's water in my boots," Khirro grumbled as they trudged across a muddy patch of ground. "My tunic is glued to my back."

"Stop whining," Elyea said. "You complain a lot for a man who made his living on a farm."

"We didn't farm in the rain. Never did I harvest a potato with water running into my eyes."

Ahead, Khirro saw Maes pull on the dripping sleeve of Athryn's shirt. The magician stopped and looked toward his brother.

"Hold."

They stopped, waiting for the magician to speak. He cocked his head, listening. Khirro did the same but heard nothing but the patter of rain drops on his soaked clothes and soon began to lose patience. He wiped water from his eyes, about to complain again when Athryn spoke.

"Horses. Someone is coming."

"I don't hear any--" Khirro began, but the others were already moving to find cover. He followed, pushing his way through a dense bush, the wet foliage dumping rain water on his head.

Ghaul pulled his bow from his shoulder and nocked an arrow as he crouched, gesturing for Khirro to draw his sword. He did and, with the black blade free, he noticed Maes staring at it instead of in the direction Athryn had indicated.

For a minute, Khirro heard only the plunk of rain impacting the leaves around him. They stared through the brush, waiting, Elyea with a dagger in hand, poised to strike as any fighter would. Athryn drew his sword while Maes stared at Khirro's weapon. Above, a leaf that had been collecting water for some time overflowed, spilling its contents down the back of Khirro's neck. He shivered, shaking the brush around him and drawing a glare from Ghaul.

Hoof beats soon became noticeable above the rain's patter. Khirro held his breath, listening closer. He was no tracker, but he could tell more than one rider approached, though how many, he didn't know. The sounds grew nearer and their pace slowed.

They're following our trail. His grip on his sword tightened.

A breeze parted the leaves briefly, blowing rain against Khirro's cheek, revealing a swatch of chestnut fur as a rider halted directly in front of them. Ghaul drew back on his bowstring as the muscles in Khirro's thighs tensed, readying to spring.

The chestnut moved out of sight and a palomino came into view, followed by a horse of deep black. This time, he saw the rider's leg and realized he hadn't seen the same on the other horses. No riders sat them. It could only mean one thing.

"I know you're there," the rider called out.

Khirro looked at Ghaul and lowered his sword.

"It's Shyn," he whispered, but the soldier's face remained set, his bow drawn.

"He might have brought soldiers."

"I can hear you," Shyn said.

Khirro cursed himself, recalling how Shyn had heard them from a distance before. Ghaul could be right.

"I'm alone. I've brought horses and supplies. If you still covet my head, Ghaul, you'll have to wait for another day."

Khirro burst forward excitedly. After two steps, something struck him, threw him forward, pain exploding in his shoulder. He pitched through the foliage, stumbling first to his knees, then falling face first on the muddy ground at the foot of Shyn's horse. The border guard jumped from his steed, sword drawn protectively as he knelt at Khirro's side.

"What happened?" Shyn surveyed the area as the others emerged from their hiding places. Athryn and Elyea joined him at Khirro's side while Ghaul stood back, empty bow dangling. Khirro writhed on the ground, blood seeping around the arrow in his right shoulder.

Twice. His mind reeled with pain, grasping for something to hold on to. *I've been skewered by arrows twice. Who'd have thought it possible?*

Bruce Blake

Shyn acted quickly, drawing his dagger and shaving the arrowhead from the shaft. Khirro bellowed in agony as the arrow slid from his flesh, drawing a gout of blood with it.

"Maes," Athryn called.

The little man pushed his way through the brush, small dirk in hand. Tears blurred Khirro's vision as he watched the little man approach, squat by his masked brother, and roll up his sleeve.

"No," Khirro said through the pain as he rolled onto his back. He wouldn't let Maes cut himself, not when it wasn't necessary. "Bandage it."

"You are bleeding, Khirro," Athryn told him. "We can stop it, make it heal more quickly."

"No."

Khirro struggled to a sitting position, grimacing at the pain of his shredded muscle as he reached beneath his tunic and brought out the vial, showing it to everyone.

"Bandage it and this will do the rest."

Elyea looked at him questioningly, but Athryn simply nodded and tended the wound. Relieved, Khirro remembered the uncomfortable feeling when Bale healed him with magic. The healing power of the king's blood was more comfortable. Shyn approached Ghaul, leaving the others to care for Khirro.

"How did this happen?" He held his sword by his side; Ghaul didn't reach for his weapon.

"He crossed in front of my bow," Ghaul said, one side

of his mouth curling in a smug smile. "The rain made my fingers slick and my hold on the arrow slipped. An accident."

Elyea paused in bandaging Khirro's shoulder.

"What kind of soldier can't keep hold of his arrow?" she demanded.

Ghaul only shrugged in answer. Shyn looked at Khirro then back at Ghaul.

"Had he not stepped in front of you, that arrow would likely be embedded in my chest."

"Perhaps."

Shyn moved a step closer and Ghaul reached for his own sword, but the border guard moved quickly, grabbing his wrist and pulling him close so they stood chest to chest. Taller than Ghaul by almost six inches, Shyn looked down into his eyes.

"Were we not being followed, we would settle this right now."

They looked at the tall soldier in surprise, except Maes who busied himself wiping the dirt from Khirro's face.

"What?" Khirro asked pushing the little man's hand away.

"Followed by whom?" Athryn added.

"A one-eyed man follows, a half-day's ride behind. There are soldiers another day or so behind him." Shyn turned his back on Ghaul and mounted the black horse. "We must make haste or he'll be upon us."

211

"How do you know this?" Ghaul asked, suspicion plain in his voice.

"I saw him. He wears the armor of a moneysword. If it's who I think, we're better not to meet him."

"Suath," Athryn said under his breath as he finished with Khirro's wound. "There could be none more dangerous on our trail."

They moved quickly, fixing their supplies to the mounts. Khirro helped, though his wound made it difficult. It would feel better soon, he knew, but would be a day or more before he could use his arm. The second time his pack slipped from his grasp, Ghaul caught it and helped him.

"I didn't intend the arrow for you," he said in a voice quiet enough only the two of them could hear.

Khirro looked into his eyes, discerning nothing from them. Was this his apology? Did he mean the rain caused his grip to slip? No matter who he pierced with the arrow, it was inexcusable if done on purpose—they'd agreed not to kill Shyn if he returned in good faith. Unsure of Ghaul's meaning and motives, Khirro only nodded in response. This man had kept him alive when he wouldn't have survived on his own, for that he owed him the benefit of the doubt. Ghaul offered his hand and helped Khirro climb onto the chestnut horse.

"Who is this Suath?" Elyea asked as they set out.

"A murderer of women and children," Shyn said

gravely. "A wretch. A devil disguised in the skin of a man."

"Why would he follow us?" Khirro's voice was breathy and weak with pain. He held the reins delicately with his right hand and held the vial against his wound with the other.

"Men like Suath do nothing without payment in gold," Shyn said. "Someone's paid him to follow us."

"But who?"

"Take your pick," Ghaul said.

They formed a rough line with Shyn leading the way and Ghaul at the rear, undoubtedly to keep an eye on Shyn. Khirro sat in the middle, with Athryn and Maes ahead and Elyea behind.

"The soldiers following Suath are Erechanian," Shyn said over his shoulder. "He may be scouting for them."

"Or they could be chasing him," Athryn added without conviction.

Ghaul laughed. "I think it best we don't find out."

"Ghaul's right. Our best chance is to be asea before we're caught." Shyn pointed ahead of them. "We are only a few days ride from the port of Sheldive. If we reach it and get a boat before he finds us, we should be fine."

"How do you know we need to get asea?" Ghaul asked. "Khirro?"

He'd revealed their journey during one of his watches while Shyn was bound to a tree, but now he remained silent, feigning exhaustion from his wound. Ghaul let the subject go, though Khirro was sure it would come up another time.

Rain beat upon them and they fell into silence as they pushed their mounts as fast as they dared through the tangle of brush and trees. The heat from the king's blood seeped into Khirro's shoulder, warming his arm to the elbow. He flexed his fingers; the movement caused considerable pain.

As they rode, his eyes on Athryn's black-cloaked back, he wondered about the man following them, but it distracted him only briefly. After weeks of being chased, he felt little concern. He'd worry if he caught them. Instead, his thoughts turned back to Ghaul. He believed the arrow hadn't been meant for him—if Ghaul wanted to kill him, he'd had many opportunities. But it bothered him the arrow might have been meant for Shyn. The border guard came back with horses and supplies, and quickly, so he deserved their thanks and trust, not an arrow to the chest. Khirro sighed. Both men had shown dedication to this cursed journey. He couldn't imagine reaching the goal without either of them, so he decided to dismiss it as an accident, as Ghaul claimed. If anyone knew accidents happened, Khirro did. The decision did little to ease his unrest.

Nearly three hours passed, time spent mostly in silence except for the frequent checks from both Athryn and Elyea to see how Khirro fared, when Shyn reined his horse to a halt at the crest of a hill. The others halted their steeds beside him.

"What is it?" Khirro asked.

The land fell away in a gentle, brush covered slope which gave way to grassland in the distance, the three days of rain slowly coaxing green back to the landscape. Farms dotted the valley stretched before them; a town sat next to a river near the center. To the south, rolling hills became mountains, peaks hidden in the billowing gray clouds.

"To the south west, the valley ends and the sea begins," Shyn said pointing to the right of the mountains. "That's where we find Sheldive. There we can hire a boat to cross the Small Sea and take us to Lakesh."

The name of the haunted land sent a chill down Khirro's spine. When the Shaman cursed him, he felt fear and despair, but the passage of time had washed much of it away. Drawing nearer the end of their travel brought it back again.

"We'll have to skirt the valley and keep to the trees," Ghaul said, directing his comment to no one in particular. "We won't be welcomed here."

"It would be best to avoid confrontation," Athryn agreed. "Perhaps we could lose our pursuers, too."

"Very well." Shyn reined his horse around. "Are you well enough to continue, Khirro?"

"I grow stronger with each passing moment," Khirro said more on faith than feeling. The intense pain in his arm

215

continued but the vial healed him before, he had no reason to think it wouldn't this time.

"Then we ride." Shyn put heels to his mount, guiding it back into the forest. "But ride with care."

Athryn followed, Maes bouncing placidly in the saddle before him. Elyea urged her horse beside Khirro's as he started out.

"Are you sure you're well enough to continue?"

Khirro nodded, sighing. Elyea smiled.

"You're a brave man, Khirro. Let me help."

She leaned over and took the vial from his hand, a gasp of surprise coming from her as she touched its warm surface. He tensed a little as she held it up to peer at the blood.

"Does this truly help?"

"It healed my leg the first time I took an arrow."

He laughed a little, wondering how many farmers could say they had twice been skewered by arrows. Elyea lifted his bandage, blood and rain tinting it the washed out pink of a winter sunrise. Khirro cringed as she tucked the glass under the cloth, its warm surface pressing against his tender wound.

"Now you can ride with the other hand and allow this one to heal."

"Thank you."

Khirro glanced at the rain running from her hair, down her face, and thought about her prancing through the forest naked. Something stirred in his stomach and he averted his gaze. She stroked her hand along his forearm.

"Let's go," Ghaul growled behind them. "The one-eyed man will show no mercy if he catches us."

Khirro clucked at his horse and the chestnut moved forward, Elyea and Ghaul falling in behind. As they re-entered the forest, the rain eased. Khirro looked over his shoulder, past his companions, at the valley beyond and thought he saw the sun breaking through the clouds in the distance.

21

"How is your shoulder?" Athryn settled himself on the log beside Khirro.

"Better." He raised his arm and made a loose fist—the best he could manage. "The king's blood does wonders."

"I should expect."

The magician rolled his mask up to uncover his mouth and bit into a piece of salt pork. He chewed thoughtfully for a moment before speaking again.

"Quite a sword you have, Khirro."

"It..." A flutter of guilt interrupted his response as he remembered the fallen Shaman—the man who both saved him and cursed him in the space of a few hours. "It was Bale's."

"Yes. The Mourning Sword."

Khirro's eyes flickered to the magician, then away.

"I'm sorry. I shouldn't have taken it." He reached to remove the sword belt, a twinge of pain running down his arm. "You take it. You knew the Shaman."

"No, Khirro. That is not why I inquired about it. The Mourning Sword chooses its bearer. Once it chose Bale, now it is yours. Quite a legacy comes with that blade."

He removed his mask and faced Khirro. The shiny pink scar distorted most of his features and Khirro tried not to stare, but there was little else to look at on Athryn's face, so he looked down at the sword and, realizing he still held the belt buckle, released it. He'd never owned a sword before, never needed to, let alone one with a legacy.

"What do you mean, Athryn?"

The magician rubbed his chin where no stubble would ever grow. Khirro let him take his time in spite of his desire to hear about this 'Mourning Sword'.

"The Mourning Sword was cast a thousand years ago, forged for Monos, the first Necromancer. During the first age, before men made countries, before loyalties existed and pacts were signed, practitioners of magic were greatly feared."

"Magic still scares me." He nodded and thought of the things he'd seen over the past few weeks.

"It is natural for men to be afraid of things they do not understand, but it was different in ancient times. People believed all magic—even healing magic—sent to our world by the devils. Anyone suspected of practicing the arts was

218

burned, drowned, thrown from a cliff, or buried alive. Cleansed by the Gods. Only a magician killed in such manner passed to the fields of the dead. Any other way and the devils reclaimed him, sending him back to our world to wreak their havoc."

"Is that true?"

"I know not. My knowledge does not extend to the land of the dead. I can tell you, though, that many people who did not know magic lost their lives."

Khirro shook his head, sighing around a mouthful of pork—such mania in the name of fear. But, until recently, had he not been deathly afraid of magic and its practitioners? His mother's stories had conjured images of magicians doing heinous things. Given such stories, he understood how people justified their actions.

"Monos lived a secret life for decades, practicing and improving his art while appearing a simple farmer." The terminology might have upset Khirro in the past, but he knew Athryn meant nothing by it. "Eventually, the persecution of the innocent became too much for him. He watched a mob drag a woman from her hut in his own village, accusing her of witchery. They erected a pole at the center of the village, stacked it with tinder and logs soaked with pitch to purify her with fire."

Athryn paused, staring at his feet. Khirro waited, trying to be patient, but he was caught up in the story and wanted to know about his sword.

"What did she do?"

"She had a birthmark on her back."

"The mark of the devils?"

"There is no such thing, Khirro. It was but a blemish. An unfortunate blemish. "

Maes came and sat at Athryn's feet, took a piece of salt pork from him, but appeared to pay no attention to their conversation.

"When Monos saw the mob, rage took him. He drew his sword—the Mourning Sword, though not yet called that— and took the townspeople by surprise. Before they knew what happened, he cut down the leader of the mob. Monos drew his power much the way mine is drawn." He paused and touched Maes' head, stroked his thick hair. The little man patted his hand in return. "As soon as blood spilled, it opened opportunity to use his power, and he did. When he finally calmed, only he and the woman with the birthmark lived."

A few yards away, Ghaul and Elyea were engaged in conversation. A sudden burst of laughter from her startled Khirro. Instead of lifting the sullen mood, the sound stood the hairs at the base of his neck on end. She obviously had no trouble forgiving Ghaul for shooting him with an arrow.

"Do you know how she repaid him for saving her?"

Khirro shook his head before he saw Athryn had not looked to him for a response.

"She feared Monos' power, feared if people discovered

he saved her, she would be put to death anyway. She went to a man called Shyctem, a warlord trying to unite the warring clans."

"The first king," Khirro interjected.

"Yes. For her troubles, Shyctem declared her tainted by Monos' magic and had her drowned. The search for Monos began immediately, and it was this common hatred and fear of the Necromancer which united people under Shyctem's banner, drew together groups who had warred for centuries. With a common goal—the destruction of Monos and all magic practitioners—they finally had a reason for peace.

"Years passed and Shyctem's strength grew. Monos disappeared, spending his time hiding, perfecting his art and training a group of Acolytes who craved his forbidden knowledge. Therein lies the genesis of the Cult of Magic."

Athryn's hand touched a medallion hanging at his throat which Khirro hadn't noticed before, a ring of iron interlaced with two snakes coiling in and out of it and over each other. As the medallion shifted with his touch, it appeared the snakes slithered and moved. Khirro blinked and the illusion ceased.

"Rumors of Monos' teachings spread, whispered from town to town. Eventually, the whisper came to Shyctem's ear. By then, he had proclaimed himself 'Protector of the People' and saw in this whisper the opportunity he needed for one more act to complete the unification and declare

221

himself ruler.

"He sent a man feigning desire to become an Acolyte to learn from Monos. Once accepted, he became Monos' best student, learning much of the arts before leading Shyctem's army to the Necromancer's sanctuary. They captured Monos as he slept, bound him wrist and ankle, gagged him and wrapped him in canvas. Shyctem took him to his keep, then went about the task of finding his Acolytes. Each one he brought before Monos and killed in such a manner as not to spill a drop of their blood. The Necromancer watched them die without averting his eyes, helpless to do anything despite his great power."

Athryn's voice had fallen to a whisper. He paused to drink from the water skin at the side of his pack. Khirro saw pain reflected in his blue eyes.

"They slew his students by way of water, fire, earth or air. Then it was Monos' turn. Word went out to every village that the Necromancer would be executed. Thousands gathered at Shyctem's keep to witness the spectacle. He would be put to death by air—pushed from the top of the highest tower to die on the Killing Stairs two hundred feet below."

"In Poltghasa?"

"Yes. Now the last of the Free Cities, where men swear allegiance to none but themselves and each other. It sits astride the no-man's land bordering Kanos and Lakesh; a city of murderers, thieves, rapists and worse.

"On Shyctem's command, they pushed Monos from the ledge, but instead of falling to his death, the Necromancer floated to the steps below like a leaf bourn on an autumn breeze. Outraged, Shyctem would not be cheated of his victory. He ordered an enormous vat constructed in the city square. Day and night he forced Monos to watch without sleep until complete, then they filled it with water and sealed Monos inside. The crowd waited for half a day to see the vat opened and the Necromancer's body extracted but, when unsealed, he still lived.

"People whispered that Shyctem had underestimated the Necromancer's dark power. Further enraged, the so-called 'Protector of the People' decreed Monos would die by the earth God—the longest and cruelest method. Normally, the accused would be buried in a pine box, left to die of thirst and hunger, but Shyctem was not patient. He buried the Necromancer directly in the dirt, ten feet down. 'Let the worms have their way with him', he said."

Khirro shook his head in disbelief and shuddered, imagining what it must have been like lying at the bottom of the grave watching his executioners fling dirt upon him. The weight of the earth would likely have killed him before they finished filling in the hole. No crime deserved such horrible punishment.

"One week Shyctem left him in the earth," Athryn continued. "No food, no water, no air, no way to move. The throngs stayed to watch, abandoning their farms and livestock for a glimpse of the magician's body. But when they dug up the corpse, it was no corpse. The previous whispers turned to shouts: Shyctem's attempts to kill Monos proved the magician more powerful than their 'Protector'. If Shyctem could not kill one man, surely, he could not be ruler.

"Shyctem's anger was beyond reckoning. Only cleansing by fire remained, so they assembled a huge pyre. They smeared the tinder with pitch and stacked kindling and brush almost to the top. It stood large enough it might have been meant to burn an entire village. Shyctem himself led Monos, naked and dripping animal fat, from his holding cell and directed the executioners as they secured him atop the pyre.

"Before setting torch to wood, all Monos' possessions were laid out with him—a few books, some clothing and his sword. Shyctem lit the pyre, touching the torch directly to the Necromancer first before setting the wood ablaze. The conflagration licked at the heavens, keeping the Gods from their sleep. The pyre burned for two days and the bloodthirsty crowd cheered each time a log shifted.

"When the fire was finally reduced to smoldering chunks of log, the people returned to their farms to find their neglected animals dead and abandoned crops rotted in the fields—Monos' final act of vengeance was not an act of magic. It would be years before Shyctem won the right to call himself ruler, and then he had to do it by force.

"When the fire burned down, the only thing remaining of the Necromancer was his sword, heated so hot they say the steel moaned as it cooled, like a living thing mourning a loss; hence its name. Shyctem ordered the blade pulled from the ashes to have as his trophy. The fire left the steel burned black and the city's best smith could not restore it. Stranger, the runes scrolled on its blade turned the color of blood. Shyctem took the sword, but it disappeared from his armory only days later."

Khirro unconsciously rested his left hand on the sword's hilt. "What happened to the sword?"

"Stolen by the man Shyctem sent to pose as an acolyte of Monos. During his time with the Necromancer, the man experienced power most men do not know exists, and he desired it for himself. He learned all he could before betraying his teacher, fulfilling his obligation to the future king. Once Monos died, he took it upon himself to continue the studies."

A puzzled look creased Khirro's brow. "Did they capture him?"

"Shyctem allowed him to live as payment for his service, or perhaps because he could not afford a second embarrassment. The man who had been both spy and acolyte devoted himself to the arcane arts, more so even than Monos. He quietly increased his knowledge and power without intervening in the affairs of men."

"What became of him?"

225

"You will see soon enough," Athryn replied with a humorless chuckle as he pulled his mask back over his face. "His name is Darestat."

22

The border guard tried to remain motionless but couldn't keep from glancing around the small room, unconsciously refusing to look at the pink hole where Suath's eye once had been. A tic jerked his right cheek occasionally, sweat ran from his temple. Suath had seen men have reactions like this to him before and their nervousness and fear satisfied him. He knew the stories told about him, the names they called him: Suath the merciless, Suath the invincible, Suath the destroyer. Most of the stories were true. The ones which weren't told were worse.

"They killed a soldier in Tasgarad." The mercenary's voice was a low, husky growl. The soldier shook his head. "And three whores in Inehsul. Burned them."

"I didn't know," the guard said, voice quivering. "I didn't see no one."

"They came this way. I tracked them within yards of your post." He pulled a dagger from his boot, fingering its tip as he spoke. "Do you think me a liar or a poor tracker?"

The man's eyes widened. "N-neither. It's my fault. I must have missed them."

"Hmph." Suath held the blade at eye level between

them. "Within the week they passed. What do you remember?"

"Nothing. A normal night. We had a couple of pints. No harm in that. Nothing unusual. Except..."

Suath waited a few seconds for the man to collect his thought and finish his sentence, but impatience got the better of him.

"Except what?"

"I... I heard a noise. When I checked, it was just Shyn on patrol."

"Who is Shyn? Where do I find him?"

"A right fuck up. A border guard, but none of us likes him. Something weird about him, keeps to himself." The guard relaxed a little, snickered. "Funny, though. Now I think of it, he's been assigned to town cause no one wanted him in their tower. He'd disappear for hours at a time. No one'd know where he went."

Suath squatted in front of the soldier, bringing them eye-to-eye. The guard glanced away quickly rather than peer into the empty eye socket. Intimidation and disgust were precisely the reasons Suath didn't cover it.

"Why was he here?"

"I don't know."

"Because he joined them," Suath roared, the unexpected volume and ferocity of his voice startling the guard, making him jump in his chair. The man's eyes flickered to Suath, then away.

"How was I supposed to know?" The guard's voice squeaked in his throat.

"It's your job. You're to halt anyone crossing the borderland without an escort."

"But--"

Suath grabbed the man by the throat.

"You allowed an enemy of the king to cross the border into Vendaria. Incompetent fool. Do you know the penalty for treason?"

The guard's eyes bulged, his face turned purple under Suath's grip as he scratched at the mercenaries arm, kicked his legs. The grip tightened in response. The thrashing and struggling soon ceased, but Suath held on, twisting the man's throat until he felt his windpipe crushed beneath his fingers. He released his grip and strode from the room leaving the border guard's body sprawled in the chair. In the anteroom, he walked past five other guards without a look.

"What happened?" one of the soldiers called after him, but the mercenary didn't answer.

His quarry was close. He'd found the horses they left behind, seen their tracks where they crossed near the guard towers, even noticed one of them had fallen and retraced his steps. He left the tower, mounted his horse and rode into Vendaria with no worry the other border guards would follow to extract revenge for their fallen comrade. They knew him.

They knew to face Suath was to peer into the eye of the reaper.

***

A circuitous route through dense forest lengthened what would have been a three day ride straight across the open valley. Trees grew so thick in places, they were forced to find their way around them. A river which would have been easily forded the previous week had flooded beyond its banks, precipitating a ride deeper into the forest in search of a safe crossing. The closer they got to the sea, the rougher and more treacherous the terrain became. A week had passed since they crested the hill and looked down on the Vendarian valley, yet Khirro felt no closer to their goal. Their food stores were low and game had been scarce.

"We will have to hunt today," Athryn said pulling his horse up at the base of a huge cedar. He lifted Maes from his seat and then slid out of the saddle.

"What about the one-eyed man?" Elyea asked. "Can we afford the time?"

"We need our strength."

"Maybe we lost him," Khirro ventured.

"Doubtful." Ghaul pulled the saddle from his mount. "He likely knows where we are going, so didn't waste time touring the entire Vendarian forest. One person moves faster than five and a half."

Maes shot Ghaul a look of disdain only Khirro noticed—perhaps the little man paid more attention than he thought.

"I'll hunt," Shyn said. "Make a fire and boil some water. I'll return with food shortly."

"Hmm, the great hunter," Ghaul sneered. "How will you produce food for us all when we haven't seen a squirrel for days? Perhaps you'll pull it from your ass?"

Shyn looked at Ghaul, a wry smile tugging at his lips. "Perhaps for you I shall."

He strode into the woods, swallowed quickly by the thick foliage.

"The fool forgot his horse." Ghaul wandered over to Khirro, crouched beside him as he cleared his horse's shoe of stones and said in hushed tones: "I still don't trust him."

"He's done nothing to make us mistrust him."

Khirro put down his dagger, tightened the fingers of his right hand into a fist then stretched them out. His shoulder had healed but stiffness remained.

"A man who wants what you carry might attempt to earn your trust first. It would be easier to relieve you of it if you weren't expecting it."

"But Ghaul, you could be describing Elyea or Athryn."

The soldier glanced at the others. "True."

"Or yourself."

"I saved your life when it was surely forfeit. Do you forget how we met in the shadow of the fortress wall?"

"I'll never forget." Khirro shook his head. "But Shyn also saved my life. Do you forget what he did at the border?"

Ghaul grunted, his face hardening. "Don't you trust me?"

"Of course I do." His hand went unconsciously to the wound on his shoulder. "As I trust Shyn. No one has given me reason not to, and I need all of you if I'm to complete the task I'm cursed with." He half-smiled. "At least none of the others have wounded me."

"Don't cross me and you'll not get hurt," he said, his words erasing Khirro's smile.

"Don't worry about Shyn." Khirro stood and saw Elyea hunting through the nearby brush, searching for dry wood, beautiful in spite of her unkempt appearance. He gestured toward her. "We all work toward the same cause."

Ghaul grunted again and left him to help Elyea in her search. Kindling would be difficult to find. Although the rain had ceased, the mossy forest floor remained damp. Khirro put his knife away and let his horse wander to find food, a task far easier for the animals than for the humans of the party.

Athryn and Maes returned from their own search for suitable wood, adding what they found to the meager pile Elyea collected. Ghaul crouched over the accumulation and fashioned the twigs and leaves into a small pyre. A soft thump on the ground nearby startled him.

"What?" He nearly fell over as he pulled his sword.

The others stopped what they were doing and went to

him. They halted short, staring at the rabbit carcass lying on the ground a yard away from him, its throat torn out.

"Good work, Ghaul. Where did he come from?" Athryn poked at the rabbit with the toe of his boot.

"I didn't kill it."

"It is certainly dead." Athryn stooped, picking the hare up by its ears. "Make your knife useful, Maes."

He tossed the carcass to his brother; the little man picked it up and took it to a rock where he began skinning it with a practiced hand.

"It fell from above," Ghaul said scanning the trees. "It might be a trap."

Khirro laughed. "Are you saying some unseen enemy flings poisoned rabbits at us?" Again, Ghaul didn't share his companion's humor. Khirro's laughter quickly fizzled. "Well, I for one am willing to take the chance."

"Me too," Elyea agreed, smiling.

Maes made short work of the rabbit, skinning and gutting it, then cutting it into pieces suitable for the pot. By the time he finished, steam rose from a pot of water hung over a blazing cook fire. As the water began to boil, Shyn burst out of the brush, two more rabbits in his hands. Ghaul sprang to his feet at the sound, drawing his sword once more.

"Careful you don't cut Khirro with that thing," Shyn said with a smile. He extended his arm so they could see the rabbits he held dangling by their ears. "Tonight we eat fresh meat."

Maes took the rabbits from him and dealt with them as he had the first. He put all the meat in the pot, then added a selection of leaves and roots he and Athryn had collected. While the others waited hungrily, he tended the pot, stirring the concoction.

"You wouldn't believe what happened," Elyea told Shyn as the aroma of the cook pot wafted to them on a light breeze. "While you were gone, food fell from the sky."

"Really? The Gods truly must smile upon us."

He saw Khirro looking at him and winked. Khirro smiled back, unsure what the border guard meant by the gesture.

"There must be some explanation," Ghaul grumbled. "Rabbits don't fall from trees."

"Perhaps it wanted to be a squirrel." Shyn laughed and all but Ghaul joined in his mirth. "Don't burden yourself, Ghaul. Unexplainable things happen all the time. Given the nature of our trip, I'm sure this will not be the last time we wonder how something has come to pass."

Maes signaled dinner was ready by banging his spoon against the side of the pot. The savory stew held the tang of a herb Khirro didn't recognize, complimenting the gamy meat. They devoured it hungrily, except Ghaul who started by taking only small tastes. Khirro considered poking fun at him over it, but decided it would be wiser not to. The outstanding flavor quickly convinced Ghaul the rabbit wasn't poisoned and he ate two helpings.

A full belly did wonders to rejuvenate Khirro. He hadn't realized how much energy had been missing until it crept back into his limbs, returning strength to his wounded shoulder. The food affected his companions similarly. After cleaning up, they set the watches and chose spots for sleeping. Shyn took the first watch and Khirro went to where he sat before lying down to sleep.

"Can I ask you something, Shyn?"

"Of course."

Khirro paused. "How did you find rabbits when we've seen no animals in a week?"

"One need only know where to look," the big man answered with a shrug. "I've been hunting rabbit longer than I can remember."

Khirro nodded, satisfied, though Shyn hadn't really answered his question.

"And what about the rabbit from the sky? How do you think that happened?"

"Sometimes the Gods provide, Khirro."

He returned to his sleeping spot no less uncertain about what had happened than when he approached Shyn. If the Gods truly did provide, he'd be heading to his bed to sleep beside Emeline, anxious about the impending birth of a child, not bedding down on the forest floor worried about a one-eyed mercenary pursuing him through a foreign country. If the Gods truly cared, the blood of the king would never have passed into his hands.

23

"Be quiet," Ghaul growled over his shoulder.

Khirro's stomach churned and twisted so much, stillness became a discomfort. He might have taken it as illness, but the feeling had become familiar. It was the place where the Shaman's curse resided in him.

"Something's wrong," he said; Ghaul hushed him again.

Khirro tried to settle himself and peer through a space between two kegs. On the other side, some yards away, Elyea stood speaking with two men. She wore the simple, clinging shift she'd worn when they met her instead of the doeskin breeches and loose chemise she donned when they left Despina's. The men's demeanor was easy and laughter spilled from the group occasionally. Elyea's deportment matched theirs as she laughed and smiled and brushed her hand on the arm of one man and then the other. Jealousy added to the knots in Khirro's gut brought on by the curse and his reticence about their plan.

The final two days of their ride, travel became easier as the land smoothed near the coast, but more difficult in other ways. Ghaul and Shyn were at each other constantly, jibing and bickering so much it surprised Khirro they hadn't come to blows. The soldier's mistrust for Shyn tainted everything the border guard did, and his refusal to engage Ghaul except through sarcasm and jest added to the soldier's ire. They'd argued to an impasse over how best to proceed when they reached the edge of the forest, each with a hand on their swords until Athryn's wisdom prevailed.

Under the cover of night, they again set their horses free and stole across the short plain to the town of Sheldive, where they planned for Elyea to use her womanly charms and a bag of coins to acquire transport across the Small Sea. Spying from behind the stack of kegs and crates, they saw her using her assets while the bag of money remained on her belt.

One man grabbed Elyea by the waist, pulled her close and kissed her hard on the lips. Ghaul's hand went to the hilt of his sword, but Athryn stayed him with a touch on his forearm. The discomfort in Khirro's belly increased. He knew Elyea could take care of herself, possibly more so than he could, but the thought didn't relieve his disquiet.

If she needs help, she'll signal.

When the man pulled his face away, Elyea laughed again, then turned to lead them behind a pile of sacks. The other man swatted her ass and she giggled while subtly waving to her companions, letting them know she was all right. They disappeared behind the pile and Khirro held his breath. Maes stood beside him, his back to the scene, eyes closed as though in prayer or meditation, or perhaps sleep, Khirro couldn't tell which.

Minutes passed. Elyea's giggles floated to them on the

salty night air. A cramp developed in Khirro's leg and he shifted to alleviate it; Ghaul looked at him but said nothing this time. On Ghaul's other side, Athryn crouched absolutely still, unmoving as though a carven image. Khirro wondered how he remained so while such a feeling of unease twisted his own gut.

"Too much time has passed," Ghaul grumbled and began to rise, but sounds stopped him.

First they heard Elyea's voice—a moan that made Khirro's heart jump into his throat. Ghaul reached for his sword but this time Shyn stopped him. The look of disdain Ghaul gave the border guard would have shivered Khirro's spine had it been intended for him and he worried Shyn might take exception. After a second, Ghaul relented.

They heard other sounds. The voices of the two men joined Elyea's and they quickly realized they weren't hearing the sounds of a struggle. Khirro blushed, embarrassed and angry.

She's a harlot. This is what she does.

Still, he felt disappointed. In the weeks they'd traveled together, he came to see her as so much more than her profession.

After a minute, the noises ceased, a fact that brought a quiet chuckle from Shyn. Ghaul favored him with a contemptuous look that the border guard ignored. Khirro strained to listen over the caress of water lapping against the dock and the creak of ropes and boards as boats

floated nearby. It seemed to him he heard sounds of a
scuffle, but he couldn't be sure. Shyn didn't react, so he
assumed he must be wrong. Then one of the men cried
out, a short bark of alarm quickly cut off. Shyn and Ghaul
both came instantly to their feet, hands on weapons, but
Athryn stopped them again, barring their way with his arm
as he stood, too.

Elyea emerged from behind the sacks, a sheen of sweat
on her naked skin shining in the moonlight. Gazing at the
hang of her breasts and the curve of her hip silhouetted
against the night sky, Khirro forgot his worry. The feeling
in his stomach remained, but he paid it no heed. When she
bent to retrieve something from behind the sacks, he saw
the dagger in her hand. She wiped it with the shirt she
picked up, then bowed her legs and wiped herself. The
action might have seemed rude to some, but Elyea made it
appear natural and business-like, something she'd done
many times before. She discarded the soiled shirt and
disappeared behind the sacks, reappearing moments later,
clothed. Khirro brushed his disappointment aside as she
crossed the dock, gesturing with a sweep of her arm
toward a small sloop.

"Gentleman, your ride awaits."

She replaced the knife in her boot, then pulled the
pouch from her belt and tossed it to Athryn. It jingled as he
caught it.

"And it cost them a lot more than it cost us."

"Are you all right?" Khirro stepped forward, but Ghaul spoke before she answered.

"Never mind that now." He pushed past Elyea toward the boat. "Others will come. We must leave now."

Shyn, Athryn and Maes followed Ghaul to the boat; when Khirro went to follow, Elyea caught his arm. He faced her, gazing into her green eyes.

"I'm fine, Khirro. Thank you for your concern." She smiled but he found he could only return it half-heartedly and she saw his unease. "It was business, nothing more. I did what needed to be done."

Khirro nodded and allowed her to take his hand and lead him to the boat where the others waited.

"Now we're here," Shyn said, "does anyone know how to sail a boat?"

Athryn nodded. "Yes. Climb aboard and I will cast off the line."

Ghaul boarded first. Shyn picked up Maes and passed him to Ghaul, then climbed on and offered Elyea his hand. Khirro came next, wavering unsteadily as he stood on the boat's swaying deck. Athryn freed the line and pushed the boat from the dock, then jumped aboard, landing softly beside Khirro.

"We must go quietly," he said plucking an oar from the deck. He placed the tip against the dock and pushed them away. "We will drift with the tide until we are far enough away to put oar to water without raising alarm, but then we must cross the sea as quickly as possible. When they notice the boat missing and the men slain, they will look for us."

"I'll take the first watch," Shyn said before Ghaul could volunteer. "The rest of you get some sleep."

Athryn nodded. "Wake us when the city lights are distant."

Khirro gathered some empty sacks littering the deck to fashion a pillow and settled down beside a canvas tarp at the stern. He lay on his back, trying to find comfort in the stars peeking through wispy clouds, but irritation still churned his gut. His muscles tensed as Elyea lay close beside him.

"You were very brave," he whispered without taking his eyes from the sky. He felt her turn on her side, facing him.

"What you do is important. The fate of the kingdom is at stake. That makes me braver than I truly am."

Khirro sighed. *Why doesn't it make me feel braver than I truly am?*

Water lapped rhythmically against the side of the boat as the tide slid them silently away from the port town. Elyea settled in, resting her head on his shoulder, and his body tensed. He didn't touch her, but he didn't move away. Her touch made him feel warm, safe; it blocked the uncomfortable feeling in his midsection, but it also stirred up guilt and longing.

Khirro closed his eyes and willed thoughts of Emeline

to mind as he dozed. He saw her standing before the farmhouse that would one day be his if he lived to return, her stomach swollen with child. Her sad expression turned to anger and he tried to comfort her, but she turned away. Grabbing her gently by the arm, he spun her toward him and took a step back. Emeline no longer stood before him, but Elyea instead, her strawberry hair lit by the sun. Khirro looked at her, at the way her bosom stretched the bodice of her white dress. Sun shone through the thin, summery skirt, outlining her shapely legs. She bent at the waist, grasped the hem of her skirt and pulled it up to exposes the patch of red hair between her legs.

Khirro's eyes snapped open, his body starting. Elyea stirred beside him.

"Is all well?"

"Yes," he answered too quickly, but she didn't notice, instead wriggling in closer, laying her hand on his chest. He looked down at the top of her head, his breath short, tempted to stroke her hair, but he didn't allow himself.

Sleep hadn't come when Shyn roused them to take up the oars.

24

As the day wore on, the heat grew, intensifying the stench of moldering canvas. Sweat streamed down Suath's forehead, soaked his underclothes, but he remained motionless, dirk in hand. He listened to the choppy

241

sounds of oars striking water and knew his quarry had little experience navigating a boat. His opinion of their skills meant nothing, he had a job to do and nothing else mattered.

When he came across their steeds milling about at the edge of the forest, he knew he'd nearly caught them. And he knew why they came this way. He had needed boats in the past, too; it was the only reason to come to Sheldive.

He crept aboard the sloop while they busied themselves leering at the whore as she fucked them a boat, forgetting to watch the prize for which they'd come. He hid under the tarp, lying in wait, not troubling a moment over why this odd group should be headed to Lakesh. Experience had taught him people's reasons can be unfathomable. He'd also learned to attack when he had the best chance for survival and escape. In Vendaria, a fight may have called attention—the militia would be on high alert with a war to the north—and he wouldn't be able to navigate the boat by himself if he killed them on the open water, so he waited. Once he killed them, he'd head up the coast and hire a boat to take him back. Or maybe he'd go to Kanos to see what price might be paid there for whatever he was retrieving. Maybe they'd pay more than Therrador.

A sliver of sunlight stole under the tarp from a spot where the rope had loosened. Suath kept his gaze on it, watching for movement. A shadow blocked the mute illumination and he tensed, ready to attack if the need occurred.

"We should send the others back," a man's voice said in hushed tones Suath almost couldn't hear. "Two of us would move more swiftly. And the journey will be perilous. You wouldn't want their deaths on your head, would you?"

A pause before a second man's voice answered.

"No," he said. Suath heard hesitancy in his voice. "It would be as dangerous for them in Vendaria, though."

"They could go north, to the sea wall," the first voice urged.

"Not with the war. They'd destroy the boat before it came within shouting distance. It's best this way. We'll need every sword, every bit of cunning. And everything Athryn has to offer."

Another slight pause. "Watch the magician, Khirro, he has his own agenda for seeking the Necromancer, and it has nothing to do with the blood of the king you carry in that vial."

Suath smiled.

Braymon's blood.

No wonder Therrador wanted the vial so badly. The Kanosee would likely pay a great deal for this. He'd have to be careful with a magic user amongst them, but magicians bled like any man, the key was to keep them from speaking.

Suath knew how to do that.

The woman called to them from the bow of the boat

but the lapping of the waves swallowed her words.

"We're almost there," the second man's voice said with a note of resignation. No warrior, this one. "Everyone comes with us unless they choose otherwise. We'll need them all."

Footsteps sounded on the wooden deck, vibrating against Suath's chest, as someone else approached.

"We should rest when we arrive, get our bearings," the new voice said in deep, melodic tones, undoubtedly the voice of a magic user. "None will follow us to the haunted land, but the journey will be difficult. We should regain our energy before we continue."

The other voices agreed, then two sets of boots clomped away. Shadow still blocked the sun. Suath blinked sweat from his eye, straining his gaze, but saw only a bit of brown leather boot—the first man still stood nearby. It would not be enough to identify the man when the time came, but he would recognize his voice. If any amongst them might be tempted to turn to his side, this would be the one.

Or he could be dangerous.

Again, footsteps clopped on the deck and sun found its way through the opening. Sweat covered every inch of Suath's exposed skin, drenched his clothes. He'd survived the sweat boxes of Estycia and the deserts of the south, as well as more wounds and tortures than most men knew existed. Discomfort meant nothing to him, he'd be paid with more than enough gold to compensate.

Half an hour passed before the ship's bow crunched against the rocky beach of the Lakesh shore. A few more hours of heat and discomfort and they'd be asleep, then he'd make his move.

It pleased Suath they made his task so easy.

25

Therrador leaned back in his seat, steepled fingers resting against his lips as he regarded the other men sitting around the marble table. For the better part of an hour, they'd argued on the same subject and he found it hard to hide his annoyance, but he controlled himself. How he acted now would insure things came out the way he planned.

"But we don't know for certain the king has perished."

A tall wisp of a man, Lord Emon Turesti's gray hair lay limp against his narrow shoulders; his impossibly long fingers fidgeted constantly. The High Chancellor never stopped moving and all these characteristics combined to give him the nickname Smoke, though few dared say it to his face.

"In the name of the four Gods, do you suppose he unarmored himself to take up a mallet and play a quick game of roque?" Sir Alton Sienhin's droopy jowls shook as he blustered, his face a startling red behind his huge black mustache. The head of the king's army had made the trip

Bruce Blake

from the Isthmus Fortress to Achtindel in order to sit with the high council. "You haven't seen the king fight, Smoke. A warrior like King Braymon would not be relieved of his armor whilst life still coursed through his veins."

How appropriate, Therrador thought, *that they speak of what runs through his veins.*

The other men at the table—Hu Dondon, the Lord Chamberlain, and Hanh Perdaro, Voice of the People—nodded at Sir Alton's words.

Turesti's lips tightened to a pale line at the use of the nickname. "Sir Alton, with no body, we cannot presume--"

"What of the Shaman?" Hu Dondon interrupted.

The oldest man sitting on the King's High Council, Dondon didn't look any more aged than his fellows. His full head of black hair showed no gray, his posture remained straight; only the droop at the corners of his eyes gave any inkling of the years he'd seen pass.

"The Shaman is dead. He--" Sir Alton began.

"Yes, we know," Dondon interrupted again, a habit those who knew him had to live with. "Found him dead outside the walls. Makes him look a traitor. What of his sworn mission?"

Sir Alton's face grew more red. "Bale died valiantly at the foot of the fortress wall," he sputtered barely controlling his rage at Dondon's inference. "Rudric and Gendred fell by his side, the bodies of eight Kanosee pigs rotting around them. Do not speak ill of brave men."

246

Dondon waved a dismissive hand at the general. "Yes, died for his country. And his mission?"

"There was no sign of it." Sir Alton leaned back, arms crossed against his barrel chest. "We have no reason to think they had it."

"Then why were they outside the fortress?" Hanh Perdaro asked.

Though youthful, little hair grew on the head of the man known as the Voice of the People. Thoughtful and sparse of words, Therrador treasured these traits and liked the man best of the King's High Council. There would be a position for Perdaro in the future if he wanted it.

"We cannot know," Lord Turesti said. "Perhaps the king was captured and they gave pursuit."

"And suppose I shat a donkey," Sir Alton blurted. "If they were in pursuit of the king's captors, there would have been a damn sight more than three of them."

"In either case," Turesti continued, his mouth a taut line of disgust at Sir Alton's words. "We should keep things quiet. It will do no good for the army to think they fight without a king and for the people to mourn their regent in the middle of a war."

"I fear it's already too late," Hanh Perdaro said stroking the thin line of beard cupping his chin. "Whispers of Braymon's death already cross the land. The people grow nervous."

"Aye, as do the king's soldiers," Sir Alton added, his

cheeks fading pink. "Not only do they fear the loss of their king, but Rudric and Gendred--"

Dondon cut him off. "Yes, yes. But the blood. What of the king's blood?"

Therrador leaned forward resting his elbows on the table top, and the others looked toward him, waiting to hear the words of the king's advisor who had remained silent as they discussed the situation. He looked from one to the next, drawing the pause out deliberately, taking in their anxious looks.

This is what it will be like when I'm king.

"There is no blood."

He watched hope drain from their faces. Hu Dondon sucked breath in through his teeth; Sir Alton Sienhin smacked a gauntleted fist on the white and red marble table.

"I have sent men searching, and they've turned up nothing. No one survived the fight beneath the walls of the fortress."

"But why were they--" Dondon began, but Therrador cut him off, taking great pleasure in doing so. He pulled a vial from his belt and tossed it onto the table to roll across the smooth surface. Four pairs of eyes followed the empty glass as it skittered to the middle of the table.

"The blood was spilled," Therrador said.

"Then all is lost." Lord Turesti said voicing what must have been on all their minds. "What will happen with no heir to the throne?"

"Civil war," Dondon said. "The kingdom will be plunged into turmoil."

"You belly-dragging son of a rabid weasel!" Sir Alton Sienhin stood so suddenly his chair teetered. "Would you have us roll over and wet on ourselves? Hand our country to the Kanosee and save them the trouble of dirtying their boots?"

"Sit down, you fool," Hu Dondon sneered. "If you and that so-called royal guard had done your jobs, perhaps we wouldn't be having this conversation."

"How dare you. We lost three--"

"You lost the king," Dondon snapped. "Nothing else matters."

"You are nothing but a--"

"Enough!"

Therrador slammed his hand on the table; the men turned their attention to him, their expressions ranging from despair to rage. As they stared, he pulled a rolled parchment from his belt and tossed it onto the table. It spun a few times, rolling to a stop against the empty vial.

"That letter contains the king's wishes if he were to fall and not be raised." He looked at them, gauging their reactions. "And the solution to our problem."

They stared at the paper, none of them speaking or reaching for it. Even the normally verbose Hu Dondon remained speechless. Finally, Hanh Perdaro looked up from the parchment, meeting Therrador's eyes.

"Why did you not tell us of this sooner, Therrador?"

"I held hope of discovering what happened, as you did. I hoped beyond hope, prayed to the four Gods our king would be returned, but time has passed. The likelihood of my prayers being answered, my hopes coming true, grows dimmer every day. It's time something is done to save our kingdom."

"What does it say?" Lord Turesti asked.

Therrador breathed deep. "It says I'm to carry on King Braymon's legacy as regent and protector of the realm, and my heir after me."

"Yes, yes. But how do we know this to be true?"

If Hu Dondon didn't realize the mistake he'd made in asking as the words passed his lips, Therrador's sudden rage made it clear.

"How dare you!" Therrador yelled. "I became friends with Braymon suckling side by side at our mothers' teats. I served our king before he became king, while the likes of you rooted at the feet of the man who held his rightful throne."

Dondon hung his head. "Apologies, Lord."

Sir Alton looked across the table at Dondon, disgust and pleasure mixing plainly in his eyes. "It bears the unbroken seal of the king," he said pointing at the roll, his mustache quivering as his camouflaged lips moved behind it. "It is the wish of the king."

Seconds passed as they stared at the king's mark. Hanh Perdaro picked up the letter, broke the seal and unrolled it. He read its words while the others held their breath, awaiting confirmation. Therrador fought to keep his rebel lips from breaking into an inappropriate smile. When Perdaro finished, he set the letter back on the table.

"It is as he says." He pushed his chair away, moved to Therrador's side and dropped to one knee. "I pledge fealty to you, my Lord. My life is yours, King Therrador."

Only the briefest moment of pause passed before Sir Alton's voice bellowed out across the chamber.

"Long live King Therrador!" The others joined in, thrusting their fists in the air. "Long live the king!"

Therrador sat back in his chair and allowed the smallest of smiles to curl the corners of his mouth.

26

The white tyger squatted on its haunches, silent but for its breath. Khirro stared into its golden eyes, unsuccessfully attempting to fathom who or what lay behind them. They sat for some time—how much, Khirro didn't know: a minute in a dream could be hours, or hours but a minute. He shifted, moving to his left, and the tyger growled deep in the back of its throat, startling him. He settled back and the beast quieted. Each time he moved, the tyger growled again, fixing Khirro in place.

"Who are you? What do you want?"

In the other dreams, the tyger seemed helpful, friendly. Not so this time. This time it acted as jailer or guard, keeping him from leaving. Khirro scanned the forest surrounding them without recognition. This was not the place of the lake and the moon. He breathed deep and leaned to his left. The tyger growled, but he ignored it this time, leaning farther. The beast bared its teeth. Khirro quickly moved back and the rumble in the tyger's throat ceased.

"Stray not from the path, Khirro." The tyger's voice rang in his head. "Danger lies on all sides."

Khirro moved directly toward the tyger. It didn't react.

"Who are you?"

"You will be safe if you follow the path. Stray not."

Without knowing why he took the chance, Khirro reached out and touched the tyger's nose. The big cat neither flinched nor moved away. His fingers brushed the soft fur between its eyes, felt the moistness of its nose. He only had a moment to notice these sensations before the animal rose abruptly and leaped away into the forest. Khirro stood, staring after it as a chill ran down his spine.

And then Khirro was walking, though he didn't remember wanting to walk or starting to do so. Trees and brush slid past and he realized where he was, where he had to go. The Shaman had shown him the path to Darestat's keep when he cursed him with this burden and he saw it clearly now, knew he walked it.

South. The path lay south. There he'd find an inland lagoon fed by a towering waterfall, beside it a ruined village. There the journey through Lakesh would start.

The trail ahead of Khirro disappeared, foliage and brush enveloping it, and a feeling he was no longer alone overwhelmed him. He scanned the thick brush hoping the tyger had returned to guide him but saw only leaves and branches. He swung back to the path and before him, where there had been only forest a moment before, was the lagoon and the abandoned village, the waterfall cascading soundlessly into a clear pool. Under other circumstances, the scene might have been beautiful, but the feeling of being stalked pressed in, brushing Khirro's cheek, filling his lungs. Everything dimmed. The huts, the lagoon, the trees, everything faded into darkness. Everything disappeared.

Khirro opened his eyes.

With the dream still fresh in his mind, he didn't understand what his eyes saw at first. Darkness, but not dark like at the end of the dream. He knew he was awake. He blinked to clear his head and focus his eyes.

Scars criss-crossed the face looking down on him. One eye glared at him menacingly, the other socket empty and pink.

The one-eyed man.

Khirro pushed himself to his elbows, sucking air in noisily. He opened his mouth to call out, but a dirk to his

253

throat stopped him.

"The vial," the man whispered.

How can he be here?

Mind reeling, Khirro stared into the man's craggy face. Pursuers couldn't have arrived already, couldn't know where they'd land, even if they knew they sought the Necromancer. The one-eyed man pushed the blade painfully against his throat.

"Give it to me."

Khirro's eyes flickered side to side.

Where are the others? Did he kill them?

Another cry for help stuck in his throat. He had no doubt this man would slit his throat and find the vial himself, would likely kill him once he had it. Khirro moved his hand toward the opening of his jerkin and the vial it hid, and the stiletto secreted beside it.

"I'll get that."

The man pushed Khirro's hand away and reached roughly beneath his shirt, searching with his fingers until he found the glass container. He pulled it out and tucked it beneath his own tunic without moving his gaze from Khirro to look at his prize, then held up the stiletto he'd retrieved at the same time.

"And just what did you think to do with this?"

Something moved behind the man. Khirro glanced away to see Athryn creeping up behind him, then quickly brought his eyes back to the one-eyed man. A smile twisted the man's scarred features and Khirro realized his mistake.

"Athryn," he called out too late. The mercenary whirled, blade flashing moonlight as it opened a gash across the magician's belly. Khirro scrambled away as he saw the dagger Athryn held fall to the sand, his body collapsing close beside it. The man turned back to Khirro, but everyone else had wakened. Shyn and Ghaul called out, rushing to them with steel in hand. The one-eyed man cursed and hurled the stiletto at Khirro before leaping away into the forest. Khirro rolled on his side and the slender blade sank hilt deep in the sand inches from his head.

"What happened?" Shyn demanded as he and Ghaul skidded to a halt beside Khirro.

"The one-eyed man. He took the blood of the king."

The two soldiers dove into the trees, leaving Khirro with hand outstretched, intending to warn them how dangerous the man was, but they were gone. He pushed himself to his knees, reaching for his sword belt, his gut burning as he determined to follow them, to get the vial back. Then his eyes fell on Athryn. Elyea and Maes already knelt at his side, the little man cradling the magician's head on his lap while Elyea hurriedly opened his shirt. Khirro abandoned all thought of pursuit and crawled to her side to help peel the blood soaked clothes from the magician's torso. As they pulled it away, a thick gray coil slid from his abdomen. Khirro caught it before it touched the sand and slid it back in, his gorge rising in the back of his throat. Memory of his father's arm twitching on the ground, blood spurting from his shoulder came to mind, the helpless feeling he had then returning with it. Athryn groaned, a low, weak sound that squeezed Khirro's chest and made him feel sick to his stomach.

"What do we do?"

He looked at Elyea. She looked back with tear-rimmed eyes and shook her head, then turned to gaze into Athryn's mask-less face.

A pained, indistinct moan from Maes startled Khirro—the first sound he'd heard the little man make. They looked at him, expecting tears and dismay, but the noise was made to draw their attention. He motioned for Elyea to switch places with him and she complied, Athryn's long hair spreading across her thighs as she stroked his scarred cheek. Maes moved beside Khirro, nudging him aside, and bent over Athryn's wound, examining it closely.

"What can I do?" Khirro asked, voice choked with emotion.

Maes shook his head, moonlight reflecting on the tears running down his stubbled cheeks. He rocked on his knees like a child come to the end of a fit of rage. Then his lips began to move. An indistinguishable, garbled chant whispered between them. Khirro stared, hypnotized by the rhythm of his rocking which coincided with the chant, and his words which weren't incomprehensible foreign words, but incoherent mumblings of a man with no tongue.

He was trying to cast a spell.

Is this possible?

Khirro looked at Elyea stroking Athryn's face. Her lips moved, too, but he understood what she said: "It's okay. Everything will be all right."

She didn't look at Maes, as though she knew what would come next. Tears stained her freckled cheeks and, when she looked at Khirro, he saw anguish in her eyes. He wanted to comfort her, to hold her; she looked away. This time, she looked at Maes and gasped. Khirro pulled his gaze away and looked to the little man.

Maes held his left hand extended above his brother's wound, a knife pressed against his wrist. Panic jumped into Khirro's throat.

What does he think he's doing?

Khirro grabbed the little man's arm to wrestle the dagger from him, but Maes didn't interrupt his chant as he pushed Khirro away with strength greater than expected. Khirro tumbled onto his back, a half-buried rock knocking the wind from him.

"No!" Elyea cried as Khirro found his equilibrium and righted himself in time to see Maes open the artery in his wrist.

He directed the fountaining blood into Athryn's wound. Khirro reached for his arm again, but the point of Maes' dagger came to rest against his throat. The little man never stopped chanting, his rocking didn't slow, yet the tip of his dirk caressed the vein in Khirro's neck, telling him to leave him be. Elyea drew a sharp breath.

"Leave him," she said, the anguish as plain in her voice as on her face. "I don't need you dead as well."

Khirro filled his lungs with salty air then stood. Maes lowered his blade as Khirro went to Elyea's side, sank to his knees and put his arm around her doing his awkward best to comfort her despite of the knot of fear and dread clogging his chest. He looked into Athryn's face, pink scar shining faintly under the moon, eyes closed, his features slack.

"Is he--?"

"He breathes." Her hair brushed Khirro's cheek as she shook her head.

Maes continued to chant, quieter now; his rocking slowed, losing rhythm. The flow of blood from his slashed wrist became a trickle.

Khirro leaned closer to Elyea. "If I can stop the bleeding, we might save him."

The man's right hand flashed up, dagger pointing at Khirro again. Khirro didn't move.

The brothers' blood combined to flow down the magician's sides, a thick river soaking everything it touched, turning the sand black in the moonlight. Khirro didn't think he'd ever seen so much blood, not when the sheep gave birth, not even when his father lost his arm. His stomach moved into his throat and he fought it back. What kind of warrior couldn't keep his stomach at the sight of blood? And, like it or not, he was nothing if not a warrior now.

The trickle from Maes' wrist had slowed to drops when he slumped forward across Athryn's midsection. Khirro moved to help, but Elyea stopped him with a hand on his shoulder.

"Leave him. He's beyond help. His blood is gone and there's no one to give him more."

"What of Athryn?"

She put a hand first to his brow, then under his nose.

"He lives for now. Only time will tell if we'll dig one grave or two."

Khirro hung his head, settling back on his knees. Could they make it to the Necromancer without the help of the magician? He chastised himself silently for the thought. At least one man who'd come to support and aid him lay dead, his life forfeit for nothing with the vial gone.

How could I let him take it? I should have done something. Something other than get Athryn killed.

Minutes passed. Elyea continued to stroke Athryn's face as Khirro brooded over yet another mistake with a high price.

That's what started this whole thing...my mistakes.

When he heard someone approaching from the nearby forest, Khirro was vaguely aware he should pull his sword but found no strength in his limbs to do so. He breathed a relieved sigh when Ghaul emerged, Shyn following closely behind.

"He escaped," Ghaul said as he crossed the beach to them. "Wake the midget, we have to go after him now."

"He's not sleeping," Elyea grated, her voice low and tinged with anger. "He's dead."

"What happened?" Shyn asked.

Elyea lowered her eyes, shoulders trembling as she sobbed quietly. Khirro pushed himself awkwardly to his feet, legs wobbling beneath him as pins and needles crawled up his calves. He guided the other men away, recounting the details of Athryn's wound and his brother's attempt to revive him.

Shyn shook his head. "Maes did that? But Athryn is the magician."

"Never mind that," Ghaul snapped impatiently. "Did it work? Did the midget succeed?"

Khirro sighed. "Athryn lives, but whether he's saved or simply hasn't expired from his wound yet, we don't know."

The muscles in Ghaul's jaw tightened. He turned and strode purposefully to Elyea kneeling beside the brothers, the little man's body lying across Athryn's midsection, hiding the wound. Ghaul grabbed the back of Maes' tunic.

"What are you doing?" Elyea glared at him. Ghaul stopped and looked at her, his fingers curled grasping the cloth.

"We can't wait here until the magician gets up and dances a jig. The blood of the king gets farther from us every second we delay pursuing the one-eyed man."

She looked away. "Be gentle with him."

Ghaul rolled Maes aside. The dagger tumbled from the little man's limp fingers to the blood soaked sand. Khirro and Shyn moved closer, but blood covered everything, concealing wounds and flesh.

"Water," Ghaul commanded.

Khirro retrieved the water skin from his pack, nearly tripping on the stiletto buried in the sand as he did. He retrieved the blade and returned with the water for Ghaul. The warrior yanked the cork and splashed Athryn's belly, the water turning pink as it rolled down his sides. It took three washings to expose clean flesh. Instead of hanging innards, a long scar stretched across his stomach.

"It worked," Elyea whispered. She looked into Athryn's face, a smile tugging the corner of her lips, then she looked to Maes and the smile disappeared.

"It seems there was magic in the little one, too—tongue or no," Shyn said.

Ghaul harrumphed and handed the water skin back to Khirro. "I'm glad one of them lives," he said, the sentiment not reflected in his tone. "But we have a thief to catch."

"We can't leave yet." Khirro stared at the spot on Athryn's belly where he'd replaced his intestines not long ago. "We have to give him a chance to recover."

261

Bruce Blake

He looked at each of his companions.

Ghaul gritted his teeth. "The one-eyed man took the king's blood," he said gesturing toward the forest. "Have you forgotten why we came to this God-forsaken land? Without it we are merely a group of fools waiting to die for no reason."

"We'll find him," Shyn said.

Ghaul shook his head. "This man is no farmer. He knows the ways of both hunter and prey and won't be easy to track." He looked at the others and Khirro refrained from showing his offense at the warrior's choice of words. "We'll leave Khirro and Elyea here to tend the magician while we find the one-eyed man."

"No," Khirro said. "We shouldn't separate. To do so in the haunted land would mean death to us all."

"He's right," Shyn said. "We'll have better luck tracking him come daylight, anyway."

The muscles in Ghaul's jaw visibly clenched and released, clenched and released. He crossed his arms, his brow furrowed.

"Every moment we spend here costs us."

Shyn put his hand on Ghaul's shoulder. "Worry not. I'll find him."

"Oh, the great tracker honors us again." Ghaul shrugged away from Shyn's touch. "Perhaps we should wait for winter. It will be easier to follow his tracks in the snow."

262

Shyn's eyes narrowed, his expression hardened.

"Did I not bring horses when I promised?" Both men's hands fell to their swords. "Was it not I who warned you the one-eyed man pursued us?"

Ghaul eyed him warily, fingers tightening on the hilt.

"Yes, tell us how you knew of the one-eyed man? He followed from a different direction than you came with the horses. How do you explain that?"

"Stop it," Elyea said. "Both of you stop it."

"No, he's right." Shyn's voice sounded different, almost relieved. Khirro gaped. Had he been wrong about the man? "I owe an explanation."

The border guard released his grip on his sword and stepped away. His gaze slipped from theirs, finding instead the ground and the pool of moonlight casting his shadow there.

At first, Khirro thought what he saw a trick of the light. Shadows crawled across Shyn's face like a cloud across the sky, distorting and discoloring it. Shyn looked up at them, eyes glowing with yellow light, then he cried out, doubled over in pain. Khirro took a step toward him but Ghaul blocked his way.

"No," he said. "Let's see what happens."

Shyn dropped to his knees, hands covering his face as he cried out again. Khirro stared, concern and curiosity locking his gaze firmly on his companion. The night's trickery continued, making it seem as though Shyn became smaller, but Khirro soon saw this was no illusion—the border guard's mail shirt hung loosely from his shoulders, his hands disappeared up the sleeves of his tunic. When he looked up, he no longer looked like the man who'd accompanied them from the border: his nose grew longer, his eyes pulled to the sides of his head. Dull gray feathers covered his face.

Elyea gasped. Ghaul's arm fell away from Khirro's chest but he no longer attempted to go to Shyn. He had to remind himself to breathe.

Half-a-minute later, the man they called Shyn was gone. His clothing lay in a pile on the sand as though discarded by someone gone for a midnight swim. A gray falcon with liquid-gold eyes stood upon the clothes. The huge bird squatted back, spread wings with a span as wide as Shyn was tall and, with a mighty leap and powerful downstroke, took to the night air. It swooped into the sky, momentarily blotting out the moon, and left them open-mouthed on the beach.

Khirro stared after the falcon until it disappeared into the night sky. His head spun, dizzying him, and he sank to the sand, sitting beside Elyea. Her eyes flickered toward his, but he didn't return her gaze.

Maes was dead. Shyn had left. The king's blood was gone.

Khirro buried his face in his hands.

27

They moved Athryn to the shade of a tree before the sun rose too high in the sky. What to do with his brother's corpse was not so easy a subject.

"We should burn him," Ghaul said. "Bury him at least." Khirro might have agreed if he thought he meant to set the little man's spirit free from its earthly ties, but Ghaul was more practical than that. "If we leave him, he'll attract animals. Or worse."

"No," Elyea said as she bathed Athryn's brow with a cloth soaked in cool sea water. "He's Athryn's brother. The magician would want to see him."

Ghaul shook his head, frustrated. "What if it's weeks before he recovers? I've seen men sleep for months after serious injuries, or never wake at all. Are we to live with the stench of the midget, risking disease and animal attack?"

Elyea nodded. "Yes."

"Argh, woman. Help me, Khirro."

Khirro looked at Athryn, his head resting in Elyea's lap much as the night before, then glanced toward the copse of trees twenty yards away, hiding Maes' blanket-covered body.

"I think it should be the magician's decision."

Ghaul cursed and strode angrily to Khirro, who shrank from him when they came face-to-face.

"Soon you'll have to leave the farmer behind and

Bruce Blake

become a warrior, or it will cost you your life. And possibly mine."

He stalked away, ignoring Shyn as he passed; he'd not said a word to the border guard since he revealed his secret. Shyn approached Khirro.

"Don't listen to him," he said. "You'll do the right thing when the time comes."

I haven't yet.

Khirro nodded silent thanks as Shyn turned and went into the forest where he would become the falcon and spend the day adrift on the winds, searching for the one-eyed man.

Khirro watched Elyea swab Athryn's forehead, pausing occasionally to dip the cloth in the water-filled helm at her knee. The muscles in her forearm rippled beneath her smooth skin as she wrung out the excess, dripping some of it onto the magician's tattooed chest.

"What do you think about Shyn?" she asked without looking up.

"Unusual, to be sure." When she leaned forward to wet the cloth again, her loose shirt hung away from her chest and Khirro had to avert his eyes so she wouldn't catch him staring at her cleavage. "Ghaul is more convinced we shouldn't trust him."

"But what do you think?"

"He's done us no wrong. What about you?"

"He scares me somewhat, but it's as you say. Ghaul

thinks he's in league with the one-eyed man but, if so, why wouldn't they have revealed themselves before we got to Lakesh?"

"No one in their right mind would come here."

Wind stirred the trees about them and dried the sheen of sweat on Khirro's brow. A checker board of sunlight fell across the mossy ground. Nearby, Ghaul drew the edge of his dagger down his cheek, taking a week's worth of stubble off with each pass.

This isn't so bad. There's beauty here.

He looked back to Elyea to find her hand idle and her eyes upon him.

"Tell me about your wife."

He swallowed hard and turned his gaze from hers. "Emeline is not my wife."

"No?" Her tone told him her smile had disappeared. "Doesn't she carry your child?"

"There's no honor in my story."

Cloth rustled as Elyea moved from Athryn to squat in front of Khirro. She lifted his chin with one slim finger. "Remember to whom you speak, Khirro. You've heard my story. How could I judge you?"

Khirro's chest loosened. Since leaving his village, conscripted to the king's army, he had told no one, save for hints to Shyn. Perhaps the time had come.

"She's not my wife, not even my woman. She's the daughter of our nearest neighbor. I admired Emeline from afar as we grew up and one night not so long ago, we shared too much ale. Two months later, her moon time didn't come." He sighed, paused. Elyea said nothing to prompt him to continue, but he saw in her eyes she wanted him to. "She does not bear my child out of love, Elyea. That's part of the reason I'm a soldier now."

Elyea giggled, but stopped when he shot her an angered look. "I'm sorry, Khirro, I mean no offense. How does she know it's yours?"

"She was a maiden before that night."

She stifled another giggle. "You spilled her maiden blood? Good for you!"

He shook his head, unable to share her mirth.

"When they discovered she was with child, her parents wanted my head. Had it been up to my father, he'd have given it to them himself, but my mother kept them from me. When the Conscriptors came, father made her give me up to them; to him, I had disgraced the family. Again."

Memories filled his mind. His mother cried a little the day he left, but his father remained stern and strong, his empty sleeve hanging at his side as a reminder why.

Elyea touched his cheek, startling him. "I'm sorry, Khirro. But what of Emeline through all this?"

"She wanted nothing to do with me—never did, never will." He made himself look into her green eyes. "She said I raped her."

Elyea's face hardened, lines creasing the spot above her

nose. "Did you?"

Khirro suddenly wished he could take back telling her the story, take back the very fact it happened.

"We drank too much ale," he said slowly. "I don't even remember seeing her unclothed."

They looked at each other a long time. Finally her face relaxed.

"I think you've done nothing wrong."

He blinked, confused. "Why do you say that?"

"Because I'm not only a woman, but a woman who understands and knows men better than most. It's not in you to do such a thing, ale or no."

She smiled again, a warm, understanding smile that made him believe her words. He tried to smile back, but met with little success.

"There is much pain in this for you, isn't there?"

"Yes." He glanced over her shoulder at Athryn. "I'm responsible for ruining Emeline's life and my own. Sometimes I wish I could switch places with my brother, like Maes did."

"Your brother?"

His eyes flickered back to hers as he nodded. "When the Conscriptors came, my parents told them they only had one son. He yet lives his life any way he chooses while I'm banished and cursed to die in a foreign land."

She touched his face again. "You're a brave man. What you do here will save a kingdom. Can your brother say

269

that, hiding behind your mother's apron?"

"I'm only here because the Shaman cursed me to be."

She leaned forward and wrapped her arms around him, pulled him close. He waited out her touch, keenly aware of her breast pressing against his chest as a tingling began in his groin. Khirro didn't return her embrace for fear it might spread, grow. Emeline was the only woman he'd been with, if he'd even been with her. Elyea released her hold but, as she pulled away, her lips brushed his gingerly, lingering a moment as they touched. Surprised, Khirro pushed himself to his feet.

"I should check on Ghaul."

"He's fine, Khirro." She looked up at him, hands folded on her knees. "Come sit with me."

He took a step away.

"I'll see if Shyn has come back. Or check our supplies."

He strode away, half hoping she'd call after him, ask him to come back. She didn't. Women like Elyea didn't have to call after men. As he walked away, he looked back over his shoulder and saw she'd returned to swabbing the magician's forehead. She didn't look up or beckon him to return. He shook his head and looked at his feet as he trudged the distance to Maes' remains. He didn't know what to think about her words or actions—he'd never needed to interpret the conduct of a harlot before.

Can I even think of her as a harlot still? I don't want to be thought of as a farmer.

He crouched by the little man's corpse, pulled the blanket away from his face. Khirro's confusion of thoughts and emotions fled. Such things became petty when looking death in the eye.

Maes' skin was ashen, the color drained from it with the blood from his wrist; insects crawled across his slack face. Khirro brushed them away in disgust. He deserved better than to lay in wait under a tree, devoured by bugs tiny piece by tiny piece.

The scars on the little man's neck made Khirro think about the kind of life Maes led, of the blood he spilled in the name of magic, of the pain and frustration he must have felt at having no tongue. Such bravery from such an unlikely person. And in the end, he sacrificed everything so his brother might live.

Did he know his words would work, or did he determine to give up his life only in the hope it would be enough to save Athryn?

Guilt filled Khirro. Here he stood in the presence of true love and courage; seeing it made him realize he didn't truly understand it. He thought he loved his family, and once thought he loved Emeline, but now saw he didn't really know. A knot formed in his throat. The sad story of his life paled in comparison to those of his companions. One had been a concubine by eight years old, one a soldier by twelve. Society ostracized the third for an affliction he couldn't control and the others spent their lives hiding, not allowed to be themselves. Why did he deserve sympathy? In comparison, his life had been good.

More bugs crawled onto Maes' face and Khirro brushed them away. Here lay a man he should strive to be more like in his life. A tear rolled down his cheek for the little man who couldn't speak but still made such an impact on those who knew him.

"Khirro!"

The tone in Elyea's voice pulled him immediately from his thoughts and brought him to his feet. He drew his arm across his face, wiping the tear away before she saw it.

"Ghaul!"

Khirro covered Maes's face and hurried across the hot sand, skidding to a halt beside Ghaul at Elyea's side. Both of them stared at the magician sitting up, blinking rapidly like a man emerged from a dark cave into bright sunlight, blinded and confused.

"Athryn."

Water from Elyea's cloth shone on the smooth surface of the magician's face; he looked at Khirro as though he didn't recognize him. The blank look didn't escape Ghaul's notice.

"Do you not know us?" he asked looming over them.

Athryn looked at him, then at Elyea, and finally at Khirro again. He turned with visible effort to scan the forest and beach.

"Where is Maes?" A croak emerged from his parched

throat. "Where is my brother?"

"You were gravely injured." Elyea moved the damp cloth to his lips, but he pushed it away. "Maes saved your life."

Athryn's expression changed; his eyes darted desperately between his companions, searching for an answer.

"But where is he?"

Somewhere in the forest, a bird sang an unfamiliar song, sad and lonely to Khirro's ear; the sound constricted his heart. How did you tell someone his brother gave his life to save him? He tried imagining what it would be like to wake and find the person you loved most in the world gone, but couldn't. He shook his head dispelling the thought as Elyea spoke again.

"... and he spoke, Athryn—he said the words to save you." She spoke quickly, emotion laid bare on her face as tears rimmed her eyes. "Because of him, you live."

Recognition dawned in Athryn's expression. He understood the cost of what his brother had done.

"Where?" he asked again, voice loud and gravelly. He grabbed Khirro's hand, pulled himself to stand on shaky legs.

"There." Ghaul pointed.

Khirro watched Athryn stumble toward the copse of trees sheltering his brother's body from the sun. He reeled across the swath of sand, stumbling, falling to his knees.

Elyea gasped, jumped up and rushed to help him. He took her hand, using it to climb to his feet, then staggered away; she followed no farther. The magician reached the trees, tore aside the blanket and fell to his knees at his brother's side.

A howl of misery broke the still afternoon air as Athryn found his voice, his sorrow stopping the bird's lonely song as though put to shame. Elyea's shoulders trembled as she wept along with her friend, feeling his loss. Was she doing as Khirro had, imaging what it would be like to lose a loved one? Was she thinking how she'd feel if she lost Aryann, or Leigha, or Despina?

Athryn cried out again, voice cracking with strain and dismay. Ghaul shifted uncomfortably from foot to foot. Khirro wondered what a warrior thought of such a display —likely that it was no way for a man to behave. Anger rose in Khirro's gut, nearly overpowering his sadness. Did this man have no feelings? If being a soldier meant dispensing with compassion, then he was glad to be called farmer after all.

Khirro shook his head realizing emotion tainted his opinion. How could he possibly know what Ghaul thought?

They waited in silence, each lost in their thoughts as Athryn unleashed his grief and sorrow again and again, cries echoing across the ocean, to be lost amongst the waves. Finally, his wailing ceased. Minutes passed. The silence quickly became more uncomfortable than his sorrowful wails.

"Should we go to him?" Khirro didn't know if he would want comfort or solitude were it him.

"No," Elyea said. "Leave him be."

Ten more minutes passed; each of them found unimportant activities to occupy themselves. Ghaul sharpened his boot knife; Elyea rolled a piece of grass aimlessly between her fingers; Khirro rubbed absently at the scar on his shoulder left by Ghaul's arrow. It was Ghaul who alerted the others with a grunt when Athryn rose from his dead brother's side.

The magician crossed the sand with slow, deliberate steps, the new pink scar on his belly gleaming in the sun. He carried Maes in his arms like a babe, the blanket which had covered him left behind. When he reached the brace of trees where his companions waited, he knelt and lay the body on a patch of yellow-brown grass as though setting down something infinitely delicate. Tears glistened on Athryn's cheeks, but composure showed on his face. He stood, head bowed.

"Tell me what happened," he said, voice raspy but stronger. No one said anything. "Please."

Elyea sucked a breath through her teeth as though inhaling the strength to tell Athryn the story. She paused, holding the air in her lungs, then told him of the one-eyed thief who appeared from nowhere in the night and his attempt to stop the man. Khirro's throat dried up as he listened, remembering how his thoughtless glance had given Athryn away. That made Maes' death his fault. How many more deaths would he be responsible for?

As Elyea told Athryn how the assassin's stroke opened his abdomen, his hand went to his belly, fingers stroking the smooth scar. Her voice broke with emotion as she described how Maes uttered indistinct words and opened his vein to save his brother, not allowing them to stop or interfere. When she finished, they stared at each other in awkward silence. Athryn's face remained slack, eyes gleaming, but he shed no more tears. Khirro shuffled his feet, disturbing the dry dirt beneath them.

"Can you bring him back?" he asked breaking the silence, feeling stupid for having asked.

"There is nothing I can do." Athryn shook his head. "I am but the speaker of the words. It was my brother who had the power of magic."

Khirro's brow wrinkled, unsure what Athryn meant. *Does he mean Maes was the magician, not he?* He opened his mouth to ask for clarification, but Ghaul put his thoughts to words first.

"But what of your burns?" the warrior asked sounding more angered than surprised. "You told us you survived dragon's breath."

Athryn sighed a breath heavy with memory.

"Maes faced the fiery breath and lived when he should

have died." He closed his eyes, reliving those memories or trying to force them from his head. "The killing breath was meant for me, but Maes saved me. I was left burned, touched by the flame, but not enough to have killed me. To gain the power of the dragon, one must live when they should have died. Maes should have been roasted alive, yet escaped unscathed."

"You lied to us," Ghaul said, his voice lowered to a growl.

Khirro glanced at him, at the anger lined upon his face, but didn't know what to think himself. Did Athryn tell them he was a magician, or did they assumed?

"It happened when we were young; Maes kept it hidden as long as he could," Athryn continued as though he hadn't heard Ghaul's accusation. "When it became clear the king would have Maes' tongue out for the magic he called blasphemy, he taught me what words he could, wrote the others on my skin. When my brother could no longer speak, we became as one magician split between two bodies, one wielding the power, the other the words." He paused as a wave of emotion contorted his face, shook his shoulders. "I believed neither of us complete without the other, until this. Until he made the ultimate sacrifice. Maes was complete."

Elyea reached out, her fingers brushing Athryn's arm, but he pulled away, stepping from the shade on to the sandy beach. Ghaul opened his mouth to say something, but a gesture from Athryn stopped him.

"He did not need me after all," he said, his voice weak. "I could not have done the same for him."

He stumbled away down the beach to be alone with his anguish.

***

The contempt in Ghaul's voice was obvious, like he spoke to a child who'd asked a question beneath consideration.

"No. It would be suicide to bring a decomposing corpse with us through the haunted land." He held up his hand, ticking off reasons on his fingers as he spoke. "It will slow us. It will make us ill. It will attract animals I'd rather not encounter. We have a thief to catch—we must move swiftly."

"The one-eyed man moves quickly," Shyn said.

He'd rejoined them at nightfall, reporting on the one-eyed man's progress as he dressed. Khirro told him what happened in his absence and soon after Athryn expressed his wish to take Maes with them.

"I must take my brother to the Necromancer," Athryn said, his voice flat. "I must bring him back from the dead, no matter the cost."

Ghaul sneered. "I'm happy to know you'd so readily sacrifice my life for the midget."

Athryn didn't react to the warrior's words.

"Could the Necromancer bring life back to a rotted

278

corpse?" Elyea's compassionate tone struck Khirro—her life would be in as much danger as Ghaul's, yet she still held concern for her friends.

"Darestat is the most powerful. I do not know he could, but I do not know he could not. When Maes put the blade to his wrist, he did not know if the magic would work, yet he drained his lifeblood to save me. I cannot do anything but try."

"You forget why we are here," Shyn said, his tone a counter-balance between Ghaul's anger and Elyea's sympathy—the voice of reason. "We must recover the blood of the king. If we fail in that, all will be lost and we may all die."

"Shyn's right," Khirro said mimicking the border guard's tone. "It's the king who's important. It's why we're here." He glanced at Athryn, hoping he wouldn't take his comments as belittling Maes' sacrifice, but he felt the pressure of time. The longer they tarried, the longer the one-eyed man's lead. "The Shaman said not to open the vial. If the blood dried up, the life would be gone. Maes emptied his blood into your wound, so a withered body will be equally useless to the Necromancer."

"If we made it," Ghaul glowered. "The smell would attract predators and carrion eaters to us like flies to shit."

Athryn stared past them into the night and the sea beyond. Khirro followed his gaze out over the ocean to the stars glimmering in the dark sky. When he looked back, a crooked smile crinkled the unscarred corner of Athryn's mouth.

"You are right, Khirro. Thank you for showing me the error of my judgment." He glanced to where his brother's body lay nearby in the sand. "Let us purify his body with fire, set his soul free to the winds for the Gods to collect."

Athryn struck out to collect driftwood for his brother's funeral pyre, leaving the others to do the same and wonder at his sudden change of heart. Khirro wandered down the beach, finding suitable pieces of wood as he followed the line of the forest, but he didn't dare stray into it. None of them did. Any forest is dangerous after dark, one in the haunted land more so. As Khirro made his way back to the spot for the pyre, Athryn joined him.

"Thank you, Khirro."

"For what?"

"What you said made sense. In my grief, I had forgotten." A tear glistened in his eye; Khirro bent to retrieve another chunk of driftwood.

"I don't understand."

"I am Maes' only chance now. I carry my brother's blood, much like you will again carry the king's."

Khirro's brow creased. He felt as though Athryn spoke to him in some foreign tongue, like when he cast a spell. His companion must have seen his confusion because he leaned closer, lowering his voice like they shared a secret.

"I have no vial of blood, Khirro. I am the vial. The blood

of my brother courses through my veins along with my own, kept alive until we reach the Necromancer. You reminded me of that."

Khirro tried to smile along with his friend, but a chill of dread crawled down his spine. Taking life from a glass container was one thing, but from a living person? Would Athryn survive, or were the brothers destined to spend the rest of their days trading life for life?

***

They trudged silently up the beach, four of them when there had been six. In addition to his own pack, Shyn's hung from Khirro's shoulder while somewhere ahead, a falcon cut through the night sky, ranging north and east to pick up the one-eyed man's trail. Behind them, the funeral pyre still burned, flames licking toward the night sky like the tongue of a snake—or a dragon, Khirro supposed.

They'd watched the fire until Athryn was satisfied his brother's soul had been released to the heavens on swirling gray smoke. As it burned, the magician who might no longer be called magician said nothing: no words of tribute, no words of mourning, no good-bye. Since telling Khirro his thoughts, he'd spoke not at tall. When Shyn talked of Maes' bravery, he only smiled sadly. When Elyea offered heartfelt condolences, he nodded. When Ghaul suggested it time to leave, he followed without complaint. The others attributed it to grief that Athryn would get over with time, but Khirro knew differently. It was hope staying

281

Athryn's tongue. Khirro wondered how far he'd go to protect the blood he carried within. Could they count on him to do what was needed when the time came to raise the king?

They followed the sand, staying clear of the forest. The thief had a day's head start, but their future would hold enough nights spent in unknown forests, so they decided to stay out of it as long as possible. Shyn tracked their quarry from the air, so he'd guide them to the best place to finally enter the trees.

Without the vial, Khirro's wounds ached and itched. He flexed his shoulder and rubbed his thigh. Athryn strode beside him silently, the black cloth mask he wore at night covering his face, hiding his thoughts and feelings. Khirro's own thoughts weighed on him, questions bouncing around in his head uncontrolled. Who was the one-eyed man? How did he know about the vial? How did he find them?

None of the possible answers pleased Khirro; most of them frightened him more.

28

Morning sun peeked over the treetops as the forest ended abruptly, opening on a vast field of yellow grass standing higher than the top of a tall man's helm. An unfelt breeze swayed the grass, sending waves across it like the surface of a soft, yellow lake. Suath strained to see over but found himself unable to determine how far the grassland stretched.

He stopped on the short patch of dirt and rock dividing the forest from the field and pulled some salt pork from his pack. For more than twenty-four hours he'd pushed on, uncaring of the tales of the haunted land Lakesh. He'd been here before and nothing happened to prove a hex hung over the land, as nothing happened this time. Companions had lost their lives here, but he saw that as a self-fulfilling prophecy—if one came to a place thinking it evil and dangerous, it would prove so. If you chose not to believe old wives' tales, as Suath chose, this was simply another foreign land of grass and trees and soil oblivious and uncaring of the comings and goings of man.

Suath chewed the tough meat and wondered at the strip of bare earth stretching away both directions, a natural border between forest and field. No plants grew on the dry, brown earth scattered with rocks of all sizes; the width of the border looked uniform, almost man-made.

Strange.

Suath swigged from his water skin, wishing it contained wine, then hung it back on his belt and touched the pouch hanging beside it to feel the hard outline of the vial hidden within. Therrador wouldn't be pleased if he knew the bearer yet lived, but he'd never find out. If the cursed country didn't kill them, he'd find them himself. Either way, he'd collect the entire reward; Therrador need not know if he swung the sword himself.

If he ever saw Therrador again.

Suath hadn't cared what the vial contained when offered the reward, but he wasn't a stupid man. He saw the blood, he overheard from whom it came. Others might pay more for such a thing.

Finishing the piece of meat, Suath crouched and rolled up the cuff of his breeches. In his haste to get away with the vial, he'd neglected something. He brushed his fingers across the flesh of his calf, tracing the bumps and ridges of the scars carved there. Finding an unmarked spot, he pulled his knife, gritted his teeth and drew the tip an inch along his leg, cutting deep.

"For the magic-user," he muttered. His finger searched for and found another as-yet unscarred area. "And here will be for the rest of them."

He nodded, satisfied, and pulled his pant leg back in place ignoring the blood trickling into his boot. After cleaning and re-sheathing his knife, he crossed the rocky ground to the edge of the field, looking up at the clear sky as he went. Overhead, a falcon wheeled and glided, its huge wings dark against the blue sky. Suath grunted. The bird had followed him off and on since he fled the beach. Some doing of the magician he left bleeding on the sand? Perhaps the counter on his leg was premature. Too bad if the magician lived, he had learned long ago the least dangerous magic user was a dead one. He dismissed the bird. It didn't matter if they knew where to find him, they had to catch him.

And then they had to take the vial from him.

Then they'll earn their cuts.

He grinned and stepped into the wall of grass, the tips of some blades brushing his cheek. Its toughness surprised him. Instead of parting easily like a curtain, each blade stood straight and strong like a reed, resisting his movement with the stubbornness of a living thing. After a couple steps fighting its firmness, he realized he'd have to cut his way across the field like a farmer harvesting hay. It would slow him, but his substantial lead gave him time. He stepped back from the grass and drew his sword.

As steel scraped leather, the grass leaned away, shrinking from the blade like a child seeing punishment coming. Suath blinked and shook his head to dispel what must be a trick of the light. The mercenary set his jaw, gripped his sword with two hands, and swung.

The sharp edge cut through the grass, though not easily, clearing a patch ten feet wide at the level of Suath's knee. A sudden wind rose, sighing through the field with the low howl of an injured dog. The uncut blades around him whipped and swirled with the wind, lashing his hands and face. Suath swung again, hewing another patch, and the wind ceased as suddenly as it had risen. He paid it no attention and pressed on, each swing of his sword extending the path before him, each stroke leaving hundreds of fallen blades of grass in its wake.

Half an hour passed. Suath's battle hardened arms ached, sweat streamed from under his helm into his bare eye socket, irritating the scarred flesh, but he kept moving. The deeper he went into the field, the more resistant the grass became. His sword swung left and right rhythmically, opening the path before him. As time stretched on, his pace slowed. He wanted to keep going but had to rest and catch his breath if he was to make it across the field—he didn't even know how much farther he had to go. He stopped, leaning on his sword, its tip inserted in the ground, and breathed deep, then stretched to his fullest to peer over the grass before him. He saw only more grass. He shook his head and looked back to see how far he'd come.

The sight behind him made his breath catch in his throat. The knee high stubs of grass were not yellow like the uncut field around him; instead, the trail of cut grass glistened crimson and rust. Suath's brow creased.

Some fluid in the blades, he thought, rationalizing what he saw. *Not blood, but like sap from a tree.*

As he turned back to his task, the wind sighed again, whipping a blade of grass against his cheek, drawing blood. Suath whirled toward it, bringing his sword to bear and another struck him from behind, opening a cut on the back of his neck. He spun back to his right to face an attacker he neither saw nor knew how to fight. An unfamiliar feeling crept into Suath's gut, curling up in the bottom and making itself at home: fear.

Heavy gusts of wind whipped the grass, flagellating his face, dancing away then reaching for his eye. Suath swung his sword, called on ingrained combat skills to quell the sickening feeling in his stomach. His steel swept left to right, right to left, each time cutting empty air as the wind pulled the grass away only to send it back with every opening. A grin crossed Suath's face; he'd never have guessed a pasture would prove the most formidable swordsman he'd ever faced.

He cut at the grass again, but this time his sword halted in its path as though striking a tree. He pulled to free it, looked down and laughed throatily. Grass wound around his steel, hundreds of blades holding it. He wrenched it, cutting some of the grass. It fell away only to be replaced by still more twining itself about his sword. Suath planted his feet and pulled again, leveraging all his strength and weight as he'd done so many times on so many battlefields.

It didn't move.

The wind rose higher, howling across the field. A wave crashed through the grass, tore the sword from his hands. He watched in disbelief as the weapon floated away on the tops of the grass as though passed hand to hand until it disappeared in the distance. The muscles in his jaw flexed; he pulled his dagger from his belt. He'd not die here—not in this country, not in this field. Too many worthy opponents had tried to take his life to die like this.

The mercenary spun, intending to retreat from the unearthly field, but nearly tumbled to the ground. Blades of grass wound around his ankle held him fast. He tried to move the other foot only to find it fettered, too. He swung his blade to free himself, but more grass caught his wrist, twisting his arm, forcing the dagger from his grip. The wind screamed, a banshee howl filling his ears, pounding in his head. The tall blades of grass bent and swirled, whipping his body, pulling him down. He fought against the impossibly strong grip, but the more he thrashed, the stronger it became.

The wind died, the howling ceased.

Flat on his back, Suath stared up at the blue sky. Tendrils of grass crawled across him, coiling about his neck and limbs, reaching up his sleeves and under his belt like so many snakes. The grip grew firmer still, pulling at him, crushing him. He laughed, the sound strangled as the blades around his throat tightened. Suath had known since the beginning of memory he wouldn't die of old age, but he'd expected to be felled by a superior foe on the battlefield, or done in by a stealthy knife in the dark. What would he have thought if he knew he'd lose his life to a weed?

His laughing ceased, his smile fled. The mercenary didn't cry out, he never had before this, he wasn't about to start now. Instead, he looked up at the sky, unblinking and unrepentant, and saw that the falcon no longer circled overhead.

29

They stood around the body in silence, but not the reverential silence with which they'd gathered for Maes. Horrified awe inspired this silence.

Athryn refused to cross the bare ground and enter the sea of grass, though he didn't say why, so he and Elyea waited for the others at the forest's edge. Khirro, Ghaul and Shyn picked their way cautiously along the knee-high, rust colored path, aware the taller grass might hide anything or anyone. No wind stirred the uncut grass; each blade drooped near the top like heads hung in mourning.

The one-eyed man's body was so sunken into the shallow grass, they didn't see it until almost upon it. Spatters of scarlet darkened the rusty grass around him. Khirro had never seen anything like this done to a man and if his companions had, they didn't say.

The man's head still clung to his neck, his scarred face laced with fine cuts. Both eyes were missing. His body lay open gullet to groin, all contents except backbone removed—organs, arteries, bones—everything gone. The husk of a man lay before them, a skin with only arms and legs and head. Khirro wiped the back of his hand across his lips and found his mouth dry as the beach they'd left behind, but his stomach didn't churn, he felt no urge to retch. The extremity of the mutilation made it seem unreal.

"What do you think happened?" Shyn asked, his tone cold. None of them took their eyes from the carnage.

Ghaul shook his head. "It doesn't matter. We have to find the vial and leave before we find out first hand."

"Where could it be?" The thought of spending time near the body searching for the vial sent a chill up Khirro's spine.

"Anywhere." Ghaul drew his sword and shifted a flap of skin—once part of the man's chest—with the tip. Under it lay his shirt and hauberk, flayed open and laid aside in the same manner as his torso. "Pockets and pouches would be a good place to start."

Ghaul and Shyn fell to the grisly work of shifting aside hanging skin and searching through blood soaked clothes as Khirro watched, his head shaking side to side slightly.

What happened here?

The sweet smell of the ripening corpse insinuated itself into his thoughts as his eyes surveyed the flaps of skin, the picked-clean backbone. Something wasn't right about this; something was oddly missing.

Where are the bugs? He directed his gaze skyward. *And the deathbirds?*

No vultures or crows circled above, no animals appeared to have disturbed the body despite the time it must have laid here before they came upon it. Not a single fly alit on the grisly flesh to feed on spilled blood. If nothing came to feed on the corpse, where had the man's insides gone?

Khirro turned from his companions and took a few steps back down the path of short, rusty grass. He didn't know what he looked for, perhaps the one-eyed man's heart, or a string of bowels, some bones, something to make sense of the gruesome scene. He saw none of them. No clue about what happened to his one-time attacker. He took another step, staring at the ground before him, when something off the path caught his attention: a patch of light brown, barely distinguishable in the yellowed grass. Khirro moved closer, crouched, then recognized it as a deerskin pouch.

"Have you found something, Khirro?" Shyn called.

"I think so."

He reached for it, but somehow it moved from his grasp, floating a few inches into the air. He stretched farther and again it moved. Khirro pulled his arm back, puzzlement allaying fear for the moment.

"What is it?"

Khirro jumped. He hadn't noticed Ghaul and Shyn come to his side. Heart hammering in his chest, he looked up at them.

"A pouch."

He turned his attention back to the deerskin satchel. It had settled back on the ground, defying him to reach for it again—he didn't.

"Is it in there?" Ghaul asked, impatience obvious in his

voice.

"I don't know. I can't get it."

"What do you mean you can't get it?"

Ghaul pushed in beside him and bent to retrieve the pouch. His fingers brushed its surface as a ripple ran through the grass, moving it out of his reach. He cursed and reached again but the pouch jumped away as though tossed hand to hand.

"By the Gods," Shyn whispered. "This place is haunted."

Ghaul scoffed and drew his sword. "Weeds need to be cut, that's all."

A breeze stirred the tall grass, calling the drooping tops to attention as they swayed with its touch. Khirro watched it move, unease growing. There was something about the wind, something unidentifiable that brought cold sweat to his brow.

"Hold, Ghaul." Shyn touched the warrior's forearm; Khirro wondered if he felt the same thing he did. "Let me try."

He pulled his gauntlet on firmly and reached for the pouch like a cat stalking a bird. Closer and closer he inched; the pouch didn't move. As his fingers touched its drawstring, a blade of grass coiled and shifted, bouncing it away from his grasp.

"Enough games," Ghaul growled. Shyn stepped aside. "I'm in no mood for this. The sooner we're away from here, the better."

He drew his sword back and the wind rose, shuddering through the tall glass, shifting it, swirling it. Khirro understood the source of his unease—the wind didn't move his hair, he didn't feel it against his cheek.

"Wait, Ghaul. I think..."

His words came too late. The sharp age of the soldier's sword cut stalks of grass. The pouch toppled to the ground at Shyn's feet. He snatched it before it bounced out of his reach.

"Got it," he said before a deafening wail rose about them.

Shyn tore his sword from its scabbard, ready for attack from some unseen animal, but Khirro knew no beast hid in the grass. The grass was the beast. It whipped and whirled about them forcing them together, pushing them back toward the man's emptied body.

"We have to get out of here," Khirro screamed. Ghaul and Shyn both looked at him; he didn't know if they'd heard him. "Run!"

He pushed his companions ahead of him, urging them down the path toward the forest and what he hoped would be safety. As he ran, he dared a look over his shoulder and saw the wall of grass at the end of the path slam down, missing his heels by inches. Six feet of grass came down on the path from all directions, engulfing the one-eyed man's ravaged corpse. When it rose, the body was gone.

They raced down the hewn trail but Khirro felt as though he ran in dream-time, his legs pumping but carrying him nowhere. Ahead, Shyn and Ghaul pulled away. He glanced down, thinking suck sand hidden beneath the grass slowed him, but it was the grass itself. Yellow blades reached from all sides, grasping at his arms and legs. He pulled away, but a few hung on, slowing him, and the slower he moved, the more blades that gained purchase. Panic flashed through his head as he realized exactly what had happened to their pursuer. If he didn't free himself, the same fate awaited him.

Khirro called for help, but the howling field drowned his cries. He reached for his sword knowing Ghaul's blade brought this upon them, so the weapon likely wouldn't help, but what else could he do? His fingertips grazed the polished pommel before the grass wrenched his arm away.

He reached again, stretching as far as his bonds allowed, but his fingers only brushed it. Struggling and straining, Khirro stumbled on; a blade of grass finally broke giving him enough play to wrap his fingers around the grip. He drew the black blade, steel singing against leather above the grassy cacophony.

The sword didn't reflect sunlight the way a normal sword did, instead sucking in the light, feeding upon it. The red runes scrawling along the length of the blade crawled and flowed like blood in veins below the surface of the steel. Khirro brandished the weapon above his head, readying to cut himself free, when the grass released him. He stumbled to the ground, disappearing into the rusty grass, then clamored to his feet with the coppery smell of blood in his nostrils. Ahead, Shyn and Ghaul reached the edge of the field and gestured him on as Elyea joined them, the concern on her face plain even from this distance.

Khirro looked back. The grass which had been holding him had retreated from the path. At the far end, where the one-eyed man had been, the tall grass on either side crashed together like waves colliding where opposing currents met. The line of grass surged toward him and he turned and ran, sword in hand, breath shallow and quick. At the end of the path, his companions moved aside, making room. He didn't dare look back. If he let fear slow him, it would mean his life.

Thirty feet from safety, he felt a rush of air at his back as the wave of grass bore down on him. The sheer volume of air being moved pushed him off balance and he lunged forward, desperate to be free of the cursed field. His shoulder struck rocky earth and he rolled with the impact, coming to rest on his back, eyes closed tight, waiting to be crushed by the deadly grass.

After a moment, he opened his eyes to see blue sky above, and then Elyea's relieved face. Her mouth pulled into a strained smile and her lips moved, asking if he was all right. He nodded as best he could then she leaned in and kissed his cheek.

30

Shyn stepped from behind the tree, fastening the final button of his tunic. He was self-conscious about transforming and had only allowed them to see it the one time.

"Well?" Ghaul asked impatiently.

Khirro didn't understand why, after all that had happened, he still didn't trust Shyn. Perhaps they'd never get along.

"There's nothing to see. The forest is too dense."

"What use is a man who turns into a bird if he sees no more than a man who can't?"

"Perhaps you'd like to try?"

"Enough," Elyea snapped. "The two of you arguing like children doesn't help us find our way." She looked at Khirro sitting on a fallen cedar, Athryn silent beside him. He read the question on her face before words left her lips. "Think, Khirro. Which way do we go?"

The forest around them was thicker and quieter than a forest should be. No bird calls shrilled the air, no animals foraged for food, not so much as a mosquito buzzed around their heads. In another place, under other circumstances, such quiet might be peaceful, refreshing, but not here. With every turn they took, every step they made, a sense of doom followed, closing in, attaching itself to their skin, filling their lungs with every breath. Khirro expelled some of the feeling from his lungs with a heavy sigh.

"I don't know, Elyea." He didn't look at her, didn't want to see disappointment on her face.

"I thought the Shaman showed you the way," Ghaul said, redirecting his frustration from Shyn to Khirro.

"He did."

"So get us where we need to go."

Khirro looked at his feet, frustrated and embarrassed. The Shaman showed him the way but he couldn't remember it. *Don't stray from the path*, the tyger had said. Now he understood the beast's warning—once off the trail, you might not find your way back.

"It is not that you cannot remember, Khirro," Athryn said. Khirro looked at him, gaping. These were the first words he'd spoken since they cremated Maes' body. "You have no reference. What is the first thing you remember Bale showed you of Lakesh?"

They awaited his answer, blame in their eyes, and anger rose in his chest. He'd neither asked nor wanted to lead this expedition. The Shaman cursed him to it. Nor had he begged any of these people to join him, each had insisted. Did they not think there may be a danger this might happen? Yet there they stood, accusing him. In that moment, he didn't want them there, didn't need their so-called help.

297

Then Elyea stood beside him, rested her hand gently on his shoulder, and the anger melted away.

How could I think that about them? They've been there for me when I needed them. Saved my life. His cheeks flushed red with guilt.

"What do you remember?" she asked, her voice soothing. He looked into her deep green eyes and nearly fell in.

"A ruined village." His hands fiddled in his lap; he made them stop. "It sits on the shore of an inland lagoon, south of where we landed on the beach, that much I know."

"South then," Shyn said. He pulled his pack on and started out without waiting for the others.

"He said south," Ghaul called after him derisively. "That's this way."

"I'm the one who flies above the trees." Shyn laughed. "I know where the sun sits in the sky."

"You wouldn't know where your ass sits without a map."

The soldiers closed on one another, both reaching for their swords. Before they got close, the ground shook beneath their feet, stopping them.

"What was that?" Elyea asked, dagger already in hand. The ground shook again.

"That way." Shyn pointed the direction he'd already begun walking.

They crept forward, Shyn and Ghaul in the lead. The

forest heaved and swelled with hillocks and buried roots, forced them to clamor over fallen logs. They moved carefully, straining to be quiet as they climbed up a hill, then down the other side. The ground shook once more, this time accompanied by a low rumble like a boulder tumbling down a distant mountain.

Cresting another hill, Ghaul stopped without warning, breath hissing through his teeth. Khirro crouched beside him peering down into the hollow at the bottom of the hill. Stumps crowded the forest floor, many of them wider across than a man is tall. Directly across from them, the next hill had been hollowed out into a man-made cave, snarled roots dangling from the ceiling.

Khirro stared down the swell trying to make sense of what he saw. His mother's stories of men bigger than nature should allow, as tall as three normal men, came to mind. These men made meals of any creature they got their hands on, devouring everything, even the bones. But surely they couldn't be true, they were merely stories told to keep children from misbehaving.

Like the stories of magicians and Necromancers and men who turned into animals.

Suddenly, he understood why they hadn't seen any animals or birds in the forest. The forest creatures knew better than to be here.

None of them wanted to be food for a giant.

***

299

The smell of dirt and peat filled Khirro's nostrils as they lay atop the ridge watching, waiting. The earth here smelled different than on his farm., altered by the detritus from the trees. Still, it was the earth's aroma and it provided him some comfort. He shook his head at the thought.

How does one feel comfort while spying on a giant?

Athryn lay beside him, breathing quietly. Somewhere above the trees, Shyn's wings caught air as he scouted a path past the giant. Disagreeing with Shyn as always, Ghaul took Elyea to find a way around the encampment from ground level. Khirro didn't like the idea but, in their effort to stay quiet, he had no chance to voice his opinion.

They watched the giant making ready for the night. The huge man stood at least the height of three tall men, his head dominated by a sloping forehead flowing straight into his twisted nose. Cracked, puffy lips parted on gapped teeth as it pulled small trees out of the ground by their roots like a child might pluck dandelions for amusement. These logs—branches in the giant's hands—it snapped in two over its knee and piled beside a well-used fire pit.

Khirro looked on, fascinated and horrified, at this creature from his bedtime stories. He'd never believed in them—or so he told himself—but they'd kept him from wandering into the forest alone, made him go to bed when told. When he grew older, he saw the stories for what they were: untrue lessons meant to frighten, to teach, to warn.

Or so he believed until an undead soldier pulled helmet from head, ready to strike him dead. Dead men walking, magic, a man who became a bird, malevolent grass, a giant: if all these things existed, did it make dragons, ghosts, demons and Gods real, too?

A rustle of leaves pulled Khirro from his musings. He rolled to his back, brandishing his dagger, and saw Shyn standing on the hill, naked and haggard like a man who'd worked for days without sleep. Athryn gathered the border guard's clothes he'd kept with him and crept down to meet him, Khirro close behind.

"Anything?" Khirro whispered as Shyn pulled his breeches on.

The bird man shot him a glance telling him not to speak, then shook his head. The forest was thicker than any he'd seen, Shyn had told them before, its canopy so dense he couldn't fly through it. They waited while he donned his clothes, then crept to the crest of the hill again, bellies to the ground. When they reached the top of the rise, Khirro's blood chilled in his veins.

The giant was gone.

Khirro's eyes darted across the clearing. No sign of the creature. Shyn looked behind them and Khirro's throat clogged with fear. Had the giant seen them? Scented them? Surely something that size couldn't sneak up on them.

"Where is it?" Khirro's whisper was barely more than a breath.

Bruce Blake

Neither man responded. Minutes passed as they scanned the forest. Somewhere amongst the trees lurked a creature who could crush them in its hand, split their bones for the marrow like a normal man snapping a twig. A shudder shook Khirro's body and Athryn gestured for him to remain still.

It felt to Khirro like they lay there a very long time before they heard Elyea cry out. Instinctively, Khirro moved to get to his feet, hand reaching for his sword, but Shyn's hand on his shoulder stopped him. He settled back, body tense.

Another shout sounded through the trees, this time Ghaul's voice, followed closely by a deep throated roar sounding more beast than man. Trees groaned and brush shook, then all noise ceased. A minute passed, two. Khirro's muscles tensed, nearly tying themselves in knots as he readied to rush to his friends' aid though; with time to think about it, the thought of such action became more difficult, foolhardy. He looked at Shyn; the border guard thankfully gestured for him to wait.

The ground shook with the giant's footsteps. Khirro wondered how this creature could possibly have been quiet enough to sneak away without their knowledge.

Elyea called out again, closer this time. The trees beside the dugout-cave shook, then parted, and the giant emerged, a crooked grin marring its flat face. It carried Elyea under one arm, her arms pinned at her sides, legs

302

flailing uselessly. The giant's other arm hung at its side. Fingers the thickness of tree branches gripped the back of Ghaul's tunic as it dragged the warrior through the brush.

Ghaul's arms and legs hung limp.

31

Therrador shifted, seeking comfort on the uncomfortable seat. The throne wasn't designed for relaxation, but he was confident he'd get used to it. He glanced around the throne room, unconsciously noting where he'd make changes: Braymon's coat-of-arms would have to go, of course, replaced by his own—a crossed sword and staff. And the tapestries would be supplanted. He and Braymon always had dissimilar tastes—in decoration, in clothes—in everything except women. He scowled at the thought and put it immediately out of his head.

Leaning back in the hard seat, Therrador wondered how the mercenary fared. He knew the man was a ruthless killer—there was no man alive more likely to follow a grisly task to its end—but could he be trusted? A man willing to sell his sword to the highest bidder didn't instill confidence in his employer. Suath would probably try to sell the vial elsewhere, even without knowing its contents, to see if he could get more than Therrador offered. Most wouldn't be interested in a vial of unidentified blood, but some might guess its contents, perhaps Suath himself. Better not to take any chances.

Hanh Perdaro's network learned of two Vendarians found dead on the dock near a slip that shouldn't have been empty. They must have made it to Lakesh, or tried to, if the Small Sea didn't claim them. Therrador never expected they'd make it as far as the haunted land—Suath would be penalized, if he returned.

The king's advisor fidgeted again. The mercenary would follow his quarry to the cursed earth. If he took the vial from them there, it was an easy trip up the coast to Kanos where a man with a vial of blood and a taste for money would have more luck finding a buyer than in Vendaria. As soon as he heard about the stolen boat, Therrador sent more soldiers after them—both the man carrying the vial and the mercenary. It didn't calm his nerves, however.

He glanced at Graymon playing near the foot of the throne—knights and dragons, as usual. The sight of his son brought a pained smile to his lips.

He looks so much like his mother.

A knock on the throne room door brought him to his feet. It was best he not be seen sitting upon the throne—not yet. He descended the three short steps from the dais and took a seat at the granite table set to the side.

"Enter."

The thick oaken doors swung inward and Hanh

Perdaro, Voice of the People, entered. He crossed halfway to where Therrador sat, then stopped and bowed shallowly at the waist.

"My Lord."

"Perdaro," Therrador replied with a nod. "To what do I owe the pleasure?"

"I need your ear, my Lord." He glanced at Graymon knocking over knights with the wooden dragon—in his games, the dragon always won. "Alone."

Therrador looked at his son again, then motioned for the door guard.

"Graymon, Daddy needs to speak to Uncle Hanh alone. Go with the young man, he'll get you a treat from the kitchen."

Graymon looked up, waving the carved dragon defiantly at the guard. "No," he cried. "No one can capture Gorgo, king of the dragons."

Shaking his head apologetically at Perdaro, Therrador rose and went to his son, crouched in front of him. Before opening his mouth to speak, Graymon lashed out with the dragon and struck Therrador's forearm painfully with its wooden teeth. Therrador's combat reflexes responded automatically. He grabbed the boy's wrist, making him drop the toy. Graymon's face turned instantly from joy to hurt, his eyes watering, mouth drooping. Therrador released his arm, regretting his reaction.

"Please, Graymon. Da needs to speak with Uncle

305

Hanh." His soothing tones had little effect on the boy's quivering lip. Therrador stroked his cheek. "The nice man will get you a treat. I bet there's cookies."

Graymon's face brightened like a cloud passing from the sun. He jumped up and ran to the door guard while Gorgo, king of the dragons, lay forgotten on the floor. Therrador watched him leave, then returned to the table and motioned for Perdaro to sit.

"What's on your mind, Hanh?"

The Voice of the People took a seat directly across from Therrador, taking a moment to straighten his tunic and smooth his sparse hair before speaking.

"There are rumors," he began. Therrador tensed at the words—Hanh Perdaro didn't tend toward dramatics. "I have heard whispers the blood of the king is bound for Lakesh, Therrador."

The king's advisor stiffened at the sound of his own name; he'd become used to being addressed as 'my Lord' and the like. The day the entire country referred to him as 'my liege', 'your highness' or 'your grace' couldn't come soon enough. But first these whispers needed to be dealt with.

"I have already told you , Hanh," Therrador said carefully controlling his voice. "Bale is dead, as are Rudric and Gendred. None escaped. You saw the empty vial. The king's blood fed the parched earth at the foot of the Isthmus fortress."

"It's not I who disbelieves. My opinion is inconsequential. I speak for the people. If not quelled, whispers and rumors become rumblings, and nothing good comes of rumblings." He paused to glance over first one shoulder, then the other—a habit born of listening to and re-telling whispers. "It's also said the Mourning Sword was not with Bale's body. Some see it as an ill omen."

Therrador harrumphed. "Pillaged, that's all. What man wouldn't want such a sword for their own, whether they knew what it was or not."

"But the people say--"

The slap of Therrador's open hand on the smooth granite table top echoed across the chamber. He glared at Perdaro and surreptitiously rubbed his stinging palm against his thigh. For this man, he had more patience for conversation than most, but he found his patience easily worn thin these days.

"There is a war being fought," he snapped. "Do the people whisper about that? The kingdom needs a king, or all will be lost. What do their rumors say about that?" He glared at the Voice of the People, scrutinizing his expression, but it betrayed nothing of his own thoughts. "That's where my priorities must lie, not in chasing a hope we know false. Braymon's dead and gone and I'm the one he named to take his place if exactly this came to pass. The sooner the people stop their whisperings and accept their new king, the easier life will be for all."

307

Bruce Blake

They looked across the table at each other, neither speaking for a minute. Therrador wondered if he'd allowed his anger to make him say too much, but Perdaro's face showed nothing. The things this man must have heard through the years—some of them enough to make most men cringe, or cry, but the Voice of the People couldn't afford such luxuries. He spoke little, listened much, and reacted not at all.

"What does my Lord wish to do?"

Therrador drummed his fingers on the table, acting as though his palm didn't still hurt. He stopped and rubbed his chin.

"Start your own rumors, Hanh," he said finally. "Tell the people what they want to hear. Whisper that we caught a Kanosee who survived the fight outside the fortress walls. With his capture imminent, he emptied Braymon's blood from the vial. Tell them we recovered the Mourning Sword from his butchered corpse and it's secreted away until there is a Shaman to replace Bale." He stared at Perdaro, looking past him, through him. "Tell them Braymon is dead, he won't be coming back, and his dying wish was for Therrador to be king in his stead."

Hanh Perdaro nodded, unspeaking. His face remained an emotionless mask. When Therrador said no more, he stood, bowed at the waist and went to leave. As his hand touched the brass knob on the oaken door, Therrador spoke again.

"And Hanh, tell Sir Alton I need to see him. There's a one-eyed man who must not enter the kingdom alive."

Perdaro nodded and left the throne room, closing the door behind him. Therrador leaned back in his chair, crossed his hands across his stomach. He glanced at the wall hangings, imagining them depicting his own acts of heroism. Perhaps one of them would show Gorgo, king of the dragons. Graymon would like that.

"Tell them the king is dead," he said to the empty room. "Tell them 'long live the king'."

32

Night fell but the forest remained illuminated by the flames from the giant's fire reaching toward the boughs high overhead, flickering and dancing higher than the height of the giant. The creature squatted at the edge of the fire pit, staring mesmerized into its depths, occasionally poking a burning log with the tip of a spear longer than any Khirro had ever seen. Several yards from where it crouched, Elyea and Ghaul sat back to back, a thick rope woven of green vines looped around them. Their chins drooped forward, touching their chests, so Khirro couldn't tell whether they were conscious or not.

Overhead, Shyn-as-falcon perched on a limb, awaiting the signal. Khirro and Athryn crept around the giant's encampment, painstakingly picking their way to a spot close to their captive companions. As the moment for action drew near, Khirro's gut twisted. He touched the vial tucked inside his tunic, seeking comfort and courage from it, but found only cool glass. Over the past weeks, he'd tasted fear like he'd never experienced. This was worse. Anticipation multiplied fear exponentially, growing it beyond the bounds he thought possible. Athryn dug an elbow into his side, urging him forward. Khirro drew a deep, slow breath, preparing to move.

Nothing happened.

He tried again, struggling to make his limbs carry him forward to rescue his friends, but they'd have nothing of it. Fear paralyzed him, froze him to the ground with his face in the dirt like the snake it made him feel.

He cursed his stubborn muscles. Both Elyea and Ghaul gave up everything to aid him on a journey not their own, risking their lives for him, yet here he lay, unable to propel himself to rescue them. Disgust and self-loathing coiled in his belly. Hadn't enough people died because of him, because of his fear? He wouldn't be able to live knowing these two perished because of his cowardice.

He was gathering his strength, focusing on one limb at a time, when the giant pulled his spear from the fire and gazed at the glowing tip. A homely grin twisted the giant's lips as it looked from spear to prisoners, a low chuckle rolling through its yellow-brown teeth. The creature extended the weapon, the glowing tip leaving a ribbon of gray smoke trailing behind, until it hovered a few inches from Elyea's cheek.

The heat brought her from her daze, wrenching her mind back from wherever it had gone to escape. She raised her head, eyes widening when she saw the glowing spear head—leaf-shaped and the length of a short sword—pressing close to her flesh. She leaned away, feet scrabbling against the forest floor sending dirt and decayed evergreen needles spraying away, but Ghaul's limp form lashed to her back held her from moving. The giant laughed at the high-pitched squeaks of fear escaping her throat and flicked the tip toward her. She flinched and the beast laughed louder.

Khirro's teeth clenched watching the giant play his game over and over: threaten her, watch her cringe, laugh aloud. Not until the orange glow faded did the giant lose interest. Khirro let out his breath as the creature drew the weapon away. Tears ran down Elyea's face leaving clean tracks on her dirty cheeks.

The giant thrust the spear once more; Elyea dodged but the point continued past her ear and brushed Ghaul's cheek—Khirro heard the sizzle of hot metal on flesh. Ghaul's head jerked up; he yelped with pain and twisted away, his weight shifting enough to tumble them on their sides. Elyea struggled against the rope and freed one hand —she must have been working the knot while she feigned unconsciousness. The giant grunted a curse and slammed his spear to the ground in disgust.

311

As Ghaul writhed on the ground beside her struggling to loose himself, Elyea freed her other hand. The giant reached for her but she avoided his clutch. The huge man ignored her as she scrambled away, concerning himself with the most dangerous threat first. He sat Ghaul up like a child playing with a doll and hit him open-handed across the face, knocking him unconscious. Khirro tensed. This was the time to act, but he did nothing as the giant closed the distance to Elyea in two strides, wrapped his arm around her waist and lifted her from the ground. The creature laughed as he brought her back to his seat by the fire. He pulled her face close to his, his tongue snaking from his mouth and up Elyea's cheek. She cringed, struggling to pull away, her face screwed up in disgust.

From above, a shriek rang through the night—Shyn had waited long enough. The gray bird swooped from the dark, talons raking the giant's head. The creature bellowed, swung its free arm wildly, but Shyn avoided the blow. Athryn jumped to his feet and pulled his sword. Khirro didn't take the time to consider his options, leaping up alongside the magician, thankful his limbs did as he asked. He drew the Mourning Sword, vaguely noticing the blade looked blacker, the red runes glowing fiercely in the firelight.

Shyn swooped again as Elyea fought the giant's grip, but there was no element of surprise this time. His fist looped at Shyn; the falcon dodged, but the blow caught

312

him mid-wing, spinning him away. In the moment of distraction, Athryn rushed the giant, sword raised to strike.

The giant saw him at the last second and brought his arm down to block the sweep of Athryn's sword; his blade separated the giant's meaty finger from his hand. The monster howled in pain and rage, nearly deafening them, but reacted immediately catching Athryn's hip with its hair-covered foot. The magician spun away and fell to the ground beside Ghaul. Khirro stepped up in the magician's place, the Mourning Sword raised above his head.

The giant's eyes locked on Khirro's, fury burning in his gaze, freezing Khirro's hand. The beast reached toward the fire, blood dripping from the stump of his finger, sizzling on the hot rocks at the fire's edge. Elyea struggled, her strength waning as the creature's grip tightened.

If I don't do something, she won't survive his grasp.

He took a tentative step forward as the giant's remaining fingers closed around a log, grasping it and swinging it in one motion, spilling the fire out of its pit. Khirro ducked as a small tree engulfed in flame passed over his head close enough to singe his hair. He stumbled back, dodging the giant's back swing, mind searching for a way to counter-strike that wouldn't be suicide.

How will I reach him?

The answer came on the voice of a falcon. Shyn dove at the giant's face, a talon raking his cheek. Khirro lunged, the Mourning Sword a black and red streak cutting the air,

313

but the tip only grazed his foe's stomach opening little more than a scratch. He dove away from the giant's retaliatory blow, sprawling on the ground. In the flicker of a second he rolled across the ground, Khirro saw Ghaul had regained consciousness and Athryn was crawling toward the fray, favoring his injured hip.

The giant brought the flaming log down in an overhead blow, its flaming end brushing the tree boughs above. Khirro rolled away as it slammed the ground, sparks exploding into the air. He caught sight of Elyea. She'd pulled a blade from her boot and was attempting to manipulate the point into the giant's ribs. Panic rushed into Khirro's chest—if she knifed the brute, he'd crush her for her troubles.

"No!"

Khirro struggled to his knees as Elyea pushed the blade with all her remaining strength. The small knife must have felt no more than a pinprick to the beast's thickly muscled ribs, but it surprised him, sent him reeling back. When his foot came down on a smoldering chunk of wood, sending him off balance, Shyn dove in. Khirro lunged, rolling under the log as the giant flailed, and swung the Mourning Sword, a prayer on his lips—if he missed, it would be his life, and the lives of his friends.

He didn't.

The Mourning Sword's impossibly sharp edge cut the flesh at the back of the giant's ankle, severing flesh and

314

muscle and tendon. The moment blood touched the sword, the glowing runes spilled out, covering the blade, turning the length of the sword red.

The beast put weight on his wounded leg and howled when he found he couldn't, then lifted the injured foot, hopping as he raised the burning club to vanquish the foe on the ground at his feet. Khirro gritted his teeth awaiting the blow as he had lying on the dirt of the Isthmus Fortress's courtyard an eternity ago.

If I'd died then, everyone else would be alive.

Before the giant struck, Shyn swooped in and buried his talons in the giant's shoulder. The creature bellowed and Khirro swung the Mourning Sword again, its blade having returned to its normal red and black. When it contacted the back of the giant's other ankle, it again blazed red as though the taste of blood lit a fire inside the steel.

The beast tottered, gravity working against him, a look of astonishment replacing the rage on its face. The giant swayed, then fell like a cut tree; Elyea tumbled from his grasp as he threw out his arms to lessen the pain of the fall. Khirro scrambled out of reach.

The ground shook as the giant crashed into the fire pit, flames melting hair and burning flesh, the smell ghastly as the creature rolled off the embers, back smoldering. Khirro stood, knowing but dreading what must happen next. In spite of the giant's intentions, he had no stomach for

315

killing the beast, not like this. He stepped forward and stopped, surprised to see Ghaul standing by the giant's head, Athryn's sword in hand.

"Bastard," he hissed through clenched teeth, blood trickling from his nose and ear.

The warrior grasped the sword's hilt with both hands, raised it above his head, measuring his blow. Something told Khirro nothing good would come of ending the creature's life but he didn't try to stop Ghaul. The giant's eyelids fluttered, recognition flickering in its rheumy eyes, but it made no attempt to protect itself. The blade came down across its throat.

Blood fountained from the wound, spraying as high as Ghaul's head. He pulled the sword free and brought it down again, again, grunting with the effort of each blow. Khirro stood limply, watching, aghast at the sight, but did nothing, said nothing. With the fifth swing, the giant's head came free from its body. Its arms twitched twice, then the once mighty beast lay still. Ghaul stood over it, lips pulled back in what might have been grin or grimace. The blood spattering his face and up the front of his clothes made his white teeth stand out against the red background.

Khirro thought if he ever saw a demon from the hells, this would surely be how it looked.

33

The few snatches of sleep Khirro managed that night

were brief, full of nightmares.

They'd argued about staying the night at the giant's encampment or moving on. Ghaul insisted they go because there might be more of the beasts but, when Shyn found a cache of meat, they finally agreed to stay. Despite not knowing what kind of meat it was, Khirro's growling stomach convinced him to eat.

Athryn lay near the fire, the vial of king's blood pressed against his injured hip. As Khirro tossed and turned searching for a comfortable position, he thought the absence of the vial against his chest might be what kept him from sleep. He'd gotten used to it being there, drew comfort from it. When he rolled to his other side, he saw Ghaul keeping watch. He'd offered the vial to him, too, but he refused. A real warrior didn't need magic to heal, he said. Shyn kept watch from the branches above.

"Thank you."

Elyea's words startled Khirro; lost in pondering Ghaul's attitude and searching for sleep, he hadn't noticed her come to squat beside him. He propped himself on his elbows and looked into her freckled face. She'd used water from one of the skins to wash the tear stains from her cheeks.

"No need."

She stretched out on the ground beside him, face to face, close enough he felt her warmth.

"If not for you, that thing would have squeezed me in

317

half." She nodded toward the giant's body still lying opposite Athryn. They weren't strong enough to move it, even with all of them helping.

"Not just me." Khirro felt blood filling his cheeks, adding to his warmth. "Shyn, Athryn and Ghaul are as much responsible."

"It was you," she whispered wriggling closer, breath touching his face.

Her eyelids fluttered and she leaned forward until her lips brushed his, the touch making his limbs tingle. He looked at her closed eyes as she kissed him. It had been so long. It felt so good. He closed his eyes, enjoying the moment, and a flood of memories surprised him: Emeline's face, his parents, his brother; how he and Ghaul found Elyea in the forest, what she did for a living. He pulled his lips away.

"I... I can't."

"Of course you can."

She shifted her hips forward so their bodies came together. He moved away to keep the hardness creeping into his breeches from encouraging her, but she pressed insistently.

"Please," he said, breathing the word. "Emeline..."

"Enough games, Khirro. You may never see this Emeline again, even if we survive."

Khirro's brow creased. "What do you mean?"

"When you're asked to leave, people don't want you to

come back."

Her tone wasn't spiteful, but the words stung. He saw she was trying to make him understand the truth, and he knew she was right, but it didn't make the revelation any less painful.

"But she... I... I have to make things right again."

The tingle of desire disappeared, replaced by hurt and disappointment.

"I see your longing and sadness when you talk about her. I understand your feelings, but when she became pregnant, they forced you into the king's army. Did your parents or hers banish you?"

Khirro averted his eyes. "Both."

She stroked his cheek tenderly.

"What happened isn't your fault."

She leaned in again, pressed her lips against his, but he didn't reciprocate. Pulling back, she looked at him, the tenderness gone from her face. Khirro shook his head.

"I can't." He wanted to, Gods knew how much he did. That night with Emeline had been the only time—and alcohol kept him from remembering it—but this didn't feel right. Not here, not now. "I'm sorry."

"Me too." An edge crept into her voice. She stood and wiped the dirt and fir needles from her clothes. "One day you'll have to stop fucking your dream and try a real woman."

Khirro watched her walk away, part of him wanting to

call her back, but he repressed the urge, buried it beneath a layer of guilt too thick to let anything else in.

Elyea sat beside Ghaul and a twinge of jealousy surprised Khirro when she leaned over and kissed the warrior. Someone would fulfill her need tonight. Ghaul returned her affection without compunction or conversation. Angry with himself, Khirro watched until Ghaul reached out to remove Elyea's shirt, then he turned his back on them. When sleep finally claimed him, it did so to the sounds of their love making.

***

Athryn and Shyn spoke occasionally while the others kept mostly to themselves, speaking only to answer questions as they prepared to leave the giant's camp. Whenever Khirro looked at Elyea, she diverted her eyes. He wanted to tell her it was all right, he understood that she had a need he couldn't fill, but he didn't. It wasn't true. Every time he looked at Ghaul, the soldier smiled broadly, like a child who stole a treat and got away with it.

They searched the camp but found nothing of use, and Khirro was surprised to find himself mildly disappointed that they didn't find any bones split lengthwise and sucked free of marrow. Many of his mother's fables had already proven to have basis in reality, he half-expected this journey to prove them all true. He glanced at the giant's headless body and his disappointment fled. How could he so quickly forget how close they came to finding out first

320

hand?

Athryn approached Khirro, only a slight limp impeding his normal grace, and held the vial out. Khirro took it from him.

"Thank you," the magician said, then went back to finish storing his gear.

In those two short words, Khirro sensed the man's great sadness. No wonder after losing his brother, but surely he still hoped the Necromancer would bring him back as he would Braymon. No, he'd lost something else, too, and holding the vial, feeling the magic swirling within, reminded him.

It will always be there. Every time there's magic, he'll want to have it back.

He wondered how Athryn felt—like a soldier losing his sword arm, or a singer his voice. Already this journey had produced such sadness.

And there would be more.

Khirro took a chunk of salt pork from his pack before fastening the flap. He chewed the tough meat and pondered the story of the Mourning Sword Athryn had told. A fantastic story, but the detail which stood out to Khirro was that Darestat had been there a thousand years ago, when the sword earned its name. Old beyond reason, an acolyte of Monos himself, betrayer, and possibly in league with the enemy. The thought of the Necromancer chilled his spine. Why would this man resurrect the king?

321

Because they asked? Khirro's head sagged. Every time he put his mind to the task cursed upon him, it became so much more than simply reaching Darestat's keep.

A noise jarred Khirro from his thoughts. He cocked his head, listening. None of the others heard. Athryn and Shyn chatted about where to find water to fill their skins while Ghaul and Elyea finished packing.

Again.

This time Shyn looked up. Something moved through the forest, something big but distant and uncaring of the noise it made. Shyn signaled the others as Khirro crossed the clearing to join them. Ghaul gestured for them to be quiet and pointed toward the hill at the south end of the encampment; they freed their weapons. Khirro looked at the Mourning Sword, realizing he had been a poor soldier and forgotten to wipe the blood from it, yet the black blade shone clean. He turned it in his hand and the runes pulsed red once then faded. When he looked up, he'd fallen behind the others; the noise was closer at his back. He hurried to catch up.

At the top of the grade, they hid behind the sparse cover of some thorny berry bushes and waited. A few minutes passed before the forest parted and a giant stepped into the glade.

Giantess, Khirro corrected himself.

She stood three feet shorter than the slain giant when a head sat on his shoulders; matted tresses hung to her waist as did the massive teats sprinkled with coarse black hairs. If not for the sagging mammaries, Khirro might have mistaken her for a shorter twin to the first giant, with only slightly fewer whiskers.

The companions froze as the giantess entered the camp, the carcass of a deer slung over her shoulder, though not any deer Khirro had ever seen—dark brown with white spots and a single three-pronged horn protruding from between its eyes. She hummed to herself, a guttural sound not as deep as the giant's voice. When she lifted her eyes and saw the campsite, the humming stopped.

For a few seconds, nothing happened. Khirro and his companions stood at the top of the hill, breath held, tensed to attack if necessary. The giantess stared.

Has she seen us? Smelled us?

Impatience got the better of Ghaul and he took a step toward the creature, but Athryn stopped him with a hand on his chest and a shake of his head.

The deer carcass tumbled to the ground as the beast's arms fell limp. She took a step, a whimper sounding deep in her throat. She cried out what might have been a name and stumbled toward the corpse, gaze fixed on the body of her slain friend, or brother, or husband.

Elyea tugged Khirro's sleeve, pulling him away from the scene, guiding him over the top of the hill. Before cresting the rise, he looked back and saw the beast collapse to her knees beside the slain giant. When she noticed the ragged flesh where his head should have been, she wailed toward the branches above, her monstrous voice filled with sadness, then slumped across the corpse, sobbing.

When the giantess passed from their line of sight, they bolted into the forest, the beast's anguished wails following on their heels, tugging at Khirro's heart.

***

An hour later, they still heard the wails of the giantess, distant and fading. She made no attempt to follow.

"Not yet," Ghaul said when Elyea commented about it.

"Ghaul's right," Shyn said. "When her grief has been slaked, she'll thirst for revenge. We best put many miles between us before that happens."

"But which way?" Elyea asked.

"South still," Khirro said without hesitation. The others looked at him, unused to his confident tone. "The ruined village is only a day from here. The tyger told me."

They stopped walking and stared at Khirro.

"What tyger, Khirro?" Elyea asked, the first words she'd spoken to him since he rejected her and, despite their tone, they lifted a weight he hadn't realized he carried.

Khirro sighed. "A tyger visits me in my dreams, tells me what to do."

Athryn grasped him by the shoulder, eyes gleaming behind black cloth mask. "When did you first dream of this tyger?"

"A month ago, I guess."

"Since the journey began? Since you have had the vial?"

"Yes."

"What does this tyger look like?" Ghaul asked. "Is it pink with wings? I might have seen it, too... when I had too much mead."

Khirro ignored him. "It's huge, with paws as big as my head. Its fur is white, with black stripes. He comes to me as a friend."

"He is," Athryn said taking his hand from Khirro's shoulder. "Each man's soul takes the form of an animal, Khirro. That is what you see in your dreams."

Khirro raised an eyebrow. "The tyger is my soul?" The thought instilled pride in him—the soul of a tyger.

"No." Athryn shook his head, dashing his conceit. "It is Braymon's soul which comes to guide you."

The vial radiated warmth against Khirro's chest, as though agreeing with Athryn's words. They stood silently; the distant wails of the giantess had ceased.

"I'm not one to argue with a man-eater," Shyn said, sweeping his arm across his body, gesturing for Khirro to lead the way. "South it is."

Ghaul shook his head but said nothing as Khirro took the lead.

34

The branches overhead offered little protection from

the deluge. The ground turned to mud, sucking at their boots as they walked, slowing their progress. By Khirro's estimation, it was mid-afternoon the day after they fled the giant's encampment, but it might well have been evening for the lack of light penetrating the trees. No one spoke as they tramped through the muck, the patter of rain on flora and armor and clothes conversing with the splash of boots in mud the only words.

So far, there had been no signs the she-beast followed them, but they pushed on as though she did. Both Shyn and Ghaul were convinced she'd come after them; since they agreed so infrequently, Khirro assumed they must be correct. They also agreed the giantess would be able to track them, given they'd seen no wildlife since setting foot on the cursed earth of Lakesh, yet the giantess returned to camp with a deer over her shoulder.

Khirro knew they neared the ruined village, felt it in the pulsations of the vial against his chest. It would be a relief to find a familiar place, one he'd seen in dreams and when the Shaman showed him the way, but he wondered what kind of people had lived in a village in the haunted land. The thought raised goose flesh on his arms.

Ahead, the seductive wiggle of Elyea's hips was gone, suppressed by her attempt to keep mud from pulling the boots from her feet. Khirro shook his head. He didn't understand women at the best of times, and she was no normal woman. Was she attracted to Ghaul or simply seeking physical satisfaction? How could he possibly fathom the motivations of a woman thrust into the life of a concubine before her first bleed?

She views her body as a commodity, something to trade for food, to earn a living with. Or maybe to say 'thank you' with.

He hadn't thought of that before. What if he tried to say thank you to someone for saving his life, only to be rebuffed? She had good reason to feel slighted, for going to Ghaul, and for not speaking to him, if that was the case. Thinking this, he hurried forward, the broad leaves of a bush slapping his face and dumping water down his collar as he fell in to walk beside her.

Elyea looked at him as he matched her stride, her hair subdued by the rain except for a stray strand stuck to her forehead, directing the flow of water down her cheek. Khirro looked at her, at the water running down her face, distorting the freckles scattered across her cheeks and over the bridge of her nose. For the first time, he noticed her slight overbite and the bump on the bridge of her nose, but her eyes remained unchanged: emerald, intelligent. She wasn't as pretty with her hair tamed by the rain, but somehow more beautiful, more real.

"I'm sorry," he said looking at his feet.

"For what?"

"For the other night."

She put a finger under his chin and raised his head so

327

their eyes met.

"It's all right. I couldn't give you what you needed and you couldn't give me what I needed. Maybe one day."

A smile tugged the corner of Khirro's mouth; his cheeks burned with embarrassment at her words and her touch. Sensing his discomfort, she moved her hand away and returned her eyes to the front. He did the same.

"You were right about Emeline," he said, boot splashing in a deep puddle of muck. "I need to let her go. She was never mine.

"I know."

He shook his head. "I just don't know what happened."

Elyea paused for a breath before responding. "Did you rape her?"

"No, I... I don't think so." He trudged along, expecting her to comment, to chastise him, but she didn't. "We drank too much. I passed out."

"Then you probably didn't. In my experience, men don't often forget their first time, no matter how much they drank. Nor do they perform well under those circumstances."

"But if I didn't, then who?"

"Could be anyone." Her tone turned sour. "Maybe your father. Or hers. That would explain why they blamed you and sent you away."

Khirro didn't want to think about possibilities like those —they were somehow worse than being accused of rape.

328

But Elyea was right that he'd likely never return to his village, and Emeline had said she didn't want to see him again, so why spend time yearning for a dream never to come true? He stole a glance at Elyea. There were other women in the world, after all.

"Up here," Ghaul shouted from ahead where he'd been scouting, his form a dark silhouette amongst gray trees a hundred yards away, ghostly arms waving over his head. "I've found the village."

***

The village turned out to be eight broken down huts, uninhabited for an unimaginable number of years. Only one had enough roof left to provide cover from the rain which continued pounding down through the night. Water streamed in through a half dozen holes, muddying the dirt floor, forcing them to huddle in one dry corner. Athryn stood in the doorway taking his watch while the others tried to find sleep.

Khirro shifted on the hard floor, back pressed against the uneven stone wall. Elyea lay in front of him, her breathing soft and steady, already asleep. He felt her lying close, her breath stirring his hair, the smell of her wet clothes filling his nostrils. He wanted to caress her, but fought to control the urge. This was neither the time nor the place. The gentle hills of her shoulder and hip were a dark silhouette against a gray background; his imagination filled in the details. In his mind he saw her strawberry hair,

329

the swell of her breasts, her soft, white skin sprinkled with freckles. His breath shallowed as a tingling began between his legs, radiating into the bottom of his gut.

One touch wouldn't hurt. She won't mind; no one else will know.

The sensation in his loins made him brave. He reached his hand toward her waist slowly, carefully. Elyea sighed in her sleep, startling him, and he pulled his hand away too quickly, smacking his elbow against the wall and sending pain shooting up his arm. He hissed a curse between his teeth. The impact made his fingers tingle—a distinctly different feeling than the one in his pants. He lay still, waiting to see if she'd wake, but her breathing remained rhythmic.

Khirro took a breath of his own, wondering what he was doing. Not so long ago, he thought Emeline would be the only one for him, now barely a thought of her came into his head. He tried not to wonder what had actually happened, it was easier to accept blame than imagine possibilities like Elyea had suggested. At least in accepting responsibility, it made sense for his parents to give him up to the army while hiding his brother. If he'd done what Emeline accused him of, he didn't have to ask the harder question: why did they want him to leave?

By the door, Athryn shuffled his feet as rain continued to fall. Khirro reached his hand toward Elyea again, feeling it shake in the darkness. Breath held, he moved his fingers closer until they brushed flesh. He drew away for an instant, then touched the tips of his fingers to bare skin again. He thought of the gentle curve of her hip but as his fingertips kissed across warm skin, he found the flesh tougher than he'd imagined. And hairy.

"Not my type, Khirro," Ghaul grumbled from the other side of Elyea where he lay with his hand on her hip. "Keep your hands to yourself."

Khirro jerked away, banging the same spot on his elbow against the same knob of wall. He gritted his teeth at the pain and cursed to himself, then shifted to face the wall. The darkness hid his embarrassment and disappointment, but he still couldn't face them. Ghaul said nothing more and his snores soon overpowered Elyea's gentle breathing.

The tip of Khirro's nose brushed the wall as he scoured his mind for soothing thoughts that might let him sleep. He crossed his arms in front of his chest and felt the warmth of the vial. Somehow, the curse thrust upon him by the Shaman had become the least complicated thing in his life. It didn't judge him for being a farmer, nor for possibly impregnating a woman not his wife. It didn't shun him for being a coward or a poor warrior. All it wanted was for him to take it to the Necromancer.

Hours later, when Athryn woke Ghaul to take over the watch, Khirro pretended to be asleep. Not long after, he managed to convince his body it was true.

***

No tyger spoke with Khirro in his dream. No one stalked him. Instead, he dreamed of a woman lying on a bed of straw, knees drawn up and belly full of child. Her face looked like Emeline one instant, Elyea the next. Khirro watched, panicky because he knew nothing about birthing a baby.

The woman screamed and cursed. Sweat streamed first from Emeline's forehead, then Elyea's. Her skirts were pulled up above her knees and Khirro peered between her legs at what his mother would have called her woman's flower. It didn't look like a flower. It bulged and undulated as the woman screamed again. He didn't take his eyes from the spot between her legs to see if the sound came from Emeline's mouth or Elyea's.

Khirro blinked his eyes firmly and knelt between her knees, not knowing what to do but feeling compelled to do something. In life, he'd only seen women's genitals four times: Emeline's, which he didn't remember; his mother's when they bathed together in his youth; Elyea's when they found her and again when she danced in the rain; and a girl from his village named Maree who made him pay with a piece of candy to see it when he was six and she twelve. He never had a close look at any of them, but none looked remotely like the one before him. It didn't look like a flower but more like the maw of some toothless animal.

Emeline/Elyea grunted and strained. Khirro stared as the slash between her legs pulsed and stretched. He reached out tentatively, hand shaking, but didn't touch it. Another scream filled his dream and a hand, small and brown, pushed out of the opening. Khirro pulled away. The tiny fingers searched the ground, grasping, dirt and straw sticking to wet flesh as it groped. The stubby fingers dug into the straw and pulled, freeing first a forearm, then an elbow.

Khirro fell back as a second hand emerged from the widening gash. If the woman still screamed, he didn't hear as he stared at the two brown arms protruding from between her legs.

Why is my baby brown?

The thought disappeared as the hands worked to extract the rest of the child. The top of a smooth brown head appeared, stretching the woman wide. Traders had come to Khirro's village once from the far south with dark skin and shaved heads, but not like this. The child's skin was mottled gray-brown, like clay or earth or shit.

The head came through, then the shoulders. Blood flowed around the baby as Emeline/Elyea's body split to the navel to make room and she screamed over and over without pausing for breath. The child pulled free, dragging wrinkled legs behind it, rolled onto its back and yanked the umbilical cord from its stomach, severing the connection with the woman whose belly it had just left.

333

The cord whipped around, spraying blood like a snake with its head cut off. Khirro's dream-self watched, unmoving, wanting to help but unable to. The babe rolled onto its stomach and pushed itself to its feet.

The child standing before Khirro swayed slightly on plump brown legs. It no longer looked like a babe but like a boy of perhaps four summers. Its entire body—arms, legs, head, face—were all the same gray-brown, its features indistinguishable except by shape. It stared at him, its wet-looking skin glistening in the strange glow illuminating the straw mattress but nothing else around them. Khirro extended a tentative finger toward the child's shoulder. Emeline/Elyea had stopped both screaming and moving; Khirro knew her to be dead, or close to it, but couldn't take his eyes from the child.

His finger touched the child's shoulder and sank to the first knuckle in the mottled flesh. Gray-brown eyelids blinked across gray-brown eyes, but the child made no other reaction. Khirro withdrew his finger. It came away covered with mud. Fleshy gray-brown lips parted revealing mouth, teeth and tongue the same color.

"Dada."

***

Khirro woke with no memory of his dream of the mud child, only a heavy feeling of dread perched on his chest. Eyes still closed, he felt the wall close to his face. A chill at his back told him Elyea must have already risen. He breathed deep, forcing the constriction from his chest, and thought of wanting to touch Elyea and of encountering Ghaul's hand.

Did he tell her?

He hoped not but, no matter how long he lay here, it wouldn't change it. Better to get up and face it.

The dawn light cast little illumination into the hut as Khirro opened his eyes. Rain no longer beat on the broken roof, yet he still heard water flowing. They hadn't seen the lagoon when they arrived, but Khirro knew it was nearby. It was the towering waterfall he heard.

As he edged toward wakefulness, Khirro gazed at the wall inches from his nose. No wonder banging his elbow hurt so much, the mortar hadn't been smoothed when they built the hut. Bumps and valleys covered its surface leaving it rough and unfinished. He moved his head back to get a better look.

At least the bumps aren't jagged, that would have really hurt.

He looked at the gray-brown wall constructed of dried mud—horrible workmanship that somehow still stood after so many years. Even a farmer like himself could have built it better than this.

The random bumps and valleys coalesced as Khirro blinked the last vestige of sleep from his eyes. Thoughts of masonry practices fled his mind and his dream rushed in, filling the void: the woman, the horrifying birth, the mud

335

child. The same gray-brown eyes stared at him from the wall, the same mottled gray-brown face, its mouth open in a frozen scream.

Khirro scrambled away, bumping against Athryn asleep on the floor. The magician stirred, perhaps said something, but Khirro didn't notice. Farther from the wall, able to see more of its surface, other faces became visible—dozens of them.

"Hey," Khirro called struggling to his feet.

"What is it?"

Athryn woke instantly, hand on the hilt of his dagger. Someone stood in the doorway: Shyn or Ghaul, maybe both. Khirro didn't look.

"The walls," Khirro whispered as though not wanting to wake the children sleeping within. He pointed with a quivering finger. "The walls are made of children."

He felt the others beside him but didn't look at them. Instead, he stared at the wall composed of face after face. Some of the younger ones looked placid, calm, but expressions of pain and fear twisted the others, silent screams mortared in their open mouths. Khirro's jaw dropped, but his eyes stared, seeing the faces while the children stared back, blind. The smallest was no more than a babe, the eldest perhaps seven or eight summers old. Their faces horrified Khirro. Corpses didn't wear such expressions—these children had been alive when sealed in the mud.

The hand on Khirro's shoulder made him jump. He'd forgotten his friends were there.

"We must go," Shyn said, his voice low, controlled. "This place is evil."

Khirro looked at him and saw sadness in his eyes, and in Athryn's, too. Ghaul's face remained stony.

"Where's Elyea?" Khirro's voice sounded small to his own ears, like all the energy had been sucked from it.

"Bathing at the lagoon," Ghaul replied.

"Gather everything. I'll get Elyea," Khirro said.

He spun toward the door and took one step before more faces staring at him, more bodies supporting the walls, stopped him. A hundred anguished children pleaded to be set free from the walls by the door.

Khirro turned his gaze to the floor and hurried out into the ruined village, a sickly feeling clawing its way out of his gut and into the back of his throat. He glanced at the other huts as he passed and saw more of the same: innocent faces—invisible in the dark and the rain when they arrived —glared at him from every surface. Where the baked mud was broken, bones showed: smooth tops of yellowed skulls, pointed ribs, shattered thigh bones.

The sound of water tumbling over the fall and into the lagoon kept him moving. He had to get Elyea, spare her from these sights. He plunged through a thicket of trees and emerged on the shore of the lagoon to see the waterfall cascading over a rocky outcropping thirty feet

337

above into water murky with silt and mud kicked up by Elyea's bathing. She stood in the middle of the shallow pool facing away from him, water up past her waist, wet hair clinging to her freckled back.

"Elyea," he called urgently. She turned to him, arms crossed in front of her bare breasts, and he remembered her face in his dream—agonized, sweaty. "We have to go."

"But I'm having such fun," she said with mock pout. "I love the water, it makes me feel free."

She dropped her hands into the water, then threw them up over her head, splashing droplets into the air to sparkle in the rising sunlight. Khirro glanced at her breasts, but the memory of his dream, and of the children in the walls, kept his eyes from lingering.

"Now, Elyea. We have to go now."

She covered her chest again. "Has something happened?"

"I'll tell you when we've left."

She'd waded only two steps toward shore when the first corpse floated to the surface: a girl of about eight summers, naked, her swollen body white and puckered with seaweed tangled in her hair. Others followed: a boy a little older, an infant. Elyea gasped. More corpses appeared bobbing on the waves created by the waterfall, and body parts—arms and legs and heads.

"Elyea! Hurry!"

She didn't move. For half-an-hour she'd bathed with

338

these things hidden in the mud beneath her feet and now she could only stare. The corpse of an infant girl, bald and sweet as a cherub even in water-bloated death, brushed Elyea's leg. She screamed.

Khirro plunged into the water, heedless of the body parts bumping his legs. Corpses and severed limbs covered the surface of the lagoon, a few of them adults with lips and nipples purple against their bulging white skin; most were children.

So many children.

Elyea had stopped screaming by the time he reached her. She stood, eyes wide, hands clamped over her mouth as convulsive sobs shook her. Khirro forced a hand under her arm and dragged her toward shore, fighting his own panic as he cleared the way of corpses. Each step brought more bodies and limbs into their path, touching Elyea's skin no matter how he tried to protect her. Fear and disgust stiffened her legs, made her difficult to move. Khirro glanced shoreward and saw his companions staring at the grisly scene.

"Find her clothes," he yelled.

Shyn and Ghaul went immediately to the task as Athryn waded into the water, extending his hand. Elyea screamed again as the head of a young boy floated against her leg, dead eyes open, staring up at her. Khirro kicked it away but lost his footing. His grip slipped from Elyea.

Water closed over his head, murky fluid found its way

into his mouth. He pushed against the bottom of the lagoon but his hand sank into mud and held him, sucked him down. The corpse of a boy in his teen years floated over him, hands seeming to grasp for his chest and the vial hidden there. Khirro kicked and struggled as the corpse sank toward him.

The boy's eyes opened.

Bubbles exploded from Khirro's lips as he yelled; the lagoon rushed in to fill his mouth. The corpse face loomed inches from his, its cheeks tinged blue; an eel-like fish slithered out of its nose and into its mouth. The corpse's hand groped his chest: searching, caressing. Then a hand on Khirro's shoulder pulled him up until his head broke the surface of the water. He spat and choked, expelling the rancid fluid from his mouth, his lungs. He looked into Athryn's masked face and for a moment thought he'd been rescued by yet another corpse.

"Come on, Khirro," the magician urged.

He released Khirro and swung his cloak over Elyea's shoulders as she shivered violently. Khirro struggled to his feet, put his arm around her shoulders and pulled her close as they moved to the shore, the waves their steps created setting the corpses bobbing and bumping against one another.

"Her clothes," Shyn said coming to their side.

Elyea stared at the lagoon and Khirro looked back, too. The body parts and dead children had begun to sink back into the depths, their bleached bodies going under as though recalled to their watery graves

"Keep them," Khirro said to Shyn. "We'll stop for her to dress when we're away from this place."

A minute later, the surface of the lagoon was clear, all of the bodies, arms, legs and heads settled back like silt after a spring rain. Elyea watched until they were gone, then turned to Khirro.

"Did you know?" she asked, her voice so quiet he had to lean close to hear. "Did you know this would happen?"

Khirro shook his head.

"No. There are other things in the village. Things you don't need to see."

He looked into her eyes and saw the last fragment of her strength disappear. He scooped her into his arms as her knees gave way and hugged her close, her body shivering against his.

Athryn put his hand on Khirro's shoulder.

"Let us go."

Khirro nodded.

"Which way?" Ghaul asked, voice unshaken. Nothing on his face, in his voice or demeanor suggested the grisly sights affected him. It made Khirro both envy and pity him.

"West," he replied steering Elyea away from the lagoon.

They moved in silence, allowing Elyea to dictate their pace as the sun rose above the trees. With some distance between them and the lagoon's corpses, they paused for her to dress. She moved slowly, distracted from the task, but they waited patiently; even Ghaul gave her privacy to clothe herself.

Shyn took the lead when they struck out again. Elyea walked beside Khirro, her arm around his waist for support.

"Thank you," she whispered and kissed him on the cheek. Khirro shook his head.

"No need to thank me. I won't let anything happen to you."

"And I won't let anything happen to you."

35

"A messenger from the Isthmus fortress, my Lord."

From his balcony, Therrador contemplated the city spread before him—his city. Curls of smoke rose from the chimneys of bakeries and smithies; people crowded the market and public houses. The city did a booming business during wartime, its population swollen by those seeking shelter in the capital, afraid for their lives. Beyond the walls, tents spread across the plains, set up by merchants from near and far come to fleece coins from the burgeoned populace.

"Send him in," Therrador said without looking away.

He breathed deep, smelled the bread from the bakeries and the oily odor of the blacksmiths' forges. The streets bustled, clean and tidy near the palace. The distant strains of a musical troupe floated on a breeze cooler now than it had been—summer had finally broken.

"My Lord."

Therrador turned to look at the messenger and it took him a moment to recognize Sir Matte Eliden, a knight of at least sixty summers who fought beside them when Braymon won his crown. The six years since Therrador last saw him had not been kind; he looked every one of his years and more. The knight's watery blue eyes always looked like they might spill tears into his neatly trimmed white beard at any moment.

"Sir Matte," Therrador said, consciously adding a note of delight to his voice. He descended the short marble stair from the balcony and embraced the old knight. "You look well, old man. What news from the front?"

"The enemy's ceased storming the wall, my Lord."

"That's good news. Push enough of them from ladders and they lose their taste for climbing, eh?"

Sir Matte neither smiled nor nodded.

"The siege continues from afar, hurling boulders and hellfire at the wall. We return the same, but for every one what falls, two more take their place." He glanced around the room, eyes watering, then leaned forward and, in a quieter voice, said: "We fight an army of the dead, my Lord.

"So I've heard," Therrador nodded and put his arm around the old knight's shoulders, guiding him to a seat. "Rest, good sir. Would you like some wine?"

343

Sir Matte wiped the back of his hand across his mouth. "We ran dry of ale a week ago. I'd welcome a tankard."

"I'll make sure the situation is remedied." Therrador clapped his hands sharply and a squire appeared at the doorway. "Bring Sir Matte a flagon of ale, and a cup of red for myself." The squire bowed and left. Therrador took a seat across from the knight. "Tell me, how is morale amongst the troops?"

"It'd be better with more ale, my Lord."

"I'll send some kegs back from my personal stores. How is it otherwise?"

The knight shook his head, sighed. "It taxes them, fighting an army of dead men. And there be the matter of the king."

"What do you mean?"

The squire re-entered the chamber, a pewter mug of ale and a goblet of wine on his black tray. Sir Matte had the ewer to his lips before it left the servant's hand. Therrador waved the youth away and took a sip of wine as he watched the knight drain half the tankard, ale dribbling from the corner of his mouth.

"Ah," he proclaimed lowering the mug, froth in his mustache like icicles hanging in the eaves of a house. "That'll put the hair back on yer balls."

Therrador laughed in spite of himself. "Even your saggy old balls?"

"I'll let you know." Matte took another swig, then his

face became serious. "Some of the men are worried the wall won't hold."

"We both know the wall will stand. It has done so for a thousand years, it will for a thousand more. But you mentioned the king. What of it?"

Sir Matte set his tankard on the table with a thunk.

"With the king by their sides, the men remembered why they fought against those monsters. Now he's gone, and none know if he's dead or not."

"He's dead," Therrador said, voice flat. He swirled his wine in the silver goblet, weighing his words. "Braymon left instructions I should rule if he fell."

The knight paused, mug lifted half-way to his lips. "This shouldn't be kept a secret, my Lo... your grace. The men need to know for whom they fight."

"And they shall, Sir Matte."

He stared past the old knight, remembering Braymon, the battles they fought and the good times they shared. The plan was going perfectly so far, but he had to admit, he missed the man in spite of the wrongs he'd done him.

"I'll come, bring ale for the men, and I shall bring them a king." He moved his gaze to the knight. "You have given me an idea, Matte. They can watch as I become their king."

"What do you mean, Ther... my liege?"

"My coronation will take place at the Isthmus Fortress. The men protecting the kingdom will see first hand for whom they fight." Therrador smiled and raised his goblet;

345

Sir Matte banged his flagon against it and drained the remaining ale.

And the Archon will see I have done as promised. Therrador's smile faded from his lips. *Gods help me.*

36

They traversed hills and valleys, plunged through thick stands of trees twisted with brambles and ivy slowing their progress, but now the land flattened, the trees thinned and travel became easier. Each step carried them farther from the grotesqueries of the ruined village, each mile from it bettering their moods. Elyea slept fitfully, calling out sometimes, but she calmed. Khirro dreamed of the mud child the first few nights, but the image faded with distance until it no longer disturbed his sleep.

It was Khirro's turn to scout, a task he didn't relish, but only Elyea was excused from the duty—against her will. As he walked, he hummed a working song his father sang in the days before the accident, distracting himself from his discomfort. He didn't remember the words—something about an aching back and a good harvest—but the melody remained. No other sounds disturbed the forest: no animals, no wind, no chirping birds or buzzing insects. Khirro stopped, listening when he thought he heard something, the melody halted halfway through a verse, but only the same silence that dogged them from the time they landed in the haunted land came to his ear. He held his breath, waiting.

The sound was quiet but, in the silence of the forest, it couldn't be mistaken. A groan made by the throat of a man.

Khirro looked over his shoulder. His companions followed too far behind to be seen or heard. He hesitated, unsure if he should investigate or wait for the others.

What would a soldier do?

Ghaul or Shyn would continue, he decided. He drew a deep breath, seeking courage in the air entering his lungs.

The noise again, ahead and to the south. Louder this time.

What if it's a giant?

The giants' sounds had been similar to a man's, but this... If not a man, Khirro couldn't guess what would make the noise. But could there be men in the haunted land?

Not friendly ones.

Khirro drew the Mourning Sword and pulled the shield from his back. Fear tingled his limbs but the past weeks had taught him to accept it and move forward. Without fear there was no bravery, no courage. One didn't dispel the other, they were inseparable, like fire and air.

He crept forward, choosing his steps carefully. Another moan, closer. He adjusted his grip on the sword. Some nights Shyn practiced with him, helping improve his skills, but as he advanced, the sword held out in front of him, it felt like it didn't belong in his hands.

Sounds behind him—his companions catching up. The moaning man must have heard because he spoke, removing all doubt as to the nature of the noise maker.

"Wha...? What's that? Dolum, did you hear something?" His voice was weak, tired. No one answered his question. "Who goes there?"

Khirro filled his lungs and thought about waiting for the others, but if he did and it turned out to be a trap, they'd be trapped along with him. He'd known the time to prove himself a soldier would come, might as well be now. Bellowing his best war cry, hoping to both frighten his adversaries and alert his friends, Khirro sprang forward at a run. He only covered ten paces when he saw the voice's source.

Five men languished before him, each held immobile in the earth, one buried to his chin, the least to his waist. Khirro halted. Without doubt, two no longer lived: one's entrails had been pulled out by something as the quickearth held him helpless; another stared skyward sightlessly, swollen tongue lolling, face purple. The eyes of the man sunk to his chin were closed, but Khirro didn't know whether he lived or not.

"Who's there?"

The man buried to his chest, one arm pinned at his

side, struggled to look over his shoulder. All the men wore Erechanian armor.

"What happened?" Khirro asked as he crept around the edge of the trees.

"Quickearth. Thank the Gods you're here. Most of my troop has perished, eaten by the very earth on which we walk."

"How many?"

"Twenty."

Khirro stopped, stared at the man and his four companions. "'But there are only--"

"The others are gone. The ground devoured them like a beast." A battle axe lay on the ground beside the man, blood dried on its edge. "There was no sign of the quickearth until we were upon it, then it sucked us down like a hungry animal."

Khirro crept to where the soldier could see him; the man's eyes narrowed.

"What are you doing here?" Khirro asked warily.

"Find a branch and pull me out."

"But you--"

"Hurry," the man snapped. "When the earth is done with the others, it will take me, too."

Khirro hunted through the underbrush, careful to stand on stones and roots and not touch the bare earth. He found a sturdy looking branch and extended it toward the man, but it didn't reach. As he pulled it back looking for a place to stand closer, he heard voices. His companions had arrived.

"Don't come any closer," he said as Elyea came into view. She halted immediately, eyes fixed on the unusual scene before her. "It's quickearth. Careful where you walk."

The others came through the trees behind Elyea. She stopped them where she stood and passed on Khirro's warning.

"What is going on here, Khirro?" Athryn asked, his flesh colored mask giving the illusion he had an elongated, drooping face.

"These men are trapped in quickearth. I'm going to try and get them out."

"Use your head," Shyn called. "Why would Erechanian soldiers be here if not to find you?"

The branch Khirro reached out toward the bound man wavered in the open air between them. The man glanced over his shoulder, then back at Khirro. A line of sweat glistened on his brow.

"Well?" Khirro asked holding the branch beyond the man's reach.

"I don't know who you are." The man shook his head too enthusiastically. "Please, just get me out."

"He's a liar, Khirro," Ghaul said. "Leave him for the birds." He looked at Shyn, snorting a laugh in his direction.

Khirro's eyes narrowed with suspicion. "Tell me why

you're here and I'll help you."

The man's face drooped. He looked at his comrade buried to his neck, then to the man whose entrails were spilled on the ground.

"Therrador sent us to find the man who assassinated king Braymon. But I don't care about that now. I want to live. I'd gladly turn a blind eye, even on an assassin, if only you'll help me. I'd--"

The arrow pierced his throat, cutting his plea short with a fine spattering of blood spraying across the ground. The loamy soil gobbled it up as the soldier slumped forward like a rag doll. Khirro looked past him at Ghaul holding his bow at arm's length, the string empty. He lowered it and their eyes met; Khirro said nothing.

"They were looking for us." Ghaul shrugged. "I guess they found us."

He nocked arrows for each of the others, regardless of whether alive or dead. Khirro averted his eyes when the arrows penetrated throats or eyes or temple. He knew this was a warrior's way of being humane, but he still didn't want to watch, nor did he protest as he might have. He knew what Ghaul would say.

"They would have killed us if they came upon us," Elyea said coming to his side. "Besides, the earth would not have let them go. Now they won't suffer."

"Roots find no purchase in quickearth," Athryn said taking the lead and skirting around the clearing cluttered

351

with dead men. "If we stick to the trees, we should be all right."

As a farmer, Khirro spent his life working with the earth beneath his feet, learned about different soil types, their unique properties and what crops each would support. He'd heard tales of animals, people, even entire towns swallowed by quickearth, but he discounted them in the same closed-minded way he disbelieved his mother's bedtime stories. If this trek did nothing else, it made him a believer.

"So Therrador has taken control of the throne." Shyn stepped over the trunk of a fallen birch. "And doesn't want you to succeed."

Khirro shook his head. "With the Shaman and the others dead, no one knows I carry the blood of the king."

Ghaul laughed. "They may not know it's you, but they know someone has it. And there's no doubt they're not coming to help. The one-eyed man was no common thief, he'd seen many battles, taken many lives."

"And now Erechanian soldiers looking for an assassin." Elyea added. "Someone knows we have the king's blood."

"And doesn't want Braymon to come back," Shyn finished for her.

Khirro looked at his feet as he walked. He didn't like what they said but couldn't argue their accusations. In the haunted land, enough things stood against him already, he didn't need his own country attempting to thwart him, as well.

"But why?"

"The power of a crown can do strange things to a man's mind," Athryn said from ahead of them.

"You think Therrador...?"

Khirro couldn't believe it. The stories of Braymon's rise to power all told of Therrador's role in securing him the crown. Why would he not want his friend back?

"Don't be dim, Khirro," Ghaul snorted. "Of course, Therrador. And likely a few generals, some politicians, the Vendarians, the Kanosee. A list the length of my arm wouldn't be enough to name all the people who'd benefit from Braymon's death. It's the same list of people who want you dead. I'm surprised there aren't more pursuing us."

A bramble caught Khirro's tunic—one more thing trying to keep him from his goal. It made sense others would harbor ambition for the throne, but Therrador? Braymon became king not long after Khirro's birth and always seemed a good and fair ruler, protecting and providing for the people of his kingdom. Wasn't that what mattered?

Around him, the others continued speaking of political plots, but he paid little attention. The conversation ended quickly and they fell back into silence, Shyn taking point. Elyea walked beside Khirro, holding his arm. She smiled and he tried to do the same, but it felt false on his lips. Ghaul made a sarcastic-toned comment from behind, but

Khirro didn't hear what he said and didn't ask him to repeat it.

A brisk wind rose among the tree tops, rustling branches, spilling loose needles and cones down through the limbs. It was the first sound they'd heard from the forest in days, a sound some might identify with peacefulness, but peace never made its way here. Instead, it was ominous, eerie—as though the trees whispered to each other in a language only they understood.

What do they say? Who are they talking to?

Khirro thought it safer if he never found out.

37

The lake itself looked as it had in the other dreams. He sat in the same place, on the same rock, yet something seemed different. He surveyed his surroundings and found them unfamiliar, like someone had picked up the lake and moved it to a different location.

The time and weather also differed. A full moon shone sporadically through clouds smudged across the sky; wind whipped the lake into waves, slapping them against his rock, throwing spray onto his naked skin. The cool air snaked around him, crawling between his arms and body as he hugged himself against the chill.

He stepped off the rock onto pebbly ground, the gravel beach pressing uncomfortably into his bare feet. The moon emerged from behind a streak of cloud, its reflection choppy and misshapen on the roiling lake; its light outlined a building on the far shore. Khirro squinted at the single barrel tower perched on a rocky hill. No torches burned in windows, no banner flew above. The moon went behind another band of gray cloud and the structure disappeared.

A sound from the forest at his back startled Khirro. He looked around expecting the white tyger to appear from the dense foliage. Nothing. Leaves quivered in the wind and another noise followed: a low, guttural sound not human or animal, but somewhere in between. Nothing making that noise could be anything but evil, dangerous.

Khirro ran.

He stayed close to the shoreline, but the forest grew right to the water's edge in places. Branches and brambles whipped his face and chest, scratched his arms and legs as he plunged through them. He ran across rocky beaches, stubbing his toes, nearly turning his ankle. It was not the kind of running he'd experienced in other dreams—the feeling of moving quickly but going nowhere. This time he ran with considerable speed, covered a great distance.

Ahead, a wide gully appeared, too wide for the waking Khirro to clear, but he wasn't the waking Khirro. His feet hit the edge of the crevice, loam squeezing between his toes as they dug into cool, soft earth, and he leaped into the air.

And he flew.

He didn't fly as Shyn did, with wings and feathers, talons and beak. Instead the wind carried him up and up and up. The gully fell away, fading to a line on the earth as he rose above the trees. Higher and higher he went until he brushed the clouds. From here he saw the size of the lake, the tower only a dot sitting beside it. Far off to his left, a bank of fog marked the shoreline of Lakesh while the rest of the land lay in darkness, nothing to see but tree tops below him. Cold air made goose flesh prickle on his arms and legs and chest.

He gazed around in wonderment floating above the world until a pinprick of light buried deep down in the forest caught his attention, and he knew it was the campfire his physical self slept beside. He estimated the fire about three days travel from the lake.

The clouds parted and the moon shone down, illuminating the land. Even Lakesh looked beautiful when seen this way. Khirro moved his arms, attempting to steer his course, to see more. Two days march behind the campfire, trees trembled and shook, moved by more than the wind. He tried to direct himself toward the disturbance, but was sucked downward and away instead. Wind buffeted his body as the ground rushed up at him. An instant later, he lay on the mossy ground staring up at the tower stretching toward the cloud-scudded sky.

Khirro pushed himself to his feet brushing dirt and bits of moss from his thighs. The moon shone on the tower's gray stone, its rough surface unblemished by doors or windows. He circled the tower, bare feet padding spongy ground, and stared in awe at the rough-hewn sides of the massive keep. No lines of mortar showed between bricks, as though the entire structure had been chipped from one enormous block of granite. As he rounded to the far side, Khirro stopped. A huge black bulk sat on the ground near the tower. He crept closer until he made out the shape of massive wings folded against a sleek body.

A dragon.

He watched, waited. It didn't move.

Curiosity pressed him forward one tentative step at a time. By the time he approached close enough to lay his hand on the dragon's forefoot, he knew it was a statue carved from the same stone as the tower: gray flecked with something shining in the moonlight.

The dragon's head was bigger than a horse's and stood yards above Khirro's head. He stooped to look at the curved talons grasping the earth, the scales covering feet and legs. The detail of the carving astounded him as he brushed his fingertips across it feeling each curve and dent. Every ridge in place, the work of a master carver who refused to bend to the whim of the rock.

A vibration shook the statue and Khirro pulled his hand away. It quivered again, accompanied by a rumbling growl. Startled, Khirro stumbled away from the dragon, falling to the loamy ground. He stared up at the head expecting it to

357

turn glowing red eyes on him, but it didn't move. He heard the growl again, this time realizing it came from behind him. Rolling onto his belly, he reached for the sword that wasn't there.

The white tyger padded silently across the mossy ground, its tail swishing insistently as it paced back and forth.

"You," Khirro said, voice louder than intended. The tyger said nothing, only continued its restless pacing. Khirro climbed to his feet feeling vaguely self-conscious about his nakedness. He looked from the tyger to the tower and back. "Is this the keep of the Necromancer?"

The tyger ceased pacing and fixed him in the gaze of its golden eyes.

"Yes," it said. "Your journey draws toward its goal."

Had he been awake, such a statement might have brought fear and foreboding but, in the dream, elation spread through him. Soon Braymon would be restored and the world would go back to the way it should be with no one hunting them and Lakesh a distant memory. Braymon would probably show his appreciation by releasing him from service, he'd heard of such things being done. The rightful king could do whatever he wanted—grant him land and a farm of his own, maybe. Khirro smiled broadly at the thought, but the tyger's intense glare chased it from his face.

"This is cause for celebration." Khirro nodded, looking

for confirmation, but the tyger gave him nothing. "Only a few more days and the danger will be done."

"Do not fool yourself, Khirro. When you reach Darestat's lair, your perils have only begun."

Khirro's face slackened, the fear and foreboding he'd expect of his physical self creeping into the dream. "What do you mean?"

"Only the seeker can face the guardian."

"What?"

"It's the only way to gain entrance."

Khirro's brow furrowed. "Stop speaking in riddles, beast. Say what you mean."

The white tyger turned away and loped around the curve of the tower. Khirro took two steps after the great cat, then stopped. A warm wind brushed his back, stirring the hair on his arms and legs and the back of his neck. Goose flesh hardened on his chest. He didn't want to look.

A stronger breeze flowed around him, and warmer. Khirro's muscles knotted as he turned slowly, holding his breath, suddenly glad this was only a dream. When he'd been flying, he wished it real so he could feel what Shyn felt soaring above the trees, but now, as the warm wind blew again, he longed for wakefulness but couldn't make it happen.

He faced the source of the warm wind.

The dragon reared on its hind legs, muscles bunched, smoke spilling from its nostrils like a blacksmith's chimney.

359

Its gray scales rippled as it moved, clacking together like waves receding from a rocky beach. Gray wings spread and retracted, its eyes shone red with glowing menace. The urge to flee grabbed Khirro but, unlike his flight along the lakeshore, this time the dream ruled, rooting him to the spot. The monster threw back its head and roared at the sky. Khirro covered his ears, shut his eyes, and willed the dream to end. When he opened them, the beast still stood before him.

Khirro's mouth moved—to plead for mercy, or ask forgiveness—he didn't know what might have come out if he found words. Instead, breath wheezed through his constricted windpipe. The dragon opened its maw revealing three rows of pointed teeth, a forked tongue, and blackness lit be a tiny spark.

Then the flames came.

They unfolded toward him like a banner unfurling in the wind. Time slowed. Khirro watched the flames—red and yellow and orange and white—as they twisted and curled, a living thing advancing upon him. The swirling conflagration hid the dragon and heat touched Khirro's face. In an instant the inferno would engulf him, ending his life.

This is the guardian.

And then he woke.

His eyes opened to flames. Startled and afraid, he cried out, scrambling against moist dirt to get away, but something pressed against his back kept him there. Elyea sat up and put a comforting hand on his shoulder.

"What's wrong, Khirro?" she asked, voice groggy with sleep.

Athryn and Ghaul, also arrayed on the forest floor near the fire, woke as well. Shyn came to them from where he'd been sitting watch.

Khirro breathed deeply to slow his thumping heart. He looked into the camp fire, recognizing the flickering flames for what they were but still chilled by the vividness of the dream. Had sleeping too close to the fire been the source of it? He looked at his companions, saw the concern on Elyea's face, the sword in Shyn's hand, the mask hiding Athryn's expression, the annoyance Ghaul didn't attempt to hide.

"A dream," Khirro said. "We can't tarry. Danger follows."

That was the guardian and I am the seeker.

38

"I've been to this place before."

The lake wasn't exactly as in his dreams. Instead of blue and clean and serene, patches of weeds and sludge floated here and there on the murky water; the rocks littering the shore were larger and more jagged. A brisk wind churned the lake's surface, splashing choppy waves against the rugged shore. And the lake was bigger than in his dream

361

Bruce Blake

with no tower standing on the far shore they could barely see. The trees were bigger, too—ancient cedars and redwoods, fir, pine and hemlocks crowded the lake, some of them large enough it would take a man five minutes to walk their circumference. Khirro hadn't known trees grew so big.

"Where do we go now?" Ghaul asked. Khirro pointed to the far shore. "How far?"

"I don't know. I saw it from here in my dream. The lake is much larger than I thought."

Elyea shivered in the cool wind; Khirro removed his tunic and spread it over her shoulders. He made no comment when Ghaul shook his head and rolled his eyes.

"There is great magic here." Athryn sat on a rock looking out across the lake, his mask removed to allow the cool wind to caress his face. Khirro saw only the unburned portion of the magician's face; if he didn't know him, he might have thought he looked like any other man. Athryn faced them, dispelling the illusion. "It is in the air and the water, the trees and the rocks. It is the power of the Gods made real."

"What of the Gods?" Ghaul spat on the rocky shore and slapped the sword hanging at his waist. "Never have I slain a foe with one of your Gods. Give me steel any day."

Khirro suppressed a smile at Ghaul's bravado—this was how a soldier dealt with fear. Over the weeks, he'd come to realize brave men felt fear, too, only how they reacted to

362

it differed. There were countries, Khirro had heard from traveling merchants, where people worshiped their weapons as gods. Perhaps Ghaul would have been comfortable living there.

Athryn turned back to the lake, saying no more. Khirro liked the man, but he'd said so little since the death of his brother, Khirro worried he'd be more concerned about raising Maes from the blood in his veins than about bringing life back to Braymon.

Raising the king took priority, nothing could get in the way of that.

They milled about in silence for half an hour before Shyn emerged from the forest. Ghaul whipped around, pulling his sword, pointing it at him. Shyn chuckled as he finished buckling his sword belt around his waist.

"Always looking for an excuse to skewer me, aren't you, Ghaul?"

"No one would be laughing if you turned out to be a wolf." Ghaul sneered as he replaced his sword in its scabbard. "What did you see?"

Shyn's smile disappeared. "Apparently our saggy-teated friend wants vengeance upon us for killing her comely mate. She follows us with two friends."

Elyea sucked a breath through her teeth. "Three of them? How far away?"

"Perhaps half a day. They move quickly."

Athryn slid off the rock and came to the others. "We

363

Bruce Blake

must waste no time." He looked at Khirro, then Shyn.
"What is the best path?"

"The shore is treacherous, more so than I dreamed.
Sometimes the trees overtake it. Following it would be
slow and dangerous." Khirro rubbed his chin. "The trees
aren't so thick in the forest, but our pursuers would track
us easily and catch us before we reached the keep."

"Let them come," Ghaul growled. "We defeated one of
their kind—me with my hands tied behind my back."

Shyn tsked. "You're very brave when the creatures
aren't standing before you, Ghaul." The muscles in Ghaul's
jaw bunched. "We had surprise on our side last time. We
have no such advantage now."

"I'd be no less brave if they crashed through the trees
this instant."

"We know you would," Khirro interrupted waving his
hand for them to be quiet. "It would be best for us to reach
Darestat's keep before the giants find us."

Athryn looked out over the lake. "Our best choice
would be straight across the water."

"Do you propose we swim?" Ghaul said with a snort. "I
don't have a boat in my pack. Do any of you?"

"Let's build one," Elyea suggested.

Shyn shook his head. "Not enough time."

"Then the forest it is," Ghaul said. "Let them come taste
my steel."

Khirro leaned toward Elyea, lowering his voice. "I wish

we had a boat."

The wind rose, howling through the trees and across the water. Waves splashing against the rocky shore sent spray over the tops of them, then the gust dissipated to a gentle breeze as quickly as it had come. The waves receded and a new sound came from the shore—a rhythmic thumping. They all stopped, listening.

"What's that?" Elyea asked. "The giants?"

"They're too far away yet," Shyn said.

"There," Athryn said, pointing between two jagged rocks.

Khirro stood on his toes to see over the magician. He saw a flash of something wooden. The prow of a rowboat bobbed on the waves, thudding against the shore.

Elyea eyed it, then looked at Athryn. "Did you do that?"

He shook his head. "My spells died with Maes. I told you there is great magic in this place."

Khirro gulped the lump from his throat.

Did I do that?

Ghaul moved toward the boat, hand on sword, followed by Shyn and the others. As they neared it, the wind died completely. The waves disappeared and the boat steadied, floating in place with no rope tethering it.

"It's empty," Ghaul said over his shoulder.

Shyn prodded the side of the boat with the tip of his sword. Two oars lay at the bottom of the boat, and nothing else. White paint flaked from the boat's surfaces, two thick boards crossed its breadth serving as seats. Khirro's uncle had owned this boat, he realized—he'd seen it once as a boy when his uncle took him fishing.

"It's solid," Shyn said poking his sword at another spot. "No rot."

"Then we should take advantage of this fortunate turn." Athryn stepped toward the boat.

"I don't like this, magic man," Ghaul said. "Too convenient."

Athryn ignored him, climbing over the side of the boat, setting it rocking precariously. Shyn sheathed his sword and grabbed the prow to steady it.

"We have no choice," Shyn said. "Any other route will leave us in the clutches of an angry giantess. Can you not swim, Ghaul?"

The soldier shot an angry glance at Shyn but said nothing. There was no other sensible choice.

Elyea boarded first, taking a seat beside Athryn at the rear. Khirro and Ghaul followed taking up position on the other seat. Finally, Shyn pushed the boat away from shore and leaped into the prow making them all grasp for safety as the boat rocked violently. When it steadied, Ghaul and Khirro wrestled the oars from the bottom of the boat and took a few minutes to get the rhythm of rowing in unison. Soon they skimmed across the surface of the water leaving both rocky shore and pursuing giants behind.

As he pulled on the oar, Khirro wondered again how

this boat appeared at the moment they needed it, at the moment he wished for one. Should they trust something unexplainable?

Only time would tell.

39

They had been rowing for less than an hour when the mist descended upon them like a blanket thrown over their heads. They could see each other, but everything beyond the gunnels disappeared in the eddying fog. The shore, the lake ahead and behind, the sky above—all swallowed by the pale white curtain that left everything it touched damp.

At least the lake is calm.

"We should stop before we get turned around."

"Athryn's right," Shyn agreed. "Without seeing where we're going, we may end up where we started. Or worse."

"Afraid of a little fog," Ghaul muttered but pulled his oar from the water without argument. Thankful for the rest, Khirro did the same.

Waves lapped the boat as they floated in silence. Khirro faced Athryn, their knees touching, the magician's black mask unreadable as he stared passed Khirro, attempting to penetrate the mist, or lost in memory, or grief, or plans. Shyn shifted in the front of the boat, setting it wobbling, and Ghaul grabbed the edge for support.

The fog grew more dense. Khirro looked over the side

of the boat at the green water hiding the depths of the lake, every bit as impenetrable as the fog enveloping the world above the water.

"Why don't you make yourself useful and see where we are," Ghaul said over his shoulder.

"It wouldn't do any good in this fog," Shyn replied, then laughed. "Besides, you know I have to unclothe to change. Did you want my bare ass pressed against the back of your head?"

Elyea put her hand over her mouth, hiding her smile. Sitting across from her, Ghaul's eyes smoldered.

"None of us need that, Shyn," Khirro said before Ghaul spoke. "You can keep your breeches on, thanks."

Shyn laughed and slapped Khirro on the back. As they settled back, a wave rolled out of the fog, buffeting the boat, sending them reaching for a safe hold.

"What was that?" Elyea asked, her smile gone.

They gazed into the fog, searching for the source of the swell, but the swirling mist disguised all. A minute passed and the ripples subsided, then they heard a splash in the distance to Khirro's right.

"A fish jumping," Ghaul said, his voice lacking surety.

"We haven't seen any wildlife since we reached Lakesh." Shyn stared toward the sound. "Why would there be fish if there's nothing else?"

Khirro leaned out over the water, straining to see something through the dense cloud, listening for something, anything. No more sounds came, no more waves. He settled back into his seat, glancing down at the surface of the lake as a shadow slid by beneath its glassy surface, disappearing under the boat.

"There's something in the water!"

The words had barely left his lips when something nudged the bottom of the boat. Elyea let out a startled yelp and Ghaul lifted his feet unconsciously.

"What is it?" Shyn called stretching to see over Khirro.

"There." Athryn pointed over Ghaul's shoulder.

They all twisted, rocking the boat again as they tried to glimpse what Athryn saw. A yard from the boat, at the edge of their limited vision, dark green skin marked with gray patches and flecked with black bulged the surface of the water, cutting through it like a knife through lard. The slick skin flashed in the mist-choked light, then it disappeared.

"What in the name of all four Gods?" Elyea's green eyes flickered with the same fear tightening the muscles in Khirro's thighs.

"I don't know, but it's time to put paddle to water again, Khirro."

Ghaul pulled his oar from the bottom of the boat and Khirro did the same, falling into rhythm with Ghaul more easily this time. The boat cut across the water, though what direction they headed, none of them knew. The water by Khirro's oar contorted as the creature's back broke the surface again, keeping pace.

369

"It follows us," Elyea said, her voice quiet.

Khirro craned his neck to see, ceasing rowing and leaving the blade of his oar in the water. A thick green loop coiled around the oar, jerking it in Khirro's hand, but he held on.

"It's got the oar," he cried gripping it with both hands.

The green spotted skin faded to sickly yellow as it curved down to the creature's belly. Its body looked like a python's, more than a foot across, and it had decided to make a meal of the oar, squeezing the life from it. Khirro pulled but the thing wouldn't relinquish its grasp. It dove, wrenching the oar from Khirro's grasp. A moment later, the paddle bobbed to the surface, floating alongside the boat.

"You have to get it." Ghaul jabbed his elbow painfully into Khirro's ribs. "With one oar, we'll only go in circles."

Khirro looked at him in horror. Raised his entire life on a farm, the fishing trip with his uncle and their flight across the little sea were his only exposure to deep water, and neither had contained a malicious creature lurking in its depths. But Ghaul was right: *he* needed to get the paddle. He couldn't ask one of the others to get it without seeming a coward.

Stay calm. Move slowly—don't rock the boat. He breathed deep. *It's not so far. I can reach it.*

He reached toward the oar and the boat lurched. He pulled his hand back, clutching at the side, heart beating in his ears.

"Get it," Ghaul urged. "Quickly, before it returns."

"Be careful," Elyea said touching his leg.

Clenching his teeth, Khirro stretched again, ready this time for the boat to shift. The oar still bobbed beyond his fingertips.

"Hold on to me."

Ghaul grabbed a handful of Khirro's tunic and he leaned out farther still, but for each extra inch he stretched, the oar floated that much farther away. He rose off his seat, fingers wiggling at the tantalizingly close paddle, when a coil of the creature's body surfaced directly under his arm, its patchy skin brushing him. Khirro cried out in surprise and fell back into the boat. Elyea yelped and held on to Athryn who grasped his seat with both hands.

"I think I can reach it," Shyn said shifting his position.

Khirro shouldered him back, having the briefest second to reflect on the dangers of pride as he stood, wobbling with the movement of the boat, and drew the Mourning Sword.

"I can get it," he insisted. "Hold my belt, Ghaul."

"Khirro, no," Elyea said, but Ghaul's fingers were already wrapped around Khirro's sword belt. He reached beneath his jerkin, pulling the vial from its hiding place and handed it to Athryn, regretting this ridiculous show of courage.

371

"Just in case," he said; the magician took it. Khirro wished for him to try to talk him out of reaching for the oar, but he didn't. Only Elyea protested.

"Ready," Ghaul said.

Khirro inhaled deeply through his nose, smelled the lake's dirty odor, and leaned over the side, stretching the Mourning Sword toward the paddle. The boat listed with his weight and Athryn and Shyn shifted to compensate. The tip of the sword nudged the oar.

"Come on," Khirro muttered through gritted teeth. "Come on."

He extended farther, pushing the tip of the sword beyond his goal. He brought his weapon down on it, coaxing it closer.

"Farther," he called to Ghaul over his shoulder.

The soldier slid over in the seat, bracing his feet against the side of the boat. The belt dug uncomfortably into Khirro's mid-section, but he ignored it; the oar floated close enough for him to reach. As the blade of the sword touched the oar, Khirro heard something thump hard against wood.

He hit the water, the coldness of it threatening to steal his breath. It surrounded him, sucking him down and away from the wan light of the surface. He thrashed and swung the Mourning Sword as though he could cut his way free. The silty water stung his eyes as the weight of armor and weapons pulled him down. He stopped moving when the creature slid by in front of him close enough to touch.

Khirro swam for the surface, the sword in his hand making his arm impossibly long for swimming. He considered dropping it, but it would be his only defense if the serpent came for him. He kicked his feet and stroked with his left arm, holding the sword straight out above him.

I've come too far to drown.

With no sun shining, he couldn't tell how deep he'd gone or see the boat above in the murky water. Weeds brushed against his face before his flailing arm sent them swirling away. Then his arm wouldn't move. He jerked his head, expecting to see the serpent's mouth wrapped around his forearm, but instead a mass of weeds twisted around it, holding him. He pulled but they tightened like a living thing loathe to let him go. His breath burned in his lungs, screaming to be replaced with fresh air.

Khirro drew the Mourning Sword's sharp edge through the tangle and the weeds released his arm. He stroked for the surface but the serpent reemerged from the murk, struck his chest forcing precious breath from his lungs.

It swam a tight circle and came at him again. For the first time he saw its head: tapered to a flat snout designed for swimming, two black eyes faced forward. Its mouth opened revealing needle-sharp teeth. A surprising calm descended over Khirro, quelling his distressed lungs as he watched the serpent rush in for the kill.

This is not my time to die. He didn't know from where the thought came. *The Gods have important things for me to do.*

He swung the Mourning Sword around, brought its tip to bear on the serpent and noticed how the runes glowed even in the turbid water. The creature spasmed to change its course, but too late.

The tip of the sword entered through the roof of the serpent's mouth and exited the top of its head. It convulsed on the end of the blade, thrashing to free itself, but Khirro maintained his grip, twisted the blade. A dark cloud spread through the water and the struggle ended.

Khirro put his foot on the serpent's snout and wrenched the glowing red blade free then stroked desperately for the surface. His arms turned to rock, each stroke requiring every bit of energy he could find. His legs faltered.

This is not my time to die.

When his head finally broke the surface, he gasped a ragged breath. Never had air tasted so good. He grabbed the oar floating nearby, thankful for its aid in keeping him afloat, and kicked for the boat, limbs heavy with exhaustion. Hands grabbed him, helped him over the side.

He lay in the bottom of the boat catching his breath and staring at the blue sky for several minutes before he realized the fog had dissipated. The sun shone bright, drying his soaking clothes.

40

Time slid by with the water beneath the boat's hull but they made little progress toward shore. Shyn and Athryn pulled on the oars, sweat running off their chins, dripping from the ends of their noses as the sun beat down relentlessly, reflected and intensified by the lake's glassy surface. Khirro's clothes—long since dried under the sun's heat—lay in a heap at the bottom of the boat with everyone else's. They all wore only enough to keep their skin from frying and rowed in no more than ten minute shifts for fear of passing out.

Elyea plunged her hand through the skim of green foam covering the water to cool herself then pulled it out quickly, a surprised look on her face.

"It's hot," she said wiping scum off her hand.

Khirro peered over the side of the boat, tempted to test the temperature himself, but he resisted. It would be a long time before he'd go in the water for anything other than bathing. In the distance, tendrils of vapor curled up from the lake, snaking toward the sky, disappearing before they became mist.

The sun takes the lake. If we survive long enough, we might be able to walk ashore.

Athryn stopped rowing, leaned over his oar to rest. In the heat, he had removed his mask and the scar on his face shone with sweat. Shyn stopped, too, and put his hand on Athryn's shoulder.

"We should make for the closest shore," he said, voice rasping in his parched throat.

The magician shook his head. "No. We are being tested. If we give up, we will never reach the Necromancer."

"To hell with the Necromancer," Ghaul said from the front of the boat. "No matter how much we row, we go nowhere. If we don't have rest and water soon, we'll die." He shifted to face them. "Why should he test us? How could he know we're here?"

"Darestat knows all," Athryn replied through cracked lips, each word a struggle to find breath. "He does not want to be found. If any man could reach him, he would never have peace from those who want of him. Or those who want him dead."

They fell silent as the boat floated without drifting. Khirro hung his head, sweat trickling down his back. For the first time in his life he felt like he had a purpose, but he'd fail, boiled to death like a breakfast egg. His mind floated like the boat, drifting back through the line of failures marking his life: the slaughter of the Shaman and the others; the death of King Braymon; his laughable training as a soldier; his banishment by his parents; the disaster with Emeline; the accident that took his father's arm, and on and on. A life of failure and disappointment. This was his last opportunity to redeem himself. He took the vial from the pocket of his tunic.

"Give me the oar, Athryn," he demanded, standing. The

swaying boat sent ripples racing away to be swallowed up in the lake's stillness. "Shyn, do you have anything left?"

"I do," Shyn replied despite the sweat soaking his thin cotton shirt.

Khirro traded spots with Athryn, his knees brushing Elyea's as he sat. He looked at her hair plastered to her forehead, at the way her sweat soaked shirt clung to her chest, outlining her breasts. She smiled weakly and brushed the stray strands of hair from her face. A warmth unrelated to the sun's heat filled Khirro's chest and, in that moment, he knew he loved her. He may never be able to tell her, or show her, but he was clear he did.

Let's go." He pried his gaze from hers and turned to Shyn. "If you tire, trade with Ghaul."

They dipped their oars into the water and pulled. The vial pulsed against Khirro's leg, throbbing in rhythm with their strokes. Water splashed and jumped from the blades each time they broke the surface, the ripples spreading farther and farther until a wake spread from the stern of the boat.

"We're moving," Ghaul cried over his shoulder.

They moved slowly at first, the trees on the bank crawling by, but their speed increased. The motion created a slight breeze that dried the sweat on their brows. The more Khirro rowed, the more energy flowed through his limbs. Shyn stroked beside him to the pace set by the blood of the king.

377

The air grew cool—cooler than should be caused by the boat's movement. Khirro watched Athryn and Elyea pull on clothes they'd removed in the heat. The hair on Khirro's forearms prickled, but he welcomed the feel of a little goose flesh after the searing heat.

Minutes later, Elyea breathed out a cloud of mist. High above, billowy white clouds painted gray on their flat bottoms gathered, blotting out the sun, throwing a shadow across the lake. The welcome goose flesh on Khirro's arm became an unwelcome chill. They stopped rowing a moment so he and Shyn could reclothe. Less than ten minutes later, Elyea let out a surprised gasp as the first flake of snow landed on her nose.

"How is this possible?" she asked turning to Athryn.

The magician shrugged. "I told you: Darestat does not want to be found."

Snow fell steadily. Elyea moved closer to Athryn, using their combined bodies to create warmth. Khirro ignored the twinge of jealousy poking his ribs and felt thankful to be rowing, creating his own heat.

"Let me take over," Ghaul offered, apparently having the same thought.

"I'm fine," Shyn replied continuing to stroke the oar through the water.

Khirro wanted to say the same thing, to keep the activity and warmth to himself, but that wouldn't be fair. If they took turns when rowing was hard, they should do the same when it was desirable. Besides, he didn't really want to watch Elyea snuggled up to Athryn, for warmth or otherwise.

"You can take my place."

He pulled his oar from the lake and balanced it across the boat. Shyn stopped rowing and gripped the oar being exchanged as Khirro and Ghaul completed the awkward dance of trading places on the unsteady boat.

Khirro settled into place on his knees at the bow. No longer rowing, he noticed his muscles aching from exertion. He swung his arm in a circle, stretching the muscles as the rhythmic splash of oars dipping into water resumed. A smile no one else saw wrinkled the corners of his mouth—when Shyn and Ghaul rowed together, it was the only time they worked toward a common goal.

The snow fell harder, swirling around them. Khirro pulled his tunic tight under his chin, squinting and blinking as flakes the size of a copper piece flew at his eyes. The shifting white curtain obscured the shore ahead, but it was growing closer.

Snow gathered on the edge of the boat and on the shoulders of Khirro's tunic. He brushed it away, but it took little time to gather again. The green algae coloring the surface of the lake disappeared, seeking warmth in deeper water. A shiver shook Khirro as he saw the scum replaced by a rime of snow. He looked at the water directly in front of the boat; the prow pushed aside a thin layer of ice as they advanced.

"The lake freezes," he called over his shoulder, teeth chattering.

Snow collected in the bottom of the boat, dusted the surface of the lake. The trees on the approaching shore wore the same white cloak. The ice grew thicker until it began to impede their progress, slowing them, making Shyn and Ghaul pull harder and harder on the oars. With the shore tantalizingly close, the blade of Shyn's oar glanced off the ice instead of finding water. He tried again and failed to penetrate it. The same happened to Ghaul. The rowing stopped and soon after the boat did, too.

"What now?" Ghaul threw his oar to the bottom of the boat. Khirro turned toward the others, knees creaking and aching from kneeling in the cold.

"The shore isn't too far," he said, though it had been a while since he could see land clearly through the veil of heavy flakes.

"How can you be sure?" Athryn asked. In the frigid weather, Khirro found himself envying the magician's mask. "Shyn, can you take to the air and see?"

The border guard shook his head. "It would be suicide to fly in this."

"So what's the hold up," Ghaul said half under his breath. Shyn glowered at him.

"We have no choice," Khirro interjected. "We'll have to walk the rest of the way."

380

"I..is the ice th...thick enough?" Elyea asked.

As if in answer, the ice around them crunched and creaked, squeezing against the hull of the boat. Khirro stood, knees popping, but the boat didn't move. He swayed from side to side, gently first, then more aggressively. Ice held the boat fast.

"It's freezing quickly." Shyn thumped the blade of his oar on the ice. "Perhaps we should wait to be sure it will hold us."

"We freeze quickly, too," Athryn said, his words carried on a plume of mist; a ring of frost encircled the mouth hole of his black mask.

"Athryn's right. My toes already lose feeling. If we wait too long, we may not be able to walk." No surprise Ghaul's words contradicted Shyn's.

"I'll go first," Khirro said, surprising himself. A gentle warmth spilled through his chest—the vial tucked into its place at his breast.

Is it the king's blood itself giving me warmth and courage, or the spell keeping it alive?

He strapped on his sword belt, threw his pack over one shoulder and the shield Athryn and Maes conjured him over the other. The boat didn't bob or sway or quiver—frozen solid. He went to step on to the ice but Shyn stopped him.

"Take this," he said handing him the oar. "Test the ice with it."

381

Khirro nodded and extended the blade over the side of the boat, prodding the ice. The tip touched and slipped to the side, twisting in his grip. He recovered and poked again. The ice proved solid.

"Let me get twenty paces before you follow." Khirro threw his leg over the side, shifting his weight carefully. "Come one at a time, ten paces between you. Follow my tracks." He looked at them and forced a smile. "Go no farther if you come upon a big hole in the ice."

"Be cautious," Athryn said.

Elyea stood and leaned between Shyn and Ghaul to hug him and kiss him on the cheek. Her body shivered with the cold, but the kiss spread warmth across Khirro's face. She sat back down, saying nothing as Khirro brought his other leg over the side.

A layer of snow more than an inch deep crunched beneath his boot; the ice creaked but held. He took one small step, then another, creeping forward, prodding the ice before him with the tip of the oar. A cold wind whipped across the lake throwing snow in his face, flapping his tunic as though the air wanted to tear it from his shoulders.

Khirro counted off step after tentative step, his jaw aching from clenching his teeth. At his twentieth step, he looked back to see who they'd send next, but the blizzard concealed the boat from sight. Likely Athryn would follow next, then Elyea, leaving Shyn and Ghaul to argue over who'd do the soldierly thing and bring up the rear.

Khirro turned his attention back to the expanse of snowy ice before him.

One foot in front of the other. Almost there.

"Almost there," he repeated aloud, his words whipped away on the howling wind's response.

He stared ahead at where he thought the shore should be, the blowing flakes dizzying him as they spun about his head. The blizzard quickly filled in the bare streaks left in the snow by his shuffling gait. He advanced carefully, distributing his weight equally between both feet, and soon saw shapes of jagged boulders lining the shore.

The snow is abating.

He moved forward more quickly. Twenty yards from shore, the ice cracked beneath his feet, loud as a thunderbolt to Khirro's ears. He halted, dispersing his mass equally. The sound ceased, the ice held. He looked at his feet, then at the shore. A tentative step forward brought more reaction from the ice, a sound like thick cloth tearing. Khirro hesitated, fear knotting his gut. The vial radiated warmly against his chest, fortifying him, prompting him on. The ice creaked again, forcing his decision.

Khirro dropped the oar and broke into a run, feet slipping in the snow and on the ice it covered; his legs pumped but carried him nowhere. The deep-throated groan of the ice grew in volume and he wondered if he

383

was destined to drown after all when his feet gained purchase and he bolted forward. Snow pelted his face as the wind attempted to push him back. His hands curled into awkward fists, contorting his frozen fingers inside his gloves. The cold air burned his ears.

He reached the shore and clamored up a boulder, feet slipping on its frosted surface. The ice's growl stopped, like an animal giving up the chase. Khirro spun around, safe atop the rock, breathing heavy mist into the waning flakes of snow and saw his companions crossing the frozen lake. He waved his arms, directed them around the cracked ice. Ten minutes later, they stood safely ashore catching their breath. Khirro hugged Elyea close, felt her body quiver against his.

"Where do we go from here?" Shyn cleared snow from a rock and sat. His cheeks were red from the cold, his gray stubble frosted.

"In my dream, the keep could be seen from the shore of the lake." Khirro scratched the sparse beard on his cheeks, scanned the area, then pointed. "That way."

"We should hurry," Athryn said. "We do not want to lose any lead we gained on our pursuers."

Ghaul snorted. "I doubt we're any farther ahead after that cursed lake," he said. "We would have been better off going through the forest."

No one responded as they reslung packs and shields. Silently, they picked their way from the shore, over icy rocks and through banks of snow, Khirro leading the way, following the memory of a dream.

41

The keep stood a hundred feet high, and nearly as wide —a squat sentinel standing alone in the woods—yet they almost walked past it.

"More sorcerer's trickery," Ghaul grumbled.

Devoid of doors and windows, the tower appeared much like Khirro dreamt it. The stone comprising it was black instead of gray, the glittering a result of hoarfrost. Despite its stature, the ancient cedars and redwoods surrounding it dwarfed its size.

Shyn placed a gauntleted hand against the wall, brushed away frost. "There are no lines of mortar." He looked up the tower's face to the gray sky above; the snow had ceased. Khirro didn't know if it was daytime dimmed by clouds or night brightened by snow. "It's like someone carved the keep rather than built it."

"Impossible," Ghaul said.

"Nothing is impossible," Athryn said. "Not for the Necromancer. How did you get into the keep in your dream, Khirro?"

"I didn't." Khirro glanced away from the others. If his cheeks weren't already reddened from the cold, embarrassment would have accomplished the task. "The dragon attacked before I entered."

Ghaul looked at Khirro. "Dragon? You said nothing of a dragon."

"It meant nothing. A dragon statue that came to life in my dream."

"The rest of your dream has proven true," Elyea said. "The lake, the keep, everything."

"I didn't dream the giants, or the serpent. I didn't foresee the heat or the cold."

"It makes no difference. There is no dragon now," Athryn said. "Had we found out a day ago makes no matter. We must find the entrance quickly."

Shyn nodded. "I'll go up to the roof," he said unbuckling his belt. "You search the wall for a secret opening. There's a way in somewhere."

He strode away removing his armor as the others split into pairs. Khirro and Elyea followed the curve of the tower to the left, Athryn and Ghaul to the right. They groped along the wall's surface searching for any hint of an opening or hidden switch. Khirro glanced back and saw Shyn at the edge of the trees naked, gray feathers pushing through his skin and looked quickly away from Shyn's stomach-turning transformation. The change back to human form was worse—feathers, talons and beak fell to the ground, rejected by his man-form. When complete, it looked as though a huge bird had been savaged by a beast.

"You should have said something about the dragon," Elyea said scrutinizing the wall above her head, scouring it with her fingers.

"It would have made our journey more difficult." Khirro thought of the tyger's words: *your perils are only beginning.* "You wouldn't have been pleased at the prospect of rushing into the jaws of a dragon."

"I'm not pleased about rushing into the grasp of a man who can raise the dead." She paused and looked at him. "But I'm here."

"You are."

They returned their attention to the wall, inching their way along its curve. His dream and Shyn's comments had been accurate: no individual bricks, no mortar. Whoever built the tower did so with incredible skill. Or magic.

Wings beat the air. Khirro whirled, expecting a dragon attack, but caught a glimpse of gray wings. Shyn landed beside his heap of clothes, then disappeared from sight as they advanced around the keep. Khirro nearly walked into Elyea—she'd stopped prodding the wall and stood staring toward the trees on her left.

"What's wrong?" Khirro asked.

Elyea extended a shaking finger. Khirro stepped from behind her to see what she pointed at.

The dragon was like the tower—the same as in his dream, but different. It stood the same size as he dreamed, towering over him with wings half-spread behind it, but was also hewn of a different material than the dream dragon. Instead of gray granite flecked with black, its

Bruce Blake

surface was translucent red stone—garnet or ruby. Black veins ran beneath the surface. No snow or frost rested on the statue's surface.

"Is that your dragon?" Elyea asked, voice quieted with fear or wonder. He nodded.

Elyea padded across the snow toward the dragon, forgetting the wall at her back. Khirro watched, awed by the sight. What would even a small piece of such a statue be worth? Dreams of decadence and opulence filled his head; castles and servants and land swam through his mind, dreams of wealth and lordships. Elyea paced slowly away as his mind wandered. The warmth of the vial flaring at his chest startled him from the daydream and he realized the thoughts didn't come from within.

A spell. A trap.

"Elyea!" He sprang forward, reaching her in three strides, and grasped her shoulder.

"It's so beautiful," she said, voice distant. "So beautiful."

Khirro spun her around, looked into her deep green eyes; they stared back blankly and he wondered if she saw him. He shook her and recognition seeped back into her face.

"What are you doing?" Annoyance tinged her tone.

"It's a spell. Another trap."

She twisted her head to look over her shoulder at the dragon, then back at Khirro. He saw she understood. She buried her head against his shoulder.

"I thought I could have it." Her voice muffled in the cloth of his tunic. "It beckoned me, offered itself."

"It's all right. Go warn the others. If they know, they won't be affected."

She nodded and went to the tower sneaking another glance at the dazzling statue. Khirro watched her stay close to the wall as she disappeared around the curve. He gazed back at the dragon but this time, instead of seeing riches, the blood red stone seemed solid fire waiting to be unleashed. He moved closer, staring at the black veins within as they seemed to pulse and pump. He blinked twice to dispel the trick of the light.

It's ash. He took another step. *Ash flows through the veins of a dragon, not blood.*

He stalked a cautious semicircle around the statue, starting in front and ending near its tail, staying ten yards away the whole time. Snow crunched beneath his feet but the ground lay bare and muddy a few yards out from the statue. The dragon crouched halfway between sitting and lying down, its belly not quite brushing the ground. Khirro stared hard, imagining he saw bones in there, the remains of its last victim. He was kneeling, peering beneath its hanging belly, when the others rounded the tower.

"This is your dragon, Khirro?" Ghaul said with a laugh. "It doesn't look so dangerous."

"It also began as a statue in my dream." Khirro didn't look up. There was something under there, something he couldn't quite see.

"What is it?" Elyea asked.

"Dragon teats," Ghaul commented; no one laughed.

"I think there's an opening."

He moved closer, feeling braver now his companions were there. A yard from the beast, he crouched again.

"There is. Right under its belly." He shuffled closer, mud splashing his boots.

"Wait, Khirro," Elyea called. He ignored her.

No more waiting.

He stretched for the opening. The dragon's belly rested six inches above the opening—not enough room for a man to get to it.

There has to be a way.

Sweat rose on Khirro's brow as he inched closer. His cheek touched the dragon's belly; it was rough and pitted, not smooth as it appeared from a distance, the stone hot. The heat on his cheek intensified but he reached farther. Another inch or two and his fingers would reach the opening, maybe confirm it the entrance to the keep.

One of his companions shouted something he didn't hear. Other voices joined the first, but he was so intent on reaching the hole, they might have spoken a foreign tongue.

A little farther. The voice in his head drowned the others out. *Just a little farther.*

The dragon's belly lurched up, revealing the opening.

Khirro saw wooden stairs disappearing out of sight before the red belly slammed down narrowly missing Khirro's arm as he pulled away. His companions' voices rose to fearful shouts. This time he heard and understood.

"Get away, Khirro! The dragon lives!"

42

They saw the fortress wall rising against the horizon while they were still leagues away. To many, the sight instilled wonder and awe, but not to Therrador. The first time he visited, in his idealistic youth full of dreams for the future, he'd felt what others felt as he'd gaped at the wall standing fifty yards high and running the entire width of the isthmus—more than two leagues. The wall had endured for a thousand years, each stone brought by wagon from quarries across the kingdom. The immensity of the structure and the complexity of building it deserved awe, but years spent behind the wall caused reverence to erode into indifference.

"How hold the troops?" Therrador asked.

"The wall holds," Sir Alton Sienhin replied from his right, his horse half a length behind.

"I didn't ask about the wall," Therrador said between clenched teeth. Traveling always made him distraught—too many times the trip ended at a fight. "The wall has stood a thousand years—I'm not concerned for the wall. How are the men?"

"It'll be good for them to have their leader amongst them. It's been difficult with Braymon gone. The officers do what they can to maintain morale and fight despair." The sound of hooves on beaten earth filled the silence as he paused. "The constant rain of rocks and fire from the Kanosee does nothing to cheer their spirits."

"They'll have their leader soon." Therrador shifted in his saddle, searching for a spot on his ass not yet sore. "We'll be there by nightfall."

"And the coronation, your grace?"

"The day after tomorrow. That will give enough time for news to spread." He smiled to himself. "News the new king has arrived."

They rode on in silence and Therrador thought about Graymon, wished he could have brought the boy, but a fortress during wartime is no place for a child. Certainly no place for the heir to the throne of Erechania. In two days, his son's future would be assured and all those years of servitude would be paid in full. Therrador smiled again as his entourage rode across the plain, a cloud of dust billowing behind to mark their passing.

***

Torches flickered in windows dotting the wall of the Isthmus fortress as Therrador and his host rode through the gates, though there were few people in sight as they entered the bailey. Only soldiers and their support remained. Most farmers, merchants and other residents of the fortress had fled at the first sign of the Kanosee army crossing the land bridge onto the salt flats, many of them camping around the outskirts of Achtindel, the rest scattered to villages in the area. Only the greediest merchants remained to take the money of the more than ten thousand soldiers housed in the fortress, but in the large stronghold, even such numbers made it feel empty.

Therrador's steed trotted down the stone boulevard, Sienhin and the rest close behind, horseshoes striking sparks in the dim light. Boulders lay strewn around, occasionally a house lay in ruins or ashes. He turned in his saddle to speak to Sir Alton.

"See this mess is cleaned up first thing. The men hear the catapult fire thumping the wall, they don't need further reminders lying in the streets."

"Yes, my liege."

"And send for some whores from Achtindel. Offer them double if you must—even whores have a duty to their kingdom. If a man's cock is happy, his head is clear. If his head is clear, he's a better fighter."

"Yes, my liege."

They wound through the streets, passing men here and there who only looked up at them. Therrador gritted his teeth but reminded himself they didn't yet know he'd be their king in a few days. When they reached the stables, Therrador dismounted first, followed by Sienhin, then the others. The stable hand took the reins from him, a smile upon his face.

"It's good you came, Lord Therrador," he said leading the big chestnut toward a stall.

"Lord for now," Therrador said more to himself than the stable hand then turned his attention back to Sir Alton. "Take me to the fortress commander. I'll know from his mouth how we fare."

He strode into the courtyard and scanned the area as Sienhin trailed behind. The state of the fortress disgusted him. Braymon would never have let it look like this, so neither would he.

"And then I'll need to speak with the chamberlain. There are many arrangements to be made."

Therrador breathed deep through his nose, smelled the scents of horse manure, burnt wood, and the sweat of the journey still damp on his body. Smells a soldier lived for and loved.

43

Khirro tightened the straps of his shield around his left arm; it felt uncomfortable, awkward.

"The tyger said the seeker must face the guardian," he said swinging the shield, testing the straps. "It's the only way to gain entry."

The dragon crouched over the opening, sides heaving, smoke spouting from its nostrils as it breathed. It hadn't moved since Shyn and Athryn dragged Khirro away, but neither had it returned to its slumber. Gleaming emerald eyes stared at Khirro. Deep inside the translucent chest, he imagined a black heart beating, sending streams of ash coursing through its veins.

It's alive. And anything that lives may die.

"This is foolishness," Ghaul grumbled and pulled an arrow from his quiver. Not many left. "You're no warrior, Khirro. What chance do you have fighting a dragon carved of stone?"

He nocked the arrow and drew the bowstring before Khirro could open his mouth to protest. The arrow sliced through the cold air to shatter upon the dragon's breast. The beast threw its head back and roared, shaking the ground and shivering the trees. Smoke billowed from its mouth.

"Very brave, warrior," Shyn said. "Are you trying to get us all killed?"

"Shut up. Someone has to kill the beast or we've come all this way for nothing."

"It must be me." Khirro tried to sound unafraid but his voice shook.

He was no warrior, Ghaul had that much right. Until the war, and then the water serpent—a kill more luck than killer instinct—he'd never killed more than pigs and chickens, and then only to fill his plate. But dinner rarely fought back. What hope did he have of slaying a dragon?

"At least give me the vial," Ghaul said. "If you must

sacrifice yourself on the whim of a dream, I want the reason I've been dragged across three countries and placed in so much danger to be safe."

Khirro shook his head. "The vial stays with me. It gives me strength. And courage."

Bale had named him bearer, so *he* must convey the vial to Darestat. If he perished, all else would be lost. The vial warmed his chest and he chuckled faintly to himself. Things were about to get much warmer.

Khirro adjusted his helm, drew the Mourning Sword, and stalked away from his companions. He didn't look back for fear Elyea's expression would melt his heart and what little courage he'd mustered. The dragon flicked its tail, canted its head to better see him. Khirro stopped some distance away, searching for a weak spot in the creature's ruby skin, but saw no fault, crack, or opening. He crept around to the dragon's rear, carefully remaining clear of its whip-like tail. The beast turned its head to watch.

Elyea and the others disappeared from Khirro's view as he padded around the far side of the creature. It looked much the same as the other—solidly armored, impossible to breach. Coldness penetrated Khirro's heart, his head felt light. How could he kill this thing? The only plausible opportunity was the most dangerous. The head. Maybe if he struck at the emerald eyes. But how to get past the mouth and the fire within?

Pacing a wide berth to the front of the dragon, Khirro

stopped ten yards from the farthest point he judged its long neck could stretch. To his right, his companions stood, weapons drawn, halfway between the dragon and the keep. He almost laughed at the dagger in Elyea's hand —so small compared to the beast. The dragon's gaze followed his.

"The eye," he called. The dragon's attention flickered back to him. "Aim for the eye, Ghaul."

In an instant, Ghaul nocked an arrow and drew the bowstring. The dragon stared at Khirro, green fire burning in its eyes. Ghaul's bowstring twanged. The dragon flicked its tail and knocked the arrow out of the air. Ghaul loosed another and again the tail flashed. A lump formed in Khirro's throat—the dragon hadn't taken its eyes off him. Ghaul pulled another arrow.

"Save it," Khirro said. He glanced at his companions. "It must be me."

With the Mourning Sword held in front of him, Khirro willed his legs forward a step. His heart beat hard at his temples and in his throat, in his chest and the palms of his hands. The forest to his left with its snow dusted trees, and the tower and his companions to his right all disappeared as the world became nothing but the dragon with its teeth and claws and fire and him with shield and sword and vial. His breath rasped loudly in his ears, but he realized it was so because he heard no other sound. The dragon snorted, smoke spilled from its wide nostrils filling the air with the

397

odor of brimstone. Khirro pushed his other leg forward. Steam rose each time he released his breath, mimicking the smoke seeping from the dragon's nostrils.

Two more agonizing steps and the runes on the Mourning Sword's blade began to glow dully. It smelled blood in the air, sensed the coming taste of flesh. Khirro looked from the dragon to the blade in his hand. The scrolling runes pulsated, writhing like snakes up and down the steel, their redness rivaling the dragon's scales.

The dragon arched its back, threw back its head; an earsplitting roar reverberated skyward as though calling to the heavens themselves. Khirro covered his ears, knocking the shield against his head, momentarily dropping his defenses.

The dragon's head shot forward, the roar still rumbling at the back of its throat, jaws snapping.

Startled but out of reach, Khirro stumbled back. Another roar tore the air. Khirro fell to his knees, hiding behind the shield. The beast reared its head, jaws gaped wide. Voices called to Khirro from a very long way away and part of him wanted to turn his attention to them, to leave this awful world where there was only him and the dragon that would kill him. But another part, a part he hadn't known existed until he fell into the lake and faced the serpent on his own, ignored them. He climbed to his feet and moved the shield from his face.

Gaping jaws, rows of sharp teeth. Deep inside, at the

back of the dragon's throat, a spark flickered, tiny and dim but dangerous. Khirro knew what the small flame meant.

He pulled the shield in front of him and curled his body into a tight ball behind it as the flame hit. The force nearly knocked him to the ground. He closed his eyes, concentrating his energy and strength on keeping his feet —if he lost his balance, there would be no more fight. Sweat streamed down his face, trickled down the back of his neck. What they'd experienced on the boat earlier in the day paled in comparison.

The pressure against his shield eased and Khirro opened his eyes. The ground was bare and steaming for yards around him, the snow vaporized, the mud beneath turned dry and cracked. His shield glowed red-orange; the red on the Mourning Sword glowed more brightly than ever.

The force ceased. Khirro dared a look over his shield, careful not to bring his cheek too close to the red hot edge. The dragon's head hung on its neck, its great ruby chest heaving. Khirro used the respite to creep closer. The cold air dimmed the heat radiating from his shield, but the Mourning Sword continued to glow fiercely. He took another step and the dragon reared back, howling. Khirro planted his feet.

This time, the dragon's breath didn't hit as hard nor last as long. When it stopped, Khirro rushed forward, closing distance before his foe recovered. His mind swirled, part of it taking control, part of it wondering what he was doing. If he stayed at a distance, the dragon would wear him down and he wouldn't be able to counter. At close range, dragon fire was useless. He'd have to contend with tooth and claw, but he could attack.

He caught the dragon by surprise, getting within arm's length before it reacted. The Mourning Sword struck it in the lower chest, shearing through ruby scales. The dragon jumped back screeching. Khirro glimpsed the opening hidden beneath it—decrepit wooden stairs disappeared into impenetrable darkness and the Gods only knew what lay beyond.

The dragon lunged forward, jaws snapping. Khirro dodged, its warm breath stirring the hairs on the back of his neck. The Mourning Sword flashed, seeming to act of its own accord, and pierced the dragon's neck, spilling gray ash from the wound. The beast roared in pain as Khirro swung for its leg but it danced aside, impossibly quick for a creature of its size, and the sword cut empty air.

A huge paw crashed into Khirro's back, razor sharp talons slashed his flesh and sent him flailing to the ground. The Mourning Sword slipped from his grasp and the old part of him—the coward farmer—flashed panic through his limbs. He fought it, clamored to reach the blade lying in the mud out of his reach. He rolled to his back, teeth grinding against the pain, and pulled his dagger—a needle compared to the dragon. The beast reared, air whistling into its lungs, and Khirro's dream jumped to mind.

How did it end?

He saw the spark flicker at the back of the dragon's throat and remembered the fire engulfing him in the dream, but did he survive? He struggled to position the blackened shield over himself so he wouldn't find out how it turned out.

The ground shook under Khirro's back but he resisted the urge to look around, see what caused the tremor. The dragon closed its jaws, cocked its head. Another quake, this time accompanied by the sound of stone crashing against stone. The dragon screamed and spit a pillar of fire over Khirro setting the trees behind him ablaze. The noise sounded again; the dragon coiled on its haunches and leaped into the sky, translucent wings spread wide. Talons dragged across Khirro's chest as it took to the air; its tail lashed, narrowly missed his face.

And it was gone.

Khirro lay on his back, dagger extended, wondering what happened. Elyea appeared at his side, hugging him, the reflection of the fire in the nearby trees shone in the tears streaking her cheeks. She said something, smiled a strained smile, but Khirro didn't hear, his mind was still occupied with the dragon and the noises emanating from the far side of the keep.

The dragon cried in anger, its howl mixed with another, more guttural noise. Wincing at the pain permeating his

401

whole being, Khirro pushed himself to his feet, leaned on
Elyea for balance. He stumbled away from the charred
earth and the opening in the ground, unsteady legs
carrying him toward the keep. Elyea grasped his hand but
he pulled away.

"Khirro." Shyn rushed to his side. "We have to get into
the keep before the dragon returns."

He shook his head. "You go. I have to see what's
happening."

The skin on his face felt tight and hot. He could
imagine how it must look, hoped he wasn't burned like
Athryn. He retrieved the Mourning Sword and shuffled
around the tower. A hand caught him under the arm,
steadying him—Shyn at his side.

"Ghaul will get the others down the stairs. I'll ensure
you get there, too."

Khirro looked at him, too tired to smile, and nodded,
then returned his thoughts to keeping his balance. They
crept around the keep, the dragon's shrieks prompting
them on. More than one voice snarled and bellowed in
answer.

The giants have caught up.

They rounded the curve of the keep and saw boulders
strewn near the foot of the wall, rubble chipped from the
tower scattered amongst them. Three giants—two males
wearing bearskin loincloths and the female they'd
encountered before—hurled stones at the dragon held

aloft above them, the mighty sweep of its wings stirring the trees like a tornado's wind. The dragon's head cocked back and the tiny spark lit the depths of its throat. The giants shouted and growled, unaware of what the little flame meant until fire belched from the dragon's jaws.

Flames engulfed one of the males and the giant's war cry became a scream of agony. It stumbled into the forest, igniting shrubs and brambles as it went and the dragon followed flame with tooth and talon, diving at the others, slashing and raking, whipping its tail.

Khirro saw no more as Shyn drew him away only half-willingly from the battle. Pride swelled his chest—he'd stood against the dragon and lived where three giants would fall under its savage attack. Distracted, he stumbled on a stone fallen from the tower wall, but Shyn's hand under his arm kept him upright, pulled him back from his self-congratulations. He righted himself and let Shyn lead him at a faster pace.

Ghaul stood at the top of the stairs leading into the ground, urging them on. As they hurried toward him, the warrior's eyes strayed to a spot over their heads. His expression changed and he rushed down the stairs. A snarl echoed in Khirro's head. He looked over his shoulder as the dragon rose high above the tower, ruby wings blocking the sky. The arm of a giant dangled from its claws.

A few more yards.

The air swirled around them as warm breath singed the

403

hair at the back of Khirro's neck. Shyn dove down the stairs pulling Khirro after him. Teeth gnashed, slammed closed like a clap of thunder, but he was out of reach.

Khirro ran down the dark stairs as fast as he dared but couldn't help but glance back at the dragon's head filling the opening, its green eyes blazing anger. Then the face disappeared, replaced by darkness.

And a spark.

Khirro leaped down the stairs, praying the bottom was close. His feet caught, pitched him forward. Abruptly, he saw every detail before him—the grain of the boards in the ancient stair, frost painting the earthen wall a sparkling white, his companions diving down a tunnel, out of sight. His world filled with light, then fire and heat, and finally darkness.

44

The tyger was not the same as in the other dreams. The black and white striped fur which looked like it would be soft to the touch was gone. Instead, the tyger stalking a tight circle around him pulsed and flowed, its shape formed by fire. Khirro shielded his eyes from the light, but felt no heat. When it halted a few feet in front of him, he reached out a shaking hand and brushed its flaming whiskers, its blazing ears. It still didn't burn him.

"Don't be afraid," it said, its voice a deep, pleasant rumble in his head. "We are one with the fire. It burns within us."

Khirro stared at the beast, at the flames flickering in its face. "Am I dead?"

"No." The great cat took a step forward, a fiery tongue flickered out and caressed his cheek. "I will heal you."

"Thank you, King Braymon."

"I am no longer King Braymon but the spirit that dwelled within him. I will remain so until the Necromancer restores me." The cat paused, head titled. "But we will both always be of the fire, Khirro."

He opened his mouth to speak, but the tyger and the dream dimmed like a taper nearing the end of its tallow: flickering, fading and finally going out.

The darkness of waking was a startling change from the light of his dream. For a moment, Khirro couldn't remember who or where he was, but memory returned quickly: the keep, the giants, the dragon.

The fire.

A torch guttered at the edge of his vision; he shifted toward it, drawn to the flame. His body ached, kept him from moving much, so he fell back with a creak of armor. The smell of something burnt filled his nose.

"He is awake." Athryn's voice. The magician appeared over him, the torch in his hand reflecting flame in his polished metal mask. Khirro looked to see himself in its surface, see what damage the dragon had done, but the torch obscured his view. "Do not try to move."

"Where are we?" Khirro croaked, his throat a desert, his words sparse water squeezed from the sand.

"In the tunnels under the keep," Elyea replied kneeling beside him.

She stroked his forehead, brushed hair from it, and the burnt smell intensified. Her eyes didn't stray from his. He blinked slowly, a vision of dragon fire filling his mind as his eyes closed. He snapped them open again, struggled to prop himself on his elbows but Athryn's hand kept him in place.

"What of the dragon?"

"We are far enough into the tunnel neither the dragon nor its fire can reach us," the magician told him.

"But it's perched on the exit," Ghaul said, an edge to his voice. "We're doomed to die here."

"There will be another way out," Shyn snapped.

Khirro brushed Athryn's hand from his shoulder and pushed himself to a sitting position. It hurt. His skin felt as though it had shrunk two sizes. Elyea and Athryn each supported him under an arm and helped him to his feet.

"Are you okay to move?" Elyea asked.

"I have to be."

Athryn nodded. "Elyea, help Ghaul and Shyn get ready while I change Khirro's dressings."

She kissed Khirro lightly on the cheek then went down the tunnel to join the two soldiers.

"How long have we been down here?"

Athryn shrugged as he unwound a bandage from Khirro's chest. "It is hard to tell without the sun overhead. Perhaps two days."

Two days!

Khirro wiped sweat from his brow though Athryn's touch felt cool. He glanced down the tunnel at the others and saw they all wore their tunics.

It's the burns making me warm. Or fever.

"How bad is it, Athryn?"

The magician didn't look up. "Your wounds are clean. They heal quickly, more quickly even than the blood of the king healed them before."

"No, I mean the burns. Do I..." He hesitated. "Do I look like you?"

Athryn stopped, raised his eyes to meet Khirro's. No tone of accusation or offence entered his voice.

"No, Khirro. You are unscarred."

He moved his head so Khirro could see his own features reflected in the mask: hair singed, eyebrows gone, but no burns. He sighed with relief—hair would grow back. But there was still the heat.

"I'm hot, Athryn. Do I have a fever?"

Khirro had seen many people in his village succumb to fever after they thought their wounds healed. A chill shook his spine. What mockery it would be to survive a dragon only to die of infection.

"You survived the dragon's fire." Athryn's tone was

407

hushed, his eyes gleamed behind his mask. "Not once, but twice."

"That's why I'm warm?"

Athryn tapped his finger against Khirro's chest. "It gets inside and burns there."

Khirro stared, wide eyes reflected and distorted in the contoured silver mask as he remembered the dream tyger's words.

"What do you mean?"

With a shrug, Athryn went back to changing Khirro's bandages. "You saw what effect it had on my brother. We shall soon find out what it means to you."

45

The dragon landed heavily on the stone floor, teetered before toppling on its side; the impact snapped a wing from its body. It lay unmoving, feeling no pain, before small fingers wrapped around its middle and picked it up from the floor leaving the broken wing behind.

Graymon held the wooden dragon up to examine the damage. He looked from the carved dragon to the wing lying on the floor and sadness welled in his eyes, but he bit his lip. How could Gorgo, king of the dragons, fly with only one wing? What good was a dragon who didn't fly? He looked at the toy, sadness turning to disgust at the useless, broken thing. No good to him or anyone now. Angry, he threw the dragon to the floor. It bounced once, the other wing separating from the body, and smacked against the wall.

The boy sank to the floor and sat cross-legged, head hung. If Da was here, he'd have fixed the king of the dragons.

Why did he go?

Nanny was no fun. She didn't like to play and mostly left him alone—like now. Graymon rubbed at a smear of food caked on his trousers since lunchtime and wondered what to play now Gorgo was hurt. He got up and walked to the tapestry covering a hidden doorway and stood close, ear brushing the woven scene of wild horses galloping across the plain. No sounds.

Maybe nanny left.

She wasn't very good company, but he didn't want to be alone, either. He pushed the tapestry aside and peeked through the space between it and the wall. Nanny sat in Da's chair snoring softly, feet up on the big red and white table.

Graymon let the tapestry fall back into place, relieved he hadn't been deserted, but still with no playmate. He retrieved one of Gorgo's broken wings, then the other, then slumped cross-legged and picked up the carven dragon. He held a wing against the body, the splintered ends fitting together like a puzzle. When he let go, it stayed in place until he moved the toy, then tumbled to the floor.

"Rrrr," he growled as he walked the wingless dragon

409

across the stone floor. "Rrrr."

The half-hearted growl came out a shadow of its former self—the once ferocious beast would never be the same without wings. A dragon unable to fly was no more dangerous than a lion. Not that lions weren't dangerous, he just already had a lion toy. Disappointed, he let go of the toy, leaving it standing on the floor, and glared at it.

He wanted his dragon back.

I want my Da.

He closed his eyes and sighed, fought to keep tears at bay once more. He didn't want nanny to come in and find him crying. She'd get mad if she found him crying. Nanny didn't like tears.

A scraping sound made Graymon forget his sadness. He opened his eyes expecting to see nanny or a guard standing in the doorway, but there was no one.

The boy glanced around his chamber, from unmade bed draped with red bedclothes that matched the frilled canopy, to wooden shelves cluttered with carved animals and tops and intricate toy soldiers, and at the armoire, so tall he couldn't reach the clothes hung inside without help. Everything looked as it always did.

Movement at the corner of his eye caught his attention: one of the broken-off wings skittered across the floor. Graymon stared. He reached to pick it up but it skirted his grasp and crossed to where the dragon stood. The other wing followed, sliding and bouncing along until it lay on the floor beside its former owner.

Graymon opened his mouth, intending to call nanny, but giggled instead. What a wonderful trick the king of dragons had done. He leaned forward to examine the three pieces but they began to shudder, so he stopped. The wings rose from the floor, rotating and moving until their splintered ends lined up against the dragon's body. The ends touched, glowed briefly with dim red light, and Gorgo, king of the dragons, became whole again.

Graymon clapped his hands and laughed. He didn't think to wonder how his favorite toy had healed itself, only felt elated the dragons would have their king again and he his toy. He rocked happily back and forth, excited to play once more, but stopped when the dragon's wings flapped.

The wood creaked as the wings raised and lowered once. Graymon sucked in a sharp breath through his open mouth.

The king of the dragons never did that before.

The wings flapped a second time. Then again. The boy giggled. The dragon's wings flapped harder and the toy rose from the floor, an inch at first, but its wings beat the air harder and it climbed higher.

Graymon's laughter stopped as nerves nibbled in his tummy. Having a flying dragon appealed to him, but he knew toys didn't move by themselves, not without gears and strings and keys to wind them. He stared as it hovered level with his head. The toy maneuvered until their eyes met. The dragon's eyes held the same red glow that had fused its wings back together.

As he gawked at the dragon, Graymon noticed the figure standing on the bear skin rug by his bed. The person didn't move. The hood of a black cloak was pulled down to cover its face while the cloak's hem brushed the fur carpet; its hands were tucked into broad sleeves.

Graymon forgot the dragon toy. Fear seized his chest, climbed into his throat, but he swallowed hard around it.

Warriors don't show others when they're afraid, his father told him more than once. *Not even little warriors like you.*

He wanted to be a brave little warrior like his Da wanted him to be, but it was hard.

"Who...who are you?" Graymon's throat wanted him to cry instead of ask questions.

"I'll not hurt you, my prince," the figure replied with the pleasant-sounding voice of a woman, one which would sound good if it took up a song. "The king sent me to take care of you."

"Da?"

"Yes, your father." Her tone soothed him, as though she crooned a lullaby. "He sent me to get you, to bring you to him."

Graymon tilted his head as he looked at the figure; she didn't move as she spoke. Da had warned him to be careful of people he didn't know, but the prospect of seeing his

412

father sooner than expected made him excited.

"But Da is far away," Graymon said, excitement in his voice. "He went to where there's a real war with real soldiers."

The person knelt in front of him, though he hadn't seen her cross the room, startling Graymon. He noticed he needed to pee.

"Your father wants me to take you to him right away."

She took one hand from a sleeve and placed it on Graymon's knee. He looked down and saw slender fingers ending in long nails painted many colors. Tiny pictures adorned each one. On one: a bunny; on another a fox was painted, then a flower and a sun. As Graymon looked at them, the bunny jumped from one nail to the next and the fox took up the chase, leaping in front of the sun, chasing the bunny past the flower. The boy gasped and giggled.

The black cloaked woman reached out a finger and placed it under his chin, raised his eyes to peer toward where hers would be if he could see beneath the hood. As if hearing his thoughts, she reached up and pulled the cowl back.

Graymon cringed, expecting something dead and decayed to appear from under the black cloth. Instead, long hair so yellow it appeared golden spilled from the woman's head, cascaded over her pleasant face. Painted lips curled in a warm smile that reflected in her dark brown eyes.

413

"We must go." She put her hand on Graymon's shoulder and squeezed lightly. He pivoted his head, trying to see the pictures on her nails. "Your father wants to see you."

"What about nanny?"

Graymon allowed the woman to help him to his feet. The king of the dragons flapped its wings and climbed higher until it came to rest on his shoulder. He smiled as the toy nuzzled his neck.

"Nanny is sleeping." She took Graymon's hand. "There is no reason to wake her. She will know you have gone to your father."

Graymon stroked the wooden dragon's ridged neck; it nipped playfully at his fingers. He didn't know who this woman was, but he liked what was happening with her around. It would be all right to go with her—Da sent her, after all.

"Will we be riding horses?" He liked horses, they were more fun than riding in a carriage. Warriors rode horses.

"No, I have a quicker way for us to get there, but you have to promise you won't be frightened."

Graymon looked into her brown eyes and smiled involuntarily.

"I promise."

"Good. And you must be quiet so we do not wake nanny."

He nodded, being quiet like she wanted. The dragon

hissed near his ear and the boy stifled a giggle. This would be an adventure like a real warrior would have. His Da would be proud of how bravely he acted. Smiling, he looked down at his hand in the woman's. Figures still danced across her painted nails, but the fox and bunny were gone. Instead, twisted men with skeleton faces and creatures he didn't want to see writhed from nail to nail. He looked away, suddenly regretting his promise not to be scared, and glanced toward the woman. He wanted to tell her he'd changed his mind about going but the black cloak whirled about him, fell over his head, leaving him in darkness.

Graymon began to cry, the black cloak swallowing his sobs as easily as it swallowed the light.

46

Once the torch burned down to nothing, guttering and spitting its last bit of light, the darkness stretched on without respite. The tunnel twisted and turned, throwing off Khirro's sense of what direction they traveled and how far they went. Against reason, it angled ever downward, away from the keep they thought their goal.

"Are you sure this is the right way?" Ghaul asked more than once, his tone becoming more angered each time he heard Khirro's response: "I don't know."

He didn't know. The Shaman showed him the way to the tower, no farther. The dream tyger told him it was he

415

who had to get past the guardian, but no more. Perhaps neither of them expected a simple farmer to make it this far.

Who could blame them?

He dismissed the thought. Both Shaman and tyger wanted him to succeed. They probably didn't know what to expect after the dragon. When was the last time anyone had passed the guardian to chart what lay beyond?

They pressed on in the saturnine dark, moving slowly to avoid walking into each other until their eyes became accustomed to the constant night inside the tunnel. Even then, they could see only a few paces ahead. When they stopped to rest and sleep, they took turns at what they insisted on calling 'watch' though they watched nothing but blackness.

No dreams disturbed Khirro's sleep—no Shaman to guide him, no tyger encouraging him, nor dragon to kill him, or women to tempt him. The same darkness that permeated his waking accompanied his sleep.

Khirro thought it must have been the second day of groping along the benighted passage when they arrived at a fork in their path. Before this, they'd passed no side tunnels or openings to confuse the path they should follow.

"Which way?" Ghaul asked. Khirro barely saw his features in the dark, but knew his jaw would be set, eyes hard.

"I don't know."

He regretted his honesty immediately as the shadow of Ghaul's face turned to a scowl. The warrior slammed his gauntleted hand against the tunnel wall, the sound echoing away until lost in the dark like themselves.

"How in the name of your Gods are we going to get out of here?" He stepped closer to Khirro, hand on the hilt of his sword.

"Calm yourself, Ghaul," Shyn said, voice more commanding than calming. "The best way to find our way is to keep our heads. Figuratively as well as literally."

Ghaul's glare slid from Khirro to the border guard. "What do you propose we do, birdman?"

The air in the tunnel gathered around them, pressing in like a bloodthirsty audience awaiting the outcome of the warriors' standoff. Khirro's skin still felt as though it belonged to someone smaller than himself and he shifted in a vain effort to loosen it.

"A breeze blows from the tunnel on the right," Shyn said finally. "It's slight, but might lead us to the surface."

They gathered around the opening to feel the wind. If it was there, Khirro didn't detect it.

"All right. Shyn and I will investigate, the rest of you wait here. Don't move until we say." The anger in Ghaul's voice had been replaced by satisfaction at having a soldierly task. He leaned toward Elyea and said: "I'll be back soon," then moved to kiss her but she turned her

417

head so his lips brushed her cheek.

"Do not stray from the path," Athryn said as they took their first step into the opening. "If there are other tunnels, stay on the straight path or come back. We do not want to lose you."

"Could we be more lost?" Ghaul sneered.

Shyn slapped him hard on the shoulder. "One can always be more lost."

They pulled their swords and stalked into the tunnel, disappearing from sight immediately. Khirro thought that Shyn's voice didn't sound as confident as usual; he sighed and wondered if this was the right thing to do.

***

Minutes dragged by, their languid pace agonizing. Khirro sat with his back pressed against the wall searching for a position to best alleviate the pain crawling beneath his skin. He healed quickly, as Athryn said, but pain still nagged him. The gashes inflicted by the dragon were deep and likely would have killed him if not for the protection afforded by the blood of the king. As he shifted, Elyea lifted her head from his shoulder.

How brave she's been.

The Mourning Sword lay balanced across his lap in the hope its glow would provide them with some illumination, but the red runes didn't glow in the darkness of the tunnel —a trick of the light, then. Athryn stood at the mouth of the left tunnel, dagger in hand, invisible to Khirro. He couldn't remember if the magician still bothered to wear his silvered mask—even it couldn't be seen in the impenetrable dark.

They're all brave. They gave up so much to accompany me on this voyage that didn't belong to them. Without them, I'd be long dead. Like Maes.

Thinking of the little man squeezed Khirro's heart. He couldn't imagine how Athryn felt losing his brother, especially the way it came to pass. Yet the magician continued, driven more by the hope the Necromancer would raise Maes than by Khirro's task. He suspected the magician was prepared to give his life to bring his brother back.

What irony that would be, like a song a troubadour might sing.

And Elyea. She snuggled closer against his side seeking the warmth he radiated. He didn't pretend to understand her life, couldn't fathom living it and being happy, but she seemed content. Yet she left behind her friends and all she knew without pause. Warmth unrelated to the dragon's breath filled his chest. If someone told him a few months ago love for a harlot would fade the image of Emeline from his mind, he'd have thought them crazy.

Finally, his mind strayed to Ghaul and Shyn—both warriors, and brave, but so different. He admired Shyn, a man ostracized by his peers for being different, though how different, Khirro didn't think he'd yet learned.

419

Through it all he remained of good spirit, caring for those about him. Ghaul, on the other hand, was more what he'd have expected from a life-soldier: hardened, tough, uncompromising. He wondered about Ghaul's motivations. Was he here out of loyalty to the crown? A glory seeker? Or something else? His joy in killing appalled Khirro at first, but it was his profession, something for which he'd been bred and trained his whole life. It didn't matter why Ghaul was there, only that he was with them, helping accomplish their goal.

But he's been so different since Shyn joined us.

Khirro thought back to when he and Ghaul had eluded their pursuers, scrambling along the bottom of the drainage ditch. So long ago. Ghaul hadn't been so angry before there was another soldier in their company.

Athryn shifted, his cloak brushing against his breeches, unnaturally loud as the darkness amplified it. They all sat with their thoughts, waiting, listening for a sign of their friends returning. Or something else.

It was hard to tell how much time had passed when the sound of metal clanging against metal echoed down the tunnel. It seemed to come from everywhere at once. Khirro leaped to his feet, Elyea close behind.

"Athryn, where did that come from?"

"I do not know." The magician moved to his side, looking first down one tunnel then the other. The darkness revealed nothing.

"Shyn," Khirro yelled. It was impossible to know if his companions were the source of the noise, but he had to assume they were and they might need help. "Ghaul! Where are you?"

Khirro's voice reverberated down the tunnels, bouncing from wall to wall, finally swallowed up by distance. No answer came. The clash of steel ceased. Breathless minutes passed. Khirro raised the Mourning Sword, ready for anything, and was startled to see the runes glowing a deep red, reflecting swirls of crimson in Athryn's metal mask.

There's blood in the air.

The thought fled as the sound of footsteps echoed down the passage, growing louder. And closer.

But from which way do they come?

***

Shyn strode along the passage as quickly as he dared, his senses tingling. He felt feathers bristling just below the surface of his skin and struggled to keep them at bay. A falcon would be of no use in an underground tunnel.

The tunnel ran fairly straight, but even Shyn's heightened vision couldn't penetrate far, and he didn't want to walk into the wall—or anything else. The farther they advanced, the stronger the breeze felt on his face. He knew the others hadn't felt it—skin used to judging wind velocity and direction based on the movement of feathers was more sensitive than the average man's flesh. As minute as the movement of air was, he relished the feel of it

421

against his cheek, allowed it to distract him from the knot in his belly.

"It grows stronger," he whispered over his shoulder. Ghaul grunted.

They walked on, their footsteps disturbing silence unbroken for centuries. Shyn probed ahead with his sword, the tip occasionally scraping the wall as the tunnel veered a little left or right. The sound of leather scraping against stone followed him as Ghaul dragged his hand along the passage wall looking for side tunnels. After a few minutes, Shyn saw a little farther, his sensitive eyes detecting a change in the level of light. Hope quelled the bird beneath his skin.

"Can you see the light, Ghaul?"

"No."

"Up ahead. It's dim, but grows brighter."

The wan light allowed Shyn to see several paces ahead. A wall soon loomed, ending the passageway.

"We've reached the end." Shyn halted. "This is where the tunnel stops."

He touched the wall and looked up along its surface. At the top was a slit smaller than a man's little finger. The tiny opening—an air hole—was responsible for the light and the movement of air only Shyn felt. He couldn't tell whether moonlight or sunlight shone through—they must be a long way underground for it to be so diffuse. The hope that had calmed him disappeared; the short hairs on the back of his neck stirred, his flesh prickled.

"This is where it ends," Ghaul said, voice low and husky.

Ghaul's tone set Shyn's nerves screaming of danger. He gripped his sword with both hands and turned, blade held before him.

Ghaul stood waiting, sword raised. He swung it down savagely, catching Shyn half by surprise, but the tip scraped the stone ceiling showering sparks twinkling into the dark. The brief flash lit the hatred on Ghaul's face like a torch to Shyn's keen eyes, and the instant of pause as steel struck stone gave him time to parry the blow from his face. He countered, their swords sparking. Shyn wondered if the meager light allowed Ghaul to see him, too.

Ghaul took the offensive, raining blows at Shyn, kicking him, driving him back against the end wall. Another thrust. Shyn parried, elbow slamming the wall. Ghaul's blade glanced off his forearm and blood filled the border guard's gauntlet. Survival instinct took over and he began to change as he dodged another blow.

Is there enough room?

He couldn't control the transformation in such situations so set his jaw and concentrated on defense until the change finished. Ghaul's next strike hit full force against his sword's guard, tearing it from his hand. There wouldn't be time to change.

Or anything else.

423

He crossed his arms in front of himself, leather and mail deflecting Ghaul's blows for a moment, but only for a moment. The steel finally slid through leather and mail, flesh and organs, not stopping until the tip touched stone behind him. Shyn sucked air in through his teeth, burning in his pierced lung. Ghaul loomed close, the hate in his eyes glowing in the darkness.

"Why?" Shyn whispered.

"I need the farmer to carry it," he said drawing his blade upward, slicing through more organs. "The others are nothing. You're the only one who can stop me."

Shyn's mouth moved as he formed another question, but only blood bubbled from his lips. The dim light of the tiny shaft overhead began to fade, but Shyn saw the blue sky and bright sun far above, felt the wind whisk through his feathers, and smiled.

***

Darkness pressed around Khirro like a cloak of fear and dread spread across his shoulders, wrapped about his body. At his elbow, Elyea's breath came short and sharp. To his left, Athryn waited at the mouth of the other tunnel, guarding against whatever might emerge. The clatter of metal striking metal died away, followed by silence. Khirro dared not call out again as he struggled to keep his hand holding the Mourning Sword from shaking.

An ache knotted Khirro's shoulder, tension burning his muscle with the weight of the sword. He wanted to stretch

424

his pained muscles, but was afraid any movement would give him away. If he let his guard down, that would be the moment something leaped from the darkness. The discomfort had become almost unbearable when they heard noises.

At first Khirro couldn't distinguish the nature of the sound or where it came from, but it soon resolved into footsteps. Hard leather slapped against stone floor, moving quickly, sending echoes bouncing down the long passageways making it impossible to tell how many feet made the sound.

The noise grew louder.

Khirro's muscles tensed further. He scanned the darkness trying to see Athryn.

Where is it coming from? In front? Behind?

The runes running up the blade of the Mourning Sword cast a mute light like the dim red embers of a dying fire. Khirro saw Elyea's strained features painted with blood by the faint glow, her jeweled dagger in hand. She didn't look away from the tunnel.

The echoes intensified, tangling upon one another until it seemed an army approached. At the last second, Khirro realized the sound emanated from the tunnel before him, the one down which Shyn and Ghaul had gone. He drew back his blade, the runes brightening at the prospect of blood like an animal salivating before it eats.

Ghaul must have seen the runes as he skidded to a halt

425

out of sword's reach. The soldier held his own blade in his hand, the steel marked by dark patches along its edge which could only be blood.

"What happened?" Khirro asked dropping his blade to his side.

Ghaul bent at the waist and gulped air in ragged breaths. Visions of monsters or undead Kanosee soldiers dogged Khirro's thoughts as he waited for him to recover.

"We must go," Ghaul panted, gasping more of the stale tunnel air. "Death lies down that tunnel. Shyn is lost."

Elyea gasped. "What?"

Athryn joined them, the Mourning Sword casting swirling fire in his silvered mask.

"They surprised us," Ghaul said finding his breath. "Came from nowhere in the dark. We fought, but they killed Shyn. I slew them, but there may be more. We can't stay here. The other tunnel is the only way."

The runes' glow faded and blackness crept back in around them. Khirro reached forward tentatively, resting his hand on Ghaul's shoulder. "Are you all right?"

"Yes."

"But we can't leave Shyn," Elyea protested.

"Shyn's dead. The rest of us need not die, too."

"But we can take him to the Necromancer. He can bring him back."

"He cannot be raised," Athryn intoned solemnly. "Only living blood can be resurrected. If his heart has stopped, it

426

is too late."

"It might not be," Elyea said clutching Khirro's sleeve, looking to him for support. He wanted to give it, wanted Shyn to be alive, but every nerve in him said it was too late. "We have to be sure."

"No," Ghaul said firmly. "There is death for all of us down that passage. We have to go. Now!"

They stood in silence, each invisible with their thoughts and emotions before Ghaul pushed past, moving to the left tunnel. Athryn's cloak stirred as he followed. Elyea's ragged breath stayed at Khirro's side. He reached his arm around her shoulders, careful not to stick himself on her dagger, and guided her toward the opening. At first her legs were stubborn, her feet dragging against the floor, but she soon followed, moving down the tunnel away from one unknown danger toward another, their companion left behind.

47

It would have taken hours to climb to the cavern's ceiling, half a day to reach the far end. A cobalt glow emanated from everything; it lit the entire area leaving no corner or crevice in darkness. They'd seen the light seeping down the tunnel and hurried forward, anxious for their journey's end, but they found no Necromancer—not here, not yet.

The cavern was empty except for stalactites hanging

Bruce Blake

from the high ceiling, large enough they'd impale a man if they fell. Many became stalagmites halfway to the floor, joining top to bottom. Water dripped lazily from most of them, plopping into shallow puddles that trickled away to nowhere.

They stood at the entrance, awed and disappointed. The torpid blue light reflected in Athryn's mirrored mask, changing it from silver to azure, the same color as his eyes.

"Where now?"

The dried blood on the edge of the sword Ghaul still grasped looked gray in the cavern's glow and Khirro cringed as he posed the all-too-familiar question. Khirro opened his mouth to answer the same way he did every time the question was asked, but Athryn spoke first.

"We should rest. We are tired and it will be easy to keep watch here." The magician's tone was solemn. Ghaul grunted in response.

They kept the wall at their backs as they entered the cavern and picked their way through scree, fallen stalactites and puddles glowing a luminescent blue more dazzling than the rest of the cavern. Ghaul called a halt when they found a spot partially hidden by a boulder.

"I'll take first watch," Khirro volunteered and received no argument from the others.

Ghaul cast his pack on the ground, cleared an area of loose pebbles and stones, and lay down with his back to them, sword within easy reach at his side. Athryn removed

428

his metal mask, stored it in his pack, and pulled on his black sleeping mask.

"We have no more food," he said pulling the cloth over his scarred face.

Khirro nodded. "At least there's water here."

His belly growled a complaint as he spoke. Water wouldn't be enough for long. In the darkness of the tunnel, shrouded in fear and danger as they fled first the dragon, then whatever killed Shyn, he hadn't noticed the hunger burning deep in his belly. Now, in the light and the open, it twisted his gut, wringing aches and groans from it.

Elyea sat on a smooth-topped rock watching Athryn make himself a place to rest, then she looked at Khirro. He smiled half-heartedly; her lip twitched like she wanted to return the same but failed. Kneeling beside her, Khirro touched her arm lightly.

"Get some sleep. You'll feel better."

She nodded and looked to where Ghaul lay. Khirro leaned in and kissed her cheek, suddenly aware of the rough texture of his stubbled face, but she didn't react disagreeably. Instead, the failed smile finally broke on her lips, though her eyes remained sad and wary. He left her clearing a spot for sleep and went to the other side of the boulder, away from his companions, where he'd have a clear view of the cavern.

Khirro sat with his back against the rock, the Mourning Sword laid bare across his thighs. The expansive cavern

429

filled his vision. He'd never have guessed a cave this size
existed. The craggy floor ran level from end to distant end,
broken only by the scattered fragments of ceiling and wall
fallen upon it untold years or centuries ago. To his right,
water droplets plummeted from high overhead, ending
their journey of hundreds of feet with a plunk in a shallow
puddle. Khirro went to it, skirting rocks the size of a man's
head, and knelt beside the pool, watched the rivulet of
liquid snake away to disappear in a crack in the floor. The
water took on the glow of the cavern, intensifying it to the
brightest blue in a world of blue.

Or perhaps it is the water which lights the cavern.

He lay the Mourning Sword aside and pulled his
gauntlet from his right hand. The air cooled his sweaty
palm as he tossed the glove to the ground beside his
weapon. He stretched his hand open and held it over the
puddle to catch the next drop like a child awaiting a
snowflake. A droplet fell, missed his hand, and sent tiny
waves across the puddle's surface reminding him of the
lake. He shuddered and adjusted his position.

The next drop spattered in the center of his palm, its
coolness refreshing his warm skin. Another drop splashed
on his hand, then another. The shallow bowl of his palm
filled with water, glowing and shimmering against his pink
flesh. Its wetness awakened him to the dryness in his
throat, hidden from him like his hunger and by his hunger.
He brought his hand to his lips and sucked the fluid

greedily onto his tongue.

It tasted fresh and clean, with a vague flavor Khirro couldn't place, not earthy or dirty like so much of the water he'd consumed in the past months. Sipping it didn't slake his thirst but made him more aware of it. He bent forward and put his lips into the puddle, slurped it like a man in a desert come upon an oasis. Drops rained on the back of his neck, slipped under his tunic, cooled his hot flesh.

Khirro sucked and slurped, drank his fill until the hungry growl in his belly stopped. He pulled away from the puddle and leaned back, eyes closed. His belly felt full yet his throat and tongue remained unquenched. He dipped his hand into the water, splashed it across his face and rubbed his stubbly cheeks and chin. Breathing deeply through his nose, he opened his eyes.

An angry red glow had replaced the luminescent blue light. It flickered around him, licking the walls like flames burning without heat. Khirro raised an eyebrow, ignoring the fear poking its way into his belly.

A trick, that's all.

His sword and gauntlet were gone. He searched the ground and noted differences from what he'd seen before: no rocks or debris scattered around him, the floor rippled and sloped, no longer smooth and flat. The cavern had shrunk until the walls and ceiling were close enough he could stretch out and touch them.

Khirro stood, knees quivering. As he straightened, the ground heaved. He pitched forward, chest slamming into the hard ground, and he lay there, nose inches from the floor, waiting to see if the earth would quake again. Under him, he saw the floor was no longer made of stone, but was translucent. Trough it, he saw a wooden stair winding away into darkness.

The fear successfully quelled a moment before bubbled through, tingling his arms and fingers, clenching his groin and halting his breath. He rolled onto his back observing every detail. The light flickered red, orange and yellow as though he lay in the midst of a fire without flames or heat. He turned his gaze to the walls, squinting, straining to see. Shapes showed through it, ghosts in red.

Trees covered in snow?

Khirro jumped to his feet, knees bent and arms extended to keep his balance should the earth revolt against his movement. A shape above and to his left caught his attention and he turned his head to see. Hanging there, appearing suspended in mid-air, a giant ruby expanded and contracted rhythmically. He reached for it, stretching his arm, wiggling his fingers only inches from it.

The ground shifted again sending Khirro skittering backward. On the other side of the translucent wall, a figure appeared. He squinted and moved toward it, forgetting caution. The man wore armor and a helm, an unmarked shield strapped to one arm, a blade in the other

432

hand. A black blade.

Recognition dawned. The color, the man's position. Khirro understood where he was.

A gust of wind swirled about his limbs, pushed him against the wall. The reek of brimstone filled his nose and twisted his windpipe into a knot. The figure before him hid behind the shield as a column of flame engulfed him. Khirro glanced up at the underside of the dragon's neck and chin, fire shooting from its mouth and nostrils. Somehow, he was inside the beast, watching his own battle from the dragon's belly.

The flame ceased, leaving shield and sword glowing red. He watched himself rush forward, swinging the Mourning Sword at the dragon, connecting against its chest. The creature roared—an earsplitting sound to a man inside it. He clamped his hands over his ears, still watching as the dragon's head shot out, lightning quick, its jaws closing around the other Khirro's head.

Khirro gasped in surprise and horror as the beast drew upward, pulling his other self's feet from the ground kicking and struggling before the head came off and the body fell convulsing to the muddy ground. Blood spouted from the severed neck, its color made invisible through the red chest of the dragon. Khirro stumbled backward in shock.

This isn't how it happened.

The dragon reared on its hind legs throwing Khirro to

his back. He closed his eyes against the pain, the scar this very dragon gave him pulsing and throbbing.

Something changed.

The smell of brimstone disappeared and a feeling of floating overcame him as the pressure of his back against the dragon's belly melted away. He opened his eyes to murky water, silt stinging them. He didn't have to guess where he was this time; he knew what hid somewhere in the tangled weeds. The surface of the lake moved above him, sunlight flashing on waves. He kicked his legs and stroked with his arms, struggling toward it.

The serpent came at him out of nowhere, its nose slamming into his stomach, forcing out what little air his lungs struggled to hold. Its tail whipped his face sending him spinning, making it impossible to tell up from down. He fought to right himself without knowing where to find right. The surface winked at him and he stroked for it, lungs shrieking for air.

The muscles in his limbs burned, tiring with the lack of oxygen, but instead of coming closer, the surface floated farther from his reach. A dark shadow cut between him and the distant surface, a long, slender body blocking what little light filtered through the murk.

The light vanished. Khirro struggled, but his arms and legs gave out. His mouth opened involuntarily, desperate for air, and his lungs drew silty water, his mouth filling with the dirty taste. He sank, closing his eyes in the

434

darkness of the lake's depths.

On hands and knees, he opened his eyes coughing imaginary water from his lungs, gasping for air. He looked down at brown pine needles and ancient moss under his hands as he panted, not daring to feel relieved. It was dark, though not dark like in the tunnel.

A scream broke the still, a cry of terror Khirro recognized as Elyea's. He scrambled to his feet and clamored to the crest of the hill, twigs and branches scratching his face and hands. A fire blazed in the small valley below; Elyea lay on the ground bound by thick hemp rope. Across the fire pit sat the giant, the tip of his spear resting amongst the flames. He pulled the weapon from the fire and jabbed it into her ribs provoking another shriek.

Khirro called out but had no voice. He rushed down the slope and a root caught his foot, sending him tumbling. By the time he stopped himself, the giant had moved to Elyea. It grabbed a handful of rope, lifted her from the ground as though she weighed nothing, and shifted its grip on the spear. Righting himself, Khirro ran, shouting voicelessly, wishing he had the Mourning Sword he so carelessly laid aside.

This isn't real. This isn't real.

Real or not didn't matter, he had to save Elyea. He loved her.

The giant smiled, lips curled back from rotted teeth as

the tip of his spear penetrated between Elyea's legs. She screamed. The beast pushed harder; blood pooled beneath her, turned the ground into a grisly mud. Khirro rushed on, though he knew it was too late. Rage boiled in him as the giant continued skewering Elyea like a turkey on a spit.

Her screaming ceased.

Khirro slammed into the beast, kicking and scratching, punching and biting. The giant grunted in surprise, then flicked him away with a backhand swing the way a man might shoo a fly. Khirro reeled backward, barely keeping his feet. When he looked up, he stared once more into Elyea's wide green eyes. The head of the spear protruded from the top of her chest. As it pierced his throat, her face was in front of him, her lips touching his one last time.

The giant withdrew the spear, taking her away from him, and Khirro fell to his knees. Air wheezed through the hole in his throat, blood flowed down his chest.

Why is it different?

The giant's laughter rang in his ears as his eyelids slid closed and he slumped forward, his lifeblood pooling beneath him. Then cold dirt pressed against his cheek—not needles or moss or mulch, just dirt: a farmer's nose knew the difference.

Where am I now?

He opened his eyes to dim light he didn't recognize as the waning light of twilight or the sign of coming dawn. He rolled to his back, hand going to his throat where he found no wound, only stubble. Wiping dirt from his cheek, he peered about to determine where he'd ended up this time.

Dried mud walls surrounded him, cracked and broken. Thatch covered half the roof, the rest open to the stars struggling to be seen in a washed-out sky. The haunted village. A shudder crawled along Khirro's spine: the giant, the serpent, the dragon were all fearsome, but there was something horrific about the village and the children trapped inside its walls.

He heard Elyea's voice again, but not in a scream of terror. He sighed, relieved. His mind recognized this was a dream, or perhaps a vision manipulated by someone or something else, but he still worried for her safety.

It seems so real.

Standing on shaky legs, he crossed the dirt floor and pushed open the broken door hung askew in the doorway. Elyea lay naked on the ground in the middle of the clearing, writhing and moaning as a corpse lay atop her thrusting, grinding its hips into her. The dead man looked up at him, bleached white flesh pulled taut across his face, eyes glazed, but he still saw the face belonged to Ghaul.

Something brushed Khirro's ankle. He ignored it, enthralled and disgusted by the sight before him. He watched embarrassed, excited and angered but unable to avert his eyes.

It's not real, he told himself again. *It's not real.*

The thought didn't ring with truth.

437

The sun rose more quickly than it should, casting harsh light on the village, forcing night and shadow into hiding. With the sunlight, Khirro better saw the hideous coupling before him and realized it wasn't Elyea lying on the ground grunting and moaning with pleasure. It was her voice but Emeline's face peered lustily up at the waxen face above her. The corpse was no longer Ghaul, either, but Khirro's brother.

He stared at Khirro, a dead grin stretching his blue lips. Emeline's swollen belly compressed and expanded beneath his weight, flattening and stretching with each thrust. His eyes met hers and they stared back at Khirro red and black and vacant, dead eyes perched above her mouth as it twisted and contorted in a mockery of pleasure. The urge to call out caught in Khirro's throat.

Something brushed Khirro's calf again and he allowed his attention to shift from the hideous copulation twisting in the dirt. He looked down on a pale hand grasping his pant leg, dirt caked under its broken nails. Khirro jumped away.

Bodies writhed on the floor of the hut: young and old, male and female. Their wrinkled, sagging flesh clung to the bones beneath, hanging in sheets with black, dirt-filled veins showing through. Khirro took a step away, hand reaching for the sword he knew lay on the ground of the cavern, wherever that may be.

A figure separated itself from the others—a man whose

flesh retained more color than the others, as though recently dead—and lurched toward him. It only took a second for Khirro to recognize Shyn.

Blood trickled from a chest wound, leaving a trail down to his waist and staining his groin. Gray feathers poked through his skin in places, giving him the look of a man poorly tarred and feathered. He held a sword; his eyes gleamed. Khirro sucked a breath in through his teeth and took another step away. His foot hit something too soft to be rock, though there had been nothing on the ground in the clearing when last he looked. Of course, he hadn't been killed by a dragon, a serpent or a giant, either. The thing against his foot twitched.

And then it cried out.

Tiny and high-pitched, the sound was unmistakable. Revulsion roiled in Khirro's gut before he looked. With time to put thought to it, he might have expected the mud child—a dream within the dream—but when he looked down, he found the baby at his foot wasn't the mud baby at all. Strings of dark blood shone against porcelain skin and blank, black eyes like pieces of coal against the snowy face stared up at him. Expectantly? Accusingly?

Khirro's body trembled. The baby was boy and girl, both tiny sex organs fighting for space between its skinny legs. The umbilical cord, still attached, trailed onto the ground and across the clearing, dirt clinging to its shiny wetness. Khirro traced its path with his eyes, already knowing where it would end.

Emeline stood at the center of the clearing, the flesh of her empty belly hanging loose like a sail awaiting the wind. The cord snaked between her legs, still attached to a dead placenta awaiting its own birth. She swayed side to side as she stared and raised her arm to point a finger at him as if saying this was his fault. Her lips parted but no moan of pleasure came from them this time, only a lifeless, soul-less croak. Khirro wanted to say something, to apologize. He opened his mouth to speak but stopped when he realized the corpse with his brother's face had disappeared, then he remembered the dead Shyn creeping up behind him.

The sword pierced Khirro's side before he turned. He looked down at the blade inserted between his ribs, saw the blood oozing around the steel, then glanced up into the face of the sword-wielding corpse. He expected Shyn, or his brother, but the face belonged to neither.

The look on the corpse-Ghaul's face might have been comical under other circumstances: unseeing eyes, leering grin, sagging cheeks. Blood flowed down Khirro's side, soaked his clothes. He felt it pulse out if him with each beat of his heart. Ghaul's gnarled hand reached beneath his tunic, pulled the vial of king's blood from its hiding place.

"Mine," the Ghaul-corpse croaked through purple lips and yellow teeth.

It withdrew the blade from Khirro's side and his

strength went along with it. His knees buckled and his head hit the ground, bounced, came to rest facing the unnaturally pale baby. Its cold, black eyes stared at him. Even as he felt his own breath fade, he knew the baby also ceased drawing air.

A tear rolled down Khirro's cheek as his eyes slid closed.

48

Therrador emerged from the tunnel into the wan light of the new moon, the fortress wall looming at his back like a huge beast ready to pounce. He controlled his breathing, taking quiet, shallow breaths that wouldn't be heard should anyone be nearby; he'd called off the skirmishers tonight, but one could never be too careful.

He pulled the black cloak close about his chest and crept away from the fortress. With no cover, stealth would be necessary to keep from the notice of the patrols atop the wall. Chunks of stone from catapult fire interspersed with the bodies of both Kanosee and Erechanian soldiers littered the base of the wall, making the footing treacherous as he moved toward the salt flats. Therrador had been a soldier too long for the sight of dead men to affect him, so he ignored the corpses and concentrated on picking his way through the clutter.

Little wind rolled in from the Bay of Tears, leaving the water smooth and glassy; a coolness had come to the air, removing any doubt summer was waning, autumn coming to the land. This business would be done before the first snowfall. As Therrador crept forward, a chill gripped him and he clenched his jaw to keep his teeth from chattering.

He stopped.

Still no wind to set him shivering. He glanced around and wasn't surprised when he saw a black-cloaked figure nearby, a vague silhouette against the dark sky. They faced each other, neither speaking nor moving, but he knew who this person was. Therrador finally broke the silence.

"Why did you summon me?" They were far enough from the fortress there was no chance any might hear, but he still kept his voice hushed.

"You think to cheat me." The voice might as easily have emanated from the sea as from the silhouette.

A woman.

He hadn't been in the presence of the Archon before, only communicated in other, more mysterious ways.

"You're mistaken."

"Do not lie to me." She moved closer.

Therrador's hand fell to the hilt of his sword as he searched the dark around them, wondering if soldiers hid in the night.

"I know your thoughts. You think Braymon's blood is lost and you have no more need of me or our agreement."

He gripped the hilt more tightly, shuffled his feet. "It's not true," he said knowing his words wouldn't convince

442

this woman, Archon or not. If she wasn't the Archon, why send a woman against him?

"We have an agreement. The kingship will be yours tomorrow. You must pay what you owe."

"And if I don't?"

He tensed as he spoke, expecting one of the hideous undead to leap out of the darkness and put a blade to his throat, but only the figure before him moved as she removed her hands from her sleeves. In the dim moonlight he could make out long nails at the end of slender fingers. She didn't respond, instead gesturing curtly with her hands.

A signal!

Therrador spun about and pulled his sword from its scabbard, but there was no one there. He looked back toward the woman to see the air between them shimmer and move. He lowered his weapon, stared at the shifting air. Colors swirled, blurred at first, then solidifying into a sight that made Therrador's breath catch in his throat.

A vision of Graymon floated before him, the boy sleeping under a woolen blanket, his breath shallow and easy. It was not his own canopied bed in which he lay, but a makeshift bed on a pile of straw. The wall behind him moved with an unseen wind, billowing the green material.

A tent.

"What is this?" Therrador demanded, but he already knew what it meant.

443

"Your son is my guest. He will not be harmed." A figure entered the vision, a decayed face peering from under a rusted helmet. It knelt beside the sleeping boy, looked at him, then peered directly out of the vision into Therrador's eyes. "As long as you do as you said you would."

Therrador leaped forward, sword flashing out at the cloaked figure. The edge of the blade passed through the silhouette but touched nothing. He might have thought the woman an apparition until her fist slammed into the side of his head sending him to the ground. He rolled to his back ready to defend himself despite of his blurred vision, but the woman only looked down at him serenely.

"Do nothing stupid and you will have your boy back in time. If not, your reason for wanting to be king will die with him."

He stared at the woman as an unfamiliar feeling of helplessness churned his gut. If anything happened to Graymon, everything would be for naught—Braymon's death, his wife Seerna's death, everything.

"I will do as you wish," Therrador said, resigned.

"As we agreed," the woman corrected.

"As we agreed."

The air swirled again and the vision disappeared as though dispersed by an unfelt wind.

"We will meet again after the coronation. Watch for my riders a week after you take the crown."

The silhouette wavered and disappeared leaving

Therrador alone sitting on the hard ground of the salt flats, staring at the empty air where she'd been seconds before. The gentle lap of water on the shore found his ear and somewhere out over the sea, a gull cried out—lonely sounds that made him miss his son.

"I will have you back, Graymon."

The gull cawed an answer as Therrador gained his feet and made his way back to the fortress.

49

The cavern glowed blue again.

Khirro blinked the rocks and distant walls into focus. He lay on his side, cheek pressed against the ground, one hand immersed in the cool water of the glowing blue puddle. Gingerly he pushed himself upright, head hurting fiercely—he must have banged it when he passed out. The light was harsh and bright to his eyes, his dry throat felt raw and hurt when he swallowed.

How much time has passed?

A dull red glow caught his eye, a warm contrast to the ubiquitous blue light. The Mourning Sword lay on the rocky ground, his gauntlet crumpled beside it. He stretched out to retrieve them, stopped by a pain shooting through his side. His bare hand came away clean when he touched the spot—no blood, only pain. He sat for a minute, shaking his head minutely, confused. Everywhere he'd been injured in his... dream? Vision? Hallucination?

Every place a deadly blow struck, his flesh hurt. Perhaps more truth and reality hid within the vision than he realized.

He drew a sharp breath as he remembered the corpse with Ghaul's face reaching inside his tunic. His hand went to the hidden pocket, grabbed for the vial.

Gone.

Khirro's gut wrenched. He jumped to his feet, ignoring his throbbing head, the pain in his throat and abdomen, and snatched up his sword and glove. The feel of the hilt in his hand comforted him, something he would have never imagined could be true. It had always been pick or shovel that fit his hand.

How things change.

The scrollwork on the black blade glowed dully until his hand wrapped around the hilt, then it brightened as though it drew energy from his touch. Grinding his teeth, he crept around the rock hiding his companions without knowing why he felt the need for stealth. Part of him expected to find they'd been slain in their sleep. Another part wouldn't have been surprised if they lay in wait to ambush him.

His foot sent a pebble skittering across the ground, a small sound made loud by the cavern's quiet. He paused but saw no sign the noise disturbed anyone. He moved again, more careful of his footing.

He rounded the curve of the huge boulder and was

mildly surprised to find his companions alive and sleeping exactly as he'd left them. Athryn lay closest to him. Khirro went to him—the only one who hadn't been in his hallucination, perhaps the only one to be trusted. He pressed the tip of his boot lightly against the magician's thigh and his eyes slid open immediately like he'd been waiting for the sign to wake. Khirro signaled for him to be quiet and follow and the magician did without question, moving with the natural ease and grace Khirro envied.

"The vial is gone," Khirro told him with the boulder safely between them and the others. Droplets of water plopped into the puddle of water from which he'd drunk, distracting him. When he looked back, Athryn had removed his black sleeping mask. He watched Khirro, a look of concern twisting his scarred face into cracks and crevasses.

"What happened?"

Khirro told him most of the vision, leaving out details about Emeline, his brother and the baby because he didn't want to think about them or what it meant. Athryn listened, brow furrowed, neither nodding nor commenting until Khirro finished.

"The water." Athryn glanced at the puddle. "Nothing is safe for us here. The very ground we walk upon resents our presence. But what of the vial?"

"It was Ghaul who took it."

"In the vision," Athryn added. "Ghaul's corpse."

447

Khirro conceded the point and thought of the slack, dead face and the ghostly pale baby. He glanced away so Athryn wouldn't see the disquiet the memory brought.

"Then we will begin with Ghaul."

Khirro sheathed the Mourning Sword and sighed, relieved Athryn didn't question what he'd seen nor think him crazy. The man was a magician and had seen and done things Khirro would have difficulty believing.

They returned to the others without worry of noise. Ghaul woke before they roused him, hand reaching for his sword as it did every time he awoke unexpectedly. The sign of a well trained soldier.

Or a man with something to hide.

As he looked at Ghaul, Khirro thought of the corpse in his vision. In wakefulness, the resemblance seemed superficial. The corpse's face was loose and drooping, its expression blank; Ghaul's eyes were hard, full of life and dangerous strength, his taut cheeks clean shaven. Perhaps his mind conjured the similarity.

"Give me back the vial," Khirro said, regretting his choice of words as soon as they spilled from his lips.

"What are you talking about?" A strange look flashed through Ghaul's eyes, then disappeared as they returned to inscrutability. "I don't have the vial, you do. Have you lost your mind?"

"The vial is gone," Athryn said in a tone free of emotion or accusation. Ghaul's eyes flickered from Khirro to Athryn and back, hand still on the grip of his sword. "Khirro had a vision. In it, you took the vial."

Ghaul's hard face became stone. "I don't have the vial. But perhaps I should. I wouldn't be stupid enough to fall asleep and lose it."

Who is he calling stupid?

The hair on the back of Khirro's neck bristled. From the corner of his eye he saw Elyea sit up, a look of confusion on her sleepy face.

"I was drugged. I saw you take it, now give it back."

Ghaul released his sword and spread his arms wide in a mock gesture of welcome.

"If you're convinced I have it," he said through clenched teeth, "then come get it, farmer."

Khirro surprised himself by leaping forward and throwing all his weight toward Ghaul's mid-section. A half-step to the left and an elbow to the small of the back sent Khirro to the ground, his shoulder banging against a sharp rock. He rolled, struggling to regain his feet. Ghaul advanced, dirk in hand. Khirro grabbed for the Mourning Sword, already knowing he wouldn't have time to draw it, but Elyea jumped between them.

"Stop it," she said shielding Khirro. "Stop it!"

Khirro stared up at her, his steel partially freed. Ghaul also halted, face twisted with anger and blood lust.

"Don't imagine it's your place to come between men, whore. It's a good way to get yourself killed."

449

Khirro couldn't see Elyea's face, but he imagined her expression must be like she'd been slapped. She closed the steps between her and Ghaul, stopping with only inches between them, and looked up into the eyes of the man who stood a head taller than her. Neither spoke. Khirro's breath caught in his throat, stopped by tension fallen on them like a shroud. Athryn finally put a stop to it.

"Darestat is more powerful than we know," he said. "His influence is everywhere. It is he who does this to us and he who has the vial."

His words broke the hard stare between Ghaul and Elyea as they both turned toward him. The air changed, grew lighter.

"Then we must find the Necromancer quickly, before he has us kill each other," Elyea said. "Put your blade away, Ghaul."

The soldier looked at her, blinking, then took a step away and replaced the knife in the top of his boot, though his hard expression remained unchanged. Khirro felt a boulder lift from his chest, though the pain in his throat and side remained. He dropped the Mourning Sword back into its scabbard.

"Let's go." He stood and brushed dust from his breeches. "But don't drink the water."

***

It was a trick of the blue light that made the cavern seem so large. After an hour walking in silence as the

450

picked their way around stalagmites and over debris, they reached the far wall. The blue light ended suddenly at the opening of a tunnel in the middle of the rough stone wall like it dared not cross the threshold.

They stood at the edge of the tunnel's mouth, peering into the darkness they'd hoped had been left behind when they entered the cavern. Khirro dreaded the idea of leaving the soft blue light behind. As threatening as it seemed after his hallucination, the black was worse. A minute passed, no one moving; Khirro's growling stomach reminded him how much time had passed since he last ate.

"There's nothing to do but go in," Ghaul said, finally breaking the hour long silence, but he didn't move. No one did. Time crawled.

What are they thinking?

Khirro longed for the comforting warmth of the king's blood against his chest. Was it the darkness before them that made him dread pressing on, or the emptiness he felt from the missing vial? He needed to have it back and moving on was the only way to get it.

Khirro pulled the Mourning Sword from its sheath and held it in both hands before him. Unbidden, his lips whispered a foreign word and the blade sprang to life. Bright white light burned up the steel, the red runes and black blade disappearing behind its radiance. The others stared at Khirro, expressions of surprise and disbelief on their faces. He looked back at them knowing his face

451

showed the same.

"How did you...?" Elyea whispered, voice trailing off.

"I don't know."

"Dragon fire," Athryn said. Blue iridescence and harsh white light flickered and fought across the surface of his silvered mask like beasts competing over their territory. "There is magic in you now, Khirro."

"No." Khirro shook his head. "Not me. It's this place."

Once, as a child listening to his mother's fables, he might have imagined himself a wizard, but those days passed with his youth. Power and responsibility were things he didn't crave. The Shaman gave him the responsibility for the blood of the king and twice he lost it. Being a farmer, being entrusted with another's love, these were all the responsibility he wanted, but his life would never be like that again. He looked at the others staring at him and the glowing sword in his hand. Some things couldn't be avoided, no matter how much you didn't desire them.

He strode into the tunnel and his companions followed.

Darkness fled before the light of the Mourning Sword like a hare before a fox. The harsh white glow lit yards ahead bringing Khirro comfort, as did the feel of the hilt in his hands. What would happen to the light if he used the Mourning Sword as weapon rather than torch? And could he make it stop, or would the sword glow for the rest of eternity? He considered asking Athryn but decided against it until they were safe.

If we're ever safe again.

The tunnel differed from the one they'd followed into the glowing blue cavern, angling upward slightly as water trickled down its walls here and there. The rivulets reminded Khirro of the thirst raking his throat but, though they didn't glow blue, he dared not touch the water to his lips. He wouldn't trust anything as long as they remained in this cursed place, not even himself.

As they moved down the passage, patches of moss appeared on the walls, sparse at first but growing thicker and more frequent the farther they went. The air changed, too, becoming fresher, less cloying. Khirro occasionally thought he felt it shift. Somewhere ahead, there must be an air shaft or an opening to the outside.

Outside.

The word sounded good. It would be a relief if they didn't have to retrace their steps through the cavern, past the dragon, to regain their freedom.

Will it be day or night when we reach the surface again? Summer or winter? He sighed as he walked. *If we reach the surface.*

Time had lost meaning since they descended the twisting wooden staircase...how long ago? Lakesh made its own rules.

Khirro walked on, parting the darkness as he went,

finally feeling like they drew closer to their goal. But it also felt like they no longer traveled alone. His companions trudged along behind him.

Do they feel it, too?

On the tunnel floor at the edge of the sword's light, a glint caught Khirro's eye. He halted and his companions stopped beside him.

"There's something ahead," he whispered, pointing with the tip of the Mourning Sword. Ghaul stepped forward, but Athryn stopped him with a hand on his shoulder.

"We go together," the magician said.

Khirro stared ahead as they crept forward shoulder to shoulder, but he knew the others held weapons in hand. He'd heard the gentle stretching of Ghaul's bowstring and the scrape of steel against leather as Athryn and Elyea drew sword and dagger. Khirro breathed slowly through his nose, felt no sense of foreboding, no fear, only emptiness.

Step by step they advanced, the light of the Mourning Sword reflecting on what Khirro quickly recognized as the blade of a sword. He resisted the urge to stop, inspect it and draw conclusions from afar. A few more steps and the circle of light cast before them fell on a booted foot. He stopped. The others did, too.

"Is it a man?" Elyea whispered.

No one answered. Ghaul stepped forward, motioning for them to follow. They moved again, taking small, cautious steps, the edge of the light crawling farther ahead with each footstep.

The leather boot led to a leg clothed in rough spun breeches. An empty scabbard hung on one side of a wide belt encircling the person's waist, a dagger at the other. The glow passed the waist, casting light on a dirty red tunic and reflecting on glimpses of mail hidden beneath. Nothing indicated it to be anything other than a man prone on the tunnel floor before them. The sense of emptiness grew in Khirro, becoming a feeling of loss. The clothes looked familiar, the armor recognizable. He knew what the sword-light would reveal and dreaded taking the last few steps before the glow fell across the man's face.

"Shyn," Elyea cried putting words to what Khirro already realized, perhaps known from the moment the light reflected on the sword.

They hurried forward, forgetting caution as they rushed to their fallen comrade's side. Elyea kneeled beside him, searching for signs of life, but Shyn's eyes stared sightlessly at the ceiling, the Mourning Sword's light gleaming dully on their glassy surface. Gray feathers poked in places from his head and neck, showed under the collar and sleeves of his tunic. A shiver ran up Khirro's spine as he gazed upon Shyn's face looking dead and half-transformed as it had in his vision.

What does it mean?

"How did he get here?" Athryn asked. He turned to

455

Ghaul. "You were not gone long enough to have traveled so far."

Ghaul mumbled something Khirro didn't hear as he concentrated on remembering his vision, but it was no use. Instead, he found grief. He'd liked Shyn, would have befriended him under any circumstances. He examined the border guard's face, his expression frozen in a skyward stare, lips pulled into a half-smile. Only a few feathers had pushed completely through his skin; most were trapped halfway so it looked as though he'd been skewered to death by a flock of birds. Khirro's eyes trailed down his chest to the wound in his belly. Dried blood caked in the rings of his mail and stained his tunic dark brown but none pooled on the ground beneath him.

"He didn't die here," Khirro said interrupting something Ghaul said.

"That's what I said," Ghaul said, annoyed.

Khirro ignored him, his gaze falling on feathers poking through the sleeve of Shyn's tunic in a testament to the violence of his transformation. No wonder he normally removed his clothes before changing. Khirro shook his head.

This doesn't make sense.

If the battle had been so sudden and desperate he didn't have time to change, how had Ghaul escaped unscathed? And why was Shyn here, so far from where he fell? As Khirro mulled over the circumstances, he noticed

Shyn's hand curled into a fist and shifted the Mourning Sword to cast its light upon it.

He held something in his hand.

Khirro knelt to retrieve it as Ghaul did the same, their hands coming to rest on Shyn's at the same time.

"It might give a clue what happened to him," Ghaul said brushing Khirro's hand away. Goose flesh rippled on Khirro's forearm. He knew Ghaul didn't speak truthfully, though he didn't know how he knew.

"We both know what it is," he said uncurling Shyn's stiff fingers. The blood in the vial glowed under the sword's harsh light. Ghaul snatched at it but Khirro retrieved it first.

"I told you we shouldn't trust him," Ghaul snarled as he stood. "The bastard stole the vial from you in the throes of your hallucination."

He kicked Shyn in the ribs, the toe of his boot landing with a dull thud. Elyea cried out on Shyn's behalf, pushing Ghaul's leg away.

"His wound is too grievous," Athryn said shaking his head. "He could not have taken it then come here to die. Someone placed them here together for us to find."

"But how?"

"Doesn't matter," Ghaul snapped. "The treacherous thief stole the vial. How he comes to be here isn't important. We have to find the Necromancer before we all end up like him."

Khirro stared at Ghaul, begrudgingly accepting his words. Whatever killed Shyn might be stalking them, but he didn't believe Shyn betrayed them. The border guard was no traitor. He had proven himself in Khirro's eyes many times over.

"We should bring him," Elyea said. "The Necromancer can raise him, like Braymon and Maes."

Athryn shook his head. Shyn's sightless eyes and frozen face reflected in the magician's mask, transforming it into a death mask as he looked upon the dead soldier.

"No. There is no living blood in Shyn. Darestat cannot bring him back."

"We can't leave him," Elyea said but Khirro could hear the resignation in her voice.

"There is nothing else to be done," Athryn said.

"Then let's go," Ghaul said. "I don't want to run into those things again."

They moved on leaving Shyn's body behind, silence born of caution and grief following their steps. Something felt wrong about this, but Khirro didn't know what. Everything had been wrong since they came to Lakesh, more so since they reached the keep. No sense of reality, no control.

Why did Shyn have the vial? How?

Ghaul claimed to see him slain, yet he still quickly named him traitor and thief. Too many questions couldn't be answered, not here, not now.

Maybe the Necromancer would provide the answers.

50

Trumpets blared and rose petals drifted from high windows as boulders thudded sporadically against the fortress wall. Therrador's horse whinnied nervously as it pranced along the narrow street, its shoes throwing up sparks as they clicked against flagstones. An enameled red eagle spread its wings across Therrador's golden breast plate, the tips touching his epaulets; another eagle perched atop his helm and a red velvet cape draped from his shoulders. The horse's blanket, spun with gold thread, matched its rider's gleaming plate.

People lining the street clapped and hooted as he rode by at the head of his entourage. He hid his disappointment at how few people there were, but what could he expect in a fortress under siege? There would be more at the coronation and the reception afterward, and well-wishers would pack the palace when he returned to Achtindel.

The Kanosee army had fallen back from the walls since Therrador's arrival, moving all but a few trebuchets out of range of the Erechanian war machines. They still launched boulders to keep the Erechanian forces from venturing out of the fortress, but they did little damage at such a distance. Soldiers marveled at the effect having Therrador there had on the Kanosee. The king-to-be let them have

459

their assumptions, but he alone knew the truth of it.

"I don't like it, m' Lord," Sir Alton Sienhin had blustered of the Kanosee's latest tactic as the two mounted their horses. "They're up to something. I think it's a mistake to take so many men from the wall."

Therrador had steamed at his words. What good was a coronation if no one shared in it? What kind of king was crowned in secret? He managed to control his words as he answered.

"They will not advance again," he said confidently. "They cower before our might."

Sir Alton had moved as though he'd say something else but then thought better of it.

Sienhin rode to Therrador's right and a length back followed by the royal guard and all those who'd make up the royal court—a hundred people in all, every one ahorse, clip-clopping along the lane, spilling into the courtyard beyond. More people lingered in the courtyard, cheering tentatively and cowering each time a boulder thumped the wall. Therrador guided his horse to the door of the great hall, waving half-heartedly. This wasn't how he'd imagined things. In his mind, he saw rabid crowds cheering and hollering and Graymon, the future king of Erechania, riding at his side. His chest tightened. He missed the boy, prayed he was safe.

The doors swung inward and Therrador urged his charger across the threshold, the wind snapping his cape one last time before he passed into the still air of the columned hall. The click-clack of hooves bounced and echoed into the high ceiling as his horse high stepped on the marble tiles. They passed under archways and into the cavernous great hall, brightly lit by the sun beaming through its massive windows. More trumpeting announced his arrival, the notes ricocheting from one wall to another, collecting and multiplying in the lofty roof. The crowd filling the room exploded with cheers and whistles, whoops and hollers turning the fanfare into a cacophony.

This is more like it. A smile tugged at Therrador's lips but the dread gnawing his gut extinguished it. *Oh, how I miss my boy.*

The ride through the hall met his expectations. Lord Emon Turesti had outdone himself with what little he had at his disposal, taking Therrador's suggestions and expanding upon them. Trumpets called and answered, doves flew overhead to perch at the edges of the high columns, maidens cast flowers at the feet of his destrier. The rest of his party came behind, afoot as they'd dismounted before entering the hall so that Therrador was the only one still mounted. He raised his hand to the crowd; they cheered, tapped spears on the floor and swords on shields. A young girl broke from the crowd and rushed to his side to offer him a single white rose—a plant of Turesti's, no doubt. He bent and took the flower from her, sniffed deeply of its sweet aroma before pushing it into the clasp holding his cape.

The short ride went too quickly. When they repeated the ceremony in Achtindel, he'd have Turesti arrange for the entire Street of Kings to be like this. That would be an appropriate reception for the deliverer of the kingdom. And, when the day came, Graymon's reception would be even greater.

Therrador reined to a halt at the foot of the marble stairs, dismounted, and handed the lead to a squire. He climbed the steps, hand on sword to steady it as he forced a measured pace despite the urge he felt to rush up two at a time. Trumpets and cheers loud enough to drown out the clank of his armor followed him as he climbed.

At the top, High Confessor Aurna waited, the plain gray cloak of his order tied about his waist with a knot of golden cord. He watched without expression, hands tucked inside his sleeves, lips moving slightly as he recited some prayer or blessing. Therrador knew Aurna wore clothes richly adorned with gold beneath the plain robe and jewels hung about his neck. The High Confessor headed the rich and powerful church and took advantage of its wealth.

I'll have to do something about that.

At the top of the stairs, Therrador drew his sword from its bejeweled scabbard and offered it to the High Confessor. When Aurna accepted it, Therrador went to one knee, head bowed and hands clasped before his heart. The cheering and whistling ceased as the blare of trumpets ended, echoes fading to silence a few seconds later.

Therrador closed his eyes; butterflies fluttered in his stomach. So many years of being the faithful servant, of waiting and planning, finally coming to fruition. He thought of Graymon, and of his poor, lost Seerna. He'd never forgive Braymon for what happened to her, but here was his vengeance, and he hadn't raised a sword. When he imagined these moments, they tasted sweet—not so now. The specter of Graymon's abduction clouded his mind, stealing enjoyment from every thought and deed. He drew a deep breath.

It occurred to him the throngs would think him praying as he knelt there like a good, Gods-fearing king should. He was praying, of a fashion, but not for the things which they'd want their king to pray. He prayed for Graymon and that the Archon would hold to her word. He silently told the Gods he'd give the entire kingdom away to get his son back safely.

The priest spoke, interrupting Therrador's thoughts.

"Earth and Wind, Fire and Water," he intoned in a deep voice practiced at addressing crowds. "The elements, the Gods, have brought before us this day our new king, to guide us and lead us in these troubled times."

A neophyte appeared beside Aurna to take Therrador's sword from the High Confessor. A second boy gave the priest a wooden box intricately carved with scrollwork on all four sides. Aurna opened the lid on ancient, creaking hinges, put his hand in and came out with a fistful of soil.

"Earth supports us, gives us food and hope as the king supports us, loves us, provides for us." He waved his hand toward Therrador sending a spray of soil first across one shoulder then the other as he remained head bowed and eyes closed. "By Earth, with Earth, do you vow to provide for and love your kingdom and all its people?"

Therrador raised his head and opened his eyes.

"As king, I swear by Earth."

Aurna nodded and returned the chest to the apprentice, brushing dirt from his soft white hands before the boy closed the lid. The next neophyte came to the High Confessor's side and handed him a wooden tube. Aurna accepted it without removing his gaze from the man kneeling before him.

"Wind guides us and moves us, brings us weather and seasons as the king guides us and steers us through times of feast and famine, abundance and drought, war and peace." He pressed the wooden tube to his lips and blew through it onto Therrador's face. His breath smelled of last night's wine and a bit of spittle landed on Therrador's cheek. "By Wind, with Wind, do you vow to guide and steer your kingdom and all its people no matter the season?"

Therrador swallowed, resisting the urge to wipe the saliva from his cheek. "As king, I swear by Wind."

Aurna nodded and passed the tube back to the apprentice, then received a lit torch from another. The torch guttered and spat in the still air, sending black smoke swirling toward the ceiling.

"Fire warms us and lights us, keeps darkness and cold at bay in the deepest night, protects us from all it holds as the king holds us close and keeps us from evil." The High Confessor touched the torch first to Therrador's right forearm, then his left. The kerosene spread upon them before the ceremony burst into flame. The crowd gasped. Therrador held his arms to the side keeping the flames from his face. "By Fire, with Fire, do you vow to be the light of your kingdom and keep the evils in the dark from your people?"

"As king, I swear by Fire."

A sheen of sweat shone on Therrador's brow and cheeks. It was good Water was the next God to be addressed. As another neophyte appeared, handing Aurna an ewer filled with clear water, the flames on Therrador's arms faded leaving a layer of black soot on his previously dazzling armor. He cursed to himself.

"Water gives us life, replenishes us and strengthens us as the king lends us strength and keeps us alive."

Therrador tipped his head back as Aurna lifted the ewer. The High Confessor sent a thin stream of cool water trickling over Therrador's face, running down his neck and under his armor. It felt good after the fire, refreshing, but would be uncomfortable until it dried.

"By Water, with Water, do you vow to give your life to strengthen your kingdom and all its people?"

"As king, I swear by Water."

He lowered his head, looked at Aurna, and felt the droplets of water running off his face. The High Confessor looked back at him with bloodshot eyes brought on by last night's wine. The church guarded Aurna's secret indulgences like a new born babe, but the king must know all for it might come in handy one day.

As a final apprentice took the ewer, the High Confessor raised his arms above his head, hands spread open, palms facing Therrador.

"By the Gods Earth and Wind, Fire and Water, the givers of life, the takers of life; the Gods see all and know all, and now they know Therrador as king, regent of Erechania, Protector of the Realm, the Life of the People."

Aurna stepped away from the new monarch, hands still held above his head. No one in the hall made a sound as the High Confessor disappeared behind a curtain at the back of the dais and Lord Emon Turesti, Chancellor of the High Council, stepped out to take his place.

Turesti wore the red robe trimmed in white ermine denoting his office; a golden belt adorned with jewels of many colors, no two alike, encircled his waist. The chancellor carried a great sword in his hands, six and a half feet long and gleaming gold. The Sword of the Realm, the

Chooser of Kings. Its edge honed daily by a master, the sword saw little work these days. Two decades had passed since it last chose a king and, under Braymon, beheadings became scarce. With war happening, the Sword of the Realm would see more work in the future as there were always traitors and enemies to be made examples of during wartime.

Therrador, still kneeling, swallowed hard as Turesti stood before him; the water Aurna splashed upon him had collected at the small of his back, causing him discomfort.

Thank the Gods this will soon be over.

"The Gods have given their blessings, Therrador Montmarr," Turesti began, his voice surprisingly loud and strong from a man so slight and frail. "But it is the Chooser of Kings who passes final judgment. Are you ready to be judged, Therrador Montmarr?"

"I am ready." Therrador kept his voice steady with effort. If he didn't flinch, if the blade didn't draw blood, he'd be confirmed king.

Therrador wondered if he should trust Turesti, who held his fate in his hands. If the chancellor didn't want Therrador to be king, all he need do was touch the sharp edge to his flesh and all would be at an end. Bringing the blade down on the right spot meant everything. A hair's breadth to one side or the other could mean the kingship, or death.

Too late for worry now.

467

Therrador breathed deep and held it, readying himself as Turesti raised the blade above his head, thin arms shaking with the effort. Sweat broke on Therrador's brow. Perhaps it wasn't trust he needed to worry about, but strength. Could the frail man wield the sword? It was the chancellor's job, no one else's.

The great hall fell into deeper silence as the crowd held their breath along with the man who'd soon be their king. Therrador bowed his head but kept his eyes on Turesti's shadow to see the blow when it came.

Light glinted on the blade and it made a faint whistle as it sliced the air. Therrador gritted his teeth, the muscles in his jaw bunching. The clang of metal meeting metal rang through the still hall. Therrador didn't move.

No pain.

The blow to his shoulder came swift but light, the flat of the blade striking against his epaulet. Turesti had done his job well. To the throng crowding the hall, it appeared Therrador survived a deadly blow. Lord Emon Turesti raised the Chooser of Kings above his head again, the shake in his arms more pronounced this time.

Only a few more moments.

The blade cut the air a second time. Therrador tensed. The flat of the blade struck his armor, harder this time, and the edge slipped under the corner of his epaulet. Years of combat and training kept Therrador from reacting, but Turesti must have realized what happened. He pulled the sword away quickly and examined the blade. After a few seconds, he nodded, signaling it free of blood.

"Rise, Therrador Montmarr," he said, some of the shake in his arms transferring to his voice. "Rise and accept your crown."

Therrador did as bidden, hoping the warm blood trickling down his chest would remain contained beneath his plate. He reached up with both hands to remove his helm and managed to keep his face free from expression despite the pain in his shoulder. His hair dripped with water and sweat as he tucked his helm into the crook of his elbow and cocked his arm so blood wouldn't flow from the tips of his fingers. He waited while Hanh Perdaro, the Voice of the People, took Lord Turesti's place in front of him.

"The gods have given their blessings," Perdaro said speaking with less effort than the others had. "The Chooser of Kings has seen you worthy."

He extended his arms above his head, displaying the heavy golden crown to all. Not so long ago, this crown had rested upon Braymon's head and, being his closest friend and advisor, Therrador knew it wasn't merely the diadem's bulk which weighed on him at times. Now that responsibility fell to Therrador and he felt a pang of regret his one time friend was gone.

"And, in the name of the people, I declare you King Therrador."

469

The room erupted with cheers and applause, the clamor bouncing from walls to ceiling, the room doubling and trebling the volume. Therrador raised his right hand, waved to the crowd as he faced them, and put on a smile he didn't feel like wearing. He drank in the adulation for a minute, then turned to Lord Turesti standing to his right. With the crowd still hollering and whistling, he raised his voice for the chancellor to hear with no danger he'd be overhead in the uproar.

"Get me out of here before I bleed to death."

51

The tunnel changed from rough-hewn gray stone to polished white marble as they neared the arched doorway. No seam showed where one stopped and the other began, like one faded into the other. Ancient runes and depictions adorned the walls, carved into the marble, including one series which Khirro recognized as the story of Monos, the first necromancer. It seemed an eternity since Athryn had told him the story of the necromancer and the Mourning Sword.

So much has happened.

They stopped in the doorway and peered into the chamber beyond. The same iridescent glow lit the chamber as had the previous one, but here the color shifted and changed. As Khirro's eyes registered one color, recognizing it, it would change to another. Under different circumstances, he'd have considered it beautiful, awe-inspiring, but here it was eerie and unsettling.

"This is it," Athryn whispered pointing to the far corner of the chamber.

A marble throne carved from the wall and stretching from floor to ceiling fifteen feet above sat empty. Pools of light ebbed and flowed about its base. Khirro blinked, unable to tell if the floor near the seat was solid.

"There's no one here," Elyea whispered.

Featureless except for the carven throne, no corner of the room was hidden from their view. One by one they stepped across the threshold. Mist swirled about their ankles like a living creature investigating their presence. Khirro looked around but saw no cracks or openings in the smooth walls, no place where the mist might enter the room. The floor, visible in spots through the moving fog, was the same polished marble as the walls. Nature had no hand in the design or building of such a chamber.

Khirro entered the room last and halted behind his companions. His breath came in short, sharp bursts as though the room sucked the air from his lungs before he had the chance to let it out. The Mourning Sword's glow brightened to a rich golden light as the mist twisted through Khirro's legs and up his body leaving the floor in the room laid bare as it swirled about him. His head felt light and the blade glowed brighter still. Athryn turned to him, asked if he was all right and the radiance from the sword washed over him. Khirro's breath caught in his throat.

Maes stood at his brother's side.

Khirro knew it for a vision immediately. The figure of the little man shimmered, flickering in and out of view before steadying. Khirro watched, mesmerized, as a younger version of Athryn joined him. A bandage covered half the magician's face, hiding what Khirro knew to be a fresh burn, cracked and oozing, healing itself into the scar Athryn tried so hard to disguise.

The two figures knelt together at the real Athryn's side, but he didn't notice. Maes' mouth moved forming words, teaching his brother an ancient language intended for only one use: magic. Khirro watched, agape, as he saw the little man speak.

A knife appeared in Athryn's hand and the brothers looked the same direction, reacting to someone outside Khirro's view. Athryn dropped the knife and held his hands up in protest before something knocked Maes violently to the floor, bloodying his nose. Begrudgingly, Athryn retrieved the knife, moving awkwardly as though forced by an unseen hand. Maes sat upright.

Khirro tried to look away when Athryn removed the tip of his brothers tongue, but he couldn't. Tears flowed from Athryn's unbandaged eye.

The scene shifted to Maes teaching Athryn again, a red froth of words and blood bubbling from his lips. The blade

472

appeared in Athryn's hand again. More blood. More tears. More tongue left Maes' head. Khirro stumbled back a step, blinking, and the vision disappeared.

"What's wrong, Khirro?" Elyea caught him under one arm as Ghaul grabbed the other.

"I... I saw Maes." He looked up at Athryn staring at him, eyes wide beneath his mask. "I saw you take his tongue from his head."

"You could not know. No one knows." The mask on his face hid the sorrow evident in his voice. "But that is what happened."

"But how could I--?"

"The light of truth shines from the Mourning Sword. Secrets are revealed in its glow."

Khirro stared at the blade in his hand, then looked at Elyea standing beside him. At her feet, a girl of perhaps five years lay on a bed of straw; tears flowed down her cheeks but no sound gave away her lament. A man appeared beside her, huge and threatening, and Khirro knew the man as her father.

The man moved toward her, pulled his shirt over his head. There was a familiarity to the act, like this wasn't his first visit like this. He knelt beside the young girl, grabbed her shoulder and flipped her onto her back. The dagger she had hidden beneath her slashed out, opened his throat. Warm blood rained down on the girl, absolving her of her sins, of his sins. The man grasped at the wound in

473

his throat, curses gurgling at his lips as he toppled to the dirt floor. The young girl stood and ran from Khirro's sight but, as she did, Khirro saw the dagger in her hand, its hilt adorned with jewels. The same dagger Elyea still carried.

Khirro gagged. The urge to throw the Mourning Sword from his hand nearly overwhelmed him, but one more truth still needed to be uncovered, one more secret revealed.

52

Graymon stared at the tent flap expecting someone or something to pull it aside but dreading who or what might come through. The lady had treated him nice so far—animals and sunshine graced the pictures on her fingernails again—but he didn't like being in a strange place. He missed his Da, he even missed nanny. Men who smelled like dead things and had no faces haunted his dreams each night. Every time he woke, he woke scared and shivering, wanting to call out for comfort but knowing no one would give it to him.

He tip-toed to the door of the tent and stopped before it, hand outstretched. He hoped he'd move the flap aside and find his father waiting to tell him that this whole thing had been a dream, but he knew that wouldn't happen. His throat squeaked as he drew a shuddering breath; his fingers brushed the green canvas. He grasped the edge of the flap and pulled it aside slowly. The woman stood as though she'd been waiting for him for a long time. Graymon dropped the flap and jumped back with a screech as she entered.

"You were not leaving, were you?" Her voice sounded sweet as it had when she collected him from the palace, but he no longer wanted to hear a lullaby from those lips.

"Where's my Da?" he demanded, anger giving him courage. "You said you take me to my Da."

The woman's smile showed white teeth; Graymon thought they looked pointier than they should. He backed away a step.

"I will, love. You must be patient, though. There are things your Da must do for me first, then you can be with him."

Someone stepped through the flap behind her and Graymon strained to see around her. He hoped it was his Dad coming to reassure him everything would be all right, telling him to be a brave little soldier, but the man was not his father. The man was not a man. The rotten-faced monster glowered at him, sending a shiver down his spine.

"If you want to see your Da, you have to do something for me, too." She put her hand on his shoulder and he looked sideways at her fingers, wondering what scenes danced and played across them today. "Do you remember what it is you have to do for me?"

Graymon hung his head.

"Stay in the tent," he mumbled, purposely

indecipherable, but she didn't make him repeat himself like nanny would have. He liked nanny better anyway, he decided.

"Now, are you going to do that for me, or do I have to have him stay with you?"

She gestured over her shoulder at the thing by the door and he tried not to look but couldn't help himself. The dead thing smiled at him with yellow teeth. Graymon looked away quickly, retreating another step from the door, from her hand.

"I'll stay."

"Good. Good boy."

A wave of her hand sent the creature from the tent, but Graymon knew it would be close enough to return and stay with him if he tried to leave again. He didn't want that thing staying with him. Anything but that. He sat down heavily on the straw mattress.

"I want my Da."

"Soon, love. You will be with him soon."

She turned to leave, her long black cloak swirling around her legs, and Graymon stuck out his tongue. She stopped and looked over her shoulder at him. Graymon sucked his tongue back into his mouth and curled into a ball on the mattress.

"I want my Da," he said again as tears began to flow down his cheeks. The dead men scared him, but there was something even worse about the woman. She left the tent and Graymon drifted into fitful sleep.

That was the first time he dreamed of the tyger.

53

Khirro's eyes locked on Ghaul and shadowy figures jumped into view around him, men in full armor laughing and jesting with one another, comrades who fought and died together. None looked familiar, though Khirro felt he should recognize something about them. The edges of the vision were ragged and vague enough to hide what he might normally see.

The scene changed to a battlefield littered with hundreds of corpses. A figure cloaked in black cape and cowl walked amongst them accompanied by Ghaul. The figure gestured and each corpse in turn rose like a marionette whose strings were jerked into place at the start of the puppet show. Death masks of pain and suffering contorted the men's faces, puss and blood dried in cracked scabs on their cheeks and foreheads, and Khirro knew what he saw was the undead soldiers of Kanos.

But who stalks between them, turning them from men to monsters? The Necromancer?

Dread crept into Khirro's limbs, but the vision faded, replaced by another. The figures of Ghaul and Shyn stood before him, clashing swords sending sparks about their heads. The tips of gray feathers poked through Shyn's flesh

477

Bruce Blake

as he defended himself, but he was trapped against the tunnel wall. The tip of Ghaul's blade found his belly and cut upward. Shyn slumped, his expression a mix of pain and relief. Ghaul laughed and Khirro saw the crest of Kanos come into view on his chest as the vision disappeared. The real Ghaul stood facing Khirro, sword in hand, his face hard and knowing.

"Traitor," Khirro growled. "Kanosee dog. You killed Shyn."

Ghaul brought his sword up in front of him, threatening, and chuckled.

"It took you long enough, dirt monger." He held his empty hand out expectantly. "Give me the vial."

Khirro shook his head.

"Don't be foolish, Khirro. We both know you're no match for my sword. Give me the king's blood and I may spare your life."

Khirro gritted his teeth. Ghaul's skill with a sword was much greater, but he'd come too far and been through too much to give the vial to the enemy. He wouldn't let Maes and Shyn die in vain.

The Mourning Sword sliced toward Ghaul, jumping in Khirro's hand on its own. Ghaul deflected the blow and countered with his own. The swords clanged sending a quiver up Khirro's arm. Ghaul struck blow after blow and each time, Khirro managed to dodge or parry, but he knew he couldn't repel him indefinitely. Ghaul deftly

478

maneuvered himself away from Athryn and Elyea, keeping Khirro between them so they couldn't aid him.

Khirro focused on the fight, pouring his energy into each stroke and thrust, each parry, but still noticed the cold wind rise within the chamber, prickling his arms with goose flesh and standing the hairs on the back of his neck on end. The flat of Ghaul's sword struck Khirro's shoulder and the soldier laughed, toying with him. The stark realization he was no match for Ghaul bore into Khirro's gut and he struggled to fight back the panic rising in his throat. He dodged another blow, steel caressing his sleeve. The cool breeze gusted again.

Then Ghaul disappeared. Everything disappeared.

Thick mist filled the chamber as completely as if it had always been there. A sword slashed the fog, missing him by inches. He jumped away and his back pressed against the chamber wall.

Khirro's eyes flickered, searching for his foe, for Elyea or Athryn, but he saw nothing but the wall of mist. The temperature dropped rapidly; a rime of frost appeared on his gauntlets. No sound. He called out, but his voice died at his lips, smothered by the fog. He held the Mourning Sword in front of him defensively, waiting to be attacked.

The mist swirled as though stirred by some unseen hand, then pulled itself into one twisting pillar centered over the marble seat and formed the shape of a man whose head brushed the ceiling fifteen feet above. A long, misty beard and thick white arms became distinct, a hazy sword hung at his side. A face twisted into being with angry, swirling eyes.

"Who dares disturb me?" The voice boomed across the chamber, amplified by the smooth walls. Khirro stared, forgetting the fight. "Who dares disturb Darestat?"

"I come to resurrect a king."

Khirro looked at Ghaul, surprised to have heard the soldier respond. He breathed in a short, sharp breath at what he saw. In the confusion and the cover of the mist, Ghaul had grabbed Elyea.

She struggled against the arm about her waist and the sharp edge at her throat, showing no fear, only determination. Khirro touched his chest unconsciously and felt the hard shape of the vial through his tunic.

Shyn's dead. Maes is dead. Is this worth her life, too?

"Give me the vial, Khirro."

He pulled it out and rolled it back and forth on his flat palm. Its deep red glow lit his glove, attracting the mist-man's attention.

"What is this?" His voice was a low rumble, though his words were as clear as the peal of a bell on a summer eve.

"The blood of the king, Braymon of Erechania, slain in battle by the walking dead of Kanos." Khirro managed to keep the quiver in his knees from shaking his voice.

He took a step toward Ghaul, hand tight on the hilt of his sword. Elyea shook her head and a drop of blood

480

rolled down her smooth throat where Ghaul's blade pressed against her skin.

"Why do you bring this blood to me? I care not for the doings of mortals."

"The Shaman, Bale, enchanted me to bring the vial here and see the king restored."

The swirling mist halted, falling away to leave a bent old man standing where the giant had been. His scraggly white hair fell past his shoulders framing a face wizened by more years than Khirro could comprehend. Despite his age, his eyes shone with vigor and knowledge.

"Bale?" The old man's voice was quieter but still unshaken and sure. "Bale sent you?"

"Yes." Khirro looked from Darestat to Ghaul. He didn't think he'd hurt Elyea, not until he got what he wanted. "He enchanted me to bear the vial to you."

The Necromancer made a clicking sound with his tongue.

"He did not enchant you, Khirro. No man can be made to do that which they would not do themselves, not even by magic. If such was possible, magicians would rule the world, not kings."

Khirro stared at the old man, his jaw hanging open.

Not enchanted? How is that possible?

He opened his mouth to ask so many questions—what about the feeling in his chest? Why did he feel the compulsion to complete the journey?—but the

481

Necromancer spoke again, cutting off his thoughts.

"Why did Bale not bring it himself?"

"He's dead."

The old man's face sagged, sadness dimming the blaze of his eyes. "That is too bad. He was a good student, and a fine son."

"Son?" Athryn said, his voice a whisper. Khirro had forgotten Athryn was there.

"Enough sentiment," Ghaul said firmly. "Give me the vial or the whore dies. Braymon will lead the dead army of Kanos."

Khirro tensed but the Necromancer continued as though Ghaul had not spoken.

"How did my son die?"

Hope sparked in Khirro. He raised his sword arm and pointed at Ghaul. "He's responsible."

The light in the chamber faded to dull pink as Darestat straightened and gestured, conjuring a vision for all of them to see. The images shifted and changed quickly. First it showed Ghaul dressed in Kanosee armor fighting, training, receiving orders from a figure in cloak and cowl. Khirro shivered. Then Ghaul wearing the cloak of a king's guard, running Braymon through as the face of an undead soldier leered on, laughing.

The light shifted and they saw Ghaul lead an Erechanian soldier into a tunnel, slit his throat and emerge in a field wearing the man's armor. The same armor he now wore. Then they saw the battle at the foot of the fortress, the Kanosee lying in wait to ambush their party and Ghaul coming upon the fight, nocking an arrow and slaying the Shaman.

They knew. Somehow, they knew about Braymon's plan. They were after us because they knew we carried the king's blood.

"It's a lie," Ghaul protested, his voice lacking its usual surety. "He killed Bale, not me. He wanted the glory for himself."

"Silence!" Darestat's voice became the voice of the mist giant again, filling the room and dispersing the vision. "The light does not lie."

"No. I--"

The Necromancer's eyes narrowed, his face became stern. When he spoke again, his voice was quieter, ominous, but tinted with grief.

"You killed my son."

Light flashed like a stroke of lightning, blinding Khirro. He gripped his sword tight and bent his knees to spring or defend but when his vision cleared Ghaul lay dazed on his back, his sword on the ground at Elyea's feet. Khirro blinked, returning his vision to normal as Elyea retrieved Ghaul's blade and placed the tip against his throat.

"Come forth, bearer of the blood. If you wish a life restored, there is a cost to be paid."

Cost? What does he mean?

483

Khirro stepped forward tentatively. Athryn walked beside him, pulling the mask from his face. They stopped a few strides from the Necromancer standing before the marble throne and awaited his terms. Darestat appraised them, his look betraying nothing of his thoughts or intent. A minute passed. Ghaul groaned, regaining consciousness; Elyea kept the sword pressed to his throat.

"I have lost my son," the old man said, his words measured. "The last of my line. If you wish me to resurrect your king, then I ask a son in return, someone whose life will become mine. To live with me, to learn from me."

Khirro felt Athryn straighten beside him. This was exactly what Athryn wanted.

Does the Necromancer know?

"The fire of the dragon touched my brother," Athryn said, emotion straining his words. "He gave his life for me, his blood courses through my veins. His soul rests with my soul." He stopped, drew a shuddering breath. "Our lives will be yours."

Elyea made a sound of protest but stopped short of speaking. This was why Athryn joined this fool's journey. Over time, it became easy to trick oneself into believing they were all there for each other, for the good of the kingdom, but in truth, none were. They all had their own selfish reasons, as did Khirro. Athryn came to advance his skills at the foot of the master; Shyn to prove an outsider, a freak, had value. Ghaul's motives were treacherous; Elyea saw it as an opportunity to atone for what others looked upon as her sins.

I thought I was compelled to come.

He knew he hadn't been, perhaps always knew. So why? To prove himself more than a cowardly farmer? Or to escape a life which hadn't gone the way he wanted? Both held the ring of truth.

"This is no small thing I ask," the Necromancer warned Athryn. "Your life—your lives, you and your brother—will belong to me. Living with me, learning from me, you will never return to your home. The rest of your days will be spent at my side. What say you to that?"

Athryn went to one knee, bowed his head.

"We are yours, master. Do with us as you will."

Darestat nodded, a satisfied look crossing his face. Elyea spoke to Ghaul, telling him not to move; Khirro resisted the urge to turn and make sure she was still all right.

She has everything well in hand.

"Then it shall be done." The old man moved toward Khirro, his face looking younger than moments before. "Put the Mourning Sword away, Khirro."

The blade flashed and flickered in the glow of the chamber, the runes first crawling red up and down the length of the sword then fading to black before springing to orange light as though drawn from the blacksmith's fire. Khirro regarded it a moment before sliding it into its

485

sheath, steel whispering against leather, and hoped he wouldn't have to give it up. He turned his attention to the vial in his other hand and held it out to the Necromancer. The thought of giving it up gnawed his gut.

"You are the bearer, Khirro. You must be so until it is done."

Khirro nodded and took the vial between thumb and index finger, holding it before him like something fragile, or something likely to bite. His head felt light with a mix of fear and anxiety, excitement and happiness, disappointment, sadness. So long he carried this living piece of the king next to his heart, he'd begun to feel it a part of him. What a triumph to actually complete this journey, and to live, yet a sad thing, too. His life had meant something these last months, but soon he'd be Khirro the farmer again, only after this he'd be unable to return to his farm.

Darestat closed his eyes, lips moving slightly as he chanted. A throb filled the chamber, pulsing the air in rhythm with the Necromancer's words. His voice rose and fell, a deep drone filling the space, penetrating the corners, nearly forcing the air from Khirro's lungs. Warmth radiated from the vial; the air moved about him, caressing him as though touched by a thousand unseen hands. Athryn remained on his knee, head bent, unaffected.

The colors in the chamber changed rapidly; pink then yellow, blue then green then red. The colors of the rainbow flashed in Khirro's vision, and colors never imagined. He wanted to be fascinated by them, intrigued enough to divine their origin or purpose, but he couldn't take his eyes or thoughts from the Necromancer. The old man's lips moved without slowing, speaking words Khirro didn't know in a language he'd never heard, yet somehow he knew what he said.

He beckoned Braymon's soul, entreating it to rejoin the world of the living.

The blood bubbled within the vial like a liquid at the boil. Khirro's hand quivered against his will and a low mist rose, swirling about their feet. The walls and ceiling of the chamber shimmered and swam.

Elyea's cry stilled the mist and solidified the walls.

At first, Khirro didn't know what the sound was or from where it came. The sound of steel rattling against stone followed and he knew what happened without looking. Alarm knotted his throat as he jerked his gaze from the still-chanting Necromancer's trance.

First Khirro saw the dagger protruding from Elyea's leg, then the blood flowing down her thigh. Too late, he saw the bow in Ghaul's hand and the arrow loaded against the taut string. The arrow pierced his hand as though it was paper, tearing completely through to clatter against the marble wall. His fingers opened involuntarily and the vial tumbled from his grasp, end over end toward the floor while the blood continued to roil and bubble inside.

487

"No!"

The vial struck the floor and shattered.

All that time, all that struggle and death. For nothing. A journey ending in spilled blood.

But instead of blood splashing across the floor and spattering his boots, red mist puffed from the broken vial, mixed with the other mist. It rolled and moved, formed a shape Khirro recognized immediately from his dreams as a tyger made of mist stood before him.

Darestat's voice grew louder, its pitch higher as his chant quickened. The mist tyger loomed before Khirro and Ghaul's bowstring twanged again. An arrow flew past slowly enough he could count the feathers on its shaft, but he moved equally as slowly, rendering him agonizingly unable to react as he watched its path.

Time sped up again, folding in on itself as everything happened at once: the Necromancer's words ceased as the arrow entered his mouth; the mist tyger roared, pouncing at Khirro, engulfing him in red mist; visions of battles he didn't fight and men he didn't recognize swirled about him then disappeared. The mist penetrated him, crawled into his body through his eyes, nose, ears, every pore in his skin, paralyzing him. Powerless, it overtook his limbs and muscles, overflowed his heart and lungs.

And then the world became white light.

Khirro knew instinctively it came from the Necromancer. The force of the light tossed him back and he hit the marble floor with a bone jarring thud that shot pain up his spine. The white light dissipated quickly and took all other light with it leaving the chamber in darkness. Khirro scrambled to his feet, feeling it would mean his life to remain on the floor. He drew the Mourning Sword and its blade glowed red as it thirsted for blood. The dark swallowed its light.

Khirro stared into the blackness waiting for his eyes to adjust. A leather sole whispered against stone, a dim blade came out of the dark toward him. He dodged and the sword tip caught his shoulder instead of the neck for which it was intended. It bit shallowly into his flesh, jarring his senses into action. He heard sounds all around him: Elyea's breath, the scrape of cloth on Ghaul's skin, three heartbeats plus his own. He heard more than he'd ever heard before, knew from where each tiny sound came.

Behind him, Athryn uttered a word and light filled the chamber. Khirro glanced about quickly. Athryn lay on the floor at the foot of the throne while Elyea crouched against the wall, blood dripping from her wound. He didn't see the Necromancer.

Khirro's distraction gave Ghaul the advantage.

He lunged and caught Khirro in the face with the pommel of his sword. His nose broke with a crunch and the blow sent Khirro to the floor, the Mourning Sword skittering from his grip. Before he recovered, Ghaul fell upon him, his foot on his chest, sword point at his throat.

489

Khirro looked up half-expecting to see the face of an undead monster, but it was Ghaul. Hatred burned in his eyes.

Athryn moved, his sword rasping against its scabbard.

"Stay put, magician, and speak no words. If your lips so much as move, I'll open his throat."

Khirro stared at Ghaul, surprised at the detachment he felt. Fear didn't freeze his limbs or steal his breath as before. Instead, a curious calm filled him. After facing death so many times, had he lost his fear of it?

"You can't have what you came for," Khirro said swallowing around the steel pressed to his windpipe. "Braymon will never serve Kanos."

"You have the truth of it," Ghaul said, a wry smile twisting his lips. "All I can do now is be sure he'll serve no one."

He drew his blade back for the final blow.

This is it: the end of the journey.

"No!"

Elyea grabbed Ghaul's arm and spun him away from Khirro, throwing him off balance. Khirro jumped up to aid Elyea, but years of battles, of protecting his life, had honed Ghaul's reflexes. He regained his balance, pushed away from her, and drew his blade across her from hip to shoulder.

Elyea's eyes widened in surprise.

Khirro stared.

For a moment it looked like only her clothes were cut, but then the blood came, rushing from her body. She collapsed where she stood.

The peace and calm Khirro felt vanished, forced from him by rage like he'd never experienced. His muscles tensed and bunched, blood pounded at his temples and in his throat.

He burst into flames.

Khirro felt it, saw it enveloping him head to foot, but it didn't burn. He lurched toward Ghaul as the warrior spun around and, for the first time in all the months of their journey, Khirro saw naked fear in the soldier's eyes. He stepped back shaking his head. Khirro advanced, mouth open to voice his rage, but no cry of hatred issued from his throat. He roared instead. Khirro sprang at Ghaul, brushed aside his blade, and hit him hard in the chest, bearing him to the floor.

Khirro tore at his throat with his teeth and tasted warm, coppery blood. It splashed across his face and against whiskers not there before. Claws tore the flesh of Ghaul's chest. The man screamed, the cry gurgling in his blood-filled throat. Khirro roared once more, raked Ghaul's legs and groin with hind claws and the soldier writhed in agony, face streaked with sweat and blood and terror. Finally, Khirro's fangs ripped into his chest, pulled free his still-pulsing heart. Ghaul's screams and flailing ceased, his body went limp. Seconds later, Khirro found himself kneeling over the ruined body, flames flickering and dimming until they disappeared completely.

The blood in his mouth made him gag.

He rolled from Ghaul onto his hands and knees and his stomach emptied what little it held, strings of thick blood hanging from his lips. He spit, clearing the taste from his tongue. Head hung, panting, he knelt there until he heard Elyea call to him, her voice tiny and afraid. He wiped blood from his mouth with his sleeve and crawled across the cold floor to her.

"Elyea."

Blood flowed freely from the wound running up her abdomen and across her chest; entrails showed through the split skin. Her eyes were glassy, her face pale but peaceful.

"Khirro." Her voice held little strength. "Are you all right? Did he hurt you?"

"No," he said brushing stray hairs from her sweaty forehead.

She nodded slightly. "Good. And the king?"

"I think he is within me."

"Two great men in one." She smiled as best she could and drew a shuddering breath. Khirro heard it bubble in her chest. Blood ran from her nose into her mouth and the smile vanished. A shiver wracked her body. "I'm cold, Khirro."

He removed his tunic and laid it across her but she

continued to shiver.

"Athryn," he called over his shoulder. He felt the magician's presence close beside him. "Help us."

Athryn knelt beside Elyea and took her hand in both of his. Khirro looked at him and saw the scar was gone from his face. The magician said nothing, only squeezed her hand.

"Thank you," Elyea said and closed her eyes.

Khirro felt his heart skip. He reached out and took her other hand, ignoring the sticky blood covering it.

"Do something, Athryn." There was a tone of command in his voice he'd never heard there before, but the magician didn't move. "Save her."

Athryn shook his head. "There is nothing I can do. Only the Necromancer--"

"The Necromancer's dead," Khirro shouted, cutting him off. "You're the only one." The magician continued to shake his head without meeting Khirro's eyes. "Damn you, Athryn. You can--"

Elyea squeezed his hand, her grip so weak he barely felt it, but it stopped him mid-sentence. He looked into her green eyes, the glimmer they normally held all but gone. Tears rolled down her cheeks.

"No, Khirro. It's all right." She forced a smile that quickly became a cringe. "This is why I came."

Her labored breathing made every word a struggle. Khirro wanted to make her stop, to tell her she'd be all

Bruce Blake

right, but he couldn't bring himself to lie to her.

"My whole life I've done what was easiest with no thought of myself or others. Finally, I've done something because it was the right thing to do. Please remember me that way. Let me take that with me to the fields of the dead. And the memory of you."

Khirro stroked the back of her hand. "But you could be with me. We could have a life for both of us, leave the old ones behind."

"I'd like that, but I think the future has more in store for you than making a life with a whore."

"Don't say that."

"It's what I am. What I was." A cough shook her and sent fresh blood flowing from her chest and mouth. "The fate of the kingdom is within you now."

"You are brave," Athryn said. "There is a special place waiting for you on the other side. Give Maes my love."

She tried to turn her head toward him but failed.

"You're whole again." He lifted her hand and stroked her fingers across his now smooth cheek. "More than whole. Don't underestimate who you are, Athryn."

He nodded, lay her hand gently on Khirro's and rose, leaving them alone. Elyea's eyes moved back to Khirro and the smile struggled back to her lips.

"You will have a great life, Khirro. I'm honored to have loved you."

The smile faded and her eyelids drooped, then closed.

The bubbling sound from her chest stopped.

"It's I who am honored," Khirro whispered. He leaned forward and kissed her on the forehead then bowed his head.

The low mist appeared again, tendrils of it twisted along the floor like a translucent white snake. It swirled about them, licked at Khirro's knees and crawled up Elyea's body. Cool dew formed on his skin, caressing him, comforting him. When it cleared, Elyea's corpse still lay before him, her hands in his, but he knew the part that made her Elyea had gone with it, whisked away on misty wings to a place where she'd finally be happy.

54

Night time.

They didn't know what time of day it was until they reached the foot of the creaky wooden stairs and saw stars shining down, clear and bright, unobscured by a dragon's belly. They struggled up the stairs carrying Elyea's body between them and emerged into a cool autumn evening.

The snow which covered the ground when they entered the catacombs was gone along with the ruby sentinel. As they set her body down, the ground shook briefly, sending Khirro and Athryn's hands to the hilts of their swords and their gazes scanning the woods. No giant shook the earth this time, no dragon. Instead, the hole in the ground closed behind them like a rapidly healing wound, sealing in its secrets and its dead.

It took them far less time to find their way out of the
tunnels than it had to reach their destination despite the
grim weight they carried. A dim glow radiated from Khirro
like an ember in a dying fire, so they could see better, but
the tunnels and the chamber had changed, too. Instead of
a huge subterranean room filled with blue light, the
chamber was only a widening in the tunnel which ran
straighter than before. Khirro wondered how it could be
but dismissed the thought quickly. Elyea had been taken
from him, there was nothing more to understand.

Khirro and Athryn carefully searched the area around
the keep but two lifeless giants, their charred flesh picked
at by unseen forest denizens, were the only sign of the
ruby dragon. No dragon, no third giant. Under other
circumstances, Khirro would have worried, but he felt
danger had passed. With no Necromancer, what need was
there for a guardian anymore?

They gathered wood for a pyre and lay Elyea and her
belongings atop it. Khirro kept one thing aside as a
reminder: her dagger. The knife had set her down her life's
path when she stood against her father years ago; a symbol
of the strength Khirro admired in her. Perhaps it would
lend him some of her strength in the days to come.

Flames danced into the night sky, sparks swirled and
twisted into the dark like lightning bugs at play. Khirro
couldn't take his eyes from the body prone at the center of

the blaze as wood crackled and spat, her clothing charred and her hair melted. The fire engulfed her, flickering over her skin, and Khirro heaved a shuddering sigh.

It's only her earthly body. She's already gone.

He stared at the flames, wondered how he looked when he was aflame and if she carried the memory of Khirro as a burning tyger to the fields of the dead. He hoped not.

Despite how close he stood, Khirro's body didn't register the funeral pyre's heat while Athryn stood behind him to avoid being burned. With his scar healed, Khirro supposed the magician would go to great lengths to keep from being burned again. Would that be possible? They were linked now and a fire burned within Khirro. Could he keep it from engulfing Athryn and anyone else around him?

Could he keep from succumbing to it himself?

When Elyea's body was reduced to ash and bone and the fire burned down to glowing embers, Athryn put his hand on Khirro's shoulder.

"We should go." He wore his mirrored mask despite his face being healed. Khirro wondered why but didn't ask. "A long journey still lies ahead."

Khirro didn't respond, only stared at the remains of the fire. A bone poked out of the ash and he fought the urge to pluck it out, hold it close and cry over it. Such actions wouldn't bring her back. Nothing would.

"Where will we go?" Khirro asked finally. "I've failed. The king is dead. There's no hope for Erechania."

"There is hope, Khirro," Athryn said squeezing his shoulder. "There is you."

Khirro snorted a laugh lacking humor. "What good to a war is a simple farmer? What good to a kingdom is a man who couldn't keep his friends alive?" He gestured toward the pile of bone and ash.

"The king is within you. You are much more than you know."

"I'm not the king. No one would believe our tale, they'd throw us both in the dungeon and think us insane."

Athryn sighed. "They will know you by what you do, not who you are. The kingdom needs you."

"What can I do for the kingdom?"

"Maybe nothing," Athryn said with a shrug. "But someone has to do something. And what else is there for you? Return to your farm?"

Khirro smiled in spite of himself. "No. I guess I'm no farmer anymore, am I?"

"No. And I am no performer of illusions."

They stood a while in silence. A cool breeze moved the trees and brushed Khirro's cheek, refreshing him.

So much time has passed, so many things have changed. I can never go back to my old life. My old life doesn't want me. But what new life lies ahead?

Khirro breathed deeply of the chill night air, strong

498

with the aroma of pine and cedar. It smelled good after being under the ground. He had no nose for the smell of dirt anymore.

"I'll miss Elyea," he said and the weight compressing his chest dispelled with the words. "I loved her."

Athryn nodded. "I will miss her, too."

"Do you miss Maes?" Khirro looked at his distorted reflection in the magician's silvered mask. The image looked older, tired.

"Maes is alive within me, as the spirit of the king dwells within you. It is a gift the Necromancer gave me before he left."

"Before he died," Khirro corrected.

"Darestat is not dead. He is gone from the world of the living for now, but he has not perished."

"But I saw Ghaul's arrow. No one could survive."

"It takes more than a mortal's arrow to slay the Necromancer. This world is very different than you know."

"I guess it is."

In the distance, a wolf howled and another answered a moment later. They were the first sounds of animal life they'd heard since entering Lakesh. Khirro didn't pause to ponder why they heard them now.

The world is different than I know.

"Where will we go?"

"We must return the king to his kingdom."

The words hung in the air between them on the mist of

Athryn's breath until Khirro nodded. He knelt and placed his hand on the knob of bone protruding from the pile of ash.

"We've lost so much, haven't we?" He expected no answer from Athryn and received none. "Good bye, Shyn. Good bye, Elyea. Thank you. We'll all meet again one day."

He stood and turned to Athryn. The magician removed his mask, baring the smooth new skin of his cheek. Their eyes met and something unspoken passed between them— a vow, an oath, a bond.

They strode away from the heap of ash Khirro once loved, left behind their dead companions, monsters, dragons, heroes and traitors. The Mourning Sword bounced reassuringly against Khirro's thigh as he walked, spreading through him a sense of peace. He didn't know what the future held—adventure or boredom, friends or enemies, life or death. He knew only one thing:

He did not fear.

55

Figures bustled across the salt flats like bees buzzing around pollen-laden flowers. Craters pock-marked the ground where boulders had struck, but the fortress's catapults and the Kanosee trebuchets had been quiet in the week since Therrador's coronation. His long purple cloak streamed behind him in the brisk ocean breeze as he stood atop the wall observing the activity below.

"We should attack, your highness," Sir Alton Sienhin urged, his voice loud and forceful. Therrador wondered if the man knew how to speak at a normal volume. "They haven't moved on us in a week. They can't starve us out, they know that, so they must be up to something. I say we catch them unawares. Crush them while we have the chance."

"There are still too many." Therrador crossed his arms to keep his hands from fidgeting, betraying his nerves. Sir Alton stood behind him and probably couldn't see, but better not to take the chance. No one could know about Graymon. "Don't doubt me, Sir Alton. Haven't things been better since I've been king?"

"Yes. Of course, my Liege," Sir Alton blustered. Therrador imagined his chubby cheeks reddening, his mustache quivering. "But we should--"

"Enough." Therrador silenced the knight with a wave of his hand. Any time now they should see riders. "I'll hear no more. We'll wait to see their next move. We have them right where we want them."

"Yes, your highness."

Therrador squinted out at the plains.

Where in the name of the Gods are they?

She said it would happen before the sun reached its zenith yet the sun showed midday. He felt Sienhin standing behind him, likely seething at the slight handed him, but Therrador had little concern for niceties and formalities. Only his son mattered. And he was king, it was the old knight's duty to obey.

Tendrils of gray smoke curled into the sky from cook fires scattered throughout the enemy camp. The days were cooler since they first occupied the land bridge and the salt flats, and the breeze off the Sea of Linghala could be biting. Cold wind had driven more than one army from the wall of the fortress in the past. But it would be two months before it became the weapon it could be, and Therrador didn't have that kind of time.

Graymon didn't have that kind of time.

Watching, waiting, Therrador wondered how Suath and the others fared at their task. Months would pass before he knew, but what little he heard before they disappeared into Lakesh was encouraging. It would be a relief when the vial reached his hands, then he'd smash it on the stones, ensuring his kingship. But all would be for naught if he didn't get Graymon back.

The wind snapped Therrador's cloak. Sir Alton shuffled his feet. Men and horses and things which once were men continued to shift and flow in the distance. Finally, riders separated from the host. A dozen men on fully armored horses trotted across the plain, the standard of Kanos snapping on a staff above them. A flag of truce flew below the country's colors.

"We didn't have to wait long to see what they were up to, did we, Sir Alton?" Therrador pointed out the riders while keeping his hand from shaking. The old knight moved to his side.

"What trickery is this?" He turned to his king, concern plain on his face. "Send them away, your highness. The Kanosee are not known for their diplomacy."

"But we are," Therrador said. Sienhin spoke truth and, under other circumstances when he didn't already know the outcome, he might have taken the knight's advice. "They fly a flag of truce. Come, Sir Alton. Let's hear what they have to say."

"But, your highness--"

Therrador silenced him with a scowl. The knight bowed his head in acquiescence and followed as Therrador swept by, hurrying down the steps.

"Assemble the generals, Sir Alton. We ride to meet them. I'll speak with their leader myself."

Sienhin nodded and excused himself. Alone, Therrador leaned against the wall for support as the strength in his legs waned. He filled his lungs with a long breath, hoping the air would force dread from his chest. It didn't. He collected himself and continued down the stairs.

"Ready my horse, boy," Therrador barked as he reached the stable. "And make it quick."

He inhaled the sweet smell of hay and manure. His head spun and he put his hand against a post, supporting himself as the stable boy readied his steed.

Oh, Graymon. I'm so sorry.

***

Therrador bounced gently in the saddle, purple cloak swirling behind him as he rode. A short distance ahead, he saw Sir Alton and the others where he'd left them. They didn't allow their mounts to wander or graze, instead standing ready to attack, or retreat; to do whatever their king commanded.

Are they also ready to be surprised?

Sir Alton spurred forward to meet him, halting as their horses came alongside. The old knight bowed his head without taking his eyes from the Kanosee party turning back toward their camp.

"My liege," he said, his voice quieter than Therrador had ever heard it to keep the conversation between the two of them. "What did the dogs have to say? Did they truly offer their surrender?"

Therrador's face remained grim despite his effort to relax.

"No, they do not surrender," he said loud enough for all to hear. He urged his horse on forcing Sir Alton to follow.

"Then what, highness?"

Therrador rode through the cluster of knights, allowing them to fall in behind him before he answered.

"An accord has been struck," he said finally, thankful to be riding ahead so they didn't see the strain in his features. "There shall be no more war."

A mumble rolled through the generals.

"When will the curs be retreating from our land, your grace?" Sir Alton asked on their behalf.

"They won't be."

Silence. None of the generals spoke: no murmur, no whisper, no grumbles. Shock or surprise stilled their tongues, but only for a few seconds before Sienhin voiced the question surely on all their minds.

"What do you mean, your highness?"

Therrador ground his teeth and forced a breath out through his nose.

"We will open our gates and welcome our new friends."

A clamor of protest arose amongst the men. Therrador steeled himself and thought of Graymon. The muscles in his cheek bunched and flexed as he clenched his jaw.

"Why, my king? There's no reason to give the fortress to these dogs. We're not beaten."

Therrador reined his horse to a stop so suddenly the others nearly rode into each other to avoid hitting him. He turned in his saddle to face Sir Alton.

"Do you question your king?" he roared, spittle flying from his lips.

His anger wasn't really for this man but at the distress of having no control. He'd planned to keep this from happening, but the Archon outmaneuvered him. His only hope was to sway them to what must be to save Graymon.

"N-no, your grace," Sir Alton stammered. "We were

505

wondering why--?"

Therrador's blade rang against leather as he pulled his sword free and placed the tip to the old knight's throat. No one made a move for their weapons as they stared in shock.

"Treason," Therrador said, his voice loud and firm to hide his true feelings. Sienhin's mouth fell agape, his eyes opened wide. "I should kill you myself for the treachery of questioning your king."

Sweat broke out on Sir Alton's brow, but he didn't reach for his sword, doing so would mean his life. The other generals wouldn't stand with him against the king, no matter the circumstances. If he so much as moved toward it, the entire kingdom would call for his head.

"Do you wish to die, Sir Alton?"

"No, your highness." Sienhin's voice was a whisper for once.

Therrador settled back into his saddle and removed his blade from the knight's throat.

"I'll deal with your treachery later. For now, ride ahead. Have them open the gates, tell them to make ready. The generals of Kanos will join us before nightfall."

"Yes, my liege."

Sir Alton launched his horse into a gallop toward the fortress. Therrador guessed he moved quickly more to get away than in haste to obey the order. A proud man, the old knight. His family had served kings for as long as anyone remembered. This would damage his pride, something Therrador didn't want to do, but it would be for the best. With this, Therrador could remove him from the council and replace him with someone of his own choosing.

Of the Archon's choosing.

He'd have to keep an eye on Sir Alton, though. He could prove a dangerous man or a great ally.

With a click of his tongue and prod of his heels, Therrador urged his steed toward the fortress. The generals fell in behind, silent but for the creak of saddles, the clank of armor and the beat of hooves. Therrador sighed, mouth pulled down in a frown. He'd hoped for happiness once crowned, as though a title would take away the wrongs done him. But there was always someone else to wrong you. His gut knotted.

It will soon be over. For better or for worse.

He sat straight in the saddle, intending to look the part of the conquering hero he wanted and deserved to be if not for the Archon. The ripe plum hanging from the tree of life waiting for him to pluck had shriveled to a prune, wrinkled and uninviting. He closed his eyes and thought of Graymon, but even that did nothing to make him feel better.

56

A thin haze obscured everything. It was a dream, Khirro knew, but it didn't look like any of the dreams he'd had in the past months. No tyger, no lake; all that was behind him now, he supposed. What lay ahead?

The cool mist attached itself to his skin, dampening it as he surveyed the nothing around him. He took a step, then another. The mist swirled away from his feet only to rush back in as the air settled. His breath stirred the tiny droplets, sending them spinning in kaleidoscopic patterns of white and gray. There were no sounds. Khirro halted, worried he might plunge from a dream-cliff, or be attacked by Gods-only-knew what. He waited, expecting the dream to resolve itself into something more than damp, eddying fog.

Then the glow began.

It took Khirro a minute to realize it came from him. A dim light which strengthened and brightened, burning away the mist before him without causing him the slightest discomfort. Yellowed grass, dry and dead, appeared beneath his feet. The view before his eyes cleared to reveal a green wall undulating at the whim of the wind.

A tent. I'm in a tent.

The green canvas flapped more violently and sound came to Khirro's dream: the snap of the wind against the tent, men shouting somewhere outside, and a whimper. He turned his head toward the last noise, not knowing whether he should expect man or beast, or which he'd prefer.

The boy lay curled on a bed of straw, shivering each

time the wind shook the tent walls. He glanced at the door flap like he expected someone to come through at any moment and Khirro realized it wasn't the wind that scared the lad. Khirro stepped toward him and the boy pulled himself into a tighter ball, gripping the wooden dragon he held closer to his chest.

"Can you see me?" Khirro asked.

The boy froze, eyes darting about the tent, but they held no recognition, as though he'd heard something but couldn't discern where it came from or what it was. Khirro crossed the dry grass and knelt on the straw beside the boy.

"Who are you?" he said, a breath of wind against the boys cheek that only made him cringe the way the wind shaking the tent did. "What are you doing in my dream?"

Abruptly, inexplicably, the boy's shivering ceased. He sat up and looked directly into Khirro's eyes, stared right through them. Seconds passed. Khirro didn't breathe. The boy hugged the toy dragon tight, then held it out before him, offering it. Khirro took it. He knew he held the toy but couldn't see his hand. He was invisible to himself, so he must be to the boy, too. A smile tugged at the lad's lips, but it quickly faltered.

"Please help me," the boy said, his voice a whimper, and Khirro knew that was what he had to do. He stared into the boy's sad eyes, wishing there was something he could do for him now, in the dream, but knowing it was

509

only that.

The temperature in the tent dropped suddenly. The boy grabbed the wooden dragon from Khirro's invisible grasp, fell back onto the straw mattress and curled into the fetal position, eyes clamped shut. Khirro straightened, the hairs on the back of his neck standing on end. He stood and turned to face the tent flap and whoever or whatever had come through.

The first thing that struck him was the woman's beauty. Her golden hair cascaded over her black cloak almost to her waist, a startling contrast to her dark brown eyes. But there was something un-beautiful about her eyes: a hardness, a cruelty. They were the eyes of someone who'd watch death without flinching, and they bore into Khirro, searching him.

"You do not belong here."

He stared at her, chills crawling up his spine. It seemed as though her words weren't meant for him but for that which dwelled within him. He didn't move as she approached, couldn't.

"Your time has passed. Do not interfere."

The flesh on Khirro's arm tingled as he felt the flame begin. The tent brightened as the sensation grew. The boy moaned on the bed behind him and the woman's lips became a taut red line across her stern face, stealing her beauty. Darkness collected behind her and the green wall of the tent disappeared.

As Khirro's incandescence grew, so too did the woman's blackness until the two pressed against each other like beasts locked in a mortal struggle. Khirro spread his legs, pushing against the pressure compressing his chest and threatening to force him back. His glow grew to a blaze as the darkness emanating from her expanded until there was nothing in the dream but him and her, light and dark.

"Leave this place," she said, her voice more a growl than the words of a woman. "Leave this place and do not come back."

Sweat streamed down Khirro's face, ran down his neck and under his shirt. His jaw muscles knotted, his lips pulled back from his teeth with the effort, but the darkness pushed forward, expelling his fire before it. The woman stepped forward until they were inches apart and spread her arms. Night flowed from her cloak, encircling Khirro, sucking the fire from his soul and the energy from his limbs. His knees gave out and the darkness took him.

Stars twinkled down from the sky as Khirro awoke, a knot clogging his throat. He clenched his fists, his fingers dug into the loamy earth upon which he lay.

Who was she?

He glanced at the trees pressing in around him. Athryn should be somewhere close, but he didn't know where. They'd chosen not to light a fire, and now Khirro regretted the decision. Having the flames to show him that light always conquered night would have been reassuring. He sat up and breathed out a slow sigh through tight lips.

"Graymon," he said, not sure where the name came from but knowing it was the boy in the dream. Thankfulness and fear mixed in his mind as he realized the dream had shown him what he needed to do next, where he needed to go.

"Graymon."

####

Map

Map by Rob Antonishen
http://www.cartocopia.com/

Bruce Blake

About the Author

Bruce Blake lives on Vancouver Island in British Columbia, Canada. When pressing issues like shovelling snow and building igloos don't take up his spare time, Bruce can be found taking the dog sled to the nearest coffee shop to work on his short stories and novels.

Actually, Victoria, B.C. is only a couple hours north of Seattle, Wash., where more rain is seen than snow. Since snow isn't really a pressing issue, Bruce spends more time trying to remember to leave the "u" out of words like "colour" and "neighbour" then he does shovelling. The father of two, Bruce is also the trophy husband of burlesque diva <u>Miss Rosie Bitts</u>.

Bruce has been writing since grade school but it wasn't until five years ago he set his sights on becoming a full-time writer. Since then, his first short story, "Another Man's Shoes" was published in the Winter 2008 edition of <u>*Cemetery Moon*</u>, another short, "Yardwork",was made into a podcast in Oct., 2011 by <u>*Pseudopod.*</u> His first Icarus Fell novel, "On Unfaithful Wings", published to Kindle in Dec., 2011, was selected as a semi-finalist in the Kindle Book Review Best Indie Books of 2012. The second Icarus Fell novel, "All Who Wander Are Lost", was released in July, 2012, and "Blood of the King", the first book in the three-part "Khirro's Journey" epic fantasy, followed in September. He has plans for at least three more Icarus novels, several stand alones, and a possible YA fantasy co-written with his eleven-year-old daughter.

Made in the USA
Lexington, KY
07 December 2014